Spectrums

Spectrums

THOMAS HALL

iUniverse, Inc.
Bloomington

Spectrums

iUniverse books may be ordered through booksellers or by contacting:

iUniverse
1663 Liberty Drive
Bloomington, IN 47403
www.iuniverse.com
1-800-Authors (1-800-288-4677)

Because of the dynamic nature of the Internet, any web addresses or links contained in this book may have changed since publication and may no longer be valid. The views expressed in this work are solely those of the author and do not necessarily reflect the views of the publisher, and the publisher hereby disclaims any responsibility for them.

Any people depicted in stock imagery provided by Thinkstock are models, and such images are being used for illustrative purposes only.
Certain stock imagery © Thinkstock.

ISBN: 978-1-4620-2464-3 (sc)
ISBN: 978-1-4620-2466-7 (dj)
ISBN: 978-1-4620-2465-0 (ebk)

Printed in the United States of America

iUniverse rev. date: 05/31/2011

For my mom, Jeanne, who continues to encourage me
every day of my life.

Acknowledgments

Thank you to my wife Marcia, who was so involved in the writing of this book that she should have been credited as the co-author, but wouldn't allow it.

Thank you to my daughters Kim MacMillan and Beth Slattery, and to my sister Bonnie Pendleton, all of whom read the first draft and offered terrific suggestions that were eventually incorporated into the book.

Thank you to my "writing buddies" – Ray Noveck, Alicia, Danielle, Eleanor, Adel, Charlie, and Tom.

And finally, a special thanks to Kathy McFarland, who loves books more than anyone I know.

The author has pledged that a substantial portion of the royalties from the sale of this book will be donated to charity.

CHAPTER 1

Jenna studied her reflection in the mirror. Surprisingly, she wasn't able to detect any sign of the tears that had been there earlier. She tilted her face even closer, scrutinizing every feature. Although the tears weren't visible, the overwhelming weariness was. And despite the fact that she felt it throughout her entire body, it was almost as if it had traveled through some invisible transit system and collected in her eyes.

She thought for a moment that maybe it was just sadness. But no, it was much more encompassing, much more deeply felt. Certainly sadness was a part of it, but . . . . Before she could complete the thought, a recurring question pushed its way to the forefront—*I'm only twenty-three-years-old; how did all this happen?* Of course there was a simple answer, one that she had come up with a hundred times before. But like most simple answers to emotional questions, it wasn't totally accurate, and it wasn't particularly helpful.

She took a deep breath, let out a sigh, and decided to lie down on the couch. She knew that if she went into the bedroom, despite the traffic noises outside, she would be more likely to fall asleep. Jenna didn't want that. She just needed to close her eyes for a few minutes.

The hall closet held a comforter that her mom had gotten for her when she was in high school. She lifted it off the top shelf and wrapped herself up like an Indian squaw. She immediately felt warmer, but contrary to its name, the comforter didn't really do its job.

Jenna seemed to be cold all the time lately. Initially, she had chalked it up to the fact that she was really still a California girl and the vestiges of winter in the Boston area wouldn't give up the ghost. But it was more than that. New England cold seemed to be different from other kinds of cold. Somehow it got into your bones and wouldn't let go. And she knew it wasn't *just* the cold. It was like the cold had formed a bond with the weariness. The weariness became the host, and the cold was the parasite feeding off it.

She closed her eyes and brought the comforter up to her chin. Except for her right arm, her whole body from her neck to her feet was covered. She rested the back of her right hand on her forehead, looking like a silent movie heroine trying to portray despair, or a character from *Gone with the Wind* with the vapors.

As she suspected would be the case, despite the quiet and the way she was feeling, she didn't fall asleep, not even a catnap. Instead, she found herself in that semi-conscious state that allowed her to think, but not really to feel; and more importantly, to not expend much energy doing it. Her mind didn't allow her to focus on anything in particular. It was moving about like Alice in Wonderland deciding which door to open. Finally, a thought began to crystallize. But it was actually an extension of the question she had just asked herself: How had she gotten here—at first, quite literally – to Boston, to this apartment? And then the question turned more philosophical, more far-reaching – to this point in her life?

Almost as quickly as the question entered her consciousness, it was replaced by a sense of disorientation. She was first aware of it physically. She really didn't know in which direction she was facing. Was the picture of the Cape Cod seascape on the wall in front of her, or behind her? Of course, she could easily solve that puzzle by opening her eyes. But even with her eyes wide open she knew that she would have no idea in what direction her *life* was headed.

Jenna decided to keep her eyes closed. She allowed herself to play the game of "which way am I facing?" She pictured all the mismatched furniture in the living room, trying to place it in her mind's eye. As she organized the layout, it occurred to her that the furniture looked just like the set of every high school play she had ever been in. Well, maybe not *Our Town*. The sides of her mouth did an involuntary upturn and she expelled a puff of air in what approached a muffled laugh.

She thought about the wall by the door where the mirror was located, and again about her reflection. She wondered how someone else seeing her in this state would describe her. Would they be able to detect everything she was feeling – the weariness, the overwhelming fatigue?

She suspected that even if they couldn't see beyond her physical features, they would certainly be able to describe her better than she could describe herself. Jenna had always been amazed at other people's ability to give detailed descriptions. It seemed as if everyone she knew was like some sort of police sketch artist.

Oh sure, she could give the vitals—5' 5", 115, brown hair, brown eyes, and, and . . . Okay, what else? What shape is my face? Are my eyes close together? Any distinguishing marks – like scars or tattoos or piercings? She allowed herself a light moment. Yeah, that's me – Jenna MacDonald, biker chick.

She decided to give the description idea another attempt, but with someone else. What about Trish? How would she describe Trish? Well, she's beautiful. She has blond hair, brown eyes, and she looks like . . . well, Trish. The smallest of smiles reached her lips, and then just as quickly, Jenna resigned herself to the fact that the exercise was futile.

Her mood shifted again, and the tears returned. She thought back to when she was a little girl and something happened that had made her cry; her mother would comfort her and say, "It's okay, sweetie, get it all out." Maybe that worked when you were little. Maybe there were a finite amount of tears when you were eight, but it seemed like this grown up version of Jenna had an endless supply.

Her mind remained blank for a few moments, and then without being cognizant she was going to, she opened her eyes. She blinked a few times and subconsciously noted that the painting of Cape Cod was in front her.

Growing up, she had always been a "get over it" kind of person, and even now, as an adult, on some days that worked. Today wasn't one of them. She began to feel her emotional pain in a pronounced physical way – like little acupuncture needles. Only these needles didn't relieve the pain, they intensified it. She knew that she was powerless to stop another crying onslaught, but she steeled herself and tried anyway.

Just at that moment she heard a stirring in another part of the apartment. She held her breath and remained perfectly still, listening intently to make sure she hadn't imagined it. No, there it was again. She rubbed her eyes with the heels of her hands and moved toward the noise, realizing that the stirring she had heard was probably the only thing in the world that could have halted her tears.

CHAPTER 2

(Three And a Half Years Earlier)

The summer in Southern California had been unusually warm. Many days the temperature had flirted with ninety-five degrees. By early August the flirtation had turned into a full-blown love affair; and for five days in a row the inhabitants of the Los Angeles area were in the midst of a genuine heat wave. Ironically, as August kicked into full gear, the mercury retreated, and the heat wave finally broke. In fact, when Jenna checked the temperatures in the morning paper, Boston's predicted high for the day was warmer than Pasadena's.

The drive to the Long Beach airport from Pasadena took about twenty-five minutes. And although the trip to LAX took about the same, Jenna and her mom, Sharon, always flew out of Long Beach. Jenna had often heard her mother say, "I like the smaller airports. LAX is just too big and spread out, just like Los Angeles itself."

For the last several months almost every conversation between Jenna and her mom had an undercurrent. Sometimes it came to the surface, like a whale breeching the waves, but usually it remained unacknowledged in the deep water. It was how they dealt with things. Jenna's transfer from UCLA to Tufts was no different

They had always been very close, but for reasons they couldn't articulate, or didn't know, they had never been able to confront any emotionally charged topic head on. But this particular dance of avoidance—Jenna's transfer to Tufts—this dance, so well choreographed by the both of them, might have qualified as an Olympic event. And Jenna and her mom would have been the odds-on favorites to capture the gold.

It had only been the last ten days or so that they had engaged in any honest discussions about it, much too late to really change anything. And the irony for Sharon was that she had been the one to initiate the idea of the transfer in the first place. What had she been thinking?

As they drove down the 710 toward Long Beach, Jenna opened the conversation. "I know you already told me Mom, but when will my other stuff get to Boston?"

"It might be there already. We sent it priority. At the latest, I'd say Monday or Tuesday."

Both Jenna and her mom knew that the brief exchange was just a means to avoid continuing the conversation they had been having just prior to leaving for Long Beach. The silence hung in the air for a few more minutes and then Sharon decided to try again. "Honey, you know it's not too late to change your mind. We can still fix this."

"Mom, I told you, there's nothing to fix. I want to do this."

"I know you do, but I also know that you want to transfer because you think that's what I want."

Jenna shifted in her seat and half-faced her mother. She had decided earlier that morning to offer at least some of what she had been holding back; her mom deserved more of an explanation than Jenna had been giving her. "Mom, I really do want to transfer. You know I've wanted to go to Tufts since I was a sophomore in high school."

Her mom broke in. "And you know we would have made it work somehow."

Jenna interrupted. "Mom, we didn't have the money. We both know that."

Sharon started to protest.

Jenna cut her off. "There *is* something else, though."

Sharon glanced away from the road and noticed a glistening in the corners of her daughter's eyes.

Jenna continued. "After Daddy died you gave up everything for me." Sharon started to say something, but stopped. Jenna composed herself and went on. "For the last eleven years you always put me first, never yourself."

"But that's what parents do."

"Not always, Mom. Not all of them." She paused, trying to gather herself for the strength to say the next few sentences—things she had

5

been unable to say for the last several months."Mom, now that you have Jonathan; it's your turn to be happy."

Sharon interrupted. "You think I haven't been happy for the last eleven years?"

"No, I didn't mean that. But this can be different. You told me you never thought you'd get married again, and then Jonathan came into your life."

"I don't see how my getting married means you should go off to Tufts."

"Mom, you're still a young woman. You and Jonathan can travel, do whatever you like."

"What does that have to do with . . . You're not suggesting that somehow you'd be in the way? You don't really believe that, do you? Jonathan adores you."

"Some of this isn't coming out right. You know I always wanted to go to Tufts. And then when you sold the house after you married Jonathan, that became a real possibility." Jenna hesitated. "The bonus is that you get to put yourself first for once. You get to live your life without having to worry about me every day."

Sharon allowed a small smile to form on her lips. "So, you think your being on the East Coast is going to stop me from worrying about you?"

Jenna smiled as well. "No, I know you better than that. But I also know that if I'm 30 miles away, I'll still be too much a part of your life. If I'm 3,000 miles away, then you and Jonathan can . . . ."

Sharon objected. "Where is this coming from?" She shook her head slightly. "Is it something I said? Did I do something that makes you think I don't want you around?"

"Of course not." Jenna paused and turned herself even further toward her mother. "You sacrificed for me every day. And part of me doesn't want to be so far away from you either." She paused again. "But I need to do this—for the both of us. Some of this is paying you back for being my mom, for everything you did for me." Tears started streaming down her face, and she couldn't continue. Sharon looked over at her daughter and began to cry as well.

Usually for both Jenna and Sharon tears born of sadness were much more intense and long lasting than tears born of sentiment—but not this time. Eventually, the tears abated and they were able to calm themselves.

Sharon found her voice first. "This kind of feels like we're fighting. I know we're not, but I still don't like it."

"I don't either."

They both retreated into silence for a few moments, and then Sharon said, "I guess it was pretty dumb to try to change things on the way to the airport, huh?" Jenna started to smile, as her mom continued. "Okay, I'm declaring a truce, especially since I can't get a damn refund on the plane ticket anyway."

Jenna's smile broadened into a laugh. "See, I always knew this was about the money." She paused, and as she leaned over, straining against the seatbelt, gave her mother a kiss on the cheek. "Thanks, Mom. I love you."

"Me too, honey."

They rode in silence for the next several miles, before taking the airport exit. The parking lot wasn't very crowded—the peak summer travel season having passed a few weeks before. Sharon helped get Jenna's bags out of the trunk, and they headed for the small terminal.

Jenna waited in the check-in line for only a few minutes while her mom went to the ladies' room. She got her boarding pass, slung her carry-on over her shoulder, and caught up with her mom at the newsstand.

"All set, honey?"

"Yeah. I'm at Gate 4, but I probably don't have to be there for another forty-five minutes."

Sharon pointed to a small fast food location close by. "Do you want to grab a quick bite here, or go upstairs to the restaurant?"

"Let's go upstairs. Is that all right?"

"Sure. That will give us some more time to talk."

Jenna threw her a glance.

"No, not about that. I told you – truce."

As they climbed the stairs, Jenna looked at the pictures and displays that depicted the aviation pioneers that had flown from this very location back in the '20's and '30's. She wasn't really afraid to fly, but as she surveyed the photos, she couldn't imagine how these men and women could have risked their lives in those early airplanes.

A hostess seated them near a window that overlooked the runways in the distance. They studied the menu, and after giving their selections to the waitress, Sharon said, "Have you heard any more from your new roommate – Patricia, isn't it?"

"It's Trish, Trish Cooper, and yeah I did. We've been e-mailing back and forth for the last couple of weeks."

"And she's a transfer student too?"

"Yeah, from Connecticut. I'm not sure why they do it that way, though. You'd think they'd put transfer students with someone that already goes there. But I'm sure it'll be fine."

"I know you haven't met her yet, but do you have a sense about what she's like?"

Jenna's face brightened. "Her e-mails are really funny. Oh, and yesterday she sent me a picture. I have it on my phone. Do you want to see it?"

Jenna pulled the phone from her bag, scrolled through some other stored photos, found Trish's picture, and handed the phone to her mom.

After considering the photo briefly, Sharon came out with her first impression. "Oh my, isn't she pretty!" Wow, the guys in Boston won't know what hit them. You two are going to take over."

Jenna rolled her eyes and gave her head a small shake.

"What?" said her mother.

"Projecting much? First, you don't want me to go, and now I'm taking over the place."

Before Sharon could respond, the waitress arrived with their appetizers. They both dropped the conversation and started to eat. After about ten minutes and some small talk, their meal arrived. Although the food was quite good, they both ate without much enthusiasm. Jenna particularly ate more slowly than usual, attempting to delay the inevitable. She hadn't anticipated that saying goodbye was going to be so difficult.

Sharon signed the credit card slip, and then had to redo it, because she initially signed MacDonald instead of Brooks. "I'm still not used to it. You know—like dating checks in January – you always write the previous year."

They exited the restaurant and headed down the stairs toward the security line. About halfway there Sharon stopped abruptly. Jenna took a few steps before she realized that her mom wasn't beside her. She looked back and saw her mom with her arms wide open. Jenna went to her and they hugged each other. They let the embrace linger for a few moments, and then they started to speak at the same time, which was followed by a few seconds of nervous laughter.

Sharon broke the embrace and held her daughter at arm's length. She hesitated to create any physical distance between them, but she needed to take in the full view of the young woman Jenna had become. "I love you so much, honey."

"I know, Mom. I love you too." She paused. "Mom, it's going to be okay."

Her mother choked up and was barely able to get out, "I know it will." She pulled Jenna close again and in a whisper filled with emotion said, "Be safe." She then separated from her daughter and gently nudged her toward the security line. Jenna clung briefly to her mother's hand. "I will," she said, as she slowly moved away. She gave one backward glance before disappearing from view.

Sharon held it together until she got outside and then she was overcome. She sat down on one of the wooden benches to try to calm herself. She went searching for Kleenex in her bag, and quickly exhausted the contents of the small package. After about five minutes she got up and crossed the street toward the parking area. She kept trying to convince herself that 3,000 miles wasn't that far, that being "close" to someone was more about feelings than distance, that cell phones and e-mails and texting (if she ever learned how) would make up for the lack of proximity.

And then she remembered a favorite saying of Jenna's father – "If you believe that, I have some swamp land in Louisiana and a bridge in Brooklyn you might be interested in."

CHAPTER 3

Jenna was her mother's daughter. At the same time her mother was trying to compose herself, Jenna was trying to do the same thing. She made a detour to the ladies' lounge to try to get her emotions at least partially under control. On the other hand, she thought, it wasn't as if the airport personnel weren't accustomed to seeing people upset. With the possible exception of hospitals, she figured that airports were probably number one on the "public display of emotion" list. Still, she didn't really want everybody gawking at her, wondering what was wrong.

Jenna had always thought of herself as an organized person—everything in its place, everything where she could access it if she needed to. Of course, doing that with physical objects didn't present much of a challenge, but pigeonholing *emotions*, storing them in some mental cubby, even just putting them away temporarily—that was not so doable.

After about ten minutes she was able to calm down. She had convinced herself that she needed to focus on all the things that lay ahead, not the sense of emptiness she was feeling about what she was leaving behind. Jenna was like some twenty-first century alchemist, believing that if she didn't think about her emotional state, it would somehow transform itself into something she was looking forward to.

Although she knew it might only be temporary, and it had required embracing every sappy platitude about new beginnings that she could channel through her mind, Jenna was able to make it work. She took a deep breath and put her carry-on over one shoulder and the long strap of her purse over the other, unconsciously creating a physical balance that mimicked the equilibrium she had just been able to muster emotionally.

The waiting area for Gate 4 was nearly full when Jenna arrived, and she didn't see a lot of options as she surveyed the available seats. She decided on the empty one next to a family of four – mom, dad, a little boy about four, and a little girl about three. Jenna surmised that the particular seat she had been eyeing was empty precisely because it *was* next to the family of four. Jenna didn't care; she liked little kids, and as far as she could tell, these two seemed pretty well behaved.

She navigated the narrow aisle strewn with carry-on luggage. And as she passed in front of the parents of the children, she smiled and sat down on the end seat. The little boy continued to stare straight ahead for just a moment, and then once Jenna appeared to get settled, he moved his attention toward her. She waited a few moments and then looked over, but before she could say anything, the little boy beat her to it. "Hi," he said, as he watched her for a second or two and then turned away. Jenna uttered, "Hi" back, surprised that the exchange appeared to be over.

A smile appeared on Jenna's face, as she remembered her mother's words from earlier today after she had seen Trish's picture – "The guys in Boston won't know what hit them." *Yeah, well, if this little boy is from Boston, I probably have a lot of work to do.*

Jenna was hoping that once she was airborne, she could catch up on some sleep and not engage in any extended conversations. She looked over at the little boy, hoping that she might be sitting next to him on the plane. The chances of any conversation with him, never mind an extended one, seemed pretty remote. On the other hand, if she were sitting next to somebody who wanted to talk, Jenna knew she couldn't say no. That was who she was.

Another smile came across her lips, as she thought about a discussion she had had with her mom a few years ago. It seemed that two of Jenna's friends were in a fight, and as usual, she was in the middle trying to mediate. Eventually, the two friends resolved their differences, but then they both got mad at Jenna. She was crushed. Her mom consoled her, but added some advice. "Jenna, honey, you're going to keep getting hurt if you try to make everybody happy. Life doesn't work that way." She put her arm around her daughter. "But I love that you keep trying. You have such a good heart." She paused and then lightened the moment. "I fully expect that if your high school has a People Pleaser Club, you'll be the president."

Jenna let out a little laugh at the memory.

Being a people pleaser was a mixed bag. Sometimes it made you feel great because you were helping people and they really appreciated it. Other times people just took advantage of you. Which was which, wasn't always clear, even long after the fact.

Jenna glanced over at the little boy just to make sure she hadn't misjudged the chance of further interaction. She decided again that it was probably non-existent. She rooted through her bag, extracted her iPod, put in the ear buds, and began listening.

The boarding call for "those traveling with young children" came about fifteen minutes into Jenna's musical retreat. The family of four got up at the father's urging. As the children gathered their stuffed animals and books, the parents policed the area where they had been sitting like campers closing down the campsite, and then moved toward the jetway. The little boy was walking next to his father, looking up at him, as if seeking permission. He then turned back toward Jenna, smiled, and said, "Bye". Even with the ear buds in, she was able to hear him. Jenna smiled as she returned the "Bye" and added a little wave. Jenna couldn't imagine what had been going on in the little boy's head. Maybe he was just beginning to practice the social graces. She laughed to herself – I guess "Hi" and "Bye" are a good place to start.

The boarding call for her row came five minutes later. She got in the line, which moved surprisingly quickly, and she was seated in 14A next to the window within a few minutes. It was unusual for Jenna to have a window seat. Whenever she had flown in the past, almost always with her mom, Jenna sat in the middle. During the online booking process, her mother would always ask which seat Jenna preferred. Knowing that her mom really favored the seats next to the window or on the aisle, she always responded, "It doesn't matter." What else would a people pleaser do, she thought?

Jenna intently watched the passengers coming down the aisle, trying to figure out which one was heading for 14B, and to a lesser extent, 14C. After a short time she saw an older gentleman studying his boarding pass as he checked the posted row numbers. He placed a small piece of luggage in the overhead compartment, ducked his head, and settled in next to Jenna. He looked over at her, smiled and said, "Hello." Next, he fastened his seat belt, took a magazine from the pouch on the back of the seat in front of him, and began to read.

This looks promising, thought Jenna.

The takeoff was smooth, and even better, the plane left the runway within five minutes of its scheduled departure. The disembodied voice of the pilot informed everyone that because of the strong tailwind, the flight would only be a little more than four hours.

During the first hour, Jenna watched the satellite TV embedded in the seat in front of her. She channel surfed, not unlike what she did with radio stations in the car. After going through all the channels about ten times, she decided she might as well implement the "catching up on sleep" part of her original plan for the plane ride. It didn't take long for her to drift off, and although the seats were somewhat uncomfortable, Jenna was able to fall into a light sleep for almost ninety minutes.

Shortly after she awoke, the flight attendants came around serving drinks. Jenna declined the offer. She had decided to use her laptop, and didn't want to take the chance of spilling anything on it.

She powered up her computer and moved the cursor to AOL to check her e-mail. There were five new ones. She usually read her e-mails in the order of interest they held for her—least to most. She tended to save the best for last, sort of like communication dessert. But this time, she went right for the chocolate cake—the one from Trish. Jenna smiled as she clicked on Trish's address – "tcup" – a play on Trish's name – T. Cooper. The smile quickly expanded as she began reading.

Hey Roomie,

It's about 3:30 Beantown time. I figure you're reading this in the airport or on the plane. If not, then we'll read it together when you get here. I should warn you though; I'll be looking over your shoulder and watching to see if you laugh at my jokes.

Two boxes of your stuff arrived. I persuaded two guys from the first floor to bring them up to our room – 209. Technically, they shouldn't have released the boxes to anyone but you, but the resident assistant said it was okay. I figured you didn't want to have to deal with that after five hours on a plane.

So, by my calculations (remember, I'm not a math major) you should be getting in around 8. I've been here since noon. I did a little housekeeping. Consider yourself lucky - it's way more than I do at home for my dad. Anyway, I set up the room, but if you don't like it, we can change it. It does seem a little bare. I took a picture, which I'm sending to Webster's to put next to the word "Spartan" in their dictionary. Actually, I kind of like our room. I mean, it's not huge or anything, but it's a lot bigger than some of the dorm rooms I've seen. It's probably because our dorm used to be a private residence. I think the Hutchinson Family owned it – hence the name Hutchinson House. Pretty clever, don't you think? No wonder Tufts has such a great reputation.

Anyway, each dorm room in HH is different. It kind of gives the place texture. I'm a big fan of texture. I can't even think about eating yogurt unless there's some fruit mixed in. But I digress. I did check out some of the other dorm rooms in the more modern buildings – no texture; they're all the same; they look like cells. I think I spotted some guys dressed like Friar Tuck copying scripture.

I just thought of something – Why don't you go to the Tufts website and check out HH? I think they show some of the rooms. Or you can just wait a few hours and see it in person. I know what I'd do. Delayed gratification's not my thing—at least in viewing dorm rooms.

Oh, remember the two guys I mentioned who brought your stuff up to the room? I think one of them might be date material; the other one not so much – unless you think you'd like to develop narcolepsy. Maybe that was a little harsh. But guess what he talked about after I knew him for a minute and a half? He got the measurements of all the dorm rooms on campus and divided the square footage by the cost of room and board to find out which students were getting the best deal. (We're in third place by the way.) But, do you see what I mean? Instead of "you had me at hello," it was "you put me to sleep at square footage."

I really am looking forward to meeting you and getting to know you better. (I got that last sentence from the book "Chicken Soup for the Cliché User – College Edition") Maybe I'll save the Dr. Phil moment for later.

So, back to business – no scheduled stuff for tomorrow or Tuesday. Orientation starts on Wednesday and classes start the day after Labor Day. You already knew all of that didn't you? If you don't read this e-mail until after you arrive here, we can skip this part.

Oh, I just remembered. I read this article about college freshmen (we count because we're transfer students). It said that one of the great ways for roommates to get to know one another faster is to share something about themselves that they normally wouldn't share until a month or two after they met. Sort of like an ice smasher rather than an icebreaker. What do you think? It's kind of like the college students' version of "I'll show you mine, if you show me yours." I'm game, if you are!

I just realized how long this e-mail has become—I'm entertaining paperback rights for the spring. Maybe it could be an Oprah book club selection.

I really do have to stop now. The guy who did the room and board analysis is coming back. He noticed that we have a loose baseboard. He said if he hammers it in, our square footage increases and we move into second place. First place looks out of the question unless we knock down a wall. I'm really not that competitive, but let's talk. See you in a few ☺ Trish

Jenna laughed out loud. It was the third time she had done that since she started reading the e-mail. She had attempted to stifle the laughter all three times, but she hadn't been successful. She supposed that if something struck you funny, you were really powerless not to laugh. Plus, it appeared that Trish knew just where Jenna's funny bone was located.

She looked around to see how much attention she had drawn. Other than the man next to her who gave her a paternal smile, it appeared to be minimal. Jenna wasn't sure why she cared, but she did. It was understandable that earlier when she was crying in the airport, she didn't want people asking, "What's the matter?" – That was too personal. But why should it bother her if someone heard her laughing and asked, "What's so funny?" I guess, she thought, explaining why you feel a certain way, even to yourself, is not all that easy.

Normally, Jenna didn't like long e-mails. She felt obligated to reread them over and over to make sure she responded to every question they contained, even the rhetorical ones. But Trish's e-mails were different. When she reread them she laughed just as hard the second time as she did the first time, and she didn't want them to end.

Jenna knew her reply wasn't going to be anywhere near as clever as Trish's original e-mail. So what was she going to do? I guess I could just wait to see her in person, she thought. But it seemed like Trish's effort really called out for some sort of a response. She started and stopped a number of times, nearly wearing out the backspace key. And then she decided to keep it simple.

Hi Trish,
Thanks a lot!!! I read your e-mail on the plane and laughed out loud the whole way through. The guy next to me gave me a look like-"So, did you skip your medication?"
See ya soon. Roomie

She quickly read her other e-mails, closed down the laptop, and put it away. She was about to take out something to read when she changed her mind and decided to just shut her eyes and veg out.

Of course just because you were trying to relax, didn't mean your brain was going to cooperate. Jenna's mind started spinning like the reels on a slot machine. It finally settled on some of the facetious questions Trish had posed in her e-mail. That made her smile. It also got Jenna thinking about how she had been feeling a few hours ago when she was so upset, and now, how her emotions had moved to the other end of the spectrum.

It struck her as strange that in a relatively short period of time you could go from one extreme to the other. She contemplated this idea for a few moments and it triggered something more philosophical in her mind. *If emotions can change so quickly, maybe they're not on a spectrum after all – with happiness on one end and sadness on the other. Maybe emotions aren't so linear.*

No substitute model initially came to her, and then an idea started taking shape. *Maybe when you were anticipating some big change in your life, or some momentous event, your mind gathered all your "potential emotion" – emotion that wasn't yet fully formed, like sculptor's clay, and sent it down a narrow path in your brain. Then, when the momentous event happened, it created a fork in the pathway, and your heart decided in which direction it should go.*

Jenna took a mental step back to reevaluate what she had been thinking. After a few moments she dove back in. The idea she had just described to herself would certainly explain how people could go from sadness to happiness in such a short amount of time. Instead of traveling all the way to the other end of the spectrum, your emotions only needed to go back to the fork and then take the other path.

The more she thought about her idea, the more she liked it. When she was in high school, she had taken an elective called "Logic and Philosophy." She had really enjoyed the course, and periodically she had engaged in an exercise similar to the one she had just done. She liked to think she had a separate compartment in her brain where she could keep her philosophical notions. She added this latest idea to the compartment and allowed her mind to move on to other things.

Her next conscious thoughts were about the new adventure her life was becoming. She would really be her own person now, making her own decisions, independent. She focused on that last word for a moment. The truth was that she had always been pretty independent. She suspected that when you're only eight years old and you lose a parent, independence kind of forces itself on you; it makes you grow up faster.

She thought briefly about the pioneer aviators who were depicted on the walls of the Long Beach Airport. Certainly this new phase of her life was nothing as grandiose as what they had done. Could you even call yourself a pioneer if the only thing you were exploring was your own life? She smiled at the notion. Jenna's reverie was interrupted by the pilot's announcement that they were beginning their initial descent into Logan Airport in Boston.

About ten minutes before they landed she thought back to Trish's e-mail, particularly the part about sharing some semi-hidden thing about themselves. She tried out a few possibilities, but dismissed them as too superficial. She continued running down her list of secrets, somewhat surprised that as she started to approach "deep dark" territory, she hadn't flinched and scurried back up the list.

And then there it was. One of her secrets jumped to the front of the line, standing out from all the others like it was encased in some sort of mental neon. This one was perfect – not too trivial, and not too personal. Wait. Who was she kidding? Of course this was personal! But then she realized that that was kind of the point. Yes, she decided—this was going to be the one she'd share with Trish.

CHAPTER 4

While Jenna was waiting for her luggage, she glanced at a map of greater Boston that was affixed to the wall in the baggage claim area. She couldn't help but be amazed at the number of colleges and universities that were designated on the map. It appeared that Boston was to colleges, what Seattle was to coffee shops – there seemed to be one on every corner.

Of course technically speaking, she was aware that many of these institutions of higher learning weren't really located in Boston. Harvard's not. MIT's not. They're in Cambridge. Brandeis is in Waltham. Even *Boston* College is not in Boston; it's in Newton. So, when she told the cab driver at the airport to take her to Tufts, he went over the Zakim Bridge into Boston and then continued out the other side toward Medford.

As Jenna glanced out the backseat window, she realized that she was a little nervous. She had always measured her degree of nervousness by how it related to the way she felt just before the curtain went up on her high school plays. Pre-performance jitters were a ten; this was a seven. Her mind wandered back to high school for several minutes, only returning to the present when she noticed a sign with the Tufts' insignia on it.

The cab driver followed the arrows to Hutchinson House and pulled up in front of a large tan building that dated back to colonial times. The cabbie helped her with her bags, accepted his fare, plus a generous tip, and drove off.

Jenna briefly took stock of her belongings, and was about to proceed when the front door opened and there stood her roommate. "Hi, Jenna," said Trish as she extended her hand.

She eyed Trish's hand, unsure whether Trish wanted to shake or help with the luggage. She was spared any awkward moments when Trish said, "Oh, forget the handshake – how about a hug?" Jenna righted her suitcases so they sat on their little plastic feet and then moved into Trish's outstretched arms. It seemed odd at first – she hadn't even met Trish before. But, the quick embrace actually felt like a natural thing to do. They separated and then Trish said, "Okay, let's get these upstairs."

"Thanks."

As Trish came forward to get one of the bags, Jenna got her first close-up look at her roommate. She was stunning. And even though she was casually dressed—a pair of khaki shorts, an oversized white peasant blouse, and a pair of sandals, Jenna thought that her new roommate looked like a model. Without doubt, the picture Trish had sent to her didn't do her justice. In fact, it probably wasn't even in the same courtroom.

"How was your flight?"

"Fine . . . fine." Jenna stumbled over the words, still caught up in how attractive her roommate was.

"Why don't we get everything upstairs? You can't get your keys yet, because Todd's not here. He's the resident assistant. But I have my keys, so we're all set."

"Thanks."

After they put the luggage in the room, Trish showed Jenna around Hutchinson House – the shower and bathroom facilities, mail pick-up, the laundry area, etc. It would have been easy, thought Jenna, for Trish to project an air of superiority; after all, she held the literal and figurative keys to the place. But her manner was so easy-going and self-deprecating that Jenna instinctively knew there was no attitude, no hidden agenda, nothing but a genuinely nice human being.

When they returned to their room, they spent the next twenty minutes talking, as Trish helped Jenna unpack and make up her bed. When they were finished, Trish said, "Jenna, you know, if you're tired, I can just go downstairs and watch TV or something, so you can get some rest."

"Thanks Trish, but no. I'm still on California time; it's not even 6:00 yet." She paused. "I'd just as soon talk some more, if that's okay."

"Sure, yeah, that'd be great." Trish smiled. "Isn't this where I say – 'so what should we talk about?'"

Jenna laughed. "Well, for starters, that was quite an e-mail you sent me."

"Yeah, I was pretty proud of that one. But to be fair, that guy with the square footage thing – that was all real."

With a straight face, Jenna said, "So which wall were you thinking of knocking down?"

Trish smiled, but before she could come up with a snappy response, Jenna's brain pushed forward something that had been percolating since the end of the plane ride – her secret. The mention of the e-mail was undoubtedly the final impetus her mind needed. Before she realized that she was going to, Jenna just blurted out, "I'm a virgin."

Trish looked at her with a puzzled expression on her face. "What? What did you say?"

A little more softly, "I'm a virgin."

"Where the heck did that come from?"

"Well, you know, from the e-mail, about sharing something."

Trish still looked puzzled and then her eyes and mouth opened wide in a eureka moment. "Oh, right, right. Wow, you kind of just put that out there, huh?"

"Well, I . . . ."

Trish started laughing, and then it was Jenna's turn to have the puzzled look on her face. Trish explained, "Actually, from what you just said, you *don't* just put it out there, do you?"

Jenna burst out laughing and started blushing at the same time.

Trish noticed and said, "Sorry, it just struck me funny."

"That's all right. Me too."

Trish leaned forward and in a conspiratorial voice said, "Okay, so give me details."

Jenna repeated her puzzled look, which caused Trish to recognize the foolishness of her request. "Oh, wait, you can't give me details. Nothing happened." The laughter started up again. When it subsided, Trish continued, "I guess there aren't too many details to a non-event – like, uh 'Tell me all about when you *didn't* go to Disney World'."

Jenna smiled. "So, you're comparing sex to going to Disney World?"

With feigned indignation Trish said, "And you're assuming I'd know?"

Jenna's faced reddened. "No, I just meant . . . ."

"It's okay. I was just teasing." She got an impish look on her face. "Yeah, I've been to the Magic Kingdom."

They both convulsed again. Trish stopped laughing first. "So, if we keep up with this Disney theme, then your sex life is—World of Tomorrow, and mine is . . . let's see. Well, the first time it was kind of like – It's a Small World After All."

That did it! Their laughter was now in pajama party territory. Jenna hadn't laughed that hard in years, and then when Trish said, "I have to go to the bathroom; I'm going to pee my pants," it got worse. Trish hurried from the room as Jenna started rubbing her face. Her cheeks actually ached from all the laughing.

When Trish returned she said, "I'm not sure when I've laughed like that. If we keep this up, it could be a tough semester study-wise."

They both took a moment to catch their breath, while continuing to smile and shake their heads in mock shame at their actions. When they made eye contact again, Jenna picked up the discussion. "I came close to going all the way once my junior year. This boy, Greg, and I had been going out for a while, and one night we were at his house and his parents weren't due home for a few hours. Anyway, things got hot and heavy, but, well . . . Greg kind of finished before he started, if you know what I mean."

Trish nodded her head as she let out a little chuckle.

Jenna continued. "I think he was really embarrassed after that, and we just sort of stopped seeing each other." Jenna glanced at Trish trying to make up her mind what to do. She decided it was okay. "So, what about you?"

"Well actually, not that much to tell – despite what's written on the bathroom walls of my high school – just kidding. My first time was the summer after junior year. It was the first time for both of us, and pretty awkward. We were like two little kids playing doctor. Then there was this college guy, Alex, when I was a senior. We did it a few times. It was better, but I don't think it was really like it's supposed to be. I mean, I think it makes it better if you really care about the guy, and I didn't. I was kind of caught up in him being in college, plus there were some other things going on in my life. Anyway, he dumped me after about a month and a half. I didn't feel real good about myself for a while. So . . . that's my story."

They were both quiet for a few moments, and then Jenna said, "You know, that was a good idea about sharing something. I don't even think my mom knows whether I'm a virgin or not, but it kind of felt right telling you about it."

Trish smiled. "Thanks, that was a nice thing to say." She paused, mentally wrestling with something. "I guess I still owe you a secret."

"No, not really. You told me about your . . . uh love life. That counts."

"No it doesn't." She hesitated. "Ever since I sent the e-mail, I've been trying to figure out what secret to share with you. You know how sometimes when you do something, it seems like a good idea at the time, but you haven't really thought it through? Well, it was kind of like that with the e-mail. But you know what—this is a lot easier than I thought it was going to be."

Jenna blushed at the compliment.

"Anyway, my secret is well . . . I don't drink." She paused. "Kind of funny, huh? Both of our secrets are about stuff we don't do."

Jenna smiled, but didn't say anything, anticipating that there was more to come.

"My mom's an alcoholic. I don't think I really knew that until middle school. She hid it pretty well, at least from me." Trish appeared to gather herself in order to keep going. "She took off about two years ago with some guy she met at the bar at the country club. It's just me and my dad now." Her eyes began to fill up as she finished the last sentence.

Jenna reached over and put her hand on Trish's. "I'm sorry."

"Thanks."

"So, when did she leave, the start of your senior year?"

"Yeah."

"That must have been tough."

"It was, but somehow, you know, you make the best of things."

Afraid it would look like one-upsmanship, Jenna was hesitant to tell Trish about her own circumstances, but Trish inquired anyway. "What about you? I noticed in your e-mails that you only mentioned your mom."

"Yeah, my dad died when I was eight – cancer."

Trish shook her head. "Aren't we a pair? I'm sorry. It sounds like you had it even rougher than I did."

"Neither one's a picnic."

Trish smiled and nodded. "Right."

They remained silent for a while and then Trish decided to expand the explanation of her secret. "I think part of the reason I don't drink is because I'm scared that I could become an alcoholic too. I know that's probably a major overreaction, but . . . ." Her voice trailed off before she changed direction. "I don't hate her. I know it's an illness, but still . . . it's like she chose to leave." Trish was quiet for a moment and then said, "I also think part of not drinking is I worry that if I drink too much I could lose control. I don't like the idea of something having that kind of power over me."

Jenna moved her hand back on top of Trish's. "I get that," she said.

They explored that topic for a little while and then moved on to twenty more—the Cliffs Notes version of their lives:

Jenna's mom was a teacher, her step dad an accountant.

Trish's dad managed a restaurant at a country club.

Jenna had signed up for a lot of education courses; she might want to be a teacher.

Trish was majoring in American Studies with a minor in communications – she might want to go into journalism.

Jenna had wanted to go to Tufts since she and her mom had visited after her sophomore year in high school.

Trish had been accepted to Tufts, but decided to go to a state school because she didn't know if, or when, her mom might come home.

Jenna's mom was great, and she liked her step dad.

Trish's dad was great, and she hadn't given up on the idea that she could forgive her mom someday.

They talked about favorite foods, favorite movies, favorite music, favorite everything. They had their very own version of a "Barbara Walters Special." At about one thirty in the morning, sleep finally overtook them. If there is such a thing as good exhaustion, they both had it.

In five short hours they had become like sisters. But unlike many sets of sisters, there was none of the messy, sibling dynamic that can often strain that particular relationship. No vying for their parents' attention. No trying to gain the upper hand. No jealousy over guys, or clothes, or stuff.

Although unspoken, it had quickly become obvious to the two of them that time and blood weren't always a requirement for someone to feel like family.

CHAPTER 5

During the next several weeks every interaction between Jenna and Trish strengthened their friendship. Every conversation, every shared laugh, every unspoken communication was like some sort of interpersonal mortar fortifying their relationship.

Their course schedules were quite similar, so for the most part they were in class during the same hours and back in the dorm during the same hours. But because they had become such good friends, neither of them objected to the lack of alone time.

They did have one course in common—a philosophy elective. Each Thursday when the class ended around 4:00, they would go back to the dorm, drop off their things, freshen up, and then take the train into Boston for an early dinner—nothing very fancy, just a chance to break up their routine, something to look forward to each week. On this particular Thursday in mid-October they were headed for a location just off Commonwealth Avenue near the Boston University campus.

As usual, the conversation on the way into Boston centered on the philosophy course they had just come from. "I really enjoyed that discussion today," said Jenna.

"Yeah, I did too. Who would have thought that John Stuart Mill and Thomas Aquinas would have gotten everyone's panties in a bunch?"

Jenna laughed. "Wow, quite the cerebral analysis."

"You know what I mean."

Twenty minutes later they got off the train and headed for their destination. One of the things that had attracted them to this particular location when they were checking out places on the Internet was the name – *It Had to B.U.*

It was larger than they had expected and much more like a restaurant than the typical spots favored by the college crowd. As Trish pointed out, it also had a lot of texture—plenty of quiet areas, some booths, and a large function room, which when not in use blended easily into the main area of the restaurant.

Shortly after ordering their meal, Trish excused herself to go to the ladies room. When she returned she had a flyer in her hand. "Look at this," she said, as she offered the paper to Jenna.

Jenna read it and looked quizzically at Trish. "A non-alcoholic night for college students only?"

"That's what it says, two weeks from tomorrow."

"And it's going to be here? Why do you think they'd sponsor something like that?"

"I don't know. But it says it's twenty bucks to get in, and this place holds what – 250, 300? Plus food. I bet they can make eight, ten thousand easy. And the colleges will love it."

"So when did you become a marketing major?"

Trish got a smile on her face. "I'm just saying, I can see all the positive publicity."

"Sounds like you're interested."

"Maybe. Might be fun. I mean, no guys slobbering all over the place, no drunks hitting on us."

"There's that. Okay, sure. Why not?"

A few miles away, across the Charles River, a twenty-one-year-old Harvard senior named Trent Engels had the exact same flyer in his hand, and was showing it to his friend and roommate, David Whitcomb. "What do you think, David?"

"Why would you want to go to this? Did you forget that you're twenty-one? You can legally drink."

Trent took the flyer back as if it was some sort of prop he needed to hold. "But think about all those naïve and innocent young co-eds who'll be there."

"You are such a tool."

"Yeah, but the sharpest one in the shed."

David laughed in spite of himself. "Not exactly what I meant." He looked directly at Trent and shook his head. "Maybe. Let me see what else is going on. Of course, you could just go by yourself."

"Not as much fun."

"Aren't the girls the objective, not my company?"

Trent ignored the question. "So what else are you going to be doing anyway? I'm only looking out for your social interests."

David shook his head again. "Right." He continued. "I'm going to have that operation, you know."

"What operation?"

"The one that removes you from my hip."

Around 6:30 on the night of the event, Trent opened the door to the off-campus apartment he shared with David, and yelled out, "Honey, I'm home, and I brought a surprise." Behind David was Jeremy Baxter, who had been a teammate of David's on the Harvard track team for the past three years. Jeremy was about 6' 2" with sandy colored hair, and a build that suggested he belonged more on the football field than the track.

David emerged from the kitchen shaking his head and rolling his eyes at his roommate's greeting. When he spotted Jeremy, he smiled and went over to shake hands. "Hey, Jeremy, good to see you. How was your summer?"

"Good, good. How about you?"

"Great." David pointed to Trent. "How did you hook up with this guy?"

"I ran into him on campus, and he said I should come over and see you guys; that you were going out to some new spot, and he thought I'd enjoy it."

David looked at Trent. "What, are you working for this place now?"

"No, I just wanted to make sure I had someone to go with in case you bailed."

"Flattering," said Jeremy.

David addressed Jeremy. "You solo tonight? Where's Karen?"

"Yeah, I'm solo. I was telling Trent, I'm gonna be solo for a while; Karen's doing her junior year in Brazil."

"That's not good."

"No, it's not."

Trent spoke up again. "I told him. It's a perfect opportunity to meet some new possibilities."

David said, "I'm sure that's exactly what Jeremy wants to hear right now."

"It's okay. I haven't been out much since Karen left. Actually, I appreciate the invitation."

Trent interjected. "So, what about it, David? Are you coming with us, or what?'

"Yeah, I'm coming. I can't very well leave Jeremy alone with you."

"This should be great," said Trent. "Three Harvard seniors descending on the sheltered co-eds of Boston."

Jeremy looked at David. "See, this is why I don't have a roommate."

David laughed, and then said, "Jeremy, if you want something to eat or drink, help yourself. I'm going to check my e-mail and clean up. We can leave in about a half hour."

"Thanks."

David emerged from his bedroom about twenty minutes later with a somber expression on his face. Jeremy noticed it first. "Are you okay?"

David puffed out his cheeks and shook his head slightly. "I was checking some things on my computer and I clicked on the online edition of the *Globe*. There's an article about my father by the investigative team."

Trent said, "How bad is it?"

"Not good, that's for sure."

"I'm sorry," said Jeremy.

"Maybe it's not as bad as you think," said Trent.

"It is. I mean they didn't use the word 'slumlord,' but they might as well have."

"Shit," said Trent.

Jeremy couldn't think of anything else to say, so he just repeated, "I'm sorry."

"It's okay." David hesitated. "But I don't think I'm up for going out tonight."

"No, sure. We understand," said Jeremy.

Trent again: "Maybe going out would take your mind off things."

"I don't think so."

Everyone was quiet for a few minutes and then Jeremy said, "I think maybe I'm going to take a pass on tonight too. Sorry again about your dad, David."

David nodded.

"I'll give you a ride," offered Trent.

"No, that's all right. It's only a few blocks."

"A few blocks? It's at least a mile."

"I used to be on the track team, remember?"

This caught David's attention. "What do you mean *used* to?"

"I just can't afford the time this year. I've got student teaching coming up."

Trent said, "So, you really are going to be a teacher? I mean, a Harvard education, and that's it?"

David allowed himself a little smile. "You know, Trent, it's not a requirement that you say everything that comes into your head."

Jeremy was smiling also. "I've known him almost as long as I've known you, David. I can tell when he's yanking my chain."

Trent responded. "You do make it easy, you know."

They were all smiling now. Jeremy went over to get his coat when David spoke up. "Oh, the hell with it. Let's go anyway. There's nothing I can do about the article, certainly not tonight."

Trent looked skeptical. "Are you sure?"

"Yeah, it'll be fine."

Jeremy addressed David. "Don't do this on my account."

"No, no; it really is okay."

"Good," said Trent, as he put his hand on David's shoulder. "Why don't we take two cars, in case you want to leave early?" He paused. "Or more importantly, in case I get lucky."

David couldn't help but smile. "I sure hope that doesn't happen."

"Why not?"

"Because that would mean some girl got unlucky."

"And you're supposed to be my friend."

David shrugged and headed toward his room. "I need to shut down my computer, and then we can go."

David came out a few minutes later. They all put on their coats and were about to leave when David said. "I was just thinking. If anybody asks tonight, I'm David *White*, not David Whitcomb."

Both Trent and Jeremy nodded. Trent asked, "You mean because of the article, and who your father is?"

"Yeah." He hesitated, as his voice trailed off. "And maybe because of who he isn't."

Jenna and Trish arrived at the restaurant at about 7:00, a little early for most college get-togethers, alcohol free or not. They sat in a semi-circle booth with their backs to the wall, facing the door. If this had been a James Bond film, Jenna and Trish's choice of seating would have easily identified them as spies – Keep an eye on the door, and don't let anyone

28

sneak up on you from behind. Their choice was nothing so nefarious, but purposeful just the same.

They engaged in small talk, sipped Diet Cokes, and periodically checked out the relatively few other patrons. By 7:30, however, the place was three quarters full, and the students finally began to seek out potential partners, at least for conversation, if nothing else. However, none of the hundred males in attendance had yet approached Jenna and Trish.

"Maybe this "back against the wall" strategy wasn't such a great idea," said Trish.

"It's still early." Jenna paused. "But it does seem like any guys thinking about heading over here would have to make a full commitment. I mean, they know we can see them coming the whole time."

Trish looked over at her friend. "So, you think all these guys have commitment issues?"

Jenna started to laugh. "Could be."

Trish glanced toward the door and noticed three guys entering. Two of them were about six feet tall, the third about two inches taller. Both six—footers had brown hair, the other one, sandy blond. Trish watched them as they took off their coats, and then pointed them out to Jenna. "It'd be nice if those guys don't have commitment issues."

Jenna chuckled.

As they were taking off their coats, David, Trent, and Jeremy surveyed the restaurant, not exactly sure what to do next. Trent stopped his survey and peered intently to his right. He then offered, "I see some people I know over there. I think I'm going to head over. You want to come?"

David said, "No, you go ahead. Anyone I know?"

"No, I don't think so. They're from one of my classes last year. What about you, Jeremy?"

"No, I think I'll just hang out here for a while."

Trent said, "Okay, I'll catch up with you guys later."

Jeremy spoke to David. "Do you want a Coke or something?"

"Yeah, sure."

Trish and Jenna watched this entire interaction, although they couldn't hear any of the exchange. Trish spoke first. "Now that there are only two of them, which one do you want?"

"What do you mean only two? All three of them left."

"I know they didn't come right over, but I think they'll be back."

"They didn't even see us."

"Maybe we should move closer; then it would only take a partial commitment."

"Will you stop? Are you sure someone didn't slip something into your soda?"

"Why don't we give it a few minutes, and then if nothing happens we should probably be more . . . what's the word – 'proactive'?"

"What is it with you tonight?"

"Never mind," said Trish, as she subtly pointed. Then in her best *Poltergeist* voice, she said, "They're baaaack!"

This time there was eye contact among all of them. Trish and Jenna watched as the two guys spoke to each other and then smiled at them. Trish leaned in toward Jenna and whispered, "You never answered me. Which one?"

Jenna got caught up in the moment. "It doesn't matter, they're both cute."

The guys started heading toward them. Trish leaned into Jenna again. "Quick, Jenna, go ask the manager to turn up the heat."

"What, are you cold?"

"No, but if it gets real hot in here, maybe the blond guy will take off his shirt."

Jenna lightly slapped Trish's shoulder, just before David and Jeremy arrived at the booth. David spoke first. "Hi, mind if we sit down?"

Trish said, "No, not at all."

"I'm David, and this is Jeremy."

"I'm Trish and this is Jenna."

Both guys nodded and sat down, David next to Jenna and Jeremy next to Trish.

The noise level in the restaurant increased dramatically over the next several hours, and what started off as a four-way conversation gradually was reduced to couples' conversations. The topics were pretty similar however – school, majors, hometown, family, music etc.

As it approached 11:00, Trent came by the booth, was introduced to Jenna and Trish, and announced that he was leaving shortly. David said they were going to do the same. He indicated he would drive Jeremy back, and offered to transport Jenna and Trish to their dorms as well. They declined, having decided even before they left Tufts that they wouldn't accept a ride from anyone tonight, no matter how nice they seemed.

As they prepared to leave, David asked Jenna, "Can I have your phone number?"

Jenna brightened. "Sure. I'll give you my e-mail address too."

"That'd be great."

While Jenna was writing out the information, David turned to Trish. "Nice meeting you."

"Same here."

He faced Jenna again, as she handed him the piece of paper. In an exaggerated formal tone he said, "It was a real pleasure meeting you, Jenna MacDonald."

Jenna mimicked David's tone. "Likewise, David White."

David cringed a little, although no one seemed to notice. He recovered quickly and said to Jenna. "I had fun." He held out the paper she had given him and said, "I'll call you."

"I'd like that."

"Are you sure you don't want a ride?"

Jenna was tempted, but said, "No, we're fine."

David and Jeremy waited out front with Jenna and Trish until they were able to hail a cab. They said their goodbyes and waved as the cab left the curb.

The ride back to Tufts took about twenty minutes. Both Trish and Jenna expressed to each other that they had had a good time, but Jenna was much more enthusiastic. "David seems really nice. I think he'll call, don't you?"

Trish smiled at Jenna's eagerness. "Yeah, I'd be very surprised if he didn't."

"Did you like Jeremy?"

"I did," said Trish. "He seems like a good guy too. Trouble is he's already got a girlfriend. She's in Brazil, but it's obvious that it was pretty serious."

"Sorry."

"Don't be sorry. That's just the way it is."

David and Jeremy had a similar conversation on the way back to Cambridge. "Nice girls," said David.

"Yeah, I agree. You two really seemed to hit it off."

"Yeah, we did. I'm definitely going to give her a call." David glanced over at Jeremy. "How about you and Trish? Boy, she's beautiful."

"She is, isn't she? She's really nice—and funny too. But, you know, I've been with Karen for two years. Even though she's in Brazil . . . ."

"I know."

David changed the topic. "I wish I hadn't lied about my last name. Jenna's from California; she wouldn't know who my father is, or care."

Jeremy offered some advice. "If you're interested in her, I wouldn't wait too long to tell her. That's the kind of thing that can come back and bite you in the ass."

"Yeah, you're right." David continued talking, although more to himself than Jeremy. "I need to give my father a call, probably tomorrow. Jeez, that article . . . I don't know what to think."

CHAPTER 6

Often when people describe their inability to sleep, they refer to it as "tossing and turning;" but that had never been David's experience. His inability to sleep never manifested itself in such a physical way. Instead, David usually remained motionless and quiet, except for the activity going on in his head. On the nights that he couldn't sleep, the activity resembled a giant fireworks display, with exaggerated "what ifs" exploding in one corner and fantasies in another, and the stuff and the people that were part of his life interspersed throughout. On this particular Friday night, however, the pyrotechnics only involved two people—his father and Jenna.

All told, David was able to accumulate about three hours of sleep, and then, only in small increments. He finally decided to get out of bed around 9:00. Considering all the mental acrobatics his mind had gone through the night before, he had expected some clarity in the morning. But that wasn't the case. The only thing that was apparent to him was that he needed to make a couple of phone calls—one to Jenna, which he was looking forward to, and one to his father, which he was not.

To characterize David's relationship with his father as complicated didn't begin to tell the story. Thermonuclear dynamics was complicated; string theory was complicated; decoding the human genome was complicated. But comprehending any of those would have been a piece of cake compared to peeling back the layers of complexity that constituted the relationship between the two of them.

If you Googled Bradford Whitcomb, you would discover that he was 69, the head of Whitcomb Realty Trust, and a multi-millionaire. He owned a substantial number of apartment buildings, triple-deckers, and commercial properties in the Boston area.

What you might not discover in the Google search was that he was currently single. His first wife had divorced him twenty-two years before; his second wife just three years ago. Both former spouses had received millions of dollars in their respective settlements. The last settlement had only stayed in the "financially reasonable range" because of a comprehensive pre-nuptial agreement.

Each marriage had produced a son. The oldest, Bradford "Brad" Whitcomb II, was currently estranged from his father. After graduating from Northwestern, and despite his mother's objections, he had gone to work for his dad. It lasted about a year, and ended badly. Brad moved back to the Chicago area and stayed there.

David was Bradford Whitcomb's son from his second marriage. David's mother was like any of the wives of Henry the Eighth. Bradford had only married her in the hopes that she would produce a male heir, since his other son, and namesake, wasn't in the picture anymore. The only reason David's mother had married Bradford was money. She pawned David off on nannies and housekeepers, and barely looked back when David turned eighteen and the divorce became final.

In truth, Bradford Whitcomb was the more involved and responsible parent, but the bar hadn't been set very high. The last several years had been much better, however. David's father took much more of an interest in his son and spent more time with him. Less charitable individuals might have suggested that Bradford Whitcomb only did this in order to exert control over David and mold him into what he wanted, hoping to ensure that his younger son didn't take off also. Of course, Mr. Whitcomb was reasonably confident that the six million dollar trust fund that he had set up for David, even with its codicils and restrictions, probably provided some insurance in that regard as well.

David grabbed his cell phone off the nightstand along with the paper Jenna had given him with her number on it. He debated for a moment, literally weighing the two items in his hands. He finally used the speed dial to place a call to his father's private line at the office. Even though it was a Saturday morning, David knew his father would be at work, especially after the previous day's article.

Bradford Whitcomb glanced at the caller ID, picked up the phone and said, "Hello, David."

"Hi, Dad." David paused. "I . . . uh saw the *Globe* article yesterday. How're you doing?"

"Oh, I'm fine. All of that was old news. Just recycled stuff; they're only trying to sell newspapers."

"This is the first time the investigative team's been involved though, right?"

"They're just reporters. A couple of them have an axe to grind. Nothing to worry about." He paused. "I'm very careful, David. The lawyers have been all over this. We've done nothing illegal."

"It didn't seem like they were suggesting that you did. It seemed more like they were pointing out that none of the apartments had been upgraded or . . . ."

"That's not illegal."

"I know. Of course not." David hesitated, not really aware that he was about to make the request until it came out of his mouth. "Maybe, could I come over and talk to you?"

There was silence on the line.

"Dad?"

"Yeah, I'm here. About the article?"

"If it's okay."

If Mr. Whitcomb was surprised by the request, he recovered quickly. "Yeah, that'd be fine. Why don't you come by around 10:30?"

"Okay, I'll see you then. Thanks."

David toyed with the idea of calling Jenna, but decided instead to wait until after he met with his father. He started to mentally outline the things he wanted to bring up at the meeting, but he was having trouble focusing. Periodically his mind wandered back to the previous night and his conversation with Jenna. The fact that she was occupying his thoughts, particularly when he was fully awake, both excited and scared him at the same time.

David ate a quick breakfast, showered, left a note for Trent, who still wasn't up yet, and headed out to his father's office in downtown Boston. He arrived twenty minutes later, and took the elevator up to the top floor where his father was waiting for him. "Hi, David. It's just me today. No secretary. I didn't want to leave the door unlocked. Come on in."

"Hi, Dad. Thanks."

Bradford Whitcomb's office was definitely old school. No steel and glass, all wood and leather. It looked like something out of a Victorian novel. And the formality didn't end with the furniture. In all the times David had been there, he had always sat on the opposite side of the mammoth oak desk, facing his father. Today was no different.

Mr. Whitcomb opened the conversation. "How're you doing?"

David nodded. "Fine."

"How's school?

"Good."

"Are you finding any time for yourself?"

"Yeah."

"And Trent, how's he doing?"

"He's good. He's . . . well, you know, Trent." His father smiled as David continued. "How are *you*? I mean, after the article and all."

"Really, I'm fine. My blood pressure is up a little, but it was up even before the article. I told you on the phone; this will blow over in a few days."

"Could you tell me some more about it?"

"What do want to know?"

"I'm not sure. Other than they said there had been no renovations or upgrades in the last fifteen years."

"Well, that's not exactly true. Everything is up to code. It's required; it has to be."

"The article seemed to indicate that it was the bare minimum."

"I'm not about to turn them into luxury apartments." He leaned forward. "Look David, even though there's no more rent control, most of these apartments are still subsidized. There are a lot of restrictions, and the tenants' organizations are very strong."

"What about doing some improvements that wouldn't cost that much?"

"Define *wouldn't cost that much*."

"I don't know. I don't think the article said."

"No, it didn't." Mr. Whitcomb paused, studying his son. "Where's all this coming from, David?"

David shook his head. "It's just that they're always painting you as some kind of villain. Maybe spending some money on the apartments would go a long way . . . ."

Mr. Whitcomb chuckled. "I'm not trying to win a popularity contest."

"Aren't most of the tenants Black or Hispanic?"

"You think this is about race?"

"No, I'm just saying . . . ."

"It's not about race; it's about economics and business. Most of this is low-income housing we're talking about. These people wouldn't have any place else to go if we didn't provide these apartments."

David weighed his words carefully, not wishing to further antagonize his father. "But couldn't some things be done that didn't cost a fortune, and maybe would make things better for the people who live there?"

Mr. Whitcomb stared at David. "I've complied with the law every step of the way—smoke detectors, carbon monoxide detectors, lead paint testing. None of that was cheap."

David knew that almost anything he said now was going to exacerbate the situation. "Okay, Dad. I didn't come here to have an argument."

Mr. Whitcomb, however, was the one who wouldn't let it go. He knew that he was on the defensive—a place he seldom visited, especially with his son. But he couldn't completely keep himself in check. "So, what would you have me do, David?"

"I'm not sure. I guess in all fairness, I really don't know that much about those apartments . . . but it seems like you ought to be able to figure out something, so the press isn't all over you all the time."

Mr. Whitcomb tried to recover his equilibrium. He sat back and relaxed his shoulders, altering his body language, and making himself appear less confrontational. His words confirmed the shift in his demeanor. "How about we do this? I'll set something up with you and a few of our site managers and you can go see things for yourself."

"Seriously?"

"Yes. We can meet after that, and see how you feel about everything then. I'm not the bad guy here, David."

David thought to himself, *Yeah, but I'm not sure you're the good guy either.* Instead he said, "Okay. That sounds great."

"All right then. I'll talk to the site managers on Monday and either call you or send you an e-mail to set up the times."

"Thanks, Dad. I appreciate this."

"You're welcome." And then as an obvious afterthought, Mr. Whitcomb added, "Would you like to stick around and have some lunch?"

"No, no thanks. I've got a few things to do."

"Okay, then I'll talk to you on Monday."

"Thanks again, Dad," he said, as he got up and offered his hand.

Mr. Whitcomb stayed behind the desk. He stood, shook his son's hand and said, "Bye, David. Just close the outer door on your way out. It'll lock by itself."

As David drove back to Cambridge, he revisited the conversation he had just had with his father. It was unusual for him to feel as if he was on equal footing with his dad. And while no one witnessing their most recent interaction would call them equals, David felt as if he had definitely moved up a few rungs on the ladder. His father was usually patronizing and dismissive toward David and his ideas. That didn't seem to be the case this time. If nothing else came out of this, thought David, at least for once he treated me like an adult.

When David arrived back at the apartment, he fished Jenna's number out of his pocket and called her. She answered on the third ring. "Hello."

"Hi, Jenna. It's David . . . from last night."

"Oh, hi."

"How are you?" he said, realizing too late that he had just seen her twelve hours before – what could have changed? Maybe I should have planned out my end of the conversation beforehand, he thought.

If Jenna believed his question was anything but reasonable, she didn't let on. "I'm fine. How about you?"

"I'm fine too." He paused. "I had a good time last night."

"Me too."

"I was wondering if you're free tonight, or maybe tomorrow."

Jenna hesitated, causing a few anxious moments for David. "Uh, I can't tonight, but I'm free tomorrow afternoon. I've got a paper I have to finish tonight."

"That's great. I mean about tomorrow, not about your paper." Jenna laughed. He smiled when he heard it. He liked her laugh. "How about I pick you up around 1:00? We can get some lunch, and then decide what else to do. Maybe a movie, or a ride to look at the foliage; whatever you want."

"That sounds nice."

"Great. Which dorm are you in again?"

"Hutchinson House."

"Okay. I'll find it. I'll see you at 1:00."

"Okay. Thanks, David. Bye."

"Bye."

David hadn't had too many Saturday mornings better than this one – an adult conversation with his father and a date to look forward to. He smiled broadly, remembering Jenna's laugh.

Jenna pressed the end button on her phone, and rushed down to the laundry room to tell Trish about David's call. Trish was alone, but Jenna wouldn't have cared if the place had been packed. She blurted out, "He called!"

Trish didn't have to be told who "he" was. "Wow, that didn't take long."

"I know. We're going out for lunch tomorrow."

"That's great, Jenna." said Trish, as she gave her a hug. Before they separated, Trish whispered in Jenna's ear with a melodramatic tone. "You know that whole virgin thing you've got going on; try to hold on to it for a while, will you?"

Jenna gently pushed back from Trish, and with a feigned expression of shock said, "It's our first date for cryin' out loud."

"Been known to happen."

"You are so bad."

CHAPTER 7

The New England meteorologists had predicted that the foliage wouldn't reach its peak for another few days. Nevertheless, it was already spectacular. The leaves on the maples ran the gamut from soft red to scarlet. The hickories and poplars were myriad shades of brown and gold. It reminded Jenna of an Impressionist painting, although it was hard to imagine that even the palette of a Monet could have replicated this panorama. Even the plain black asphalt of Route 93 didn't detract from the beauty. Instead, it served as the center aisle of a mammoth outdoor bazaar where Mother Nature displayed her wares.

David had suggested that they postpone their lunch until they arrived in New Hampshire, sensing that Jenna would especially enjoy the foliage in the early afternoon sun. She eagerly agreed. The conversation in the car was light and superficial, mostly because of the distraction of the scenery.

Shortly before 2:00 they left the highway and found a quaint little restaurant that had been at the same location for the past fifty years. In all that time, the basics of the menu had changed very little. New Hampshire folks tended to be no-nonsense types. And since the restaurant had been around for the last half century, David felt certain that the food would also be no-nonsense, and very good as well.

"That was a great idea about the foliage. I've never seen anything like it," Jenna gushed. "I mean, I've seen photos, but they don't really show how vibrant the colors are."

"No, not even close. I've lived here my whole life, but it's still amazing every time." He paused. "I'm glad you liked it."

Jenna smiled and then glanced down at the menu. "I guess we should figure out what we want."

"Got any ideas?"

"Actually, I was thinking of getting some breakfast."

"That's funny; I was thinking the same thing."

Jenna pointed to the menu. "Oooh, French toast. I love French toast . . . sourdough bread and Vermont maple syrup."

David expressed some surprise. "From the looks of you, I can't imagine that you eat anything like French toast very often."

Jenna blushed. "I splurge every once in a while, but not too often. I guess I was kind of lucky that I didn't put on the freshman fifteen." A pause. "I'm just hoping there's no such thing as the sophomore twenty."

David smiled. "I wouldn't worry about it; you look great."

"I wasn't fishing for a compliment."

"I didn't take it that way." David paused. "Well then, French toast it is, *oui, mademoiselle?*" Jenna smiled and nodded as he continued. "That about wraps it up for my French. But it does sound good, doesn't it?" He looked embarrassed. "I mean the French toast, not *my* French."

The waitress showed up at that moment and took their order. After she left, they both started to talk at the same time.

David said, "Go ahead, you first."

"I was just going to thank you for calling, and . . . uh for today. You know, for everything."

"Well, you're welcome."

Jenna hesitated, trying to come up with a topic to move the conversation along. "I know you told me that you grew up around here, but we didn't really talk that much about our families. Do you have any brothers or sisters?"

David knew he had to be careful as they moved into more personal territory. Earlier in the day before he left to pick up Jenna, he had envisioned telling her his real name and why he hadn't been truthful. But then he kept vacillating, like some metallic bear at a carnival shooting gallery, heading in one direction and then abruptly reversing itself.

It had been stupid not to tell her at the end of the evening on Friday; then it would have been easy to explain away. But now that he had waited a few days, telling her that he had lied could be the kind of thing that would end a relationship before it even had a chance to get started. When he first met Jenna, he liked her immediately. And somehow he instinctively knew that he wanted to give his feelings an opportunity to develop into something more.

Maintaining the deception was going to put that opportunity in jeopardy. But despite that realization, in the split second before he spoke, he decided to hold off telling her. "Yeah, actually I have a brother-well, a half-brother,

41

Brad. He's a lot older; lives in Chicago. I've only met him a couple of times." David didn't have much more to add to the sparse biography, so he directed the same question to Jenna. "How about you, any siblings?"

"No, just me and my mom, and now my step-dad. My real dad passed away when I was eight."

"Oh, I'm sorry." When Jenna didn't elaborate, David said, "My mom and dad got divorced when I was eighteen, right after I graduated from high school. My mom lives in New York now. I don't see her very often; we aren't that close."

"How about your father, are you close to him?"

"Somewhat, at least lately. He was always pretty busy when I was growing up, you know with his business and all."

"What does he do?"

"Real estate."

Here was the perfect opportunity, thought David. Just come out with it, she'll understand. He felt himself tense up, and then was unable to form the words. Instead, he shifted the conversation to Jenna's family. "Okay, your turn. What does your mom do?"

Jenna filled in the details about her mom, her step-dad, and about growing up in Southern California. Then it was David's turn again. The table tennis exchanges continued for several more minutes and then their food arrived. Jenna sensed that David was being a little guarded, but couldn't put her finger on why.

In between bites of French toast, they continued getting to know one another. Eventually, they got around to their friends. Jenna initiated it. "So how long have you known Jeremy and Trent?"

"Trent's been my roommate since freshman year. He's a real piece of work, as you could probably tell, but I love him like a brother. He's a great guy . . . it's just that he hasn't completely grown up yet. I mean socially, he's about sixteen. In terms of academics, that's a different story. He's going to graduate with a 3.8."

Jenna became a little wide-eyed. "Really? That's pretty impressive." She paused. "What about Jeremy?"

"We were on the track team together. He's terrific too. He wants to be a teacher, like your mom . . . and maybe you, right? Trent rags on him all the time about that, but I think it's great that he knows exactly what he wants to do. I wish I did." David paused and reflected back on Jeremy for a moment, searching for another piece of information to keep the conversation going.

He blurted out the first thing that came into his mind. "I think freshman year he did some modeling for a while."

Jenna hesitated, not having any idea how to respond. "Really?"

David appeared flustered. "I'm not sure why I remembered that all of a sudden." He paused, and shook his head in a self-deprecating manner, as a smile found its way onto his face. "Telling you that Jeremy was a model, probably wasn't the best strategy to impress you on the first date, was it?"

Jenna laughed. "It's okay, I'm already impressed."

David continued to smile. "With me or with Jeremy?"

"Both of you."

David decided it was all right to continue teasing her. "So, you do think he's good looking?"

"I don't know how I'm supposed to answer that."

"It's okay; I'm the one who brought it up. Just be honest." As the word "honest" left his mouth, David blanched.

Jenna picked up on the change in his expression, but assumed it was because he felt uncomfortable talking about Jeremy's looks, so she shifted the topic slightly. "Well, as long as we're being honest, the two of us are pretty much in the same boat. I mean, I don't know if Trish has ever done any modeling, but she certainly could, don't you think?"

Now David was at a loss for words. It was one thing for him to acknowledge that Jeremy was handsome, but how should he respond about Jenna's roommate? Well, he thought, at least maybe I can be truthful about something. "Yes. She's very attractive." He paused. "But I hope you're not selling yourself short in the looks department."

Jenna smiled, and slightly nodded her head. "Good save."

David returned the smile. Then he followed up. "Was that some kind of test?"

"No. But I do have to admit, I am curious about something. On Friday night when you and Jeremy came over to our booth, you headed directly to sit down next to me. How come?"

"I'm not sure. I guess it was just a gut feeling." He smiled. "Boy, that was a romantic explanation, wasn't it?"

Jenna let out a little chuckle. "Well, whatever the reason, I'm glad you did." She started blushing.

"So am I."

On the drive back, David asked, "Can we do this again? I mean, would you like to go out again?"

"Yes, I'd like that."

"I guess the weekends are probably best, huh?" He glanced over at Jenna, and then added jokingly, "Although, I could make time tomorrow, or Tuesday, or Wednesday. I'm not coming on too strong here, am I?"

Jenna smiled. "I think it will have to be Fridays or Saturdays. Although, depending on what I've got due for school, we might be able to work something else out."

David had a thought. "How are Thursday nights for you? I've got a real light schedule on Fridays, so Thursday nights would work."

"Thursdays aren't good. We go out to dinner on Thursdays. I mean Trish and I."

David got a questioning expression on his face, but his mouth displayed a smirk. "You mean the pretty one?"

Jenna broke up.

David smiled. And then thought to himself—*God, I love her laugh.*

They finally agreed to go out on the following Friday. David said he would call during the week to arrange the specifics. "I might have to call every day or possibly twice a day, just to make sure I haven't forgotten anything."

David had two early classes back-to-back on Monday morning, so he didn't get a chance to check his e-mail until nearly noon. When he did, he found one from his father.

Hello David,

I've spoken with three of the site managers. Since I didn't know your schedule, I arranged the visits for next Saturday. I've attached all the pertinent information for each one in a separate file. If you have any questions, let me know. Dad

David opened the attachments, which listed each apartment building, its address, the site manager's name, and the time of the scheduled meeting. The rest of the files contained apartment specifications, dates of inspections, and a lot of other legalese. The rents weren't included, but David didn't really expect that they would be. He could get that information from the site managers anyway.

As he read the files over, however, he began to wonder what he had gotten himself into.

CHAPTER 8

As he had promised, even if said half-jokingly, David called Jenna every day leading up to their date on Friday. A number of times when she was at school and her phone was off, he left a voice message or he texted her. Jenna learned the hard way not to read the text messages while she was in class—she had to cover up her laughter in the middle of a lecture by faking a coughing spell.

Nobody outside of Jenna's family, and certainly no member of the opposite sex, had ever paid this much attention to her. Not surprisingly, she loved it. But it wasn't just the attention; it was the person giving it to her. David had a gentle, sensitive way about him, and a great sense of humor. He seemed to exude confidence, but he was self-deprecating as well. As all of this went through her mind, Jenna smiled, and thought to herself – *Stop analyzing everything, and just enjoy it.*

For his part, David thought about Jenna every day. And while there had never been a shortage of girls in his life, no one had ever affected him quite like this, especially in such a short amount of time. Certainly, he had been infatuated with some of his other girlfriends, but this felt different, and he wasn't sure what to make of it. However, he had a similar thought to the one Jenna had – Don't analyze it. Enjoy the situation, and let whatever's going to happen, happen.

That notion led him to consider the dilemma he was still facing – when and how to tell her the truth. He tried to convince himself that his anxiety over the issue was disproportionate to the reality. *Maybe it's not that big a deal.* But then he thought of all the preparation he had to do to maintain the deception—he couldn't mention the name of his father's business; he had to carry enough cash so that he didn't have to sign credit card slips in front of Jenna, and he had to avoid talking about any topic where his last name might come up. Lying was obviously much more work than telling the truth.

David refrained from using the word 'lying' in his mental deliberations, however. The use of that particular word seemed to propel things to a higher level of wrongdoing, and his feeling of self-worth in the opposite direction. Instead, he thought about his deception euphemistically. He knew it was a semantics sham, but it provided a comfort level he had been able to live with—at least until now.

He began to realize that as often as Jenna was on his mind, so was the issue of his dishonesty and how she might react once she found out. That scared him. He finally resolved to remove the mental burr and come clean. He decided that he would tell Jenna the truth next week – once the site visits were out of the way.

David picked Jenna up around 6:00 on Friday night. They decided to stay local for dinner. And since Medford has more pizza parlors per square mile than almost any other city in Massachusetts, their choice of cuisine became a foregone conclusion.

Jenna suggested Denucci's, a place that she and Trish ate at occasionally. And although Jenna enjoyed the food, she had another motive to go there as well. There was a chance she'd run into somebody she knew from school, and then she'd have the opportunity to show David off.

Just prior to being picked up, Jenna asked Trish if the idea of showing David off made her shallow. Trish had replied, "Probably . . . but it's exactly what I'd do." They both smiled.

Denucci's Pizza had been a fixture near the Tufts campus since the early sixties, and whether you stepped inside then or now, the stereotypes surrounded you – red and white checkered tablecloths, scenes of Rome and Venice on the walls, and one of the Denucci clan twirling pizza dough by the oven. The restaurant did an equal amount of business between take-out and dining-in, and also between college kids and neighborhood families.

On this particular Friday night, it was about three-quarters full when Jenna and David arrived. There were tables available, but since they preferred the intimacy of a booth, they chose to wait. Jenna scanned the restaurant, looking for some familiar faces. She didn't find any. *So much for the showing off idea*, she thought.

A young woman approached them a few minutes later, seated them, and indicated that their waitress would be right along. David looked around and said, "This seems like a nice place."

"It is. Trish and I come here sometimes."

David picked up his menu, and with an exaggerated formality said, "And what would you recommend?"

"The veggie pizza is great, or maybe the calzone. Also the . . . ."

David started to smile, and then shook his head.

"What," asked Jenna?

"The other day French toast, tonight pizza—where the heck do you put it all?"

Jenna gave a small laugh. "I told you, I only splurge once in a while. You just happened to catch me both times this month. Actually, most days I eat pretty healthy."

"I wasn't criticizing."

"I know."

David appeared pensive before he spoke. "How about next week we go some place fancy?"

Jenna looked coquettish. "Are you asking me out again?"

"As a matter of fact, I am."

"Well then, I accept."

"Is next Friday good?"

Jenna appeared to be mentally checking her calendar, although that was only for David's benefit. "Yeah, Friday's fine. Where were you thinking?"

"In Boston. Maybe, Chez Cezanne."

"Really? That's awfully expensive, isn't it?"

"Don't worry about it." He paused. "Besides, they probably have French toast."

She reached over and slapped his hand. "Shut up."

They moved on to a discussion about the courses they were taking. After a few moments the waitress showed up at their booth. "Hi, Jenna."

"Oh, hi Samantha."

"I haven't seen you in a while. How are you doing?"

"Fine, I've just been busy with school, eating on campus a lot." Samantha's gaze shifted to David, as Jenna continued. "I'm sorry, let me introduce you. Samantha, this is . . . uh my friend, David. David, Samantha."

David smiled. "Nice to meet you, Samantha."

"Same here." She took out a pencil and said, "So, what can I get you guys?"

The veggie pizza arrived about fifteen minutes later, and initially, they did more eating than talking. Then Jenna happened to look across the restaurant and noticed an older couple. "Look at that, David."

He glanced over and saw the man patting his wife's hand in an obvious display of affection. Jenna spoke again. "That's really nice."

David smiled. "Yeah, it is." He caught Jenna's eye as she turned her focus back toward him. And before he realized what he was saying, he whispered, "That could be us in fifty years."

Jenna tried to read David's expression, but he was obviously having trouble figuring out why he had made the comment also. Finally, he broke the tension. "Well, that was awkward."

Jenna was still trying to come up with something to say, when David continued, attempting to rescue the moment. "I only meant that when we're that old, I hope we have someone we care about like those two. At least I think that's what I meant."

Jenna smiled. "Whatever you meant; it was sweet."

"So, the next time I start to say something stupid, will you please stop me?"

"It wasn't stupid. I told you, it was sweet."

Samantha came over and prevented any additional awkwardness. "How's your pizza? You two need anything else?"

"Very good. No, I think we're all set," said David.

They continued eating and talking, but avoided bringing up David's remark again. Periodically, however, they glanced over at the older couple; and it brought smiles to both their faces. Samantha came back ten minutes later and brought their check. "No hurry, whenever you're ready."

"Thanks," said David.

As Jenna watched Samantha leave their booth, she leaned forward and squinted, looking past David's left shoulder. "It looks like it's starting to rain."

"Really? I didn't think to bring an umbrella."

"It's probably okay. It doesn't look that bad."

David turned around in the booth. "It doesn't look that good." He turned back to face her. "Why don't I go get the car and bring it around?"

"You don't have to do that."

"It's better than both of us getting wet."

"Are you sure?"

"Yeah, no big deal. I'll just go up front and pay the bill, and then I'll get the car."

"Okay, I'm going to go to the ladies room."

"I'll meet you out front."

When Jenna exited the restroom, she saw David leaving out the front door. As she headed in that direction, Samantha was at the cash register with a big smile on her face. When Jenna got close enough, Samantha said, "I think he's a keeper."

Jenna returned the smile. "We only met about a week ago, but I really like him." She paused. "And he is kind of cute, don't you think?"

"Yeah, he definitely is, and . . . ." Her voice trailed off as she looked directly at Jenna, obviously trying to decide something.

Jenna sensed it, and asked, "What?"

"Well, I don't know if I should tell you this, although he didn't say I couldn't. You see that couple over there?" Samantha was nodding toward the older couple that David and Jenna had been observing. "That's Mr. and Mrs. Antonelli. They're in here all the time. They've lived in the neighborhood even before this place opened. Anyway, your boyfriend gave me an extra forty dollars and told me to pay for their meal and keep the rest for a tip. I'd say that qualifies him as a keeper."

Jenna's expression was a mixture of pride and surprise "Wow, really?"

"Yeah, he just said not to let them know until the both of you had left."

Neither David nor Jenna brought up the topic of the Antonelli's bill on the ride back to the dorm. But for Jenna's part, David's actions reinforced the good feeling she was having, not only about him, but also about the potential for whatever was going on between them to turn into something more serious. As the car approached the Hutchinson House, David said, "I'm just going to drop you off out front, otherwise, you're going to get soaked."

"That's fine. Thanks, David." She looked over at him. "I enjoyed myself again."

"I did too. How about I call you during the week about next Friday?"

"Okay"

Jenna unbuckled her seat belt, hesitated, and then instead of opening the door, she drew closer to David, put her hand on the side of his face and gave him a kiss that lingered for just a moment. Immediately, they were both aware that the kiss was far more intimate than any other physical contact between them had been. All of their goodbyes prior to this had ended with a peck on the cheek or a quick kiss on the lips, more platonic than passionate. As they separated, David moved toward Jenna until the seat belt pulled him back. "Wow, I didn't see that coming."

Jenna had a large smile on her face as she exited the car.

CHAPTER 9

David got up about 9:00 on Saturday morning, showered and shaved, got some papers together, and drove to the first of the site visits in Dorchester. He arrived a few minutes before the scheduled 10:00 appointment, parked the car in a visitor's spot, and headed for the entryway. As he approached the front door, a short man in his forties holding a clipboard emerged and glanced over at David. "Mr. Whitcomb?"

"Please, it's David. Are you Mr. Sanchez?"

"Yes. And it's Alex," said the man as he offered his hand. "Nice to meet you."

"Same here."

Alex took David on a tour of the property—first the outside grounds, followed by two vacant units, and then Alex's own apartment. David had protested the last visit, not wanting to intrude on the man's privacy, but Alex had insisted. They also looked at the boiler area and the storage facilities. David's impression was that the building was clean, somewhat adequately maintained, but very tired. The appliances in the apartments were outdated; the carpet in the hallways and common areas was stained, as were some of the ceilings.

David also realized that some of the tenants must have turned on the heat to take off the early-morning chill. He could hear the clang of the pipes as the hot water surged into them. It was loud enough that he could hear it in the corridors, not just in the apartments themselves.

Initially, Alex Sanchez came across as affable, cooperative, and knowledgeable. However, when David asked more pointed questions, Alex became guarded and somewhat defensive. Additionally, no matter what question was asked, he took the opportunity in his answer to praise David's father. He even went so far as to say the *Globe* article was a total "pack of lies."

David's 11:00 appointment with Jamal Atkins was a carbon copy of his visit to the first property – same itinerary, same areas visited, same praise of David's father. However, the second apartment building was even older than the first one, and it showed. The common areas were clean, but they had an industrial soap smell about them. David suspected that over the past week in anticipation of his visit, extra care had been taken to make everything look and smell as clean as possible. It was a noble effort, but there were a lot of things you couldn't cover up, literally and figuratively. The apartments David visited at the second building were not just tired; they were exhausted.

As David was driving to the third appointment, he began to feel like he was on a fool's errand. And to make it worse, much of it had been his own doing. When he pulled up to the parking area, however, he was immediately impressed. He saw a well-maintained lot, painted lines for the parking spaces, and a border of shrubs and fall flowers. He glanced out the window and saw that the rest of the grounds seemed to be similarly cared for.

As he exited the car, he saw a tall black man talking to a couple of children near the front door of the building. The man looked over as David approached, and said something to the kids, who scooted off. The man then moved in David's direction. As he got closer, he said, "Are you David?"

"Yes."

The man held out his hand. "Darnell Smith. You're early."

David shook hands and checked his watch. "A few minutes. I finished early at the other building."

"Which one was that?"

"Crestview, with Jamal Atkins. And before that, Hollis Street with Alex Sanchez."

"That must have been enlightening."

David was surprised by the sarcasm. "Why would you say it like that?"

Darnell eyed David, obviously considering something. "Well, I don't expect you found out anything particularly useful, did you?" He continued to study David, and before David could answer, Darnell elaborated. "Those two are so far up your father's ass, they'd need a proctologist to get them out."

David laughed, but Darnell's expression remained serious, his eyes never changing their focus. Finally, David filled the void. "What do you mean?"

"You don't know what a proctologist is?"

David let some impatience enter his voice. "Yeah, I do. But you know that's not what I'm asking."

"Can I trust you?"

What the heck is this? thought David. His first instinct was to blurt out "yes," but he held back. Instead he said, "I'm not sure how to answer that."

"Pretty simple – yes I can, or no, I can't."

David looked directly into Darnell's eyes. "If I couldn't be trusted, wouldn't I just say 'yes' anyway?"

"Fair point."

"Why are we playing these games?"

"I need to find out if *you're* the one playing games."

"I don't get it."

"What are you twenty-one, twenty-two . . . . ?"

"Twenty-two."

"I get a call from your father, and he says to show you around. He doesn't tell me why, not that it's any of my business, unless, of course, it is. Like he's checking up on me or something, or maybe you're taking over the family company. Or maybe it's just that you've got nothing better to do. I'm just trying to get a feel for the situation."

"I'm not playing games . . . at least I don't think so." David could tell from Darnell's change in expression that he appreciated the qualifier. David elaborated. "You know about the article?" Darnell nodded. "I went to see my father to talk about it." He paused still trying to assess Darnell. "Anyway, to make a long story short, I told him it seemed to me that if he spent some more money on these buildings he'd help himself out with the media, and at the same time help the people who live here."

"You told him that, huh? How'd he respond?"

"Not well at first, but then he set up these visits."

"So what do you think is going to come out of all this?"

"I'm not sure. But if I can figure out some things that aren't too expensive, maybe he'll listen." David felt like he was spilling his guts, and he wasn't sure why.

Darnell didn't respond for a moment. There was a slight upturn of his mouth and then he said, "Okay, let's go."

The tour that had taken forty-five minutes at the other sites, took an hour and a half at this one. Nothing was off-limits, and Darnell was very forthcoming about the building, and himself.

When the tour was finished, they sat in Darnell's kitchen, where he did most of the talking. He explained that he had gone to college to be an engineer, had gotten involved in drugs before he graduated, finally got himself squared away after a few years, and started working for Whitcomb Realty Trust as a maintenance man. One day while he was on the job, he met David's father. For whatever reason, Mr. Whitcomb had taken a liking to Darnell, and when there was an opening for a manager a few months later, he was offered the job. According to Darnell, David's father knew his history, but didn't care.

It was approaching 2:00 when Darnell said, "Listen, David, I've got a couple of errands to run, but if you're interested we can talk some more next week. I already showed you the preventive maintenance plan we have here, which would be really simple to put in place at the other buildings."

"They don't use it?"

"No. Each building has its own budget, and Atkins and Sanchez didn't want to spend that kind of money upfront. It made things tight when I first put it in, but now we're starting to save money." Darnell hesitated before continuing. "Just a second." He got up and walked over to the other side of the kitchen, opened a drawer, extracted some papers that were stapled together and gave them to David. "Why don't you take this with you and give me a call after you've read it."

David glanced at the cover and then skimmed a few of the pages. He turned from the papers and looked at Darnell with a puzzled expression on his face. "This looks a lot like the suggestions that were in the *Globe* article."

"Where do you think they got them from?"

CHAPTER 10

David felt overwhelmed. He was not able to get a handle on all the things that were pressing on him – the site visits, Darnell's report, a follow-up meeting with his father, school, and most overwhelming of all—Jenna. In the past, whenever he had experienced a similar sensation, his strategy had been to compartmentalize things. Put them all in separate boxes and deal with them one at a time. That strategy seemed woefully inadequate now.

There appeared to be so many facets to each issue that every time he felt like he had figured out a way to deal with one of them, another side of it that he hadn't considered came to light. The last several weeks of his life were like an intricate collage. Even if he studied it for hours, there was bound to be a small piece partially hidden that he had missed.

The most straightforward of the issues bombarding him was school. He hadn't totally neglected those responsibilities, but he certainly had started to fall behind. He took pride in his 3.5 GPA, and wasn't about to blow it senior year. So, the rest of Saturday and all of Sunday were spent on catch-up. He was so focused that even Trent's begging about going to the late afternoon Harvard football game fell on deaf ears.

The only thing David allowed himself to do other than schoolwork on Saturday was respond to his father's voice mail. Instead of calling him back, however, David e-mailed him indicating that he wanted to make another site visit before the two of them met. He chose e-mail because he was afraid his father would be able to detect something in his voice about Darnell and his possible link to the *Globe* article. And certainly, if his father started asking questions on the phone, the chances of something slipping out were even more likely.

David was somewhat concerned that his father wouldn't be satisfied with just the e-mail. He would probably want to know David's impressions immediately. If patience was a virtue, his father was the least virtuous person David knew – and it was possible that impatience was only the tip of the "lack of virtue" iceberg. Fortunately for David, no follow-up phone call came.

When Monday rolled around, David decided he wasn't ready to directly tackle any of the other issues that were bearing down on him, but he did need to at least take some baby steps by creating a timeframe and a way to proceed. Even those token actions made him feel better.

In the afternoon, David gave Darnell a call and told him it would have to be next week before he came back out to see him – he needed additional time to review the report Darnell had given him. David held back the urge to ask Darnell to elaborate about the last comment he had made, but decided it would be better to wait until after he had gone over everything before traveling down that road.

And then there was Jenna.

It didn't matter what other issue David attempted to focus on, he had trouble keeping thoughts of Jenna out of his consciousness. And every time his mind succumbed, it triggered thoughts of the kiss she had given him, producing the same stirring sensation that he had felt when it first happened. Hearing her voice on Tuesday night when he called only intensified it. He told her he had secured reservations at Chez Cezanne, and although she mildly protested, it was obvious from her tone that she was excited.

On Wednesday night David fought the impulse to call again, deciding to go with an e-mail instead. As he had promised himself, it was time to put things in motion to tell the truth. The e-mail started out light, but turned more serious when he indicated that he had something important to discuss with her. Just as with his father, David didn't trust himself not to divulge something over the phone. Besides, telling her in person gave him a better opportunity to gauge her reaction, not to mention that a face-to-face apology was the right thing to do. And while he felt true remorse for deceiving Jenna, he had to admit that he had chosen to apologize in a restaurant because it afforded him some protection in case things didn't go well. The public nature of the place would most likely inhibit Jenna from making a scene. He had tried not to entertain the idea that everything could blow up in his face, but Chez Cezanne provided some insurance. Under the worst of circumstances David reasoned, things would be salvageable if no shouting took place.

Finally, by Thursday David felt back in control of his life.

A few miles away, Jenna's roommate Trish was in the Tufts library doing some research. She had been at it for about forty-five minutes when something on the computer screen caught her attention. She moved closer to get a better look at the image that was displayed. As she read the caption under the photo, she brought her hand up to her mouth, and in a muffled voice said, "Oh, no."

She became teary-eyed as she printed out the image along with a few other pages. She gathered her belongings and headed for her next class. While crossing the campus, she had only one thought – *How do I handle this?*

Trish might as well have skipped the class. Her mind was elsewhere. She even went so far as to reread the pages she had printed out and study the images on them. The photos were not as clear as they had been on the computer screen, but there was still no doubt. *What a mess*, she thought. *If I tell her at all, I'm going to wait until tonight after we get back.*

Jenna and Trish had not missed a single Thursday night of eating out in Boston since they had started the routine right after school began. And even though David had begun to occupy more and more of Jenna's time, this particular ritual remained intact, actually more because of Jenna's insistence than Trish's.

All of that notwithstanding, someone who observed the two of them and what was happening in their lives might have assumed that Trish was jealous of Jenna, or at least of her situation. But anyone coming to that conclusion didn't understand the depth of their friendship.

In many ways, Trish understood Jenna better than Jenna understood herself. Trish knew there was little doubt that disclosing what she had discovered would devastate Jenna. Someone with more experience in relationships would probably either slough it off or get angry. But, Trish was certain that neither of those would be Jenna's primary reaction. Regardless of that however, Trish came to the conclusion that Jenna had to know.

It was obvious to Jenna that Trish was not herself on the train ride into Boston. She saw additional signs that something was bothering her friend during dinner, despite Trish's constant denial. Her roommate was the funniest, most upbeat person she knew. Those qualities were all but absent the whole evening.

When they got back to their room, they both changed into what passed for pajamas. Trish attempted to busy herself by going through the bag she used to carry her books and papers for school. Jenna recognized this activity for what it was – a meaningless task to avoid talking. "Trish, what's going on?"

Jenna expected another denial. Instead Trish closed her bag, sat on the edge of the bed and faced Jenna. She shook her head, not in denial, but rather to indicate that she was having trouble getting the words out. Jenna went over to sit next to her. "What *is* it, Trish?"

Before she spoke, Trish let out a deep breath. "This is so hard."

Jenna could only say "What?" She couldn't begin to imagine what could be causing this.

Trish continued to look down. "I found out something today . . . about David"

Jenna shuddered. "About David? What? He's not hurt, is he?"

"No, nothing like that." She glanced over at Jenna. "You know that course I'm taking – Contemporary Media?"

"Yeah."

"Well, a few days ago the professor gave out this article that had been in the *Globe* a while back. It was about this real estate guy, Bradford Whitcomb, like an investigative piece. Anyway, the professor assigned us to evaluate the article; do some research to determine what sources the writers might have used, so we could figure out how it was put together, and whether it was balanced, or not."

"What's that got to do with David?"

"I started doing the research and came across a photo from last year showing this guy Whitcomb and his son at some charity event." She paused. "It was David in the picture. David is this guy's son."

Jenna didn't immediately see the connection. She looked inquisitively at Trish.

"David's last name's not White; it's Whitcomb. I don't know why, but he's been lying to you about that."

Jenna felt like she'd been punched in the stomach. She turned away from Trish and stared straight ahead. She waited a moment and then turned back, "Are you sure?"

Trish just nodded, but she reached over into her bag and extracted the papers she had printed up in the library and handed them to Jenna, who shuffled through them until she came to the photo. She looked at it for only a moment, but there was no doubt; it was David. "Why would he do that?"

"I don't know, Jenna."

They sat in silence briefly and then Trish spoke up. "I'm so sorry. You had no idea?"

"No. He did tell me that his father was in real estate. What does the article say? Is his father a criminal or something? Maybe that's why he didn't tell me his real name."

"No, he's not a criminal. The article's pretty negative, but nothing about any of it being illegal."

"This doesn't make any sense."

"I know."

"What am I supposed to do? We have a date tomorrow night."

Trish knew that Jenna's last comment really had nothing to do with their date. It was about their whole relationship. "I wish I knew what to say, how to make this better." She reached over and hugged her roommate, as tears began to form in Jenna's eyes.

A few moments elapsed, and they separated from each other. Jenna appeared a bit more in control. "I don't think I want to talk to him. I'm just going to send him an e-mail."

"What are you going to say?"

"That I never want to see him again."

Trish grasped Jenna's hand. "I know this really hurts, and I'm not the one who's been lied to, but . . . ."

"But what?"

"I've had a little more time to think about this than you have. Don't you think you should give him a chance to explain?"

"Not the way I'm feeling right now."

"Maybe that's the point. Maybe, if you gave it some more time, you'll see things differently."

"I'm supposed to go out with him tomorrow night!"

"I know. But what harm is there if you wait until the morning? You know, sleep on it."

"It seems like you're defending him."

"You know better than that."

"I'm sorry. I shouldn't have said that."

"It's okay." Trish paused. "Listen, you've got to do what feels right for you, but it doesn't seem like you lose anything by letting him explain. If it doesn't pass the sniff test, tell him to go to hell."

That brought a smile to Jenna's face. "I need to think about this some more. Do you mind if we keep talking?"

"What do you think?"

Jenna smiled again, and then cocked her head as something occurred to her. "In David's e-mail yesterday he said he had something important to tell me. I wonder if it was this."

"Maybe."

In a hopeful voice she said, "That might change things."

They talked for another hour. Sometimes they went off on tangents, but they were never far away from the topic of what Jenna should do. There was no question that her outlook had softened, in large part because of the realization about how much she cared for David. And since she couldn't undo what had happened, she decided to opt for the next best thing—If David could give a reasonable explanation for his actions, one that she could forgive, then she would give him another chance. She had almost no experience in things like this, but her instincts told her that she had to try to use her head as much as her heart.

Despite a fitful sleep, punctuated with doubts and second-guessing, by morning the decision to go on the date seemed like the right one. Jenna also decided that it would be best not to confront David. She would see what he had to say first. That would be very telling.

Jenna didn't know if she was up to attending her classes on Friday, but decided to give it a try. She continued to have butterflies in her stomach every time she envisioned what might unfold later that night. But she got through the day emotionally intact.

She avoided reading her e-mail, not wanting to take the chance that there'd be a message from David. She got ready earlier than necessary, just for the sake of having something to do. Sitting around waiting was making her even more nervous. As she started getting dressed, she thought back to earlier in the week when she was planning what to wear. There really had been little doubt—it would be the simple black dress, the delicate pearl necklace, and matching earrings. She loved the way she looked in that outfit. But now it didn't seem to matter anywhere near as much.

The half hour before David was scheduled to arrive, Jenna and Trish continued to talk over what Jenna was going to say, and even whether going on the date was still the right thing to do. Jenna wondered if she should raise the issue of the lie, if David didn't bring it up.

"I think you need to be spontaneous," offered Trish. "And just do whatever feels right. I think if you trust yourself, it's going to work out okay."

"I'm only nineteen. How did my life turn into a soap opera?"

Trish smiled. "A starring role in *The Young and the Restless*?"

Jenna smiled back at her, and gave her a hug. "Thanks, Trish."

Jenna wrapped herself in a shawl, picked up her purse, and went down to the lobby to wait for David. He came through the door ten minutes later. As he eyed Jenna from head to toe, he smiled and said, "Wow, you look terrific."

Jenna responded with a polite smile. "Thanks, you too."

"Just a suit." He expected Jenna to say something else. When she didn't, he said, "Ready?"

"Yes."

The conversation on the drive into Boston was stilted. However, Jenna periodically expanded her comments so that David would not sense that anything was wrong. It was a major effort, but she was able to carry it off.

David had a valet park the car, and then escorted Jenna inside. The décor was understated and quite elegant, but Jenna hardly noticed. They were seated within minutes, and given menus that consisted of a single page of calligraphied writing. Jenna understood enough French that she had no trouble making a selection, and David had been to Chez Cezanne enough times that he knew what the options were.

David made small talk about what they were going to order, and then he asked, "Would you like some wine with dinner? I can order it if you'd like. I don't think it'll be a problem."

On any other night Jenna would have simply declined. But tonight, she overreacted to David's remark, ascribing an arrogance to it that wasn't there. She let him know how she felt. "That wouldn't impress me."

David was somewhat taken aback by the shortness in her tone. He decided to make light of it. "So, what would impress you?"

Jenna hadn't meant for it to start this way, but she wasn't about to hold back. "Honesty," she said.

David stared at her, quickly realizing the implications of her response. He expelled a breath, continued to make eye contact, and in a resigned voice said, "So you know?"

"Yes."

"How did you find out?"

"Does it matter?"

"No, I guess not." He paused. "I was planning on telling you tonight."

"That's convenient."

David leaned forward. "I know it looks that way, but it's the truth."

"Oh, so you do know about the truth?"

"Come on, Jenna." He had prepared to tell her in a certain way. Now he had to reconstruct and reorder everything. "Why would I choose this restaurant where the whole staff knows me, if I wasn't going to tell you?" Then something else occurred to him. "And the e-mail. What about the e-mail?"

Just at that moment their waiter approached. He knew David, but he just addressed him as "sir" when he inquired if they were ready to order. David deferred to Jenna by raising his eyebrows.

She interpreted David's expression as if he were asking whether she intended to *stay*, never mind order. When she told the waiter what she wanted, David was visibly relieved. He indicated he would have the same thing. It's not what he intended, but he wanted the waiter out of the picture before Jenna changed her mind.

The brief interaction with the waiter allowed Jenna to consider what David had just said, especially about the e-mail. She was going to say something, but held her tongue waiting for David to continue.

"I'm so sorry. I really am. I was such a jerk for not telling you. Will you give me a chance to explain?"

She was able to appear much more in control than she felt. "Go ahead."

David continued to apologize and explain for the next few minutes uninterrupted. He tried to read Jenna's expression and body language to get a sense about how his explanation was being received, but he couldn't tell.

Although David's words were starting to have an effect on Jenna, she wouldn't allow herself to show it. Instead, she looked directly into David's eyes. "Do you have any idea what it felt like to find out you lied to me?" She paused. "I understand about the article, and why you might have lied in the beginning. But then you just kept it up. That's the worst part."

David looked beaten down. "I know. I was trying to figure out a way to tell you, but . . . ." David decided that making excuses was not the way to go, so he said, "Can you forgive me?"

Jenna felt her emotions welling up, but she managed to say, "I don't know yet." When she saw the negative effect her comment had on David, she threw him a lifeline. "But I'm still here."

He grabbed it. "Can we at least keep talking? I'll answer any questions you want to ask me." He leaned forward again. "I really like you, Jenna. I did something stupid. Can't you give me another chance?"

There was no doubt in Jenna's mind that David was sincere, and she hoped with all her heart that she would be able to get past this. She didn't answer him directly. Instead, she returned to the question that was at the center of her misgivings. "I'm still having trouble understanding why you didn't tell me the truth later that night, or Sunday in New Hampshire, or any other time."

"I don't know." He paused, and then things snowballed. "I meant to, and then we started going out and it became more difficult. I was afraid what might happen. And then I started to rationalize. I told myself, that I didn't really lie to *you*; I lied to a group of people I just met for the first time, not specifically to *you*."

"And that would have made it okay? That's supposed to make me feel better?"

"What I meant was that I've never lied to you directly. I kept up the dishonesty after I lied to some people I just met. I told myself that it wasn't the same thing as telling you a lie once I got to know you." He paused, realizing how his words must be coming across. "It sounds like I'm trying to make excuses. I don't want that. There are no excuses. I was wrong, and then I made it worse by not telling you the truth once we started going out."

"I would have understood."

"I know that now, but . . . ." He stopped, realizing that he was falling back into excuse mode.

The back and forth continued on for several minutes before their meal arrived. David said, "I can't say I have much of an appetite."

"Me either." Jenna leaned forward. "Can I say something?"

"I wish you would."

There were tears starting to form in Jenna's eyes. She was actually surprised that they hadn't appeared earlier. Jenna hadn't rehearsed any of what she was about to say. It just came together as she attempted to explain her feelings. She knew it would make her more vulnerable, but she needed to say it. "I like you David." She tried to gather herself. "I've been pinching myself for three weeks, not willing to believe that someone like you could have any interest in me. And then just when I began to accept that it was actually happening, I find out that maybe you're not who I thought you were." David closed his eyes, and his lips became tight. It was obvious that he was becoming emotional as well, beginning to understand the pain he had caused. Jenna watched him for a moment and then continued. "The only reason I came here tonight was to find out if the David I got to know over the last few weeks is the real one."

"And?"

"I want to believe it."

David closed his eyes again. When he reopened them, Jenna said. "I don't want to give up on this, but I need time. I can't just flip a switch and then everything's back to the way it was. Can you understand that?"

"Of course."

She leaned back. "I'm sorry to waste all this food, but I think I want to go back to the dorm now."

"Don't worry about that. I understand."

Jenna felt like she needed to be more reassuring. Anything less would appear as if she were trying to punish him, trying to exact some emotional toll. She reached across the table and put her hand on his, knowing that the physical contact would reinforce what she was going to say. "David, I really hope this is going to be okay. And I think maybe it will, but that doesn't change the fact that it's going to take me a while to sort this all out."

It was the most hopeful thing Jenna had said all night, and David responded with all the humility he was feeling. "I'm not sure I'm in a position to ask for anything else . . . or deserve it, for that matter."

CHAPTER 11

Over the next several days, David had to fight the urge to contact Jenna. While she had made it clear that she needed time, David wasn't the kind of person who could usually just let things be. In this situation, however, his instincts told him he needed to do just that.

He checked his e-mail frequently—at least every hour, even when he was in class. There was nothing from Jenna—until Wednesday.

Dear David,

I've rewritten this e-mail ten times, trying to come up with just the right words, but none of them seemed to say what I wanted them to. I've replayed everything in my head over and over. And then finally I decided to just write what I was feeling. The truth is I miss you. Next week I'm going to Trish's house in Connecticut for Thanksgiving. I think I'd like us to start seeing each other when I get back. I hope you feel the same way.

I know people always say they want to move forward and not look back, but I really feel like that would be best thing to do. I don't need to talk about it anymore. I understand why you did what you did, and I just want for us to start over.

I'll talk to you after next week—I hope.

Jenna

When David first began reading the e-mail he felt disheartened, and then he came to "I miss you." Although he tried to concentrate on the remainder of the message, it was little more than a blur. He had to reread it two more times before it registered. He replied to Jenna immediately, thanking her, and expressing the same sentiments that she had. When he finished, he sat back in his chair, closed his eyes, and let some of the relief he was feeling wash over him.

Having his personal life somewhat back in order energized David. He reviewed Darnell's report, and then sent out e-mails to him and his father about setting up meetings. Darnell got back to him right away and attached some additional ideas, as well as a cost analysis concerning the suggestions in the report. Darnell also agreed to a meeting on Saturday morning.

About an hour later, David's father sent a short reply confirming their meeting for late Monday afternoon. In the second half of the e-mail Mr. Whitcomb brought up Thanksgiving, indicating that he would like David to join him. It might not have been intended that way, but David took it more as a summoning, rather than an invitation. The last line of the email read: *You can also bring Trent and that other young man that came a couple of years ago.* David's father was referring to Jeremy.

Sophomore year there had been a surprise snowstorm just prior to the Thanksgiving break, and long distance travel was out of the question. David had invited his roommate and Jeremy to join him at his father's townhouse. Ironically, it was the closest thing to a family Thanksgiving atmosphere David had ever experienced.

David suspected that there was an ulterior motive behind these latest invitations. His father probably wanted Trent and Jeremy to act as a buffer between the two of them. On the other hand, it was Thanksgiving, and he had sensed that there was the slightest shift in his father's outlook on things. He decided that he'd extend the invitations and give his father the benefit of the doubt. Still, he couldn't help but think that oil and water had nothing on Bradford Whitcomb and altruism.

On the way over to Darnell's on Saturday morning, David stopped at Dunkin' Donuts and picked up some coffee and a bag of munchkins. When he pulled up a few minutes before ten, Darnell was waiting outside the building, as he had been the last time. He spoke up as David approached. "You're early again. Gonna make that a habit?" He smiled as he said it.

"I miscalculated how long I'd be at the donut place," David said as he raised the Dunkin' Donut bag. "No lines. It must be my lucky day; that never happens."

Pointing to the bag, Darnell asked, "Is that a bribe?"

David laughed. "You for sale for a bag of munchkins?"

"Could be. What kind are they?"

"See for yourself."

Darnell took the bag and peered inside. "Very tempting." He then offered his right hand. David shook it, and Darnell said, "Let's go inside." They opened up the coffee and settled in at the kitchen table. Darnell made some additional room by sliding some papers and folders out of the way.

David had sensed from his first visit that Darnell took the measure of someone immediately, and either liked them or didn't. There wasn't a lot of middle ground. The silly exchange over the donuts seemed to confirm that he placed David in the former category. From their last conversation he also sensed that Darnell felt the same way about Mr. Whitcomb, but that assessment wasn't as rock solid. He decided to explore the issue, but not directly. "Before we get started, can I ask you something?"

"Sure. Go ahead."

David picked up a copy of the report off the table. "What you said last time about how the reporter got the suggestions that were in the article, what did you mean by that?"

There was no hesitation from Darnell. It appeared that he not only liked David, but trusted him as well. "The reporter that came here was kind of an asshole. He wanted dirt, something he could pin on your father, make him look bad." He paused momentarily. "Your father and I don't always see things the same way, but he's always been fair with me, and upfront. I had already shown him those suggestions months ago, and he said he liked some of them, but they were too expensive. It's his money, who am I to argue? Anyway, I could see what the reporter was trying to do. He started turning things all around, changing everything I said into something other than what I meant. So, I threw him the suggestions and made it sound like your father was just waiting for the right time economically to put them in place."

"That's not the impression the article gave."

"No. And I really didn't expect anything different. But I think it did force the reporter to tone the article down."

"Does my father know what you did?"

"He's a smart man. I'm sure by now he's figured out how the suggestions wound up in the paper."

"But not *why*?"

"Probably not. If he asks, I'll tell him."

"He didn't call you after the article was in the *Globe*?"

"Nope." Darnell took a sip of coffee and leaned forward. "Your father's a businessman. I do a good job. He makes money. Why would he want to screw that up?"

David thought about things for a moment before he spoke, and then gestured toward the papers on the table. "So why are we doing this? It sounds like he's already turned all this down once; he's not going to go for it now."

"Not right away, certainly. It would look like the article forced him into it. But some of the newer stuff I sent you—like the solar panels, I could see him going for that. It'll save a lot of money down the road."

"So, you think there's a chance?"

"I'm not much for wasting time. I wouldn't be doing all this if I didn't think there was a chance." He took out a munchkin from the bag and popped it in his mouth. "Bribe or no bribe."

David smiled. "Okay, where do we begin?"

For the next two hours Darnell explained his ideas in detail. The primary focus was on five apartment buildings – the three David had visited, and two more his father owned. Darnell was familiar with all of them because of his initial work as a maintenance man for Whitcomb Realty Trust.

The expanded report recommended a three-phase approach—first, an appliance upgrade for every apartment; second, the installation of solar panels and other energy efficient measures; and third, exterior refurbishing and grounds beautification.

David asked a few questions along the way, but mainly listened. Just prior to Darnell getting to how much all of this would cost, David asked for some clarification. "Why not start with the energy efficiency phase? You said there are tax incentives and credits with that."

"Good question. But, by starting with the appliance upgrade, the tenants get an immediate benefit, something that can be seen right away. Solar panels and new boilers aren't very sexy, if you know what I mean."

David smiled. "Makes sense." He eyed Darnell across the table. "So, the moment of truth. What's the bottom line? How much?"

"You want it phase by phase, or all together?"

"All together."

"About 2.8 million."

"Whoa. I was afraid you were going to say something like that."

"It is what it is."

"I don't think I'm going to be able to convince my father with a price tag like that."

"Maybe not."

David eyed Darnell. "What would you do? I don't mean if you were me. I mean, if you were my father. Put yourself in his shoes."

"Tough one. This will eventually make him money, but it's going to take seven, eight, maybe even ten years. Might be shorter if the tax credits get increased. He can start raising rents once the individual leases are up and he's put in the new appliances. I don't know, I guess maybe I'd do it." He paused. "But the thing is, I wouldn't mind waiting for the return on the investment. I'm a lot more patient than your father."

"There's an understatement. Kids on Christmas are a lot more patient than my father."

Darnell smiled. "So, now that you've heard all this, you think you're going to talk to him about it?"

"I think so. Yeah, I am."

Darnell nodded his head. "Good for you. And maybe good for everybody."

David gathered his things and shook hands with Darnell, who walked with him outside. As he was about to move to the parking area, David hesitated. "I meant to ask you. The article didn't say they found anything illegal, but what about cutting corners, or something unethical? You ever see any of that?"

"No. I told you. With your father, it's all about business and the bottom line. He's usually got tunnel vision about those things. But as far as I can tell, he's honest."

"That's good to hear. Of course, it doesn't really help me with this."

"No, it doesn't. But, I still think it's worth a shot."

As they shook hands again, Darnell continued. "Even if nothing comes of this, you can still come by to say hello." He paused. "Bring munchkins, though."

David was still smiling when he reached the car.

He spent the rest of Saturday writing a couple of papers for school. He would have much preferred calling Jenna and maybe going out somewhere. He considered making the call a number of times, but self-preservation, or rather the preservation of their still tenuous relationship won out, and he left his phone on the table.

On Sunday, he and Trent watched a little football, and David reviewed all the material Darnell had given him in preparation for the meeting with his father the next day. He gave Trent the short version of what he was doing. It was more for the purpose of being able to express his thoughts out loud rather than soliciting advice from his roommate. "I still don't think my father's going to go for this."

"From what you've told me, I doubt it. How long did you say it would take to make a profit? Ten years?"

"About that. Maybe less."

"What's he gonna be then, late seventies, early eighties? Will he even still be working?"

David looked at Trent. "You're kidding, right? He's never going to retire."

Trent appeared to be considering something before he spoke. "Well, if that's true, he shouldn't care about how long it takes. I'd say that's something in your favor."

David realized Trent had a point. The ten-year wait for profitability was probably not going to sink the proposal. On the other hand, the nearly three-million-dollar price tag might not even let it leave port.

At halftime of the game, David remembered his father's request about Thanksgiving, and he called Jeremy to invite him to dinner. As David had expected, Jeremy had made plans to go to his parents' house in upstate New York. Likewise, Trent declined—He was driving home on Thursday to be with his family in Rhode Island.

David couldn't help but wonder what Thanksgiving would be like with just his father and him, especially after their meeting tomorrow. He figured he might have to immerse himself in the football games if things became awkward. Watching football didn't require a lot of interaction. You just yelled at the TV, instead of each other.

David arrived at his father's office at exactly 4:00, and the secretary told him to go right in. Mr. Whitcomb was glancing out the window at the Boston skyline. When he heard the door open, he turned away from the view, went over to his son and shook hands. "Hello, David."

"Hi, Dad."

"How's everything?"

"Fine."

Mr. Whitcomb gestured toward the chair in front of the desk, as he headed behind it. "Have a seat."

"Thanks."

"Before we get started, I was wondering if you had a chance to invite Trent and that other young man for Thanksgiving."

"Jeremy."

"Right. Jeremy."

"I did, but they can't make it. They're both going home for a couple of days."

"Oh, of course." He paused. "It'll just be the two of us then. I'll have something sent in—turkey, stuffing, the usual, maybe around 2:00; that okay with you?"

"Yeah, that's fine."

With the pleasantries out of the way, Mr. Whitcomb got right to the purpose of the meeting. "So, tell me about the site visits."

David spent the next twenty minutes doing just that. He described the three buildings he visited, trying to offer a realistic picture while emphasizing how tired the structures appeared to be. Mr. Whitcomb took it all in without saying anything. David surmised that there wasn't very much in his description that was news to his father.

As David was winding down, but before he brought up anything having to do with the suggested improvements, Mr. Whitcomb interrupted him. "What was your impression of Darnell?"

David thought it was interesting that his father's first question had to do with Darnell, and not the properties themselves. But he didn't let on. "I like him a lot."

"As do I. I assume he was the most helpful out of everyone you met."

"Yes, I'd say so."

"So, are these ideas you're about to show me the same ones that were in the newspaper article?"

"Some." David could sense that his father was fishing for something, but he didn't know what. "And some new ones too."

David presented the three phases of the proposal, but not in the order he and Darnell had discussed. Instead, he led with the solar panels and the energy tax credits. He didn't hold out much hope, but if his father were going to entertain any of this at all, David felt that the tax credits might be the one thing that would pique his interest. David followed up with the other two phases, and where appropriate emphasized that there were some smaller tax credits to be had in those phases as well.

Mr. Whitcomb asked some questions along the way, but remained fairly stoic throughout, so David had no idea what he was thinking. David was just about to get to the price tag when his father said, "About eighty percent of this is from the article, so I assume you got the specifics from Darnell."

David couldn't hide his surprise, and his father read his expression. "It's not too hard to figure out, David. These ideas are similar to the ones Darnell showed me a while ago."

"You knew about the connection between the article and Darnell?'

"Yes."

"You're not upset?"

"No. I trust Darnell. If he fed that information to the newspaper, he must have had a good reason."

"I think he did." David hesitated. "So, does that mean you sent me there to spy on him?"

"No, of course not. Besides it's not spying if you already have the information." David shook his head, as his father continued more emphatically. "I didn't send you there to find out anything for me. If I wanted to confirm what I suspected, I would have just called Darnell."

Actually, that makes sense, thought David. He decided to leave it alone and move on to the financials. He gave a short summary of each of the phases again, and highlighted as many positive aspects as he could think of. Then it was time. "So, anyway, this is the bottom line . . . ."

Mr. Whitcomb interrupted. "Let me guess – two point five million."

"A little higher – two point eight."

Neither of them said anything for a moment, and then Mr. Whitcomb broke the silence. "Very well presented, David. You kept using the word investment. That was a good strategy, and for the most part accurate." He paused. "To be honest, I anticipated most of this, although the solar panel idea was a bit of a surprise. That was your best argument, by the way." He paused again. "So, what do you think I'm going to say?"

"I hope you say 'yes'."

"You didn't answer my question."

"I don't know."

"You must have some idea."

David was starting to get annoyed, although this verbal dosey-do was nothing new when dealing with his father. He calmed himself and said. "I guess I didn't have high hopes when I walked in, but I felt more encouraged as things went along."

Mr. Whitcomb smiled. "You still haven't answered the question."

"What do you want from me?"

Mr. Whitcomb held up his hand. "Okay, let me turn it around." He looked intently at David. "What would you do?"

This annoyed David again, but his enthusiasm for the proposal trumped that. "I'd do it."

"Just like that?"

"Yeah. In the long run, it's financially sound; and in the short run, it's good public relations."

"I know. I heard your arguments. Your response is quite impetuous though, don't you think? That won't serve you well if you decide to go into the business world."

The condescension was back, thought David. His father was treating him like a little kid again. David didn't trust himself to speak. Instead, he just shrugged his shoulders.

Mr. Whitcomb continued. "My first inclination is to say 'no,' however you have made some interesting points. I'd like to study these papers; may I have them?"

"Yes."

"I'll make up my mind in a week or so."

David couldn't help but think that this was all a ploy, designed to illustrate that his father, the successful businessman, was never impetuous. David chose a response that reflected that. "You're not just taking the papers for show are you?"

Mr. Whitcomb smiled. "No. I understand why you might think that, but no."

They finished up their meeting with some small talk, shook hands, and confirmed the time for Thanksgiving dinner on Thursday.

David called Darnell when he got home and filled him in about the meeting with his father. He steered clear of any mention of their discussion concerning the article or Darnell's feeding information to the newspaper. David figured that whatever dynamic was going on between his father and Darnell, he wanted no part of it. Navigating those waters required far more seafaring savvy than he had. Plus, he would probably have to save all of his navigational skills for Thanksgiving.

At similar holiday get-togethers in the past, David's emotional state often resembled a giant tug of war. The red flag in the middle of the rope would move one way and then the other. Sometimes just a casual remark or a raised eyebrow triggered the shift. And when the event was over, the flag rarely ended up in the center. More often than not, the advantage went to his father.

It was halftime of the first NFL game when David arrived at his father's townhouse. The delivery person showed up fifteen minutes later. The food was very good, which moved the red flag in one direction, but the conversation was forced, which moved it back again.

Mr. Whitcomb, never one to let a national holiday get in the way of business, brought up the topic of David's presentation. "I've been doing a lot of thinking about your proposal."

David wasn't sure why, but he felt like he had to correct his father. "It's not really *mine*."

"Okay, *the* proposal."

David watched his father closely as he continued. "I have to say, I was much more impressed the second time through, after I had a chance to study things more carefully." Mr. Whitcomb couldn't help but see his son's hopeful reaction, and then just as quickly the about-face when he finished his remarks. "But I can't see my way clear to committing that much money up front."

"You'll get it back."

"Maybe. But even if I do, it's going to be a while. Also, what happens if the tax credit benefits change?"

"That doesn't seem likely."

"Neither did Enron going under."

David knew this wasn't going to be an argument he was going to win, but he persisted anyway. "Did you figure in the good publicity this would generate?"

"Some. But you can't base business decisions on how popular they'll make you."

"So you've told me." He paused. "I guess that's the end of it then."

"I know you're disappointed, but I have to say no."

There was silence in the room except for the muted sounds of the game in the background. Mr. Whitcomb watched his son for a moment, and then spoke up. "I've asked you this before, but I'm going to ask you again—You'd do it, if it were your money?"

"The answer's still the same—Yes. I know that makes me *impetuous*." David actually smiled slightly when he said this, as did his father. "But I've done my homework. Granted it's only been a week or so, but . . . ."

"I don't doubt that you know what you're talking about. I told you I was impressed with the presentation, otherwise I just would have said 'no' in my office." He paused. "Let me ask you something. Do you really believe in this, or is this really about something different—you know . . . about the two of us?"

David was somewhat surprised by his father's directness. "I . . . uh . . . No, it's not about anything else."

Mr. Whitcomb studied his son for a moment. "Okay, I can accept that. I believe you." He sat back, never taking his eyes off David. Then he leaned forward again. "Despite what you might think, I really have given this a lot of thought, and I've come up with an idea that might be of interest to you."

"What do mean?"

"Well, I took you at your word the first time we spoke—that if it were your money, you'd do it. So, I talked with one of our company attorneys and with Alan Fenton. You remember Alan; he's my personal attorney. Anyway, I can make arrangements for this to happen, if that's what you want."

"What are you talking about?"

Mr. Whitcomb got a self-satisfied expression on his face. "I'll arrange for you to access money from your trust fund."

David wasn't sure he had heard his father correctly. He didn't speak for a moment, and then asked, "You're serious?"

"I am. But the real question is, 'Are *you*'?"

David met his father's gaze. "No strings attached?"

"Only that the money has to be used for the proposal. As you know, you're not scheduled to get the trust fund until you turn twenty-seven, but I can change that, and make half of it available now, if that's what you want."

This had come out of the blue. David couldn't have foreseen this possibility no matter how wild his imagination had gotten. "I think I need to take your advice."

"What would that be?"

"Not to be so impetuous. I need to find out more about this."

Mr. Whitcomb smiled. "I think that's prudent."

"So, this is kind of like – put your money where your mouth is?"

"I wouldn't have phrased it quite like that. But yes, I think it is."

They spent the next hour going over some of the particulars. None of Mr. Whitcomb's money would be used; it would all come from David's trust fund. When any profits started to be made, seventy-five percent would go back into the trust fund, and twenty-five percent would go to his father's company. The first phase would start next summer, and the other two phases would begin once the first phase was completed.

David asked a number of questions, some of which his father couldn't answer. "Listen David, you need to call Alan Fenton, and he'll put you in touch with one of the company attorneys as well. Then you can make an informed decision." He paused. "There's one more thing that you'll have to consider."

"What?"

"If you want to go through with this, I'm going to insist that you oversee everything. That means putting graduate school on hold." Mr. Whitcomb met David's eyes as he continued. "Part of your salary will come from the money that was set aside for grad school, and if you want some help, you can enlist Darnell and augment his salary out of the money from the trust." He paused again. "You've got a lot to think about."

David's initial reaction was one of excitement. However, that was quickly tempered by the realization that this could simply be the means by which his father manipulated him into joining the company. David responded. "Yes, I guess I do." And then with a mixture of sincerity and skepticism, he continued. "I really do appreciate what you're offering. Thanks . . . I think."

David felt that the red flag on the tug of war rope had moved back and forth quite a bit. But at the end of the day, surprisingly, it was dead center.

CHAPTER 12

David was going to have his apartment and his life to himself for the next several days. Trent wouldn't be back until Sunday night, and he surmised that the same timeframe applied to Jenna. To some extent, David was actually looking forward to being alone, except for the emotional solitude of not having Jenna back in his life. That was another matter. And it was even more unsettling because he wasn't sure whether Jenna was supposed to contact him or vice versa.

He retrieved the most recent e-mails she had sent him and looked them over to make sure he hadn't missed anything. The "getting back together" part was pretty clear, but the logistics of how that was going to be accomplished was not. He decided to wait until Sunday, and if Jenna hadn't made the first move, he would.

All of this time to himself allowed David to reflect on the Thanksgiving Day discussion with his father. No matter how many ways he viewed what had transpired, however, he came to the same conclusion – as usual, his father was attempting to manipulate things.

For the last several years, Mr. Whitcomb had been pushing David to make a commitment to join the business, but David had resisted just as strongly. He knew that eventually he might decide to do that. But at this point, with his whole life in front of him, he wanted to keep his options open. So, every time the issue was raised, David begged off.

To his father's credit, thought David, he paid for all of his college expenses, and was prepared to pay for graduate school. He had also set up the six million dollar trust fund, apparently with no quid pro quo. On the other hand, David didn't have access to the fund until he was twenty-seven. Could that have been his father's strategy all along? – postpone giving him the trust fund until he could entice him to join the business. And then if he didn't, would his father have just extended the carrot year after year until he did? And now with this new proposal, the money from the trust fund was actually being put back into the company, and the money for graduate school was going to be used for his salary. David began to view these seemingly magnanimous gestures in a different light.

He couldn't help but feel that if he agreed to oversee the project as his father had insisted, then the die was cast; he was part of Whitcomb Realty Trust, and it would be difficult to extricate himself from that any time soon.

David did try to look at the situation objectively. Maybe all of this was just coincidence, just a matter of everything coming together in such a way that it provided an opportunity for his father to get what he wanted. But he couldn't shake the notion that his father was a master puppeteer, and he had just begun to pull the strings.

David tried to push himself in the other direction again – It shouldn't really matter how everything came to pass. The proposal that his father had outlined should rise or fall on its own merits, not on whose idea it was, or what might have been behind it. And in an ideal world that was probably how he would have assessed things. But David didn't reside in an ideal world, and most assuredly, neither did his father. In fact he doubted that his father had ever even visited.

By early Sunday morning, he was as torn as he had been when his father first broached the idea. One thing had become clear, however. He needed to contact his father's attorney and get a better idea of what all the ramifications of jumping on board would be.

But more immediately, he felt as if he needed to try to put all of this out of his head, at least for a few hours. He picked up the *Globe* crossword puzzle and went to work. Ironically, after only a few minutes, two of the answers he filled in brought him right back to thinking about the very things he was trying to avoid – Seven down was "Master Manipulator". David wrote in Machiavelli—Bradford Whitcomb didn't fit. The clue for twenty-two across was "Translation Key" – (2 wds.). David filled in Rosetta Stone and smiled. *Yeah, that's what I need, he thought, the Whitcomb family version of the Rosetta Stone to help me decipher what the hell my father is trying to do.*

Shortly after he finished the puzzle, David dozed off for about an hour. The musical ring tone of his phone woke him up around 11:00. He snatched it off the end table, and groggily said, "Hello."

"Hi, David. It's Jenna."

In his half awake state he almost said, "Who?" but caught himself in time, and just responded, "Hi."

"How are you?"

"I'm good. How about you?"

"We just got back."

"From Trish's?"

"Yeah."

"Did you have a nice time?"

"Yeah, I did. Trish's dad is really nice."

"I'm glad."

"How about you? Did you have a nice Thanksgiving?"

"It was fine; just me and my father, but it was nice." David knew he was painting a rosier picture than what had occurred, but if he tried explaining what really had gone on, he would have run out of monthly cell phone minutes.

There was silence on the line until David broke it. "Jenna, I know you said we shouldn't talk about what happened, but I want to tell you again how sorry . . . ."

"You don't need to apologize again. I don't want to talk about it anymore." There was no anger in her voice, only resolve.

"Okay, if you're sure." He paused. "You're something else, you know that?"

Jenna didn't say anything for a moment. When she did speak, she decided to ease the tension. "Does that mean you might be willing to take me out for a Sunday drive?"

"Seriously? Today?"

"Well, it is Sunday."

"I know. I guess I'm just a little surprised. Yeah, I'd really like that. What time?"

"Whatever's good for you."

"Around 1:00?"

"Okay."

"Jenna?"

"Yes."

"Thanks for making the call. I was debating what to do . . . ."

"It's fine." She hesitated. "I probably shouldn't tell you this, but I just walked in the door. I haven't even taken my coat off yet."

David smiled. "I'm not sure how I got so lucky. But like I said, you're something else."

He could hear the embarrassment in her voice. "I'll see you at 1:00."

Jenna watched out the front window in the lobby of Hutchinson House. When she saw David pull up, she went outside before he even had a chance to exit the car. As he closed the driver's side door, he noticed Jenna coming down the steps. He had been mulling over how he should greet her ever since he left his apartment – a kiss on the cheek, the lips, a hug, what? Jenna made the decision for him. It was obvious from her outstretched arms that she wanted a hug. He opened his arms as well and they embraced. Jenna said, "I missed you."

"I missed you too." He gave her a quick kiss on the lips, and then asked, "Where would you like to go?"

"Why don't we just drive for a while?"

"Sure."

The first few minutes were like the initial moments of a blind date –statements about the weather and school, verbal fumbling, and some awkward periods of silence. But before too long they settled into a rhythm. They started to joke and laugh. The questions and answers became more natural, and not as measured. They were comfortable with each other again. It appeared that they were back.

"Want to get something to eat?"

"I'm not hungry for a meal, but some dessert or ice cream would be great."

There was a highway sign advertising a small restaurant off one of the exits on Route 2. It mentioned homemade pies. That cinched the deal. The restaurant didn't have booths, but they found a quiet table in the back. After they placed their order, Jenna asked, "I told you what I've been up to for the last ten days. What about you?"

David wasn't sure how to answer that. Was talking about his father's business off-limits? Probably not, but he still needed to be careful. He felt like he was on a topical tightrope. One slip and he might end up falling into the very subject that Jenna had made clear they weren't supposed to be discussing.

David decided to go ahead without a net. He told her the whole story – the meetings with Darnell, the three-phase proposal, his father's idea for funding it, and the dilemma he now found himself faced with. A number of times he asked Jenna if she were really interested in all of this. She assured him that she was, and he believed her.

During his explanation, when he arrived at the part about his six million dollar trust fund, he considered either reducing the amount substantially, or pretending it didn't exist, and making up some story about how the project would be financed. That idea lasted about a nanosecond as he remembered what had gotten him into hot water to begin with. The mention of the trust fund did cause Jenna to raise her eyebrows, but when David didn't elaborate or dwell on it, she appeared to take it more in stride than he had expected.

When David finished, he asked, "So, what do you think?"

"I think you've been busy." David smiled as Jenna continued. "It looks like you can get a lot accomplished without me distracting you."

"I much prefer the distraction."

She smiled. "Do you have any idea what you're going to do?"

"No clue. Any advice?"

She looked at him, not sure whether he was serious or not. He read her expression and nodded his head, signaling for her to offer whatever she could. "I really don't know much about these kinds of things, at least the business part . . . ." Her voice trailed off, and then it picked up again. "Only that . . . when I was listening to you, it seemed like the idea that your father was forcing you into this really bothered you."

"It does."

"But didn't you tell me that you were the one who called him first?"

"That's true. But you don't know my father. As soon as he saw an opening, a chance to get what he wanted, he jumped right in."

There was silence, but David recognized that Jenna wanted to say something. "It's okay. Tell me what you're thinking."

"What I'm thinking is that it's either a good idea or a bad idea, and why your father is doing it shouldn't make any difference."

"I guess you just cut to the chase on that one."

Jenna smiled. "Well, you asked."

David smiled too. "I did, didn't I?" He watched her for a moment before he spoke again. "So, you think I'm a little obsessed with what my father's motives might be?"

"Obsessed is probably too strong. But when you talk about it, it's pretty obvious that you're having a tough time letting it go."

"My father has that effect on me."

"When do you have to let him know what you're going to do?"

"Not right away, I've probably got at least a month or two. If we're going to go ahead with it, we need enough time to solicit bids; that's all."

"If there's no rush, then you should try to put it out of your head, and then maybe when some time has passed, you'll see things more clearly."

David stared at her, and got a smile on his face. "Beautiful *and* smart."

She smiled. "I thought you promised not to lie to me again."

When he heard the word "lie," it shook him slightly, but then he realized that if there were any residual tension between the two of them, Jenna's remark had made it disappear.

For the next several weeks, they saw each other every Saturday and at least once or twice during the week as well. There was a growing sense of intimacy, even if their only contact was through some electronic device.

David certainly wanted more of a physical relationship, but he knew that Jenna was a virgin, and didn't want to move as quickly. It was difficult, but he wasn't about to push things until she was ready.

The decision about using his trust fund to finance the apartment renovations and joining his father's business took a backseat to what was happening between the two of them. David rarely even thought about the decision he had to make unless he got a call from his father looking for an answer. To get him off his back, David told him that he would decide by February. His father didn't like it, but he had little choice.

During the second week in December, when David was about to drop Jenna off in front of Hutchinson House, she turned to face him. "David, I'm going home to California over the Christmas break. I hope you understand. I haven't seen my mom since August."

While David had been expecting this, it still rattled him to hear it out loud. "I know. I guess I was hoping that since we hadn't talked about it, somehow it wasn't going to happen. So, when are you leaving?"

"Classes are done next Friday, so Saturday morning."

"Can we squeeze in some extra time before then?"

"Sure."

On the ride back to his apartment, David tried to find something positive about being alone for the next three and a half weeks. The best he could come up with was that it would allow him to concentrate on his decision about the proposal. It seemed like a small consolation.

As he was reflecting on all of this, something he had not expected started to enter his consciousness. He realized that his suspicions about his father's motives were nowhere near as strong as they had been. But, he also knew that once he started to immerse himself in considering what he should do, his original thoughts about being manipulated would most likely resurface.

CHAPTER 13

In the few days leading up to the Christmas break, David and Jenna spent nearly every free moment together. David even broached the subject of going out to California. And although Jenna initially got excited about that possibility, she recognized that she owed the time to her mom.

David drove Jenna to the airport for the Saturday morning flight. She delayed going through the security line until the last possible moment. When it was finally time to go, Jenna gathered her carry-on and stood facing David. He took the bag out of her hand and placed it back on the seat. "You can't give me a proper goodbye if you're holding that."

She smiled, as he put his arms around her waist and leaned in to kiss her. She kissed him back, and then threw her arms around him. "I'm going to miss you," she said.

"Me too."

While they were still embracing, David whispered in Jenna's ear. "Promise me something."

She tried to separate herself to look at him, but he continued to hold her so close that she couldn't. Jenna asked, "What?"

"Promise me you won't say anything for the next thirty seconds."

"Why?"

"I just need you to promise."

"Okay . . . I guess . . . I promise."

He broke the embrace and stared into her eyes. He took hold of her hand, leaned in and kissed her. He then pulled back slightly, "I think I'm in love with you," he said.

Jenna's eyes got big and she started to speak. "David . . . I . . . ."

He slowly moved backward a few steps and released her hand. "Shh, you promised." As she tried to say something again, he put his index finger to his lips and shook his head. After a few more backward strides, he turned and headed toward the waiting area exit, glancing back only once with his finger still on his lips, and a broad smile there, as well.

Tears started forming in Jenna's eyes, blurring her vision. She couldn't see David very clearly as he opened the door and disappeared. What *was* clear however, were the words that he had spoken, and also the significance of when he had said them – not in the midst of a passionate moment, or in some romantic candlelit restaurant where feelings got exaggerated. This had been said in the light of day. And if any talk of love can be reasoned and measured, she knew that this was.

Jenna went through the security line in a bit of a daze. She had recovered enough when she got to her departure gate to try to call David. There was no answer. She was going to leave a message, but decided to text him instead.

I'm not going to text the words that I want to say to you. I want you to hear my voice when I say them. I'll call when I get to CA.

She replayed the entire scene with David in her head fifteen or twenty times on the plane ride; she thought of little else. David's words kept echoing in her head, as if he had said them outdoors near some giant rock formation, and they kept reverberating in the air.

As usual, Jenna was reluctant to analyze what had transpired, other than to reaffirm in her own mind that David was expressing the way he truly felt. She knew that for her, this wasn't some infatuation; this very well might be the real thing. But she hadn't allowed herself to try to interpret what David might be feeling. And now she didn't have to.

She smiled as she realized that she had probably known she was falling in love for quite a while, but had been unable to articulate it—almost like she was part of some nineteenth century novel where the young heroine could never express her feelings before her suitor did.

The pleasantries in Jenna's head made the cross-country plane ride seem like the Boston to New York shuttle. Before she knew it, they had landed and she was about to exit the aircraft. Jenna figured her mom was probably already at the luggage carousel waiting to pick her up. However, Jenna knew she couldn't possibly put off calling David until she got home, and she wanted some privacy, so the car ride back to Pasadena wasn't an option either.

Fortunately for her, the Long Beach Airport was set up in such a way that arriving passengers had to pass through a waiting area before retrieving their luggage. Jenna found a relatively private spot off to the side, and pressed the speed dial. It barely completed its first ring, when David answered. "Hi."

"Hi."

"How was your . . . ."

"No. No small talk. It's my turn now. You have to promise not to say anything."

He laughed. "Okay, I promise."

Jenna's voice caught for a moment, so her words came out more haltingly than she intended. "I love you, too. I've felt that way for a long time, but for some reason, I couldn't say it out loud." She paused. "I wish I were there with you right now."

There was silence on the line for just a moment, and then David said, "Is it okay for me to talk yet?"

She laughed, but there were tears forming in her eyes. "Yeah, it's okay."

"I really meant what I said. I do love you." Almost as if he knew what she was going to ask him, he continued. "After I told you how I felt, I didn't want you to say anything, because I didn't want you to just repeat the same thing back, you know, like some reflex action. I needed to hear it from you the way I just did." He paused, and then eased the tension. "Of course, I didn't really think it through enough to realize that when you said it back to me, you'd be three thousand miles away."

Although the last sentence made Jenna laugh, it was through a stream of tears, and she had trouble responding. Finally she found her voice. "David, I'm so happy."

"I am, too."

Neither of them spoke for a moment, and then Jenna said, "I don't know what else to say, I just wish I could kiss you and put my arms around you."

"I know; I feel the same way." David hesitated before he continued. "It's going to be a tough few weeks."

Jenna tried to offer something to lessen their sense of separation. "Maybe I can get an earlier flight back to Boston."

She could hear the smile in his voice. "You owe this time to your mom, remember? Take care of that, and then I'll have you all to myself when you get back."

"I like the sound of that." She paused. "I do have to go meet my mom, but I'll call you as soon as I get to my house."

"Okay . . . I love you."

"I love you too . . . but it's not fair; you said it first again."

He laughed. "All right, next time I'll be more chivalrous—ladies before gentlemen . . . Bye, Jenna."

"Bye."

As Jenna ended the call and closed her phone, she was shaking. For Jenna, emotions on both ends of the spectrum affected her in a physical way. David's words in Boston and this follow-up conversation filled her with the excitement of all the future possibilities. She thought back to four months ago when she was literally in almost the exact same location, also thinking about what might lie ahead. It was as if the August departure from Long Beach and her arrival today were emotional bookends, except nothing was ending. She knew in her heart that this was all about beginnings.

Jenna maneuvered her way out of the gate area and headed to find her mom and her luggage. Sharon was waiting just on the other side of the door. As soon as she spotted Jenna, she rushed to her and extended her arms. Jenna did the same.

"Oh, honey, it's so good to see you."

"It's good to see you too."

Sharon pulled back slightly. "Let me get a good look at you." She did a quick assessment. "Still beautiful as ever."

"Oh please, Mom."

Sharon noticed some tears in her daughter's eyes, but since she had some of her own, she didn't think anything of it. Still, it looked like more than simply reunion tears. "Are you all right? It looks like you've been crying."

Jenna started to deny it, but she was bursting to tell someone, and that emotion won out. "Yes, but it's not anything bad."

"What is it?"

"It's about David and me."

Jenna had told her mom about meeting David and a number of their follow-up dates, but hadn't indicated how serious it had become. That wasn't possible; she hadn't completely admitted it to herself.

Sharon smiled. "So, things are moving along?"

"You could say that."

Sharon hugged her daughter again. When they separated, Sharon said, "After we get your luggage, why don't we go upstairs to the restaurant. I want to hear all about it." She put her arm around her daughter. "If you try to tell me on the ride home, I might drive off the road."

Jenna smiled. "Okay. I don't want my love life to be the cause of an accident."

When they were seated in the restaurant, Jenna told her mother the whole story, even about David's lie. Although Sharon had heard some of it before, she never interrupted. Jenna was beaming, and Sharon didn't want to take the chance of saying something to change that. When the story came to a close, Sharon smiled and said, "I'm so happy for you, sweetie. You should see your face when you talk about him."

Jenna's smile got bigger. There was a brief pause in the conversation, and then Sharon's expression became more serious. "I know it's not really any of my business, and . . . it's a bit indelicate, but . . . ."

"It's okay. I know what you're wondering. And no, we haven't slept together." Jenna knew her mother's unasked question was pragmatic, not prurient, so she had no qualms about answering it. She blushed a little as she continued, "At least not yet."

"I wasn't asking to be nosy."

"I know." And she did know. One of her mom's best qualities was that she was never judgmental.

Sharon spoke again. "It just seems that if this is as serious as it sounds, maybe . . . I can't believe I'm saying this . . . you should see Dr. Roberts. You know, about protecting yourself."

"Actually, I was thinking the same thing."

Sharon eyed her daughter, wondering if she dared press things further. She decided to ask permission before jumping in again. "Can I offer some advice?"

"Of course."

"You need to be sure, honey, or as sure as you can be. I just don't want to see you get hurt."

"Me neither. I know it's only been a few months, but I'm in love with him."

"Well, if it's possible to judge that by the expression on your face, then I'd say you definitely are. But still, you need . . . I'm starting to repeat myself. Forget it. I trust you. I know you'll make the right choices."

Jenna smiled. "Thanks, Mom."

Sharon shook her head. "Somehow, I think I'm supposed to try to talk you out of this." She paused. "But the truth is, I had only known your father for three months when I was sure. And while Jonathan was a little longer, I still knew pretty quickly that he was the one."

Jenna continued to smile at her mother's reminiscing. "I can't wait for you to meet him.'

"I can't wait either. After all, we have a lot in common." Jenna looked at her mother quizzically, and then Sharon said, "I love you . . . and evidently he does too."

Over the next several days leading up to Christmas, Jenna and David spoke at least once a day, sometimes more. Every conversation ended with "I love you" or some variation. It was as if David's initial pronouncement had opened the floodgates. Jenna had to admit to herself that the first few times she had said those words, it was awkward; not because she didn't believe them with all her heart, but rather because it was hard to imagine that this was really *her life*, and not some movie script. It didn't take all that long, however, for the words to come more naturally and more automatically, but never with any less meaning behind them.

On Christmas morning, although on opposite ends of the country, Jenna and David did the same thing at approximately the same time—they opened the gifts they had sent to each other. Jenna had selected a light blue jacket from L.L.Bean for David. He sent her a gold necklace with a single diamond pendant. They both put on the other's gift right after they opened them. For the next week, David only removed the jacket when he was indoors. Jenna never took off the necklace.

Later in the day when they spoke, they expressed their feelings about the gifts, and about each other. David had spent part of Christmas with his father and told Jenna it went as well as could be expected. His father hadn't pressed him too hard about the decision he was contemplating, seemingly willing to accept the February 1st deadline. David had also reminded his father that he hadn't even talked to Alan Fenton yet. That was scheduled for a few days after Christmas.

Jenna had an appointment to see Dr. Roberts on the same day that David was scheduled to meet with Alan Fenton. David had told Jenna about his meeting, but she hadn't mentioned anything to him about her doctor's visit. If things worked out the way she expected, he'd know soon enough.

CHAPTER 14

David arrived at Alan Fenton's office shortly before 9:00. He sat in the waiting room for about five minutes, and then Mr. Fenton opened the door to his office, greeted David with a handshake, and invited him inside. He had met Mr. Fenton a half dozen times before, and had heard his father speak of him often, but he hadn't formed a definite opinion about the lawyer; their interactions had been much too infrequent to allow that. He did sense, however, that Mr. Fenton was more open and personable than his father. This feeling was borne out immediately when he invited David to sit across from him at a small round table in a corner of the office. There was no mammoth desk separating the two of them.

"How are you doing?" began Mr. Fenton.

"I'm fine. Thanks for taking the time to meet with me."

"I'm glad to do it." He paused. "Would you prefer me to explain about the trust fund, and how this would all work, or do you have some questions you'd like to ask me first?"

"I think I'd rather have you go over everything first, and then if I have questions along the way, I'll just ask them if that's all right."

"That'll be fine. I probably should tell you that your father has instructed me to be as forthcoming as possible without breaking any confidences or divulging privileged information."

This last statement surprised David, and he was sure it showed in his body language. But if Mr. Fenton noticed, he didn't react; he just continued with the preliminaries. "I also spoke to one of the attorneys for the business to make sure I understood how the funds would have to be used, and the best way to transfer them. Obviously, this is all predicated on your decision. Nothing has been put in motion yet." Mr. Fenton looked more intently at David before he continued. "I can arrange for you to talk with any one of the attorneys directly if you'd prefer that."

"No, I don't think that'll be necessary, at least not for now."

"If you change your mind, just let me know."

"Okay, thanks."

Mr. Fenton reached for a couple of folders on the table and handed one to David. "I've prepared some material so you can follow along as I outline how we're going to proceed, that is if you give us the go-ahead."

David opened the folder as Mr. Fenton began the explanation. "As you can see, your trust fund is worth $6 million, payable in a lump sum when you turn twenty-seven. However, this new provision allows you to accelerate the process and take out $3 million immediately to fund the proposal you're considering." Mr. Fenton glanced at David to see if he had any questions before he resumed. "If you choose to go forward with this, and then before all the phases are completed, you change your mind and stop overseeing the project, you forfeit the $3 million you withdrew, and the terms of your trust fund change."

"To what?"

"The remainder of the trust fund is decreased to $1 million, payable in ten yearly installments of $100,000."

David raised his eyebrows and shook his head. What raced through his mind was that while his father certainly was under no obligation to give him *anything*, Mr. Whitcomb had laid things out very cleverly to make sure David would join the company.

Mr. Fenton didn't react to David's head shaking. "Any questions so far?"

In a slightly sarcastic tone, David responded, "No, I think I understand everything very clearly."

Again, Mr. Fenton didn't react. "The next few pages contain some information I think you already know. The $3 million has to be used for the project; and after it turns profitable, seventy-five percent goes back into the trust fund and twenty-five percent goes into the business."

"Yes, thank you. I was aware of that."

David could see that Mr. Fenton was trying to ease himself into saying something else. David waited him out. Finally, the lawyer leaned forward and spoke. "There is one more thing."

"What's that?"

"Your father's will."

"His will?"

"Yes. He said I could share this information with you." David didn't react, so Mr. Fenton continued. "If anything happens to your father, you inherit everything, *provided* that you are working for the company at the time of his death. If that's not the case, then it all goes to charity."

David rarely thought about financial matters, except most recently, and then only in the context of this proposal; but his curiosity got the best of him. Plus, he wanted to be sure he had heard things correctly. "I want to make sure I understand this . . . At the risk of seeming insensitive, if my father . . . uh . . . passes and I'm working for Whitcomb Realty Trust, then I inherit everything. But if I'm not working for the company . . . ."

"It all goes to charity."

David pondered this information for a moment. "Can I ask you something?"

"Certainly."

"Has my father's will been updated recently?"

Mr. Fenton mulled this over for a moment before speaking. "I guess I can answer that. About two weeks ago."

"Were most of these provisions added at that time?"

"That I'm not at liberty to divulge. You'll have to talk to your father about that."

"Another question?"

"As many as you like."

"You said at the beginning that I can access $3 million of the trust fund to finance the project and the other $3 million will remain in the account until I turn twenty-seven. What happens if I decide *not* to go through with this? Is the trust fund still worth $6 million when I turn twenty-seven?"

Mr. Fenton hesitated. When he finally spoke, he chose his words carefully. David wasn't sure if Mr. Fenton was trying to do him a favor, or if his father had anticipated this question and instructed his lawyer to answer it in a specific way. Nevertheless, the intonation in the words Mr. Fenton spoke provided David with all the information he needed. "I haven't been instructed to make any changes to your trust fund if you decide not to fund the project . . . *as of yet.*"

After a few more minutes of discussing some logistical matters, Mr. Fenton offered his hand. They shook, and as David was leaving, the lawyer said, "I'm sorry I couldn't be more helpful with some of your questions, but please don't hesitate to call, if you think of anything else. I'll do whatever I can."

"Thank you. I appreciate the difficult position you're in."

He nodded. "Goodbye, David."

"Goodbye."

On the drive home, David created a mental balance sheet concerning his father's actions. He remained troubled by the paradox. On the one hand, at least for the time being, there was a substantial trust fund once he turned twenty-seven. On the other hand, nearly every other positive option was contingent on joining his father's company.

Probably the most perplexing of all was that it appeared his father believed that David was motivated by money. How could his father possibly think that? David knew in his heart that the prospect of inheriting millions of dollars at his father's death would never be a major factor in his decision.

But then he thought to himself—I guess if your mind thinks along those lines, as his father's certainly did, then you probably assume everyone else's does also.

CHAPTER 15

Jenna headed back to Boston a week earlier than she had originally planned. It was actually her mom's suggestion. With both Sharon and Jonathan back to work, Jenna was by herself all day. "Of course, it's not only that," said Sharon. "You look like you're going to burst every time you're on the phone with David." And then with some pseudo drama in her voice she added, "Far be it from me to stand in the way of young love."

"You're sure you don't mind?"

Sharon smiled and shook her head.

"Thanks, Mom. You're the best."

If the plane ride out to California went by in a blink, the return trip seemed like an eternity. Jenna had decided to surprise David and hadn't told him that she was coming back early. Her flight was scheduled to arrive around 4:00 in the afternoon. She figured she would call when she landed, and if she couldn't reach David, she would take a cab to Tufts and keep trying his cell until she caught up with him.

At about 4:30 after Jenna had collected her bags, she punched in David's number. It rang five times and was about to jump to voice mail when he picked up. "Well, hi there. I didn't expect to hear from you for another couple of hours."

She tried to keep the excitement out of her voice. "This is the new impetuous and mysterious Jenna, full of surprises."

"I didn't think there was anything wrong with the old one."

She chuckled. "Well, for one thing, she wasn't spontaneous enough."

"If you say so."

"You're very agreeable today."

"Always."

"What are you doing?"

"I was reading, but I must have dozed off. What about you?"

With a sense of intrigue in her voice she said, "I'm waiting to meet up with someone."

He decided to play along. "That does sound mysterious. Should I be jealous?"

She couldn't contain herself any longer. "Why don't *you* come and meet me?"

"What are you talking about?"

"I came back early. I'm at the airport."

"In Boston?"

"Yup."

"Are you kidding?"

"No."

"This isn't a joke?"

"No joke.'

"Wow . . . I don't know what . . . Okay, I'm on my way."

She yelled into the phone. "David, David wait!"

She just caught him before he ended the call. He responded, "What?"

"You don't even know where to pick me up."

He laughed. "Details, details."

Jenna laughed too. "Terminal C Arrivals."

"Okay, fifteen, twenty minutes . . . you are unbelievable!"

She smiled. "Just hurry up."

David made the trip in eighteen minutes. He parked in the short term lot, left his keys in the ignition, and sprinted through the center doors of the terminal. He saw Jenna right away, ran to her, wrapped her in his arms, and lifted her off the ground. They kissed each other over and over, neither of them needing to speak. When they finally realized that they were creating a bit of a scene—although all the people watching them had smiles on their faces—David gathered Jenna's luggage, and they moved outside and got in the car.

As David followed the exit signs out of the airport, every other word out of his mouth was "unbelievable." He asked Jenna how this had all come about—why she hadn't told him ahead of time and at least ten other questions. When all of it finally had sunk in, and David was able to calm down, he asked, "Do you want to go to your dorm and get settled? Maybe then if you're not too tired, we can go get something to eat."

She didn't answer right away.

"Jenna?"

"Is Trent back from break yet?"

He looked over at her with a questioning expression on his face. "What? No. He's not due back for a few more days."

"Why don't we go to your apartment then?"

David started to ask "why?" and then realized what Jenna was suggesting. He looked over at her. "Are you sure about this?"

Jenna returned his glance and nodded.

The car was silent for a few moments and then David repeated his question. "Jenna, you must know that I really want this to happen, but I also need to know that you're sure."

"I am."

David could feel his stomach clench and his pulse start racing. He tried to calm himself, but with little success. He decided to lighten the moment. "I have to say, I really like this new spontaneous Jenna."

Her laugh momentarily broke the tension for both of them.

David waited a few seconds and then spoke more seriously. "I think maybe I should stop at the drug store, and you know . . . ."

"You don't need to. I went to a doctor while I was in California; it's okay."

David didn't say anything. He took his right hand off the wheel and reached for her hand. They continued holding hands until they arrived at his apartment. Once they were inside, and Jenna removed her coat, she started shaking. David couldn't help but notice. He went to her and held her. "Are you all right?"

"Just nervous."

He continued to hold her, as he subconsciously looked around the apartment. He hadn't meant to say it out loud, but it just escaped. "Obviously, I wasn't expecting you to come back here; this place is a mess."

All of Jenna's nervousness exploded into a laugh. David joined in. When the laughter ended, he took her hand, and they went into his bedroom.

Initially, Jenna felt self-conscious and embarrassed by her nakedness and her lack of experience. And while she had made the unequivocal decision to be with David, she still felt physically and emotionally vulnerable. But those feelings didn't take long to dissipate. David was gentle and tender, and Jenna began to respond in ways she couldn't have possibly imagined.

In the few moments when she wasn't just *feeling*, and she allowed herself a conscious thought, she remembered her high school friends, and even Trish, telling her that the first time was not necessarily very good. They had been wrong.

David and Jenna made love once more that night and fell asleep in each other's arms. They didn't wake up until nearly 8:00 the next morning. A simple good morning kiss started things again. And every time they thought they were physically satiated, the newness of each touch and the responses it triggered fueled the desire for more.

And while the passion in the apartment was palpable, they both understood on some level that they weren't simply having sex; it was more than that. It was a distinction that they didn't articulate, but that they knew in their hearts was critical to where they believed this was headed.

By Saturday night however, the looming reality of roommates returning, and school resuming insinuated itself into their thoughts. As they were lying on David's expansive couch in the living room only half watching a movie, they could hear the ticking of the old-fashioned clock in the apartment's vestibule moving its hands toward Sunday.

Jenna broke the relative quiet with a question. "A penny?" She didn't need to add "for your thoughts." Over the last several weeks the comfort of their relationship had spawned its own shorthand lexicon.

David responded. "Only that I wish this wasn't going to end tomorrow."

She smiled and snuggled in closer to him, but didn't add anything. That her feelings were the same as his was obvious. They remained silent for a long time, their breathing soft and in unison.

Eventually Jenna asked, "Have you given any more thought to your father's proposal?"

David decided to tease her with his response. "Not in the last couple of days. I've been a little pre-occupied, or hadn't you noticed?"

She gave him a gentle elbow in the ribs. "So, that's what I am – a pre-occupation?"

"Not a bad thing to be."

"What? You are so dead!" With that, she turned to face him and with mock indignation landed a few soft punches to his chest.

He smiled and grabbed her wrists. "Okay, truce . . . All right, you're not a pre-occupation . . . I was *fully* occupied, there was no *pre* about it."

Jenna continued to smile. "That's better . . . I think. You are quite the romantic, you know that?"

"What can I say? It's a gift."

She chuckled, and then moved to give him a quick kiss on the lips. She then turned and rested the side of her face on his chest. He kissed her hair several times, and they fell silent.

A few more moments passed and David spoke again. "Actually, I have made up my mind."

"What did you decide?"

"Are you sure you want to talk about this?"

As she answered the question, she raised herself and started to sit up. "Of course I do."

"I wouldn't have brought up the subject, if I knew you were going to change positions."

She pulled on his arm trying to get him to sit up, and playfully said, "Come on, we've been lying down for three days!"

He pretended to fight the move. "That doesn't have to change."

"Yeah, it does . . . at least until I hear about your decision."

He righted himself and shifted the tone in his voice. "I'm going to do it."

"I kind of thought you would."

"I'm not sure I have much choice. My father's not going to give up until I at least give the business a chance."

David went on to explain most of the additional things he had learned from the second visit to see Darnell Smith, as well as his meeting with Alan Fenton. As he was finishing up, he said, "So, it seems to make sense to access the money now. After all, I did like the idea from the beginning; I was just put off by my father trying to manipulate me. In the end, it's just like what we talked about. It's either a good idea or not; my father's motives shouldn't make any difference."

Jenna leaned over and kissed him.

"What was that for?"

"For being so smart."

"Well, I guess we'll see, won't we?"

"Are you still having some doubts?"

"No, not really. But there's no way to know for sure how it's going to turn out."

"I think you did the right thing."

"Ah, another unbiased opinion."

She moved closer and rested her head on his shoulder.

David continued. "I was thinking of asking Trent and Jeremy to work with me during the summer."

"Would they be interested?"

"I think Jeremy definitely would. Even if he lands a teaching job, he won't start until September. I'm sure he could use the money. With Trent it might be a different story. He's got an interview with a New York brokerage firm coming up. If they hire him, he'll probably start right after graduation."

Jenna appeared somewhat surprised. "I know you told me that Trent did well in school, but do you really think it's likely he'll get hired that quickly?"

"Yeah, I do."

They were quiet for a brief time, each contemplating something different. Jenna spoke first. "I guess we should talk about what happens with *us* this summer. We've still got spring break to sort out, but the summer is a bigger issue."

David didn't speak right away. Jenna sat more erect and faced him. After she settled in, David said, "I suppose I was hoping you could stay in Boston for most of the summer. I know that's selfish, but . . . ." He hesitated. "And if you can't stay at the dorm for some reason, then you could stay here."

She looked a little surprised. "I'm not sure I can stay in Boston the *whole* summer; I want to spend some time with my mom. Let me check out what the dorm possibilities are, maybe for one of the months." She paused. "There's a big part of me that would love to live here with you." She smiled. "Like it's been for the last three days . . . but I'm not sure, you know, we're ready to do it full time, are we?"

David stared into her eyes before he answered. "As usual, you're probably right."

"You know this doesn't have anything to do with how I feel about you. It's just that all this has happened so fast; I'm not sure I have my bearings about things."

"I know . . . Why don't we check out all the possibilities, and see how everything shapes up? . . . Don't say, 'no' just yet, okay?"

"Okay." She paused. "I don't know whether it's my turn to go first again or not, but . . . I love you."

David smiled before he leaned in to give her a kiss. "I don't think it was your turn." He got an exaggerated judgmental tone in his voice. "You probably cut the lunch line in your high school cafeteria too."

Later that afternoon, David drove Jenna back to her dorm. On the ride over he remembered something he had meant to ask her earlier. "There's a charity event coming up for Children's Hospital. My mother used to have my father buy a table each year, and even after she left, he still makes a donation. Anyway, there's dinner, a silent auction, and some awards. What do you think?"

"That sounds nice. When is it?"

"I'm pretty sure the last Friday in January."

"Yeah . . . uh, okay."

"You don't sound that interested."

"No, it's not that. It's just that it'll be the first time I meet your father."

"That's exactly why I think it's a good idea. I mean he's going to love you anyway. But if I tell him about my decision to join the company a couple of days before the charity event, then he'll be in a great mood, and maybe on his best behavior."

She gave a little laugh. "Sounds like you've got this all planned out." She continued to smile. "Remind me again which one of you is the manipulator."

CHAPTER 16

Early the next morning before Trent was scheduled to return from break, David started to clean the apartment, although somewhat reluctantly. Jenna's scent still lingered everywhere, and he knew that the cleaning solutions he was about to use would overcome the sensual remnants of the previous three days.

Although he could readily conjure up individual moments and bits of conversation, her gentle scent intensified everything he felt, and he was hesitant to do anything that might cause that to be erased. The last item he decided to clean was the pillowcase where Jenna had rested her head. Before he placed it in the washing machine, he brought it up to his face and inhaled.

The relatively small macho strand of David's personality struggled to exert itself and prohibit the gesture. But it didn't have a chance. His heart was fully engulfed, and that now dictated nearly everything he did.

When Trent arrived later in the day, he and David talked about what had been going on since they last saw each other. Initially, the conversation was light and full of good-natured joking, as it usually was between them. When the catching up had run its course however, David revealed that he and Jenna had spent the last seventy-two hours together. David offered no details, making it clear that any additional information was off-limits.

His tone and bearing also signaled to Trent that this was not some sort of juvenile conquest to be bragged about or trivialized. Trent picked up on where the parameters had been set, and didn't push things.

As David was finishing up, Trent said, "From what you're telling me, and the way you talk about her, I'm guessing things are pretty serious."

"Yeah, they are." He paused. "I told her that I was in love with her."

"Wow! You're that sure?"

"I am."

Trent repeated himself. "Wow!" He looked at his friend and could see nothing but sincerity. "Hey, if that's what it is, then I'm really glad for you. I really mean it."

"Thanks."

They were both at a loss for words after that. Trent went into his room to unpack and emerged after fifteen minutes. He sat on the couch a few cushions away from David and said, "Actually, I have some news too. Not as big as yours, but still news."

David shifted to face him "What?"

"I've got two interviews."

"Two?"

"Yeah, one next week and one in February."

"What are your chances, do you think?"

"Hard to tell. I think the Macmillan Group, that's the first interview, is a better fit for me; plus I know some people there. But if either one makes me an offer, I'll probably jump at it."

David smiled. "Maybe there'll be a bidding war?"

"Yeah, right. That's only in baseball. Although, come to think of it, I am a free agent."

They both laughed.

David changed the subject and told Trent about his decision to access the trust fund and join his father's company. When he finished, he brought up the possibility of Trent working with him during the summer.

"That's really generous, David. If nothing comes through before graduation, I'd like to take you up on that."

"You got it."

Trent got a smirk on his face. "Unless . . . ."

"What?"

"Unless you want to join the bidding war. You've got three million to play with; you'd be the odds-on favorite to garner my services."

David leaned over and punched him in the shoulder.

While it was on his mind, David gave Jeremy a call and outlined the same summer employment opportunity that he had just offered to Trent. As David had suspected he would, Jeremy said, "yes" immediately. "I really can't afford to sit around this summer, even though I'd like to take it easy before September."

"Do you have a position lined up yet?"

"No. But, there are going to be a lot of openings, so I feel pretty confident. Anyway, I really appreciate the offer. Count me in."

"Great." David changed the subject. "When do you start student teaching?"

"Next week. Have you heard of Standish High School on the South Shore?"

"Sure. That's where you're going to be?"

"Yeah, for about ten weeks."

"Well, good luck. I'll give you a call when I have some more details about the summer."

"Okay, thanks."

In Jenna's dorm room at Hutchinson House, the late afternoon sun caught one of the windows at just the right angle, and a spectrum of color formed on the far wall. Jenna was lying on her bed listening to music as she watched the brief rainbow effect start to fade. The iPod selection ended, and the image on the wall disappeared at the exact moment that Trish bounded through the door.

"Hey you," she said, as she deposited her luggage at the foot of her bed and went over to give Jenna a hug. As they separated, Trish asked, "When did you get back?"

Jenna hesitated. "A few days ago."

"Earlier than you thought, huh. So, what have you been doing with yourself?"

"I've been back in Boston . . . but not here at the dorm."

Trish looked puzzled. "What do you mean?"

Jenna started to become emotional. She tightened her mouth, leaving just enough room for the words to escape. "I've been with David . . . at his apartment."

Trish's mouth dropped open. "Really!"

Jenna was only able to nod. When she had sufficiently recovered, she recounted what had occurred over the last three days, but mostly in general terms. She wasn't reluctant to talk about the way *she* felt or about David's expression of love. But she didn't offer any details concerning their physical relationship, or even their conversations. She felt as if describing those intimacies would taint what had transpired. It would reduce everything to the level of high school girls snickering next to their lockers about some backseat sexual escapade.

When it was obvious that Jenna wasn't going to continue, Trish hugged her again. "I'm so happy for you. It sounds like it was wonderful."

"It was." She smiled. "And part of it was because of you. If you hadn't told me to give David a second chance . . . ." Her voice trailed off.

"You would have done that on your own. You're giving me way too much credit."

"I don't think so."

"Well, it doesn't matter anyway. I'm just glad it all worked out." She smiled. "You know, even if you hadn't told me what happened, I would have known. You look different somehow."

"I think I'm in love with him. Maybe it shows."

"Maybe."

Jenna continued to talk about how she was feeling, and about how the time with David had changed her. After several more minutes of describing the previous three days, Jenna realized that if she opened up any further, she would be crossing a line that she didn't want to cross. Trish recognized that as well. So at a break in the conversation, Trish said, "How about we go out and get something to eat? I want to hear more about this, but my stomach thinks my throat's been cut."

Jenna smiled, not only at the remark, but also at Trish's sensitivity to Jenna's reluctance to keep talking. "Sure. We could go to Denucci's."

"Great idea. I've been thinking about their pizza since I left Connecticut."

They put on their coats, locked the door behind them, and took the stairs to the lobby. On the way down, Trish kept the conversation light. "I have a question for you. Now that you're more experienced in romance than I am, do you think I'm using food as a substitute for not having a love life?"

Jenna pretended to seriously consider the question before she delivered her response. "Well, pizza is considered comfort food."

Trish looked over at Jenna. "I may have to eat a whole pie to feel as comfortable as I'd like to!"

On the last Wednesday in January, two days before the charity event, David went to see his father and told him that he had decided to take him up on his offer concerning the trust fund and the proposal. David had fooled himself into believing that his father might actually display some happiness at the news. But that was not to be. Mr. Whitcomb maintained his staid manner and shook David's hand in a very perfunctory way, never acknowledging that this was exactly the outcome he had been hoping for. The only statement that Mr. Whitcomb made that even approached a modicum of approval was "I think you've made a wise choice." *I guess that will have to suffice* thought David. *He is who he is.*

They continued to discuss some of the legal issues that still had to be addressed, as well as the upcoming bidding process. Mr. Whitcomb assured David that the company attorneys and the construction managers would handle all of that. "I'll instruct them to keep you informed of everything until after you graduate and come on board full time."

As the meeting was winding down, David raised the topic of the upcoming charity event. "Would it be okay if I brought a date? I know it's a little late to ask, but our table's not usually full."

Mr. Whitcomb raised his eyebrows. "Anyone I know?"

"No. We've been going out for a few months. Her name's Jenna MacDonald. She goes to Tufts."

"I see. Is it serious?"

David bristled. He wasn't about to answer that question, and he somewhat resented his father for even asking it. Other than through casual small talk, his father rarely showed much interest in what David was up to unless it involved school or the company. David deflected the question and simply responded, "It's just a date, Dad."

Mr. Whitcomb studied his son momentarily, and then said, "Of course she's welcome to come; there's plenty of room." And then as David expected he would, his father followed up with the obligatory and less than sincere—"I'm looking forward to meeting her."

David realized that he wasn't cutting his father much slack. On the other hand, he had agreed to join the company, something he knew his father wanted very badly. So, why couldn't his father find some way to say thank you?

The charity event was being held at the Royal Bostonian near the Boston waterfront. When David and Jenna arrived, David could see from a distance that his father was already at the table. Before heading over, he and Jenna surveyed the silent auction items, many of which were sports memorabilia featuring the Red Sox and the Patriots.

In addition, there were at least five all-expense-paid weekends at various bed and breakfast sites in New England. David smiled at Jenna as he wrote down a very substantial bid on one of the New Hampshire locations. "It would really be great to win one of these, but only if you promise to come with me."

Jenna blushed, and then spoke softly. "Isn't that a little too public. I mean, if you win, won't you have to go pick it up in front of everyone? And then they'll think it's for the two of us."

"Well, it is . . . but don't worry; that's not how it works. If you win, they e-mail you." He pointed at the bid sheet. "See, I wrote down my e-mail address." He smiled at her. "You still haven't answered my question. Do you promise to go if I win?"

The thought of an entire weekend with David gave her chills. She smiled back at him. "Yeah, okay. I promise."

David picked up the pen lying adjacent to the bid sheet. "Maybe I should up my offer."

"Stop it," she said jokingly.

He put the pen back down, and got more serious. He glanced over at The Whitcomb Realty Trust table and said, "Time to meet my father. Are you ready?"

"I guess."

They zigzagged through a dozen tables arm in arm. David acknowledged a number of people he knew, but didn't stop to talk. Mr. Whitcomb had just completed a conversation when David and Jenna arrived. "Hi, Dad."

Mr. Whitcomb turned, taking in both Jenna and his son. "Hello, David."

"Dad, this is Jenna MacDonald. Jenna, this is my father, Bradford Whitcomb."

Jenna wasn't sure if she should offer her hand. The rules of etiquette in that regard were always changing. She decided not to, and said, "Nice to meet you, sir."

"Nice to meet you as well." He continued to stare at her, which made Jenna uncomfortable. Not because she sensed anything inappropriate in his gaze, but rather because it was obviously one of assessment. Jenna interpreted the unspoken question in his look to be: "Should you be dating my son?"

Jenna broke the momentary silence. "I've never been here before. It certainly is beautiful. And Children's Hospital is such a worthwhile charity."

Mr. Whitcomb's facial expression appeared to soften in every place but his eyes. "It is a beautiful room, isn't it? If I may boast a little, I had a small hand in the design."

David jumped in. "I didn't know that."

Mr. Whitcomb responded. "You'll have to excuse my son, Miss MacDonald; he assumes he knows everything about me."

"Why didn't you ever mention that before?"

Mr. Whitcomb nodded at Jenna and smiled, although it seemed to her that he had to work at it. "Nobody ever commented on how beautiful the room was before."

Jenna also smiled, but hers came naturally.

David remained silent, but slightly shook his head.

"Before we sit down, let me introduce you to the other people at the table" said Mr. Whitcomb. When those amenities were completed and the three of them took their seats, Mr. Whitcomb proceeded to steer the conversation for the next half hour. Initially, it revolved around Jenna, then David and Jenna, then finally about David's decision to join the company. And even though Jenna knew a lot about the last topic, she remained quiet throughout that part of the discussion.

From David's perspective, the evening was going better than he had anticipated. His father, while not overly friendly, had certainly been more than civil. From Jenna's perspective, she wondered if David had been viewing his father too harshly. Her first impression was that Bradford Whitcomb was quite formal, and a bit full of himself. But she didn't see the signs of manipulation that David talked about. *Of course,* she thought, *I've only just met the man.*

At around 10:30, the day caught up with Jenna. She inconspicuously signaled to David that she would like to go. They said their goodbyes, and Mr. Whitcomb indicated that he hoped he would see her again. Jenna responded that she hoped so as well. David watched the exchange and thought that although it was somewhat mechanical, to be fair, his father had made the effort to be gracious.

Mr. Whitcomb watched as David and Jenna exited. As soon as he was sure they were gone, he took out one of his business cards, wrote something on the back, and then started to scan the other side of the giant ballroom. It took a few moments, but he finally spotted the person he was looking for. He maneuvered through pockets of attendees who were finishing up the last of their drinks and conversations until he reached the other side of the room.

The focus of his attention, Alan Fenton, looked like he was about to leave. Without any preliminaries, Mr. Whitcomb thrust the business card in Alan's direction. "Have one of your people check out the young woman whose name is on the back of the card."

Alan reached for it as he said, "And good evening to you too, Bradford." He turned the card over and read aloud. "Jenna MacDonald. Tufts student. Pasadena." He looked away from what he had just read and asked, "Who's she?"

"Someone David is seeing."

He started to return the card, but Mr. Whitcomb didn't take it. "We're not in the business of following people around, Bradford. We're lawyers, not private investigators."

"I don't want her followed; I just want to know something about her background."

"It says here she's a student. She's probably not even twenty-one. She doesn't have a background."

"I want to know about her family then—things like that."

Alan looked at the business card again. "I guess I can have one of our young associates do a computer search."

"Will that give me the information I need?"

"I don't know. I don't know what you need." He studied Bradford Whitcomb for a moment before he spoke again. "Is it possible that you're overreacting to this? Do you really think David is serious about this girl?"

"I'm not sure if *he* knows it yet, but I do."

"Even if that's true, why the cloak and dagger stuff? What's the problem?"

Mr. Whitcomb got a condescending tone that he usually reserved for David. "As you know, Alan, David's agreed to join my business and use his trust fund for the project. I don't want anything distracting him."

"How would having information about this girl change that?"

"I just want to know what I'm dealing with."

CHAPTER 17

David watched the snow falling outside his bedroom window. It had begun accumulating shortly after midnight, and twelve hours later showed no signs of letting up. It seemed as if every winter, despite his love of Boston, David (and most of the other inhabitants of the region) asked themselves – "Why do we live here?"

Of course thought David, the "Why do we live here?" lament was not limited to people living in the Northeast; it was often voiced by citizens in other parts of the country as well – people on the West Coast because of earthquakes, Southerners because of hurricanes, and Mid-Westerners because of tornadoes.

None of this shared discontent provided much comfort to David however, especially because this particular February had been so brutal. The wind chill factor rarely moved out of single digits; the collective backs of the citizenry were sore from weeks of shoveling; and getting anywhere took two or three times longer than usual.

To make matters worse, each of the first two Fridays of the month saw more than a foot of snow bury any plans David and Jenna had to see each other, including their first Valentine's Day together. When David called to officially cancel, he could hear the disappointment in Jenna's voice. It continued for a few more minutes, but then her tone shifted, and she became more philosophical. "I guess we don't really need to be together on Valentine's Day. After all . . . it's just another day, right?"

Their relationship had grown so strong that David didn't hesitate to inject humor into their conversations, regardless of the topic. Of course, he mainly did it in order to hear Jenna laugh. It was his favorite sound in the world. "Now if I had said that, you would have figured I was just trying to get out of buying you a gift."

Jenna chuckled, but turned the tables on him. "No gift? No gift? Let's not *completely* downplay the significance of today."

There was some additional back and forth banter, which had recently become more and more the norm whenever they spoke with each other. It was always good-natured—never tinged with sarcasm, never calculated or hurtful. It was the verbal equivalent of month-old puppies wrestling and pawing at each other. It was who they had become.

Despite the weather, February proved to be an amazing month for David, Jenna, and their friends. There was one good piece of news after another.

Trent's interviews had gone well, and both firms offered him a job. It wasn't exactly the bidding war he had joked about, but it was great to have two companies interested in him. He had until the middle of March to make up his mind.

Jeremy's student teaching was off to a great start. The principal was so impressed by what he had seen and heard, that Jeremy was offered a replacement position for a teacher going out on maternity leave. Jeremy was able to get approval from the dean to extend his student teaching assignment, and was able to accept the offer. The principal also indicated that if Jeremy performed well in the leave replacement position, he would be hired for September.

Trish landed a summer internship at a Boston TV station and made arrangements with Tufts to continue to live at Hutchinson House for the two months she would be interning. Once Jenna heard that news, she quickly followed suit, and signed up to take some additional coursework during the early summer session. This served two purposes – Jenna would accumulate a few extra credits, and it ensured that she'd be in Boston for David's graduation.

The bidding process had started for the apartment project, and everything was going smoothly. Darnell had accepted David's offer to assist him in overseeing phase one, and Jeremy was also on board.

The icing on the cake occurred when David got an e-mail indicating that he had won the silent auction for the New Hampshire bed and breakfast weekend. He and Jenna made plans to go in late March.

While neither David nor Jenna mentally listed all of the positive things that were happening, they had an overall sense of amazement at the good fortune that continued to come their way.

Undoubtedly, their euphoria would have been greatly tempered, had they known what was transpiring with David's father.

About a week after the charity event, Alan Fenton called Mr. Whitcomb to let him know that the report on Jenna had been completed. "Do you want me to e-mail it to you, send it regular mail, FedEx it? What would you prefer?"

"Why don't you give me a quick summary over the phone, and then e-mail it to me?"

Alan shook his head and thought—*It's two pages; it's already a summary.* He tried to keep the frustration out of his voice, but was unsuccessful. "It's pretty much what I expected. She turns twenty in a few weeks. There's not much to tell. It's not as if she's one of those pre-teen rock stars that have biographies written about them when they're twelve."

Mr. Whitcomb didn't respond. He hoped that his silence would signal to Alan that he should proceed, but without the petulance. Alan sensed his client's displeasure, and continued more matter-of-factly. "She's from Pasadena, lives with her mother, who recently remarried. The mother's name is Sharon Brooks now. The stepfather is Jonathan; her biological father passed away when she was eight. She went to UCLA as a freshman, and then transferred to Tufts this year. She's a dean's list student. No car registered to her here or in California. A few other things you can read for yourself, but that's about it."

There was a pause on the line before Mr. Whitcomb spoke up. "That really doesn't tell me very much."

This time Alan didn't even try to hide his frustration. "I told you, Bradford, unless there's some public scandal or some family skeleton in the closet, most nineteen-year-olds are pretty anonymous."

"Nothing about the family's financial situation?"

"Her mom's a teacher, and her step-father's an accountant. Unless he's cooking the books for some big company, they're average middle-class."

"What about her character?"

Alan was even more exasperated, but he dialed it back. "Computer searches don't usually tell you much about a person's character, unless, as I said, there's something that hits the newspaper." He paused. "I'm sorry, Bradford. I know this is evidently important to you, but I'm not sure how we can provide you with what you're looking for. Didn't you get a sense of what she was like when you met her?"

"Everybody tries to make a good first impression. It's highly unlikely she would have revealed anything unseemly about herself, even unintentionally."

"Do you think there's actually something that this young woman is hiding, or are you just being overly cautious?"

"There's no such thing as being *overly* cautious. But to answer your question—no, I don't have anything specific." Mr. Whitcomb hesitated before he continued. "I've pretty much made up my mind what I'm going to do however."

"What's that?"

"I want to modify some of the provisions in David's trust fund."

"Again?"

"Yes. The presence of this young woman complicates things."

There was silence for a moment before Alan spoke. "Is there something more to this that you're not telling me?"

"No." Mr. Whitcomb glanced at the calendar on his desk before he continued. "I'd like you to come to my office next Thursday to finalize this."

"You haven't even seen the report yet."

"From what you've told me, there's not much there—certainly nothing to alter my decision. So, are you available next Thursday?"

"Let me check." After a moment Alan said, "I've got an opening from 3:00 – 4:00, but that won't give me enough time to travel back and forth to your office and review the changes you want to make, depending on how extensive they are."

Mr. Whitcomb was reluctant to go to Alan's office. Whenever he dealt with attorneys, he preferred his own turf. But since he wanted this taken care of immediately, it didn't appear that he had much choice. With a total lack of sincerity he said, "If it would make it easier, I could come to your office."

Alan recognized that this offer was one of expediency and had nothing to do with making *his* life any easier. Nevertheless, it provided him with a leg up in the obstacle course competition that now constituted his relationship with Bradford Whitcomb. "That would be fine. I'll see you next Thursday at 3:00."

As Mr. Whitcomb hung up the phone, the final wording of the changes he was contemplating became more formalized in his mind. He reached for the pen on his desk and began to write them down. When he was finished, he scribbled a large question mark at the bottom of the page.

Despite his self-assured attitude on the phone with Alan Fenton, Mr. Whitcomb had definite misgivings about what he was planning to do. He looked at the question mark he had drawn on the paper, realizing that it wasn't the appropriate punctuation for the grammatical construction he had formulated. But it very much reflected the mental conflict that he was experiencing.

Over the next week, Mr. Whitcomb met with David to review some particulars about how the first phase of the project was going to proceed. The decision had been made to go with the original plan of upgrading appliances and standardizing all the air conditioning units. Assuming there were no problems with any of the bids, the first phase would begin around July 1st.

David felt good about the meeting. There was nothing strained in the conversation, nothing that they disagreed about. Everything seemed to go smoothly. Of course, unbeknownst to David, that had been carefully orchestrated by his father. Mr. Whitcomb was a master at putting on a congenial face while hiding things that he didn't want anyone else to know. He had been particularly careful during this interaction. He knew that if David somehow sensed what he was considering in regard to the trust fund, all of his machinations could end up backfiring.

Whenever Mr. Whitcomb had an important meeting scheduled, he prepared meticulously, leaving nothing to chance. And it wasn't limited to the paperwork involved. He would decide ahead of time which attitude and posture he would assume, how he would phrase certain questions, what he would wear, and sometimes, even where he would sit.

The preparation for his upcoming visit to Alan Fenton's office was no different. For this meeting, he decided that he would take charge immediately, emphatically outline the changes he expected to be done, and thereby convince Alan that he knew exactly what he wanted and how he intended to get it.

He reluctantly acknowledged to himself however, that much of that was bravado. But in the past it had served him well to decide on a meeting strategy ahead of time and never waiver. He couldn't bring himself to alter those tactics now, considering the success they had always brought him.

In keeping with his strategy of immediately taking control, he considered intentionally arriving late to Alan's office, and thus establishing some sort of psychological upper hand. But he recognized that doing that might not provide enough time to complete the changes he wanted to make. Pragmatism eventually won out, and he showed up at precisely 3:00.

Alan welcomed Mr. Whitcomb a minute later and directed him to the same seat in his office that David had occupied a few weeks earlier. After Mr. Whitcomb declined the offer of a drink, Alan opened up the conversation. "We're a little pressed for time, so we probably should get right to it."

"That's fine," said Mr. Whitcomb as he extracted some papers from his briefcase and handed them to his attorney. "I prepared these myself. I didn't want my secretary involved."

The last comment piqued Alan's interest even further, but he accepted the papers without any comment and began to read. When he had perused enough of the document to get the gist of what was intended, he looked up and caught the eye of Mr. Whitcomb. "Is this what you really want, Bradford?"

"It is."

Alan stared directly at his client. "Can I talk to you as your friend and not your attorney?"

"I didn't think they were mutually exclusive."

Alan ignored the remark. "I don't get it. Why are you doing this? David's a good kid, a little idealistic maybe, but still a good kid. He's agreed to join the company, and in essence, he's funding the whole project with his trust fund. Haven't you already gotten what you want?"

"This is simply some insurance. I'm just trying to protect him."

"From what?"

"Possibly himself." He paused. "We do agree on one thing. He is a good kid, but he's also impetuous. That's what I'm trying to protect him from."

"You must realize that he's not going to like this. You're taking an awfully big chance. This may make him change his mind about everything."

"Only if he finds out."

"You're not going to tell him?"

"No." A pause. "And neither are you."

Alan chose to look at the document in his hand instead of saying anything. He found the particular few sentences he had been searching for and read them aloud. "If David marries before his twenty-seventh birthday, he forfeits the entire trust fund."

Mr. Whitcomb nodded as Alan continued. "In addition, if he stops working for the company prior to his twenty-seventh birthday he also forfeits the entire trust fund, including the $100,000 a year for ten years provision."

Mr. Whitcomb nodded again, but this time added, "Correct."

Alan shuffled the papers. "What additional surprises are on pages two and three?"

Mr. Whitcomb didn't like the tone of the question, but he still answered calmly. "There's a change in my will also. If he marries before he turns twenty-seven and I pass away in the interim, everything goes to charity." Mr. Whitcomb barely skipped a beat as he moved on. "The rest of the papers contain some changes in language that the company attorneys insisted upon. The language has to do with the payback of the $3 million to the trust fund once the improvements start to become profitable."

The office was silent for a moment, and then Alan said, "Obviously, as your attorney, I'll do whatever you want me to do in regards to all of this. But I feel compelled to say one more thing before I drop it." Alan knew he was pushing it, but when Mr. Whitcomb didn't object, he kept going. "David's not you, and he's not your other son either. He's his own person. Let him make his own decisions." He paused. "It looks like the project is going to take about two or three years to complete. From everything I can tell, David's committed to seeing it through. Shouldn't he be allowed to decide for himself how he wants to live his life after that?"

"He can. I'm simply providing some incentive for him to make the . . . best decisions possible."

"How can you consider it an incentive, if he doesn't even know about it?"

"When the time comes, I'll tell him."

"When what time comes?"

"If he indicates that he's thinking of leaving the company, or if he wants to get married, then I'll tell him."

"You do realize that none of this is a guarantee? He's going to feel blind-sided. He might become so upset when he finds out, that he'll decide to do the very things that you're trying to prevent."

Mr. Whitcomb remained stoic, despite the fact that the words he had just heard made sense—primarily because Mr. Whitcomb had said them to himself. But like some high school debate team member, he tried to score some rhetorical points instead of acknowledging the validity of his opponent's argument. "So, you do concede that he has choices?" Mr. Whitcomb forced a self-satisfied expression on his face as he continued. "In my experience, large sums of money tend to motivate people to act in a way that ensures that they have access to it."

"I'm not so sure David is like most people in that regard."

For the first time, Mr. Whitcomb permitted himself to give a softer response. "I truly hope I never have to find out."

Alan debated whether to continue to voice his opinion. It didn't appear to be getting him anywhere. He didn't want to see David treated like this, but he acknowledged to himself that he probably wasn't doing him any favors, so he left it alone.

Mr. Whitcomb wasn't done however. He regained his former tone and said, "Am I correct that you handle the lease arrangements on the apartment that David lives in while he's at school?"

"Yes, we handle that."

"I believe the lease is over on July 1st."

"That's correct, a few weeks after graduation."

"I'd like to draw up a new lease. David can still live there for free, and I want you to add his friend. I think his name is Jeremy something. I'll get you the specifics. He can pay the same rent that David's roommate Trent was paying. This Jeremy is going to work with David over the summer, and evidently Trent's got a job in New York, so he's moving out."

"Do you want the lease just for the summer?"

"No. Let's do it for a year." Mr. Whitcomb knew he probably shouldn't elaborate, but he could never resist trying to impress people by showing them that he was always thinking a few moves ahead, like some chess grand master. "I want David to have a roommate, so he doesn't think about having this young woman move in with him."

Alan couldn't resist. "This is way over the top, even for you."

A twinge of anger crept into Mr. Whitcomb's voice. "As my attorney, I pay you to give me advice, but in this instance I simply want you to comply with my wishes."

"I'm well aware of my responsibilities, Bradford. But as your friend, I'm going to repeat what I said before. I think this is a mistake, and you're going to regret it."

Neither of them spoke for a few moments. The silence allowed Mr. Whitcomb to consider what had just been said.

Alan sensed that there was an opening for further discussion, so he took a chance. "Bradford, what's your objective here?"

Mr. Whitcomb knew that he could end any further debate by refusing to answer the question, but he decided not to. "You mean about the changes?"

"No. I mean overall, from the beginning. What is it that you want?"

Mr. Whitcomb fought the urge to try to reassume control and bully his way through the rest of the meeting. Instead, he answered truthfully. "I want David to join the company."

"He's already agreed to that."

"And to stay with it."

"For how long?"

"Obviously, I'd like it to be permanent."

"That might not be realistic." Alan eyed his client. "It seems that the way you've set things up, you'd settle for him to be with the company until he turns twenty-seven."

Mr. Whitcomb continued to respond with uncharacteristic candor. "That's why I finally decided to make everything contingent upon that. If he's not interested in staying with the company after working there for four or five years, then he'll be allowed to make his own decisions."

This was a side of his client that Alan rarely saw, so he tried to press the advantage by throwing out an idea. "David's almost twenty-three, correct?"

"Yes, in a few months."

Alan nodded. "So, why not just offer him a four-year contract, and forget about all this other nonsense?"

Alan regretted using the word "nonsense" as soon as it left his mouth.

He could see Mr. Whitcomb bristle before he responded. "I don't consider it nonsense." He paused. "Besides, if I offer David a four-year contract, he's going to get suspicious. He knows the project will be completed long before that, and I don't want him asking questions. The less he knows about this the better."

"You aren't negotiating a business deal, Bradford."

"I'm well aware of that . . . but it is *family* business."

"So, your mind's made up."

"Yes."

Alan was silent as he studied Mr. Whitcomb's facial expression and body language. He had gotten better at reading both of those over the years. But for the most part, Bradford Whitcomb remained an enigma. Alan leaned back and said, "One last question: Why the marriage restriction? What's your concern?"

Mr. Whitcomb didn't hesitate. "This young woman might be after the money."

"You really believe that?"

"I don't know." He paused. *"I've* been burned twice; I don't want that happening to David."

Alan didn't say anything. Instead, he looked down at the documents in front of him, a silent acknowledgement that he was done pleading his case. After a few moments he said, "I'll take care of this as soon as I can. It should take less than a week."

Mr. Whitcomb stood up and offered his hand. "Thank you."

As they shook, Alan thought *I hope for your sake, Bradford, you know what you're doing.*

Ironically, Mr. Whitcomb's thoughts were not dissimilar to those of his attorney.

David and Jenna reluctantly agreed that Jenna should go home during spring break. Jenna hadn't been back to California for a couple of months, and since she was planning to stay in Boston until the end of June, waiting that long without a trip to see her mom didn't seem right. Besides, they both reasoned, they'd have a whole weekend together at the end of the month.

However, when Jenna returned from California, she was somewhat under the weather, and their New Hampshire trip looked very much in doubt. Jenna had to skip all of her classes for two straight days, and remained in bed to try to shake whatever she had. But it didn't work. When her fever went north of 101 degrees, and even the small amount of food she was able to consume wouldn't stay down, Trish took her to the Health Services office.

The doctor on duty ran a few tests, but indicated to Jenna even before the results were back that he was reasonably sure it was the flu. The preliminary diagnosis was confirmed forty-five minutes later, and Jenna was given some medicine to try to relieve her symptoms. There was little change in her condition over the next several hours so the medical personnel advised Jenna that they thought she should be transferred to the local hospital to spend the night. She resisted the idea, but then realized that if she returned to the dorm, she was putting Trish's health at risk.

Her hospital stay lasted two nights. When David found out, he naturally wanted to visit, but Jenna insisted that he not come. Their New Hampshire trip was less than a week away, and she was definitely on the mend. She was confident that she'd be well enough to go. But if David caught whatever she had, the trip would have to be cancelled anyway.

Forty-eight hours before they were scheduled to leave, Jenna was about eighty per cent back to normal, but the excitement of the trip easily made up for the other twenty per cent. David had suggested that they postpone, but Jenna would have none of it. "I really am fine, David. The doctor said I'm not contagious; I just need to drink plenty of liquids and avoid over-exerting myself." She paused and began to smile. "The liquids are not a problem, but . . . I'm not so sure about the not over-exerting myself part."

David returned the smile. "It sounds like you *are* feeling better. And exactly what did you have in mind?"

Jenna continued to smile. "Well, I thought maybe we could . . . oh, I don't know, go skiing."

David decided to play along. "That's exactly what I thought you meant. Maybe we could even try out the intermediate slope." He paused. "So, should I pack my skis?"

"You better not, unless you're intending to go by yourself!"

CHAPTER 18

Their New Hampshire getaway felt like a honeymoon. There was no fixed schedule; no place that they had to be at a specific time, no parameters. This sense of freedom set the tone for their lovemaking as well. Any inhibitions Jenna had shown in the past were gone. She not only initiated most of the sex, she couldn't seem to get enough.

"Hey, believe me, I'm not complaining," said David after a particularly ambitious marathon. "But what the hell did they give you in that hospital?"

Jenna smiled. "I don't know. Maybe it's the New Hampshire air."

"That can't be it. We haven't even been outside for two days!"

This time Jenna laughed. "Maybe it's the water then."

David shook his head. "You know, actually, I don't care what it is. But I think we should seriously consider moving up here."

Jenna started to laugh again as David continued. "I know it would be a long commute to Tufts. But I'd be willing to drive you every day."

"I don't think that'll be necessary. I'm pretty sure the way I've been feeling is easily transferable to other states." She tried to get a more serious expression on her face. "On the other hand, New Hampshire has no sales tax and no income tax. That's mainly what you were talking about, right?"

"Get over here."

When they returned home, both of them settled back into their regular routines. For David however, it was a bit more hectic; – it involved finishing up all his coursework before graduation and doing some preliminary work on the project he was going to oversee.

Despite that, he made sure that the two of them had plenty of time together. Whatever had triggered Jenna's new found "appetite" had seamlessly crossed the border into Massachusetts, and they both wanted to take advantage of it as often as possible.

Jenna was still not ready to move in with David, but her reservations were rapidly disappearing. Sharing an apartment sometime in the next year seemed all but inevitable.

The Harvard graduation was scheduled for the first week in June. It was always held outdoors, and the University's archivists claimed it had only rained on the ceremonies four times in the three and a half century history of the event. The archivists (with their tongues firmly planted in their cheeks) suggested that this was additional evidence that even the deity that controlled the weather was awestruck by the completion of a Harvard education. Evidently however, the current deity didn't get the memo. The rain began in the early morning, and by the start of the ceremony it resembled a full-fledged monsoon.

Jenna and Mr. Whitcomb were scheduled to sit beside each other, primarily at David's urging. Jenna was more amenable to that arrangement than Mr. Whitcomb. David did have to acknowledge however, that his father had been much more solicitous over the last few months. And if he had any momentary reluctance over graduation seating protocol, it could be overlooked.

Jenna hadn't been feeling well all morning, but she knew how important it was to David that she be there. So, despite the atrocious weather, she was determined to stay until the last notes of the recessional.

Both Jenna and Mr. Whitcomb had brought over-sized umbrellas that logistically limited their conversation. Jenna was grateful for the respite. Besides feeling ill, there was something gnawing at her that wouldn't have allowed very much meaningful interaction anyway.

The graduation lasted several hours. But when Jenna heard David's name announced, and he went up to get his diploma, she felt that it had been worth all the discomfort that she'd had to go through.

Following the ceremony, Mr. Whitcomb hosted a reception in his apartment. Trent and his parents, along with Jeremy and his parents were all in attendance, as were Alan Fenton and some other business associates of Mr. Whitcomb's. David introduced Jenna to all the guests who didn't already know her. And despite how she was feeling, she did everything she could to come across as poised and gracious.

121

David could tell that Jenna was not herself however. And after some prodding, Jenna acknowledged that she wasn't feeling well.

"Is it the flu again?" asked David.

Jenna hesitated. "Yeah, probably."

David was a little suspicious of her response, but he didn't press her any further. "Come on, I'm going to drive you back to your dorm."

"You can't leave. This is . . . ."

It was too late. David was already heading for the door. He excused himself, and indicated that he'd be back shortly. His father wasn't too pleased, but everyone else seemed to understand.

There wasn't much traffic, so the ride to Tufts took less than fifteen minutes. As they approached the campus, David said, "I wish you had told me sooner, Jenna, I would have taken you back earlier."

"It's okay. I probably just need some sleep."

"Were you sick at the graduation?"

"A little."

"Are you sure you're going to be all right? It seems like something else is bothering you."

"I'll be fine, David. Really."

"You're not very convincing, you know." He looked over at her as he pulled in front of Hutchinson House. "Promise me you'll get some sleep, and I'll check up on you tomorrow."

He started to give her a kiss, but Jenna turned her face. "Not on the lips, just in case it is the flu."

After David kissed her cheek, Jenna reached over and caressed his hand. For the first time since they had left the party, her face brightened. "Congratulations again. It was a great day. I'm really proud of you." She paused. "And I could tell that your father was proud of you too."

"It did seem that way, didn't it?"

There was a brief silence, and then Jenna tried to reassure David by being more upbeat than she felt. "If I'm up to it tomorrow, maybe we could do something?"

"That sounds good." He started to kiss her again, but pulled back. "Oh, sorry. Old habits die hard."

She mustered a smile. "I'll talk to you tomorrow."

Trish had been invited to David's graduation party, but had decided to spend some extra time at the TV station instead. She thoroughly enjoyed every minute of being there, even though for the most part, she was little more than a gofer. It also didn't hurt that there was a cute twenty-three-year-old news writer who was showing a lot of interest in her.

Trish had arrived back at the dorm a few minutes before Jenna. "Hey there," she said as her roommate walked in. "How did everything go?"

Jenna responded somewhat unenthusiastically. "Fine."

"What's the matter?"

"I'm just not feeling well."

"Sitting out in the rain probably didn't do you much good."

"Probably not, but I wanted to be there for David." She forced a smile. "It really was impressive though. I'm glad I went."

Trish studied Jenna for a moment, sensing that she was holding something back. "Do you think you should go to Health Services?"

"I don't think so. They're closed now anyway, aren't they?"

Trish glanced at her watch. "Yeah, you're right."

"Let me see how I feel tomorrow."

"What classes do you have?"

"Nothing heavy. I can squeeze in a visit if I have to."

Trish was still uneasy about the way Jenna was acting. "Why don't I skip going to the station tomorrow."

"No. Don't be silly. It's probably just a bug."

The next morning Trish again offered to stay home from her internship, but Jenna insisted that she was feeling better. It wasn't true, but she didn't want to worry her roommate. On the way out the door, Trish said she would check in later on.

Jenna cut her first class and slept in for an extra hour. She turned her phone off just in case David tried to call. If he did, and her phone switched over to voice mail, he would simply figure she was in class. She wasn't about to worry him either.

Finally, when she did get up, Jenna took her time showering and getting dressed, trying to convince herself that if she did everything more slowly, she'd feel better. It didn't work.

After debating with herself for a few more minutes, she decided to head to Health Services. It was already nearly seventy degrees, but for some reason, Jenna felt the need to put on a jacket. As she approached the building that housed the medical facility, she paused momentarily, but then kept walking.

As she left the campus, she didn't have a specific destination in mind, at least not consciously. After a few blocks she came to a strip mall with a drug store anchoring the far end. She acknowledged that quite possibly this had been her intended destination all along. *I'll just pick up some over the counter medication to help me get rid of this.* If she had been able to be honest with herself however, she would have admitted that something else was going on.

With a bit more outward resolve, she entered the drug store and began a methodical tour of the aisles. She picked up some Dayquil, Motrin, and cough syrup, and placed them all in the basket she was carrying. Next came a box of tissues and a couple of magazines.

Jenna walked down the next to last aisle, pausing a number of times to pick up various items. She glanced at them, and then returned them to the shelves. Toward the end of the aisle, near the back of the store, she picked up a small box, and tried to appear casual as she studied it. A moment later she placed the box in her basket and started down the aisle. She stared at the box briefly, and then removed it from the basket. She retreated a few steps and began to return it to its proper location. Instead, she turned slightly and checked to see if anyone was watching her. And then almost involuntarily, she put the box in her jacket pocket.

As she started to move down the last aisle, she nervously pulled some additional items off the shelves and put them in the basket, not even paying attention to what they were. She delayed going to the register, trying to calm herself as much as possible.

The notion of being caught shoplifting terrified Jenna. She had never stolen anything in her life – not even a candy bar as a little girl. What had she been thinking? The answer formed quickly in her mind, but she felt it more intently in her stomach – she just couldn't have endured the judgmental stares of the cashier. That was potentially much worse than being caught. On any rational level, that made no sense. But Jenna knew deep down that from the moment she had walked past Health Services, she was operating on pure emotion.

As it turned out, the young woman who rang up the items barely looked at Jenna, allowing her to relax ever so slightly. However, by the time the cashier handed the plastic bags to her and uttered the obligatory "Have a nice day", Jenna was shaking.

On the walk back to campus, Jenna continued to finger the box in her jacket pocket. The reality of its presence forced her to finally come to terms with what she had suspected for weeks.

After she entered her dorm room, she locked the door, and began to put away all of the items she had purchased, as if somehow those actions would bring order to things. She returned to her bed where she had placed her jacket, removed the box from the pocket and stared at it for a moment. She took a deep breath, opened the box, and read the directions. After she reread them two more times, and was sure that she understood everything, she closed her eyes and lay back on the bed.

A few minutes passed and then Jenna stood up, put the box in her purse and went to a lavatory down the hall that had a lock on the door. Once she was inside, she closed her eyes and tried to steady herself. After a few moments she read the directions again, and then followed them explicitly. Despite a rising sense of panic, she waited the specified time and then forced herself to look at the stick she was holding. A plus sign was clearly visible—as she had known on some level, it certainly would be.

CHAPTER 19

Jenna gathered everything she had brought with her so that there was no trace of the pregnancy test left in the lavatory. She returned to the dorm room, put all the materials in a plastic bag, and stuffed it under her bed until she could dispose of it later.

The last thing Jenna wanted to do was to think about the test results and what they meant. She attempted to put it out of her mind by busying herself with other things. She checked her phone messages—two from David and one from Trish. She realized that there was no way she could talk to David at this point, so she e-mailed him, indicating that she still wasn't feeling well, and that she would call him tomorrow. She figured that the e-mail had bought her twenty-four hours. By then she hoped she'd have some sense about what to do. She decided not to respond to Trish's e-mail. She would just wait until Trish got back from the station.

As soon as Jenna ran out of mundane tasks, the magnitude of the situation hit her all at once. She started to cry, not from sadness, but more from a sense of feeling lost. It was as if her life had been traveling along a familiar path and then suddenly all the landmarks had mysteriously disappeared, and she found herself in the depths of a forest with no discernible way out.

She got under the covers, still fully clothed, and sobbed into her pillow. Every time she was able to calm herself, a new question pushed its way to the front of her brain – *What's David going to say? How do I even tell him? How do I tell my mom? Should I even have the baby? Should I keep it? I'm on the pill; how did I even get pregnant?*

Jenna knew that any one of those questions taken individually was overwhelming. Cumulatively, they made her feel like her entire body was weighted down. She had trouble catching her breath, which brought on even more panic. After a few moments, she began to focus on the last question she had posed to herself – *How did I even get pregnant?*

The flow of tears subsided, and even though the answer to that question was the least critical of them all, attempting to understand how this had happened provided the impetus she needed to move forward.

The pill was virtually 100% effective. Was her pregnancy some miniscule mathematical aberration? Had she and David beaten million to one odds? That was possible she thought. But she had a hard time simply ascribing all of this to chance.

And then it came to her – the time she had the flu. She hadn't been able to keep anything down for a few days. Her body wouldn't have been able to distinguish between food and birth control pills.

She got out of bed, found her laptop, and typed in "birth control pill effectiveness." There were a large number of links. She chose one with a Boston connection and began to read. The third paragraph provided all the information she needed – *Skipping as few as two days in a row reduces the pill's effectiveness by 50% or more for the next 7-10 days.* Their weekend in New Hampshire had been less than a week after her hospital stay.

Jenna found it ironic that the weekend, which had been nothing short of amazing, had ultimately led to what she was now facing.

The knowledge of how her pregnancy had occurred satisfied Jenna's curiosity, but nothing more. She had deluded herself into thinking that once she had solved that mystery, it would somehow help with everything else. It didn't. In fact, it made things worse. Jenna started to blame herself for not knowing about the pill's limitations.

After a few minutes, she shut down the computer, closed her eyes, and tried to think of what to do next. Her thoughts were interrupted by the sound of a key being inserted into the lock on the door to the dorm room. Trish was back.

As soon as Trish saw Jenna, she knew that something beyond "just not feeling well" was going on. Before Trish could say anything, however, Jenna spoke up, trying to mask the anxiety she knew she was projecting. "You're back early."

"I was worried about you. I thought you had probably gone to class or to Health Services and shut off your phone. But then when you didn't call back . . . ." Trish saw traces of Jenna's tears. "What's going on?"

Jenna didn't answer right away. She brought her hands up to her eyes, took a deep breath, and said, "I'm pregnant."

Trish looked stunned. She went over to Jenna and put her arms around her. "Oh, Jenna. Are you sure?"

Jenna nodded. "I took a home pregnancy test."

"Those aren't always accurate, you know."

"I know, but it all makes sense. The way I've been feeling . . . just everything . . . ." Her voice trailed off.

There was silence for a few moments, and then Trish asked, "Does David know?"

"No. After I found out, I didn't want to talk to anyone. That's why I didn't call you back." She paused. "I've got to figure out how to tell him. I can probably put it off until tomorrow, but not much longer."

"Do you have any idea what you're going to do?"

"No. I'm still trying to get my head around it."

They continued to talk for another hour. Jenna explained about not taking the pill for a few days, about feeling guilty, and about trying to predict how David was going to react. "I don't really know how *I'm* supposed to feel about it. So I don't have any idea what to expect from David."

Jenna started to cry again. Through her tears she said, "I think the worst thing is having to tell my mom. I know she'll understand, but . . . ."

Trish held her. "Can I make a suggestion?"

"What?"

"I think you should go see a doctor, just to be sure."

"I don't want to go to Health Services; everybody knows me there."

"Okay. We'll find someplace else. Let me check it out on the Internet."

The brief diversion of the computer search allowed Jenna to calm herself. After a few minutes, Trish pointed out a few possibilities.

"It doesn't matter. Whatever you think," said Jenna.

"Here's a clinic in Boston; it says it encourages walk-ins."

"That's fine."

"Okay. Let's plan on tomorrow morning."

Once some of the logistics were worked out, they continued to talk about the situation. Even though it wouldn't be officially confirmed until the next day, Jenna knew she was pregnant, so the discussion proceeded as if she were. In actuality, it was less a discussion than it was Jenna thinking out loud. Trish just listened.

Unspoken was the knowledge that Jenna and David would have to work things out together. Anything "decided" before David even knew, would have been done in a vacuum, and would lack any finality.

When Trish and Jenna were all talked out, Trish suggested that Jenna take a nap. She could see the physical and emotional exhaustion on Jenna's face.

"Actually, that sounds good," said Jenna.

"I'm going to go for a walk. I'll be back in an hour or so. We can talk some more, if you'd like. Or get something to eat, if you're up to it."

"Let me see how I feel." She paused. "Thanks, Trish."

Trish smiled. "I'll see you in a while."

Despite all the ideas racing around in her head, Jenna was able to enter into a light sleep for about forty-five minutes. When she awoke, her first thoughts were that everything had been a dream. That was quickly dispelled as a wave of nausea washed over her. She fought the sensation, and somehow willed the discomfort to pass. It took a few minutes of lying perfectly still and taking short breaths, but it worked. Any thought of eating something in the next few hours, however, was out of the question. Jenna called Trish's cell phone to suggest that she eat something while she was out. Jenna didn't think she could even look at food at this point.

When Trish returned, they started up the discussion again. This time it focused on telling David.

Jenna said, "If I don't call him tonight, he's going to be suspicious that something else is going on. I did e-mail him and tell him that I'd talk to him tomorrow. But if I don't call tonight, he's just liable to show up. I'm not ready for that."

"I agree. I think you should call tonight and set up something for tomorrow. Are you up to talking to him?"

"I'm going to have to be."

Jenna spent the next few minutes scripting her remarks. Finally, she took some deep breaths and pressed David's number. He answered right away. Before he could say very much, Jenna jumped in and indicated that she was feeling a little better, but needed tonight and tomorrow morning to fully recover. Without skipping a beat, she suggested that David come by around 2:00.

David tried to interject a number of times, but Jenna cut him short, fearful that any additional words between the two of them would make her too emotional. David continued to push for more details about how she was feeling, but then he seemed to accept that she probably just needed to rest.

When Jenna heard David say "I love you" she almost lost it, but recovered just enough to repeat the words back, and end the call.

Trish and Jenna waited about thirty minutes at the clinic before being seen. Jenna was given a comprehensive exam, and then she was ushered into a small waiting room. The doctor who examined Jenna was an older man who Jenna assumed must have made thousands of these pronouncements. She figured that the degree of enthusiasm with which he delivered the news depended upon what he saw in the eyes of the patient in the moments before he told her.

Since Jenna had no idea how she felt about all of this, her expression remained neutral. As she suspected, the doctor's expression mirrored her own. Finally, he said, "You're probably about eight weeks along." Jenna nodded as she did some quick math—the New Hampshire weekend had been almost nine weeks ago.

The next day, a few minutes before David was scheduled to arrive, Trish and Jenna went down to the lobby. Trish wished Jenna good luck, and told her she would see her later that night. David showed up shortly after Trish left.

"Hi, Jenna," said David, as he came over to give her a hug and a kiss.

She forced a smile, as she returned the greeting. "Hi."

"Are you feeling better?"

Jenna had momentarily forgotten about her cover story; she hesitatingly responded, "Uh, yeah." She next spoke the lines she had rehearsed for the last few minutes. "I forgot my cell phone in the room. Why don't you come upstairs with me while I get it?"

"Sure."

Jenna had decided that she needed to tell David in total privacy, certainly not in the car, not in a restaurant, not anywhere where they could be overheard or interrupted. Whatever emotions spilled out from either one of them shouldn't be done in public.

When they entered the dorm room, Jenna closed the door behind her, went over to her bed and sat down. She gestured for David to follow. There was a quaver in her voice when she said, "I didn't really forget my phone. I need to talk to you." She pursed her lips, fighting her emotions. "Well, actually to tell you something."

The concern was evident on David's face, and before he spoke, a number of thoughts cascaded in his head. *Is she breaking up with me? Is she leaving Tufts? Did something happen to her mom? What?* With trepidation in his voice he said, "What's wrong, Jenna?"

Jenna looked directly at him, and then down at her hands. "I'm pregnant."

In the split second before the words registered, David actually felt relief that it wasn't a breakup or a three thousand mile separation, but then the meaning of the words sunk in. "What?"

Still not looking at him, Jenna gave a slight nod of her head and repeated more quietly, "I'm pregnant."

"How? . . . I thought . . . you know, you were on the pill."

Jenna looked at him with sadness in her eyes. "I was. But I think when I got sick and I missed a couple of days, and then we went away . . . ."

David didn't know what he was feeling, or even what he was *supposed* to be feeling. Just as the doctor at the clinic had done, he looked to Jenna to give him a signal about how to react, but there was nothing in her expression that he could pick up on.

Silence filled the room for a few moments before David spoke. "I don't know what to say."

"I know. I still don't think it's completely hit me yet."

It was hard for David to imagine that he could experience this many conflicting emotions at the same time. The only words that finally found their way to his mouth were, "What do you want to do about it?" He shook his head. "I'm sorry. That didn't come out right. I'm just stunned. I don't know what I'm saying."

"I know. Me too. I still can't believe this is happening to us."

David stood up and blew the air out of his cheeks. "Wow! I sure didn't see this coming."

He started pacing the dorm room floor. After a moment he looked over at Jenna and she was crying. He recognized that he had to try to comfort her before he said or did anything else. He sat down next to her and allowed her to cry against his chest as he kissed the top of her head.

David knew it was going to be nearly impossible to bring any logical or systematic framework to what had happened, but he decided to try anyway.

"Why don't we just keep talking, and try to sort some of this out?" He looked toward Jenna, and she nodded before he continued. "How did you feel, you know, when you first found out?"

Jenna tried to find the words, but didn't have much success. "It was a blur. I think if this were a few years from now . . . ." Jenna started to feel embarrassed. "I'd be excited, but . . . ." She looked at David. "You know I love you; it's not that."

David held her again. "I know. I love you too." He paused, sensing that he needed to at least appear more in control than he felt "We'll work this out. It's going to be okay." But the words seemed hollow, even to him.

They talked for another half hour, still unable to express what they were feeling. And despite the openness they had established with each other over the last several months, neither one of them could bring themselves to say anything definitive. Finally, David bit the bullet.

"Jenna, obviously I want to have some say in all of this, but I think you need to be the one to make the decision. I'll support whatever you want to do." He paused. "You're the one who hasn't finished school . . . ."

"It's more complicated than that. I can't decide this by myself."

"I didn't mean that you should have to. I just meant that you should have the final say. Whatever you decide, I'll be okay with it."

There was silence again, as David continued to run things through his mind. He didn't know if what he was about to say was out of a sense of obligation, or what he truly wanted.

"I love you, and I know you love me." He looked directly at Jenna. "Maybe . . . we should get married."

Jenna looked stunned. Possibly buried deep in her subconscious, she had considered that this could be the response that David would come up with, but not on any realistic level. Jenna finally started to say something, but David cut her off.

"If we get married then it won't matter what's decided." He smiled for the first time. "I would have asked you to marry me eventually; this just speeds up the process."

A slight smile found its way to Jenna's lips, but the left side of her brain tempered things. She had barely accepted the idea that they would possibly be moving in together, and now they were going to get married. Her life was moving too fast.

"I don't know . . . ." She started to cry, and David took her in his arms.

Once Jenna calmed down, they continued to talk things through, and finally were able to make some decisions. Initially, it seemed as if the decisions were simply borne out of a sense of needing to do *something*. Eventually, however, they were both able to look into each other's eyes and know that this is what they truly wanted.

They were going to get married.

If they decided to have the baby, then they'd have a small ceremony in Boston during the summer, before school started. Jenna was just old-fashioned enough that she wanted the appearance of propriety when she returned to Tufts. She knew that regardless of how open-minded people were, as soon as they recognized that she was pregnant, their eyes would immediately jump to her ring finger. If they decided not to have the baby, then they would wait until later in the fall to get married.

Jenna told David that the decision whether to have the baby or not, would have to be made soon. An abortion close to the second trimester would complicate things for her, medically and morally.

They also agreed that Jenna should go back to California at the end of June as planned. This would give her a chance to tell her mom. David would stay in Boston to begin work on overseeing the apartment upgrades.

The emotional trauma of the pregnancy news and the ripple effect it would have on their lives was overwhelming. And yet, once the decisions had been agreed upon, it brought a peaceful resolve to both of them—something that seemed impossible a few hours before.

Ironically, the very afternoon that David and Jenna were starting to come to terms with everything, Alan Fenton was filing papers related to David's trust fund and his father's will. The two events were on a collision course that nobody could have foreseen – with the possible exception of Bradford Whitcomb.

CHAPTER 20

Jenna and David didn't see each other for the next three days. It wasn't a conscious decision; it was simply that they weren't able to place the other facets of their lives in suspended animation as they tried to adjust to the reality of Jenna's pregnancy.

David helped Trent move out of the apartment, finalized the preparation for the project he was overseeing, and provided twice-a-day updates to his father. Jenna finished up her summer course work and got ready to go back to California.

The seventy-two hours apart provided an opportunity for some of the disbelief and anxiety over their situation to fade. Both Jenna and David in their own way were able to put things in perspective.

When Jenna was much younger, especially right after her father died, like many little girls, she had dreamed of a fairy tale life – a Prince Charming, children, and a beautiful home. And while the current route to that fairy tale was not what she had envisioned, the potential for "happily ever after" still seemed like a real possibility. She loved David; he loved her, and they were expecting a baby together. Did it matter that it hadn't come about the way she had dreamt it would when she was eight?

That premise allowed her to focus primarily on what her life would be like if she went ahead and had the baby. And although she may have been viewing everything through rose-colored glasses, it became more and more apparent to her that she wanted to marry David; she wanted the baby; she wanted them to be a family.

Jenna acknowledged to herself that it was important that David come to the same realization that she had, but on his own. She didn't want him to feel pressured. She briefly drifted into thinking about the practical side of all this – Where would they live? What about school? How would they afford everything?

And then ironically, the very thing that she was dreading most – telling her mom—provided some peace of mind. Her mom would help her come to terms with all of this. She would help Jenna make the right choices. And for the first time in almost three days, Jenna felt like everything might be okay.

Even though David was scrambling to take care of all the preliminaries before the apartment project started up, Jenna was never far from his thoughts. He was a bit jealous that Jenna had Trish to talk to, and he didn't have anyone. Trent was gone, and Jeremy hadn't moved in yet. His self-pity disappeared however, as he acknowledged that coming to grips with this situation was something he had to do by himself anyway.

Just twenty-four hours after Jenna had told him that she was pregnant, he realized that somehow the weight of impending fatherhood and marriage felt less burdensome. He decided, however, not to say anything to Jenna. If he saw any sign that she was feeling the same way, then certainly he would speak up. But imposing what he wanted onto Jenna wouldn't be fair.

David and Jenna were able to spend a few nights in the apartment before she had to head back to California. Again, the freedom in their lovemaking continued even more unabated. It was almost as if now with Jenna's pregnancy, they could give themselves up to each other with no restriction or hesitation.

And while they talked about various possibilities, they agreed that no decision should be made until Jenna spoke to her mom and heard what she had to say. Still, David sensed that Jenna was feeling the same way he was. He began to find himself smiling every time the thought entered his mind.

There was an emotional goodbye at the airport as David saw Jenna off. She promised to call in the next few days to let him know where everything stood. That afternoon David helped Jeremy move in. He welcomed the company much more than he had anticipated.

The move didn't take very long. There were no large items to wrestle with, not even a bed. All the furnishings that had been bought after freshman year were still in good shape and belonged to the apartment. When Jeremy was finished putting away some personal items in his bedroom, he came out and sat on the couch with David.

"I know I've told you before, but I want you to know how much I appreciate what you and your father are doing. You know, the job and the apartment."

"You're welcome. But it's great for me too. I've got someone I can trust working with me, and then with Jenna away, I've got someone to hang out with."

"How long is she going to be in California?"

David hesitated before he spoke. "A month or so. Maybe a little longer."

"Listen, David, you've got to tell me if I'm in the way here. If you two are planning on moving in together, you need to let me know. I'll find another place."

"Thanks, but right now a lot of things are up in the air. I just don't know what's going to happen." David hadn't planned on telling anyone yet, but the words just spilled out. "Actually . . . I think we may be getting married."

"What? Seriously?"

David nodded.

"Wow. I mean, I think Jenna's terrific, but I had no idea things had gotten that serious."

David hesitated again, but he realized that since he had gone this far, he might as well tell Jeremy the rest. "Jenna's pregnant."

Jeremy got wide-eyed. "Really?" He looked carefully at David, trying to get a read on his feelings. When he wasn't able to, he asked, "How do you feel about that?"

"I wasn't sure at first. But, I think I'm getting to like the idea."

"When is she due? . . . What about school?"

"She's due in December." David wasn't about to bring up the possibility that Jenna might decide not to have the baby. Instead, he said, "She wants to go to school right up until she's ready to deliver. It's possible we could get married even before school starts."

"That soon? Wow. But hey, good for you two." He paused. "I thought Karen and I were headed in that direction, but then she met that Peace Corps guy in Brazil, and . . . ."

"Sorry, man. I forgot about that."

"It's okay."

David hesitated before he spoke. "Listen Jeremy, I haven't told anyone else about any of this. So if you could keep it to yourself, I'd appreciate it."

"No problem."

"And don't worry about the apartment situation. I think once we get married, either Jenna's going to continue to live in the dorm, or we'll look for some place closer to Tufts. But no matter what, you'll be able to stay here, certainly until the baby's born."

"Are you sure?"

"Yes, positive."

"I really appreciate that, David. But if you change your mind, you've got to tell me. It won't be a problem."

"I know. I will."

Jeremy shook his head. "I have to say, David, you're handling all this, especially the pregnancy, a lot better than I think I would be able to."

David gave a half-smile. "I've had some sleepless nights, but . . . we were probably going to get married anyway; it's just sooner than we thought. I really am okay with it now . . . better than okay, actually."

"It still must feel weird."

"Sometimes. Especially when I try to put it out of my head, and then it jumps back in."

"Have you told your father yet?"

"No. And I can't say I'm looking forward to that conversation. No telling how he'll react."

They were quiet for a moment and then Jeremy spoke up. "I think I'm going to finish putting my stuff away."

"Sure."

Jeremy headed toward his room. Before he got there, David called out. "When you're done, would you like to go over some of the details about the project?"

"Yeah, that'd be great. Give me five minutes."

As David went into his bedroom to get the project folders, he reflected on the last few minutes, and realized how good it actually felt to talk with someone else about his situation. He smiled to himself, as he thought – *Even the Lone Ranger had Tonto.*

A few minutes later David opened the folders and began to outline Jeremy's job responsibilities. "The project is going to start at the apartments where Darnell Smith is the manager. You'll like Darnell; he's a great guy.

He's also going to help us out at the other sites. That's why we're starting there, so we can work out any bugs. Anyway, here's a blueprint of the entire complex with the names and phone numbers of all the residents. What I'd like you to do is contact each of them and schedule a day and time for the installation of the new appliances. You probably should call ahead, let them know when you're coming, and tell them to be thinking about what's most convenient."

"That's it?"

"Well, that's the nuts and bolts. You'll obviously have to be on site when the installations are going on, and troubleshoot any problems. Also there's bound to be scheduling conflicts; you'll have to resolve those. But yeah, that about sums it up." David looked at Jeremy. "Not bad, huh? You get to play Santa Claus in July."

"I think I can handle it."

"No doubt."

The second night after Jenna was back home in California, David's cell phone rang a little after 6:00 P.M. He glanced at the incoming number and recognized the Pasadena area code. "Hi, Jenna. How are you doing?"

"Hi. Actually, better than I thought. I told my mom."

"How did that go?"

"She said she knew as soon as she saw me, but she's been terrific about it."

"That's great. I'm really glad."

"Yeah, me too. If I had seen any disappointment in her eyes, I'm not sure how I would have handled it. Anyway, we had a great talk this afternoon, and she said she'll support whatever we decide."

"You know, I still haven't met her. But she seems pretty special."

"She is."

There was silence on the line for a few moments before Jenna broke it. "I think you probably already know how I'm leaning, but I want to see my ob-gyn before the final decision."

"That makes sense."

"It might take a few more days to get an appointment."

"Whatever you need to do."

"I'll call as soon as I know more."

"Okay."

Jenna shifted topics. "So, when do you start the project?"

"Tomorrow."

"How's Jeremy working out?"

"You know Jeremy, he's terrific." He paused. "I told him by the way. I hadn't planned to, but we got talking and it kind of felt like the right thing to do."

"I'm glad you did. I had Trish to talk to and now my mom. I felt badly that you didn't have anyone."

For some reason, David didn't want to acknowledge that that was part of the reason he had told Jeremy. "It's not really a guy thing, though."

"Probably not most guys. But you and Jeremy aren't like most guys."

"I guess that's a compliment."

"Of course it is."

They talked for ten more minutes, said "I love you" to each other, and then hung up. Although it was left unsaid, they both knew that the decisions they made in the next few days would no doubt shape the rest of their lives.

During the following week, David and Jeremy worked twelve-hour days, but neither of them seemed to mind. The tenants were so excited about the new appliances and the air conditioning upgrades that the schedule at the beginning of the month was tremendously overloaded.

Jeremy suggested that David try to convince the suppliers to work on weekends. He was able to negotiate a deal which accelerated the installations. The tenants' association was ecstatic. Darnell joked that if David or Jeremy had run for association president, they would have been elected in a landslide—and they were management.

David didn't delude himself into thinking that the whole project was going to go as smoothly as this phase had started out. But for the time being, he was happy to bask in the appreciation coming his way from everyone at the site.

David was shocked that his father wasn't a constant presence at the apartment complex. On the other hand, David was required to give his father updates twice a day, and he was sure Darnell was being asked to do the same. For most people that would be considered micromanaging, but for David's father, that was akin to laissez-faire.

David talked to Jenna every night, and often e-mailed her as well. Her appointment was scheduled for Monday afternoon, and she indicated that she would probably have a good idea about what she wanted to do a day or two later.

It didn't take that long, however. She knew immediately after meeting with the doctor what her decision was going to be. She called David as soon as she got home.

After they exchanged a quick hello, Jenna started right in. "I just got back from my appointment."

"Everything all right?"

"Yes, the doctor said everything's fine."

"That's terrific." David paused, trying to form the words of the question he wanted to ask. But they wouldn't come.

It didn't matter; Jenna answered as if the question had actually been asked. "I want to have the baby, David. I saw the ultrasound . . . the baby's heart beating . . . ."

David could sense that she was having trouble continuing. He jumped in. "I'm so glad you said that, Jenna. That's exactly what I want too."

She told him about the rest of the visit. And about how emotional her mother had gotten as well, thinking about her first grandchild. Jenna also expressed that she couldn't imagine that she had ever seriously considered ending the pregnancy.

It was a tremendous relief to both of them that they wanted the same thing. Toward the end of the conversation, David brought up the idea of setting a wedding date. "You know, if you'd like, we can get married out there. I don't think my father would be too thrilled, although I haven't told him anything about any of this. But I'm not going to worry about that now. If it's better for you, then let's get married in California."

"What about the project? How can you take time off?"

"Actually, things are going great. We're way ahead of schedule."

"That's sweet, David. But, off the top of my head, it seems that if we hold it out here, the wedding is going to have to be bigger. We'd have to invite all my mother's friends, and . . . I really appreciate what you're trying to do, but, let's just keep it the way it was. My mom's got the summer off. She doesn't mind coming to Boston."

"Okay, if you're sure?"

"I am."

"In that case, how about the middle of August?"

"Seriously?"

There was laughter in his voice, as he said, "Are you having second thoughts?"

Jenna's voice was also light when she responded. "Of course not. But how can we arrange everything so quickly?"

"Let me see what I can do."

Jenna hesitated, only because she had trouble believing that this was really going to happen, and in less than a month. "Okay. I guess. I don't know what else to say . . . ."

"You don't need to say anything." David paused. "I'm going to go see my father in the next few days to let him know everything, but I want to get things started before I talk to him."

"That's probably a good idea." She paused. "How do you think he'll take it?"

"With my father, who knows? But it really doesn't matter." David said the last sentence as if he actually believed it, but Jenna knew it *did* matter to David more than he would ever admit. Nevertheless, she left it alone. They talked for a few more minutes, mainly about the wedding details. David promised to call as soon as he had any news.

Over the next several days, David carved out a few hours during his lunchtime to begin to organize the logistics for the wedding. The fact that he and Jenna had agreed to keep things small – no church, no large reception hall – certainly made everything easier. And by Friday the plans had started to come together.

David decided to wait until Monday, however, to broach the subject with his father. The past week at the project site couldn't have gone more smoothly, and he wanted the euphoria of the project's success to be front and center in his father's mind before they spoke.

David called his father's office around 10:00 on Monday morning, asking if he could come by around noon. After a brief interrogation, which David deflected, his father agreed to see him.

Mr. Whitcomb's secretary had gone to lunch by the time David arrived. The door to the inner office was open however, so he just walked in. When his father spotted David, he smiled more broadly than David had seen him do in some time. He came out from behind the desk, and offered his hand. "Hello, David."

"Hi, Dad."

Despite this newfound collegiality, Mr. Whitcomb returned to the other side of the desk and motioned for David to have a seat.

His father opened up the conversation by making an uncharacteristic attempt at humor. "I know things have been going well, but you can't be here about a raise already."

David smiled. "No . . . not yet anyway. I know I already mentioned it to you, but Darnell and Jeremy are doing a great job. That's one of the reasons things are going so well."

"That's good to hear."

David looked away from his father's gaze momentarily. When he started to speak, however, he resumed eye contact. "Actually, this doesn't have anything to do with the business. It's . . . uh . . . more personal."

Mr. Whitcomb arched his eyebrows, but didn't say anything.

David paused briefly, and then just came out with it. "I'm getting married."

David had rarely seen his father show surprise, but it was easily recognizable as soon as his words had registered. Before Mr. Whitcomb spoke, it appeared to David that his father was not only trying to calm himself, but also to suppress some anger. "This is quite sudden, don't you think?"

As usual with his father, David found himself on the defensive. "We've known each other for eight months, and we're in love." David knew he sounded like a fifteen-year-old, but he couldn't control how the words came out.

"What's the rush? The girl hasn't even finished school yet."

David's defensiveness turned to annoyance. "Her name's Jenna, and she's going to stay in school."

Mr. Whitcomb shook his head. "And who's paying for that?" He didn't wait for David to answer before he continued. "I think this is a huge mistake. You need to rethink this."

David ignored the tuition question. "This isn't about what *you* think. It's about my life, and Jenna's life. It's about what we want."

Mr. Whitcomb widened the divide between them. "You're twenty-three; and she's what, twenty? And you think you know what you want?"

David was becoming more and more incensed, but he tried to keep it in check. "We're old enough to know that we love each other, and we want to be together."

Mr. Whitcomb smiled, but it was one of condescension. He waited a moment and then asked. "Is she pregnant?"

David knew he shouldn't have been surprised by the directness of the question, but nevertheless he was. He almost chose to answer "no," just to see the smug expression leave his father's face. Instead, he gathered himself, looked directly at his father and said, "Yes, but that has nothing . . . ."

"Are you sure it's yours?"

The words hit David like a punch in the stomach. He couldn't have held back even if he wanted to. "Fuck you!"

Mr. Whitcomb was stunned. His face became contorted in an expression of shock and anger. He returned David's stare, and after a moment said, "Perhaps my question was a bit intemperate, but I still expect you to show me proper respect."

David didn't hesitate. "Fine. Fuck you, *sir!*"

Mr. Whitcomb realized this confrontation was quickly deteriorating, but he still couldn't bring himself to be any more conciliatory. "I think it would be best if you left, David. Come back in an hour or so, when you've calmed down."

David got wide-eyed. "You are unbelievable. You insult Jenna *and me* . . . and then you make it seem like I'm the one who's overreacting."

David got up from his chair, placed both hands on his father's desk and leaned in toward him. "Okay, I'll be back in an hour. That'll give me time to type up my resignation. I'm done taking any more shit from you." He turned his back on his father and walked out of the office.

Mr. Whitcomb started to say something, but his pride and the sharp pain radiating up his arm toward his chest prevented any words from emerging.

CHAPTER 21

David fully expected to hear his father call after him. When he didn't, it made him even more incensed. Whether through happenstance or more likely through manipulation, his father had gotten everything he wanted. David, on the other hand, felt as if he had put himself first just this one time, and this is how his father had reacted.

David could barely focus on what he was doing. As he entered the elevator, he accidentally hit the button for the wrong level. He then lashed out with the side of his hand, striking three more buttons, none of them the correct one.

"God damn it," he said out loud.

One of the buttons he had struck was for the next floor down. When the door opened David got off, deciding that taking the stairs was a much better option; it lessened the chances of coming in contact with anyone.

Halfway down, David stopped on one of the landings, took out his phone and shut it off. Besides not wanting to run into anyone, he didn't want to talk to anyone either. When he resumed his descent, a number of thoughts began to push themselves forward, but his anger wouldn't let them crystallize. The one thing he was able to acknowledge, however, was that some of the anger he was now feeling should have been directed at himself – *How could I let my father get to me like that?*

When he reached the garage level, he strode toward his car, clicked the key fob and got behind the wheel. He closed his eyes and leaned back against the headrest, trying to figure out what he should do next.

On some level he knew that he didn't want to quit, but how could he ignore what had just happened—the contempt in his father's voice when he had asked that question – "Are you sure it's yours?" David raised his right arm and back-punched the passenger seat. *What the hell is wrong with him?*

David knew he not only needed to calm down, but he also needed additional time to think things through. He couldn't bring himself to go back to work just yet, and he certainly wasn't about to go back upstairs. His apartment seemed to be the only place that made any sense.

Although his anger was still simmering, David kept to the speed limit and made it back to Cambridge a few minutes before 1:00. He fumbled with the keys to the apartment, dropping them twice, and had to take a deep breath to prevent himself from losing control.

Once inside, he headed straight for the refrigerator, found a bottle of water and downed the whole thing. He then went into his room, stretched out on the bed, and for the next thirty minutes tried to focus on the decisions he had to make. He knew he had to remove his anger and the resentment he felt from the equation, but that was easier said than done. Eventually, his logical and practical side won out.

I'm going to work for the company, but I'm going to treat my father like the boss, not my father. I'll keep everything businesslike. No special phone calls, no special updates, no friendly chitchats. If he wants things to be different, then he's going to have to apologize.

And Jenna and I are still going to get married, just like we planned. We'll invite him. If he chooses to come, fine. If not, then that will tell me something too. He'll have to decide whether he wants me and Jenna as part of his life . . . and also his grandchild. Maybe that'll make a difference. Maybe things will change when his grandchild comes along.

This last thought forced David's mind in a different direction. *In less than six months I'm going to be a father. What in the world is that going to be like?* The thought of the baby placed a smile on his face. That involuntary response, he realized, told him all that he needed to know about the way he was truly feeling.

And then the phone rang.

The sound jolted him. He initially reached for his cell phone, before realizing it was the landline on his nightstand. He still didn't want to talk to anyone, especially his father. When he glanced at the incoming number, he didn't recognize it – not his father, not Jeremy, not Jenna. It was a local area code however.

Despite his misgivings, he picked up on the fourth ring. "Hello."

"David?"

"Yes. Who's this?"

"It's Alan Fenton."

In the split second before David responded, he imagined that right after the incident in his father's office, his father had called Alan to get him to act as some sort of intermediary. Assuming that to be true, David's voice took on an edge. "Yes. What is it?"

"They just took your father to Mass General. His secretary found him unconscious and called 9-1-1."

"Oh, my God. What happened? Is he all right?"

"The doctors are in with him now, I don't know much more."

"Okay. I'm on my way."

David raced out of the apartment, jumped in the car, and made the trip in less than fifteen minutes. The entire ride over, only two intertwined thoughts occupied his mind – *This is my fault. God, I hope he's going to be all right. If I hadn't . . .* His brain wouldn't allow him to finish the last sentence.

When David arrived, he quickly spotted Alan Fenton sitting in the emergency room waiting area. "How is he?"

"No one's been out yet."

"Can I see him?"

"I don't think so. There's a team of people still in there with him." Alan momentarily looked down at his hands before resuming eye contact. "He hasn't regained consciousness as far as I know."

"That's not a good sign."

"I'm afraid not."

Neither of them spoke for a moment, and then David asked, "How did you find out?"

"Your father's secretary. She said she came back from lunch; his door was open, and he was slumped over his desk. She doesn't have any idea how long he was like that. She called 9-1-1 and then she tried your cell phone, but it went to voice mail. She called me right after that . . . I'm listed as his health proxy."

David took his phone out, turned it back on and glanced at the screen – one new voicemail.

Alan noticed that David's eyes were starting to moisten. "Why don't we take a seat? Do you want some water or something?"

David ignored both questions. "This is my fault."

"What are you talking about?"

David hesitated for a moment. "I went to see him at noontime. We had an argument, and I stormed out of the office . . . ."

Alan extended his arm and attempted to usher David to someplace with more privacy. "Come on David, let's go over here and sit down." This time David acquiesced, and they headed toward the back of the waiting area.

Once they were seated, David told Alan most of what had transpired in his father's office. When he came to the part about wanting to get married, and threatening to resign, Alan flinched. David was too wrapped up in the telling of the story to notice.

As David was finishing up, Alan's mind went into attorney mode. He realized that he needed to get some specific information from David about both the resignation and the wedding. The first order of business, however, was to try to relieve some of David's guilt. "You do know that your father was taking a number of medications for high blood pressure?"

"Right. And the one thing his doctors told him was to avoid stress. I didn't exactly help him out in that area did I?"

"He's also seventy years old, David."

David looked at Alan with a gentle expression on his face. "I appreciate what you're trying to do, Alan . . . but I still feel responsible for this."

It was obvious to Alan from the story David had just related that he didn't know anything about the changes to his trust fund. And while Alan certainly wasn't about to get into any of that right this minute, he did need to get some clarification from David as soon as possible.

He thought of a way.

"It's not exactly news that you and your father don't always see eye-to-eye on things." David managed a smile as Alan continued. "Right?" David nodded. "But, your father was ecstatic about the project, and the fact that you were working for the company." Alan paused to deliver the next sentence with the appropriate tone. "And you didn't actually resign, correct?"

"No, I didn't. And the more I thought about it, I probably wouldn't have."

Alan had the first part of what he needed. "Your father knew you were upset. I'm sure he didn't believe you'd go through with the resignation. You shouldn't be blaming yourself for what happened."

David shook his head. "This argument was different; it was much more . . . personal. I've never sworn at my father before."

"If that's true, you might be the only one in the company that hasn't."

That got another smile from David, but it disappeared quickly as he looked over at Alan. "Why does he always want to control everything I do?"

"I don't have an answer for that."

"I know." He paused. "I just told him that I wanted to get married, and you'd have thought . . . ."

Again, David provided the opening Alan needed. "You haven't actually gotten married, have you? I mean, could it be that your father sensed from what you said that you had already eloped or something?"

"No. We were planning on getting married in a month or so, but . . . ." His voice trailed off.

Alan started to feel his own sense of guilt. But he knew that one of his strengths as an attorney was his ability to separate his emotions from the needs of his clients. And although David wasn't technically his client, David's needs and those of his father were very much tied together.

Alan decided that he could live with a little guilt if it would prevent David from doing something he would later regret, especially since David had been making decisions without having all the information.

There was silence for a few moments and then David got up out of his seat. "I need to check with the front desk to see what's happening."

"I'll go with you."

On the way over, David stopped short. "Did anyone call my father's cardiologist?"

"Yes. He's been notified. He may already be in with your father."

"Dr. Ross, right?"

"That's right."

They resumed walking. Once they reached the front desk, they had to wait a few moments before one of the nurses finished writing something and looked up. "Can I help you?"

"My father, Bradford Whitcomb, was brought in a little while ago. Nobody's been out to see us yet. Can somebody tell us how he's doing?"

"Let me check and see what I can find out. Please have a seat, and I promise someone will be with you as soon as possible."

Alan and David found a couple of chairs near the front of the waiting area. About ten minutes went by and then David noticed a tall gentleman in a sport coat and tie approach the front desk. David continued to watch as the nurse pointed in his direction. The man nodded and headed over.

"David Whitcomb?" he said as he extended his hand. "I'm Dr. Ross, your father's cardiologist."

David returned the handshake. "Hello, doctor. Can you tell us anything? How is he?" David saw Dr. Ross eyeing Alan. "Oh, I'm sorry. This is Alan Fenton, my father's attorney."

Dr. Ross nodded and shook Alan's hand as well. "I just saw him briefly. The emergency room doctors are still with him." He paused. "It presents itself as a heart attack; all the symptoms are consistent with that. He still hasn't regained consciousness however. We need to stabilize him and then run some additional tests to get some sense of how serious it is."

Alan could see that Dr. Ross' words were having a strong impact on David, so he took over. "Are you concerned that he's still unconscious?"

"No, not necessarily. Sometimes that's the body's best defense—shut everything down while it regroups. It's just hard to tell right now."

David was able to compose himself, but just barely. "Is he going to be all right?"

Dr. Ross eyed David closely. "I don't know. His overall health is good, but at this point we don't know enough to answer that question with any degree of certainty." He hesitated before continuing. "I don't believe in sugar-coating things; it's not in anyone's best interest." He paused again. "We don't know how long his brain may have been without oxygen."

Dr. Ross saw the effect his words were having on David, but he continued with the same degree of candor. "The next forty-eight hours will be critical. Right now, I'd estimate his chances of survival at 20 or 30 percent. If he gets through the next two days with no additional trauma, then that estimate doubles."

David tried to speak, but couldn't.

Alan filled the void. "Can we see him?"

"Not until he's stable. Maybe tomorrow, certainly not tonight." Dr. Ross turned toward David. "I know how difficult this is, but he's in one of the finest hospitals in the country." He smiled slightly. "And as you know, your father's pretty tenacious. I wouldn't count him out."

As devastating as Dr. Ross' initial words had been, his last comment put a smile on David's face. "Thank you."

Dr. Ross reached over and put his hand on David's shoulder. "I'll check in on him every few hours before I leave around 7:00. Are you still going to be here?"

"Yes."

"Okay. I'll come out each time and give you an update. I've also left word for them to contact me if there's any significant change. I'll see you in a couple of hours."

"Thanks again, doctor."

After Dr. Ross left, David slumped in the chair and closed his eyes. Alan watched him for a few moments, but didn't offer any conversation. A full five minutes passed before David opened his eyes. He glanced over at Alan. "I'm going to stay, but if you want to go back to your office . . . you must have things to do."

"Nothing that can't wait." He paused. "I think I should stay, David. I signed all the necessary papers when I came in, but if any other decisions have to be made . . . then I think we should make them together."

Alan's words hit David hard – *if any other decisions have to be made.* There was no escaping what that might mean.

David's voice was barely above a whisper "Thank you, Alan, I appreciate that."

About ten minutes later, David excused himself and went outside to call Jeremy and let him know what had happened. He started to call Jenna, but stopped. It was still fairly early in California. If he waited to make the call in a few hours, maybe he'd have more information. He could only hope that it would be something positive.

He put his cell phone away and found a bench a few yards to the left of the emergency room entrance. He looked up at the clear afternoon sky and shielded his eyes from the sun. His thoughts jumped back to the exchange in his father's office.

A part of David again tried to convince himself that it wasn't his fault, but it was a lost cause – *If I hadn't lost my cool, my father wouldn't be in there fighting for his life.*

Even if his father survived, David felt sure that the confrontation in his father's office would be something he always carried with him. And although he believed it was possible for people to suppress some of their memories, he doubted very much that you could suppress those that involved guilt.

He thought back to when he was a little boy and he had gone swimming at a friend's pool. There had been a multi-colored ball floating in the shallow end. David had grabbed the ball with both hands and pushed it under the water. But no matter how hard he tried to keep it submerged, it always exploded to the surface.

He suspected guilt was a lot like that.

CHAPTER 22

Dr. Ross made three more visits to see Mr. Whitcomb before he left for the day, updating David and Alan each time. In essence, however, there was nothing new to report. David's father was still critical and had not regained consciousness.

During the final update, Dr. Ross suggested to both David and Alan that they go home. "There's nothing else you can do here tonight. It's possible you'll be able to see him in the next day or two, probably not sooner than that. I've left instructions that if there's any change to contact me, and I'll get in touch with you if that happens."

Reluctantly, both David and Alan took Dr. Ross' advice.

During the last several hours in the waiting room, David had been able to force the guilt he was feeling to the periphery of his brain. But now that he was alone in the car, heading back to his apartment, it moved front and center again.

Despite the complicated relationship he had with his father, David loved him, and had trouble imagining his life without his father in it. The notion that his actions – what he had said and done during the argument—might ultimately lead to his father's death began to overwhelm him.

As David opened the door to the apartment, Jeremy got up off the couch, waited a moment and then said, "How is he?"

"No change. He's still unconscious."

"I'm so sorry, David."

"Thanks." David paused. "Things are going to be touch and go for a while." He fought to keep his voice steady. "It's possible he may not make it."

Jeremy was at a loss as to what to say or do. Finally, he suggested, "Why don't you sit down?"

David nodded and moved toward the couch. He was unable to bring himself to talk to Jeremy about the guilt he was feeling. It wasn't that he was trying to hide anything; it was just that continuing to beat himself up over his part in what had happened was taking its toll. He needed some time to recover before he could even discuss it again. He'd eventually tell Jeremy everything, but not yet.

David made an attempt to steer the conversation elsewhere. "How was everything at the apartments today?"

Jeremy looked surprised. "Uh . . . fine. No problems." He hesitated. "You shouldn't be worrying about work, David. You've already got enough to worry about."

David didn't respond for a few moments. "I really appreciate everything you're doing. I'm not sure . . . you know . . . when I'll be able to be back full time."

"It's okay. Darnell and I have got it covered. If we need something, we'll let you know."

David could only nod as tears began to form. They sat in silence for a few moments, and then David got up and said, "I'm going to go call Jenna."

David sat on the edge of his bed and started to review the past eight hours, but then stopped himself. He didn't want his emotions to be raw when he spoke to Jenna.

He took a few deep breaths, tried to clear his mind as much as possible, and began to formulate what he was going to say. After several minutes, he picked up the phone and pressed Jenna's number.

"Hi, David. I was just thinking about you. Well actually, I do that most of the time." She let out a little laugh. "So, anything new on the wedding plans?"

The question caught David by surprise. "Uh . . . well . . . Listen, Jenna, I've got some bad news."

"What?"

"It's my father. He was rushed to the hospital."

"Oh my God. What happened?"

Just as he had with Jeremy, David made the initial decision to keep any mention of the argument out of the conversation. "It looks like a heart attack."

"That's awful. Oh David, I'm so sorry. Is he going to be all right?"

"They don't know."

"Do you want me to come back to Boston?"

"No. No, there's nothing you can do."

"I could be with you."

David had trouble speaking. "Jenna, I appreciate that, but until we know more . . . ."

"I don't mind, really."

"I know. But right now, I just need you to take care of yourself . . . and the baby."

They stayed on the phone for fifteen more minutes. David told her a slightly different version of what had transpired that afternoon. He finally mentioned the argument, but led her to believe it was work-related. He had promised not to lie to her again, but he couldn't bring himself to tell her about his father's question.

For the next several days, David forced himself to go into work for a few hours in the morning before he headed over to the hospital. By Thursday afternoon there was a slight upgrade in his father's condition, and he was moved into a private room just outside the ICU. David was finally allowed to see him.

Dr. Ross suggested that David brace himself before going in. "He's been through a lot, David. He's still in a coma, and hooked up to a ventilator and a feeding tube. He's stable, and his chances of survival have improved greatly, but he's not out of the woods by any means."

In spite of Dr. Ross' warnings, David was taken aback by his father's appearance. It had only been three days, but he seemed so small and frail in the hospital bed. David could never remember his father looking that vulnerable. It frightened him.

Despite his discomfort, David stayed in the room for twenty minutes, talking to his father the whole time. David knew it was debatable whether people in a coma could hear or understand what was being said. Nevertheless, expressing things out loud offered David some solace. Just before he left, he kissed his father on the forehead and said softly, "I'm sorry, Dad."

On Friday morning David was talking with Jeremy and Darnell outside one of the apartments when his phone rang. He fished it out of his pocket, recognized Alan Fenton's number and said, "Excuse me a second, guys."

"Hello, Alan. Is everything all right?"

"Hi, David. Yes. It's just that when I stopped by the hospital yesterday, they said you were going to be able to see your father. I was wondering, how that went?"

David described his reaction to seeing his father, and the fact that he talked to him for twenty minutes. He didn't mention the apology.

After they discussed Mr. Whitcomb's condition for another few minutes, Alan said, "Are you available this morning. I need to talk to you, and I'd prefer to do it face-to-face."

"That sounds ominous."

"I didn't mean it to sound that way, but it is important."

"No hint about the subject matter?"

"It's related to everything that's been going on."

David could tell from Alan's tone that he needed to make the time to see him. "Okay, give me a half hour, forty-five minutes."

"I'll see you then."

David closed his phone and tried to imagine what Alan needed to talk to him about. It didn't seem that it was related to his father's health, at least not directly. Then what? Nothing sprang to mind.

Alan was in the doorway of his office when David arrived. They exchanged some pleasantries, and then Alan ushered David to the same chair that he had sat in on his previous visit. The table between them contained even more folders and files than the last time.

"So, what's this all about, Alan?"

"There's no simple answer to that."

David got a puzzled expression on his face as Alan continued. "I've been debating with myself how best to handle this. I'm going to suggest something to you. It's a little unorthodox, but I think it's the best way to proceed."

David's interest was piqued further. "What?"

"I want you to hire me as your attorney."

"What? Why?"

"If I'm your attorney then anything we discuss is privileged, and ethically I won't have to worry about crossing any lines."

David looked confused.

Alan continued. "I think this will all make sense once we go through it." He paused. "If you agree, then I need for you to sign the contract I've prepared and pay me a dollar as a retainer."

"You're serious? A dollar?"

"Yes. That's sufficient to make it legal."

Alan extracted a sheet of paper from one of the folders on the table and handed it to David. The first few lines read just as Alan had said—the contract retained Alan Fenton to be David's personal attorney for one year at a cost of one dollar.

"It's pretty straight forward, but once you're done reading, we need to discuss something before you sign it."

David nodded, and then went back to reading. He took his time, partly so he could try to assess the degree to which he trusted the man sitting across from him. Once he finished reading and decided that he did in fact trust Alan, David took out his wallet, found a single, and offered it to him.

"Hold on to that for a minute. Hear me out first." He leaned forward. "Before you sign the contract, you need to know that if there should ever be a conflict of interest in any legal matter between your interests and those of your father, I have to proceed in such a way that protects your *father's* interests." David started to say something, but Alan put up his hand to signal that he wasn't finished.

"That's primarily because he's incapacitated. Since I have power of attorney, I have to act on my knowledge of what I know to be his wishes. And since I can't talk to him about whether he wants to reconsider something, I have to assume nothing has changed and act accordingly."

"I'm not sure I understand."

"As I told you, this is a bit unorthodox, but it boils down to this: If, for example, you wanted me to make changes to some document, but I knew the changes were against what your father had in mind, despite the fact that I have power of attorney, I couldn't ethically make the changes. Look, David. I'm not trying to be coy here. I . . . ."

David interrupted. "Does this have to do with the trust fund?"

"Partially."

"I thought we already discussed that months ago."

Alan didn't say anything, but David picked up on his uneasiness. "He changed it again, didn't he?"

155

Alan nodded. "I really can't say anything more until I officially represent you."

They stared at each other for a few moments. Finally, Alan said, "Here's what you can do, David. Hire me for a dollar. If things go south in your mind, you can fire me just as easily. This way we're both protected."

That made sense to David. But even if it hadn't, he was ready to sign anyway just to find out what else his father had done. For a moment his mind flashed back to the sight of his father in the hospital bed, and some of his anger evaporated.

David picked up the pen, signed the contract, and pushed the dollar across the table. "So, what changes did he make?"

Alan could see that David wasn't as upset as he had been a few minutes before, but he still decided to ease into things. "Remember on Monday when we were talking in the ER waiting room and I asked if you had actually resigned?"

"Yes."

"That wasn't idle curiosity. One of the changes to your father's will was that if you no longer work for the company and something should happen to him, his interest in the business would go to charity . . . and you'd forfeit the entire trust fund."

David felt his anger returning, but he didn't allow himself to show it. "Anything else?"

"Yes. And I suspect this is more problematic."

"Tell me."

"He wanted a marriage clause added."

"A what?"

"If you marry before your twenty-seventh birthday, you also forfeit your trust fund."

"WHAT?"

David got up out of his chair and started to pace. His mind again went to the image of his father in the hospital bed. But this time it didn't have quite the same effect.

"This is unbelievable," he said. "Of course, now I understand why he got so upset when I told him I wanted to get married. He was going to lose control." He shook his head and then turned back to Alan. "You know, at this point, I don't care about any of this. I don't even want the trust fund."

There was silence for the next minute, and then Alan spoke up. "I know how upsetting this is, but . . . ." Alan tried to diffuse things by assuming an officious tone "As your newly hired attorney, I would advise against that."

David forced a smile. "It just seems that every argument between my father and me is about the damn trust fund. Any chance we have at a normal relationship goes by the boards every time we talk about it. Why shouldn't I just say 'the hell with it' and get on with my life?"

"I understand why you feel that way, but I don't think you should decide anything while you're still upset." He paused. "Can you see your way clear to holding off making any decisions until we know more about your father's prognosis?"

"I told you, Alan. Jenna's pregnant. We've already started to make plans for the wedding."

Alan looked surprised, but he spoke calmly. "I know that her pregnancy makes things more urgent. But, and please don't take offense, a lot of young people today have children and aren't married."

"That's not what we want."

"I understand. But given what's happened with your father, and now with what you just found out about the trust fund, wouldn't you consider postponing things?"

David looked defiant. "Not because I might lose the trust fund."

Alan decided to take another tack. "I think you should talk to Jenna about all of this? Is she still in Boston or did she go back home to Pasadena?"

David looked at Alan curiously. "How did you know she lived in Pasadena?"

Alan realized his mistake, but covered it up well. "You must have mentioned it."

"I don't think so."

Alan spoke with a sense of confidence he didn't feel. "How else would I know?"

David dropped it. "I guess. Anyway, she's home." He shook his head. "It's just that so much has happened all at once. Jenna finds out she's pregnant, and I can't be with her right now. We've made the decision to get married, and now I have to tell her it's off."

Alan was relieved that David hadn't pursued the Pasadena question. He felt certain that there was no way he could tell David about his father's investigation of Jenna without David totally losing it.

"All I'm suggesting is that you don't do anything immediately. Don't resign and don't get married, at least until we know more about your father's situation."

David stared at Alan for a full thirty seconds, neither of them blinking. Finally a look of acceptance came across David's face. "My father says I'm too impetuous for my own good . . . All right. Okay, I'll hold off."

David offered his hand, and the two of them shook. As the handshake ended, David thought of something. "You told me that in addition to the health proxy you have general power of attorney for my father, right?"

"That's correct."

"So, you could rescind the marriage clause, couldn't you?"

"It's not that simple. As I mentioned to you when we first sat down, because I know what your father's specific intent was, I can't ethically change anything that goes against that." He paused. "Even if it would benefit another client and even if I happen to believe it would be the right thing to do."

David accepted the explanation with more good humor than he felt.

After David left, Alan poured himself a drink and reflected on what had transpired over the last several days. He finally allowed himself to think about the fact that one of his oldest friends was lying in a hospital bed in a coma. He hadn't permitted himself the "luxury" of feeling anything up until now. Instead, all of his energy had gone into protecting Bradford Whitcomb's interests, and those of his son.

After a few minutes, his thoughts turned back to the meeting with David. Other than the Pasadena gaffe, things had gone as well as he could have hoped.

Of course, there was still a lot of work to be done, especially in light of what he had found out yesterday when he visited Whitcomb Realty Trust.

CHAPTER 23

David was sitting next to his father's hospital bed late in the afternoon, nearly a week after his conversation with Alan Fenton. Dr. Ross knocked on the metal doorframe before he entered. "Hello, David."

David stood up and crossed the room to shake hands. "Hello, Dr. Ross. Anything new you can tell me?"

"No, I'm afraid not. It's a real puzzle. As I mentioned to you, the tests don't indicate any loss of brain function. His heart seems to be rebounding. He should be waking up. Frankly, I'm at a loss."

"Are there any other tests you can run?"

"None that are going to tell us why he's still in a coma." He went over to the bed, lifted one of Mr. Whitcomb's eyelids and flashed a penlight into the exposed eye. He then shook his head and turned back to David again. "I've e-mailed some colleagues of mine to see if they know of any similar cases."

They were quiet for a few minutes, and then Dr. Ross spoke. "One thing I'd like to consider is taking him off the ventilator." David's face clearly showed his concern, but he let Dr. Ross continue without saying anything. "Everything suggests that he should be able to breathe on his own."

"But why take the chance?"

"We'd have a medical team right in the room in case anything went wrong." He paused. "Being on a ventilator increases the likelihood of infection, and muscles start to atrophy. Plus, if we remove the ventilator, it may trigger something and get him out of the coma. It's a long shot, but . . . ."

"How much risk is involved? How dangerous would it be?"

"There's always some risk. But honestly, I believe it's minimal."

"How soon were you thinking about doing this?"

"Well, I've got to notify Mr. Fenton, and then I'd like to have the two of you meet with me to discuss it in more detail. If you give us the go-ahead, then probably we'd remove the ventilator by the end of the week."

"That soon?"

"There's really no reason to wait."

David nodded, almost to himself. "Okay, I can meet this week. Just let me know when."

"There is something else we need to discuss."

"What?"

"If we take him off the ventilator and he starts breathing on his own, but remains in a coma, then I'd like to move him to a rehab facility."

"Why would you do that?"

"Two reasons. First, he wouldn't require the ICU level of care he's currently receiving. And second, a rehab facility provides daily stimulation to patients that are comatose. Here at the hospital we can't continue to do that long term."

"Are there any rehab facilities close by?"

"Yes, there are a number of them in the area that I could recommend." He paused. "But, we're getting ahead of ourselves here, David. Let me talk to Mr. Fenton and set something up so we can discuss it further."

They shook hands again, and Dr. Ross left.

David remained in the room for another half hour. Periodically, he carried on a one-sided conversation with his father. But most of the time he sat silently next to the bed, contemplating what Dr. Ross had suggested.

Toward the end of the visit, David's thoughts turned to the conversation he was going to have with Jenna in a few hours. Only Alan and Jeremy knew all the details about what had happened in his father's office, and it was probably going to have to stay that way, at least for the time being. *I just can't tell her everything. Certainly, not the question my father asked me. I can't do that to her . . . maybe face-to-face when she comes back to Boston . . . but I'm not sure, even then.*

That same afternoon, Alan Fenton arrived at Whitcomb Realty Trust for an appointment with Joe Halpin, one of the company's attorneys, who had assumed the day-to-day operations during Mr. Whitcomb's hospitalization. And despite the fact that Alan considered Joe Halpin a friend, he knew that Joe would not have been able to give him the information he needed if David hadn't retained him as his attorney.

After they were seated, Joe opened up the conversation. "We've been able to get periodic updates about Bradford's condition, but it sounds like there's not much to be optimistic about."

"I'm afraid not. That's part of the reason I'm here. He paused. "As I mentioned on the phone, I now represent David Whitcomb as well as Bradford."

Joe acknowledged this with a nod, as Alan continued. "I only mention that because shortly after Bradford took ill, I became aware of some things concerning Whitcomb Realty Trust that could impact both Bradford and David.

Alan looked for a reaction. When none was forthcoming, he went on. "Anyway, now that Bradford is incapacitated, I need to get more specific details in order to protect both of their interests."

"Okay. What is it that you would like to know?"

Alan smiled. "I assume you're familiar with the phrase, 'You don't know what you don't know'?"

Joe smiled back. "Touché. So, how do we work this out?"

Alan paused briefly. "Well, I recently discovered that there have been some changes to the structure of the company over the past year and a half. What about if you tell me some of the specifics, and if I have any questions, I'll ask?"

"That seems reasonable. Most of what I'm able to share with you is public record anyway."

"I know, but this will save me from rummaging through a lot of documents and trying to ferret out what I need."

For close to an hour, Joe Halpin outlined what had been going on for the past eighteen months at Whitcomb Realty Trust. Alan interrupted only a few times to ask for clarification.

Alan had always been good at reading between the lines, but in this instance, it wasn't necessary. There was little question that as the meeting progressed, Joe was steering him in a particular direction.

Eventually, Alan was able to piece everything together. And as he did, the situation became more and more troubling. He would have to have a follow-up conversation with David much sooner than he had anticipated.

When Alan arrived back at his office there was a message to contact Dr. Ross. He placed the call immediately, and after an abbreviated discussion concerning what Dr. Ross had shared with David, they agreed to meet the following afternoon.

Alan and David arrived within a few minutes of each other at Dr. Ross' office. The receptionist indicated that the doctor was running a little late, but that she expected him shortly.

The waiting room was empty except for the two of them. Alan opened up the conversation. "You probably know more about this than I do. What's your impression?"

"I'm not sure. I go back and forth. I trust Dr. Ross, though. And if he thinks it makes sense, then I guess I'm inclined to go along with it. But you have the final say."

Alan shook his head. "I told you, David, we'll decide everything together."

David acknowledged the comment with a nod, as Alan continued. "But from what Dr. Ross told me yesterday, I tend to agree that it seems like the right thing to do. But I still have some questions."

"I do also."

They remained silent briefly. Alan broke it with a question. "How's Jenna?"

David's face brightened momentarily. "She's doing okay. I think she was a little disappointed about having to postpone the wedding, but she understood."

"That's natural," said Alan.

They were quiet again, giving Alan a chance to think about the ramifications of what he had learned from Joe Halpin. *The timing of my conversation with David has to be just right. Maybe we can get through today; we'll make the decision about Bradford . . . and assuming things work out, I can let the other shoe drop. This is going to be tough on David—one thing right after another. Not much choice; can't be helped.*

Alan's mental deliberations were interrupted by Dr. Ross' entrance. He invited them into his office, and got right to it. "As I told both of you, we're somewhat baffled. We simply don't know why he's still in a coma. I've spoken to a number of my colleagues from around the country, but they haven't been able to shed any light on it either."

David and Alan asked questions for the next twenty minutes. When they finally ran out, Dr. Ross again made his pitch for taking Mr. Whitcomb off the ventilator. David and Alan hadn't had strenuous objections to start with, so they ultimately gave Dr. Ross the go-ahead.

The removal of the ventilator was scheduled for early Monday morning. Mr. Whitcomb would be monitored for several days, and if there were no complications, a move to a rehab facility would follow shortly.

David had trouble maintaining his composure as he left Dr. Ross' office and said goodbye to Alan. He had convinced himself that taking his father off the ventilator was the right thing to do. That wasn't what was making him so emotional; it was the move to the rehab facility.

The hospital had become a familiar place. It was where he had confidence that his father would get better. Moving him to this rehab facility felt like his father was being "stored" someplace until the end. This last thought started tears rolling down his face.

The ventilator was removed at 7:15 Monday morning. Mr. Whitcomb's body shuddered a couple of times and his eyelids twitched, but his vital signs remained strong. A third shudder came five minutes later and caused some concern for the medical personnel in the room. Eventually however, he settled into a natural breathing rhythm, and the stand-by team left the room and went on to other things.

At almost 8:00 Dr. Ross came out to tell David and Alan about Mr. Whitcomb's status. "It went very smoothly. He's been breathing on his own for more than half an hour. All of his vitals are good. At this point we're not anticipating any problems."

"Did he regain consciousness, even briefly?"

"I'm afraid not. As I told you, it was a bit of a long shot, especially to happen right away. Our hope now is that he'll come out of it over the next few days."

David asked another question. "If he does comes out of the coma, does that mean he wouldn't have to be transferred?"

"It could. We'd have to reassess things at that point."

They talked for a few more minutes, and then David offered his hand, as did Alan. After they shook, Dr. Ross headed back toward Mr. Whitcomb's room. Alan patted David on the back, and indicated he would call him later. David sat down briefly before going in to see his father.

He had hoped for a miracle. Actually, he was still hoping for one. He tried to imagine what his father was feeling. The phrase "in limbo" came into his head. *That must be what it's like to be in a coma. You're not really alive. In fact, you're probably closer to being dead. What if he stays like that? Isn't that even worse than being dead?* He tried to put that idea out of his mind, but without much success.

By the end of the week, with no improvement in Mr. Whitcomb's condition, the decision was made to move him to a facility in Braintree, about twenty miles south of Boston. Although the necessity of the move troubled Alan, the resolution of the issue allowed him to refocus his attention on the follow-up conversation he needed to have with David.

They met on Saturday afternoon in Alan's office. From the phone call setting up the meeting, David had assumed that it was strictly to discuss his father's situation. But after only a few minutes, Alan moved the conversation to a different topic. "I wanted to talk to you about your father's company and some information that's come to my attention."

"Okay."

Alan removed his glasses and sat forward in his chair. "About a year and a half ago, your father decided he wanted to branch out, acquire some additional properties, primarily in New York." Alan paused. "Were you aware of that?"

"I don't think so. If my father mentioned it, I don't remember."

"Anyway, as it turns out, he entered into a partnership with Jenkins Properties."

David looked surprised. "A partnership?"

"Yes. Evidently, your father didn't have enough capital to acquire Jenkins Properties outright, so they formed a partnership. Your father maintained overall control, and continued to have the primary responsibility for the Boston operation. Philip Jenkins, the president of Jenkins Properties, was primarily responsible for the New York operation."

"This is all news to me."

"And to me as well. As you know, for the most part, I only handle your father's personal matters. Sometimes there's an overlap, but not that often."

Alan put his glasses back on, and opened one of the folders in front of him before he continued. "Over the past twelve months, the New York properties have weathered the real estate downturn much better than the

Boston holdings. That may have been one of the reasons that your father was so excited about the new project you're overseeing."

David shrugged his shoulders, and finally expressed what was on his mind. "As I said, this is all news to me, but I'm not sure where you're going with this."

Alan stopped beating around the bush. "With your father being incapacitated, Phil Jenkins is coming to Boston to take over."

"I thought Joe Halpin was in charge."

"Not as of next week."

"Really? That's a little surprising. But, how does Phil Jenkins taking over change anything?"

"That's what concerns me. Joe Halpin was primarily a caretaker, but Phil Jenkins is a different story. He'll have almost as much power regarding the company as your father did. He can do pretty much anything he wants."

"Anything?"

"If he deems it's in the best interests of the company." Alan paused. "For example, he could decide that more resources should go to the New York operation." He paused again to make sure he had David's attention. "Like the three million dollars that's supposed to fund the project you're overseeing."

David sat upright. "How can he do that? That money's from my trust fund!"

"That's where it *came from*. But it's the company's money now, and the head of the company decides where it goes."

"We've already started phase one. We've got contracts with suppliers, and . . . ."

Alan held up his hands to slow David down. "I don't think he'll do anything to stop phase one. But as far as phases two and three are concerned, who knows?"

"You can't be serious."

"All I can tell you is that Joe Halpin said Phil Jenkins has a history of shaking things up. He also said, and I'm quoting, 'He's got the reputation of being a real bastard.' And I suspect the standard to qualify as a *real* bastard is fairly high in New York."

David shook his head. "How much of this is actually likely to happen?"

"I don't know. Joe Halpin couldn't tell me anything directly. He just led me in the direction of the possibilities." Alan paused again. "I wanted you to be prepared that there might be a lot of changes coming."

"But probably not during phase one?"

"Well, probably not as it affects the project, but I wouldn't be surprised if Jenkins made some other moves."

"What else?"

"Phil Jenkins has already made some inquiries about your apartment for instance."

"My apartment? What's that got to do with anything?"

"The company owns that apartment. You don't pay any rent, and your roommate pays a reduced rate. Jenkins could argue that the lease agreement is invalid. And he might have a point. When I drew up the lease, I didn't know anything about the partnership. Your father probably didn't have the right to enter into the new lease."

David was speechless. When he finally found his voice, he asked, "Does that apply to my father's townhouse as well?"

"No, not exactly. Technically, the townhouse is owned by the company, but as the president, your father lives there rent free."

David remained quiet, trying to absorb everything he had just been told. Alan waited briefly to see if David was going to ask him anything else, and then he spoke again. "I don't want to frighten you, but it could get even worse." He looked directly into David's eyes. "Once phase one is completed, you could be out of a job."

"WHAT?"

"You were hired to oversee the three phases of the project. If Jenkins pulls the plug on the other two, there's nothing to oversee."

David got out of his chair. "This is unbelievable."

The office was silent again for a few moments before Alan spoke, "Obviously, a lot of this is conjecture. And if it comes to pass, we'll fight it. But that would take a lot of resources, and I don't know how successful we'd be."

David remained standing. He put his hands on the back of the chair and addressed Alan. "So what do we do?"

"Obviously, if your father recovers, then it all becomes moot."

David's mind flashed briefly to the image of his father in the rehab center. His thoughts were interrupted by Alan's voice. "As of now, none of us knows how likely that is, so I've come up with a few recommendations in the mean time."

David returned to his chair and waited for Alan to continue.

"First of all, you absolutely shouldn't resign."

"I told you, I wasn't planning to."

"I know, but I wanted to make sure that that was still the case." He paused. "For the time being, Phil Jenkins probably wants you working for the company anyway. Remember, if your father should pass away, and you're not employed by Whitcomb Realty Trust, then your father's share of the company goes to charity. That would greatly complicate things for Jenkins."

David took a few moments to consider something before he spoke. "Then why do you think he would consider letting me go after phase one?"

"At some point, if he believes your father is out of danger, then I suspect that could alter his thinking in that regard."

David shook his head in agreement as Alan continued. "Besides not resigning, I'm going to offer one additional piece of advice – you shouldn't get married, at least not for the foreseeable future."

"Why not?"

"Unless your father comes out of the coma and changes the terms of the trust fund, you'll forfeit everything."

"I told you, I don't care about that."

"Well, you should." David started to protest, but Alan cut him off. "Wait. Listen to what I have to say. If Jenkins does what we talked about, you could be unemployed, with no place to live, with a wife and a new baby to support . . . and no trust fund."

Alan's words pulled David up short. He hadn't had time to process what all this meant, and he certainly hadn't thought about it in the way Alan had just laid it out. But he wasn't about to simply cave in. "If all that happens, then I'll get another job."

"David, with all due respect, don't you think you're being somewhat naïve. There's no question you're bright, and you've got a Harvard diploma. But jobs making $80,000 a year to start, for someone with no specialized skills, in this economy . . . ."

David didn't take offense. Alan was right, but David still wasn't done. "I don't see how holding on to the trust fund helps me, since I can't access it until I'm twenty-seven."

"It might be possible to borrow against it."

"Can you do that?"

"I can look into it."

David continued to try to find holes in Alan's argument. After a few moments, one final idea came to him. "If Jenkins fires me after phase one is over, I'd no longer be working for the company; I'd lose the trust fund anyway. So it doesn't matter whether I get married or not."

Alan looked directly at David. "I considered that before I offered you my advice." He paused. "Since I have power of attorney, if you end up not working for the company *through no action on your part*, then I could see my way clear to changing the terms of your trust fund. I know what your father's intentions were in regards to that." He eyed David sympathetically. "But the marriage clause is something entirely different."

As Alan's words started to register, David's thoughts turned to Jenna, to the look on her face when he had suggested they get married, to the laughter in her voice when he first mentioned planning for the wedding. What would her expression look like when he told her this news?

When David finally spoke, Alan was surprised that there was no anger or frustration in his voice. But then as he listened further, he heard something more disturbing. Even though his words were measured, David sounded beaten down and defeated. "I need to think about this some more."

And then he left.

CHAPTER 24

After leaving Alan's office, David drove around aimlessly, trying to clear his head. When he finally started to pay attention, he was about to get on the Southeast Expressway—the same route he always took to visit his father. He nodded to himself in acknowledgement that his "aimless" driving had probably been more purposeful than he thought. He completed the rest of the trip in less than twenty minutes.

When he entered his father's room, David looked for some sign that things had changed. There were none.

He moved a chair closer to his father's bed, spoke some words of encouragement, and then leaned back and closed his eyes. During the last few weeks David had felt as if everything had been coming at him much too quickly. He barely had time to process what he was feeling about one life-changing event when the next one hit him.

All the ingredients for the perfect emotional storm found their way into his thoughts – *guilt* over the argument in his father's office; *resentment* toward his father for changing the trust fund; *anxiety* about what Phil Jenkins might be planning; and *doubt* that any decision he made would be the right one.

Although his conflicting emotions were overwhelming, toward the end of the visit, an idea pushed its way to the forefront. *Maybe I need to go see Phil Jenkins in person. Find out what he's planning to do. If he's going to screw me over, at least he'll have to do it to my face.*

This last thought began to set David's mood on a more even keel. As he started to leave, he kissed his father on the forehead. "Maybe things are going to work out, Dad. Maybe it's going to be okay. But no matter what, I'm not going to just sit back and let it happen." He went back to his father's side and kissed him again. "I'll see you tomorrow."

David had spoken the words with a sense of confidence he didn't feel, but saying them out loud seemed to give them more substance.

Despite feeling slightly more upbeat, David postponed his daily call to Jenna for a couple of hours. He wasn't ready to share anything concerning Phil Jenkins with her just yet, and he wanted to be sure that no residual anxiety about what was going on found its way into his voice.

When he did finally make the call, Jenna answered right away. "Hi, David. I'm on the other line with Trish. Just let me hang up with her and I'll be right back."

Less than a minute later, Jenna was back on the line. "Hi, again. Trish says to say 'hello' and to tell you how sorry she is about your father."

"Next time you talk to her, tell her I said 'Thanks'. How's *she* doing, by the way?"

"She's fine. She's still got a couple of more weeks interning at the station." She paused. "How's your dad?"

"The same."

"They still have no idea what's causing him to stay in the coma?"

"No."

"Shouldn't someone be able to figure it out by now?"

David spoke more sharply than he intended. "His doctor is one of the leading cardiologists in the country, Jenna. If he doesn't know . . . ." His voice softened. "I'm sorry. I didn't mean to jump at you."

"It's okay."

They were quiet for a moment before David changed the subject. "So, how are you feeling?"

"I saw the doctor this morning, and everything's great." She paused. "Of course, most of my clothes don't fit, but at least there's a good reason for that." She paused again. "Oh, I almost forgot. My doctor gave me a referral, someone he went to med school with who is part of a family practice in Massachusetts. His office is somewhere on the South Shore – Brainwood, or something like that."

"Braintree?"

"Yeah. That's it."

David hesitated. "That's where my father is."

"Really? That's quite a coincidence."

David didn't respond right away as his mind flashed to his father. "David?"

"Sorry."

"Are you okay?"

"Yeah, yeah I'm fine. I'm just tired."

"How's work?"

David hesitated a second longer than he should have. "It's fine, too."

"You're not all that convincing, you know. Anything you want to talk about?"

"No. It's nothing to worry about."

"So, there is something?"

"I didn't mean it that way. It's just an expression."

Jenna wasn't buying it. She decided not to press him any further, but David's responses had cinched it. She was going to head back to Boston earlier than she had planned. Something was going on, and she needed to be there.

On Monday morning shortly after he arrived at work, David called Whitcomb Realty Trust. He spoke briefly with Joe Halpin, who confirmed that Phil Jenkins was indeed coming on board in a few days.

Joe then transferred David to a secretary who made an appointment for David to meet with Phil Jenkins on Thursday. As soon as David hung up, he called Alan Fenton and outlined what he was planning.

"Do you want me to come with you, David?"

"No, I don't think so. I appreciate the offer, but I think it's better if I meet with him by myself. I just wanted to let you know what was going on, and to make sure there wasn't anything else I needed to know."

"Nothing that I can think of. Can I offer some advice?"

"Don't worry. This is all about sizing up the situation. I'm not going to resign."

Alan laughed. "Then I think you're probably right, you don't need me at the meeting."

When Thursday rolled around, David and Jeremy went to work together in the morning, and then shortly after noon David headed over to Whitcomb Realty Trust.

This would be the first time he had been back there since the incident with his father. The flashback shook him, as did the fact that Phil Jenkins was using his father's office. But by the time he arrived on the eighth floor, he was able to calm himself down.

As David walked in, Phil Jenkins was at the secretary's desk waiting for him. Jenkins appeared to be in his late fifties, a shade over six feet, with a George Hamilton tan. David's only thought was – *smooth*—and not in a good way.

Jenkins shook David's hand and invited him into the office. Ironically, he suggested that they sit in the less formal area of the office rather than on opposite sides of the desk where David and his father had always sat.

David opened up the conversation. "Thanks for seeing me, Mr. Jenkins."

"Please, it's Phil. And I'm glad you called to set this up. I was about to do the same thing." He paused. "Before we start, how's your father doing?"

"About the same."

"I'm sorry to hear that"

They were silent for a few moments before Jenkins spoke up. "Are you a student of history?"

David looked puzzled. "I guess . . . somewhat. Why?"

"Well, when I first heard about your father, and I finally accepted that I'd have to come up to Boston, I thought about what Lyndon Johnson said after JFK was killed." He stared at David for a few moments before delivering the quote—"I'd give anything not to be here."

Jenkins paused again, looking for a reaction from David. When he didn't get one, he continued. "I don't mean to be overly dramatic, but I really like your father. We got along great right from the beginning. I truly wish none of this had happened."

David sensed that everything Phil Jenkins had just said was rehearsed. Something about his tone and delivery suggested that he was putting on an act. David searched for the most neutral response possible. "Thank you. I appreciate that."

Jenkins nodded his head, leaned forward and patted David on the knee. "So, what can I do for you, David?"

"Well, with my father's situation and all, and you taking over . . . I wanted to find out where things stood."

"I'm not sure I follow."

David decided to be more direct. "As you must know, I've been overseeing the upgrade of a number of apartment buildings." Jenkins shook his head up and down to signify that he knew all about it, as David continued. "Anyway, there were scheduled to be three phases. Is that still going to happen?"

Jenkins made a steeple out of his index fingers, and studied them briefly. "I honestly don't know."

David doubted that. But at least Jenkins hadn't shut the door completely.

Jenkins continued. "I'm just getting up to speed on all of this." He paused. "Let me say this. There's no question about completing phase one. And by the way, I've heard nothing but great things about the job you're doing." He patted David's knee again. "Anyway, I'd say we're totally committed to seeing phase one all the way through."

"And phases two and three?"

"As I said, I'm still learning the ropes in Boston. I'm not ready to commit to anything beyond phase one. We'll have to see how things play out."

David felt that if he hadn't been paying attention to Jenkins' body language, then his response would have seemed very reasonable. Instead all David could think was – *I'm getting a bad feeling about this.*

David tried to sound sincere. "I appreciate your honesty." Before he spoke again, he debated whether to bring up where the funding of the three phases had come from, but Jenkins made the decision for him.

"I'm aware that part of your trust fund was transferred to the company to pay for this project, and I'll take that into consideration when I make my decision." He paused. "But I have to do what's best for the company in the long run."

David had expected this, but still wasn't able to disguise his disappointment. Jenkins picked up on it. "I'm sure this means a lot to you, David, but there may be some other options that would be just as good."

"Like what?"

Jenkins leaned forward. "I'm not in the habit of sharing my ideas with other people until I've thought everything through, and I'm ready to act on them."

David thought – *That's the first thing he's said that I completely believe.*

Jenkins leaned forward even more, as if sharing a secret. "I can tell you this, however. One of the ideas I'm considering would increase profits dramatically, and that would put money back into your trust fund much more rapidly."

"Would this involve the New York properties?"

It was obvious to David that the question surprised Jenkins. "Nothing's been decided yet, so I really can't answer that."

A number of thoughts entered David's head. *You already did. That money's headed for New York. I'm sure you thought that the idea of quick profits going back into the trust fund would appeal to me. But evidently, you aren't aware that I can't access it for four more years.*

Jenkins fumbled for the right things to say. "I'm going to explore all options . . . I owe that to the company."

David needed some additional information so he asked a related question. "If you decide to use the resources elsewhere, where does that leave me?"

Jenkins relaxed a bit, and gave David an avuncular smile. "As I told you before, from everything I've heard, you're doing a great job. As long as that continues, there will be a place for you, no matter what's decided."

"What would I be doing?"

"Since I haven't made a decision yet, my answer would just be speculation."

David knew he wasn't going to get a straight answer, so he decided to move on. As he was formulating another question, Jenkins spoke again. "There are a couple of other things I wanted to talk to you about, unless you have more questions."

"No, that's okay. Go ahead."

"These next two subjects are a bit awkward." He paused. "It concerns your apartment and your father's townhouse."

David figured that the discussion would eventually get around to his apartment, but the mention of his father's townhouse was a surprise. He did his best not to let on, waiting for Jenkins to continue.

"As far as your apartment is concerned, as you probably know, we could charge $3000 a month. Instead we're getting $500. And that's from your roommate . . . Jeremy, is it?"

He's certainly done his homework, thought David. "Yes, that's right."

Jenkins turned on the charm again. "David, I don't want to make things difficult for you, but I have a fiduciary responsibility to the company to rectify situations like this."

David kept any emotion out of his voice. "I understand."

"This isn't personal."

David wondered why everybody said things like that, especially when it was obvious that it was. If where you lived and how much you paid for rent wasn't personal, than what was it? Of course, David knew what Jenkins really meant. He wasn't singling David out; he would do the same thing to anyone.

And of that, David had no doubt.

Jenkins continued. "Anyway, to try to be fair about this, we could allow you to stay on through December? That'll give you four or five months to find someplace else." He smiled that smile again. "Or if you decide that you'd like to stay there, we could discount the rent to $2500."

He's not trying to do me any favors here. He just doesn't want the legal hassle of trying to negate the lease. David kept his tone even. "I'll have to think about that."

"Of course, take your time."

"You also mentioned something about my father's townhouse."

"Yes. Listen David, we all hope and pray that your father comes out of this and is able to return to work. But in the meantime, the townhouse is just sitting there." Jenkins held up his hands. "Now, don't worry, we won't be renting it out. Instead, I'll be moving in, and if . . . or rather, when—let's be optimistic—your father comes out of the hospital, I'll be happy to give it up so he can move back in."

This one hit David between the eyes. He recovered enough to say, "What about his things?"

"We'll put everything in storage; you won't have to do anything."

"But what about his personal papers and things like that?"

"We have a company on retainer that will handle all of that. I'm told they're very reliable"

"When is this going to happen?"

"Next week sometime. If you need to go into the townhouse before then, feel free to do so."

David couldn't help but think back to a few weeks ago when he had felt that the move to the rehab facility was like putting his father in "storage." And now, all his father's possessions would be in storage too. His father deserved better, but he had no idea how to stop any of this.

David's next words came out with an edge to them. "Is there anything else?"

"I can see that this has been difficult for you. Maybe we should save the rest for another time."

"No, I don't think so. Might as well get it all out there."

Jenkins glanced at some papers in front of him, but David knew that it was just a device to gather himself. Whatever Jenkins was about to say had been practiced, just like everything else today.

"This is about your salary, David."

It took a lot, but David remained stoic.

This time Jenkins didn't smile. "Don't worry, nothing's going to change while phase one is still going on." Jenkins looked down at the papers again. "As you might know, your position during phase one is a personal services contract. Technically, you work for your father, not the company. And a portion of your salary comes from his personal finances. Were you aware of that?"

Not exactly, thought David. But he wasn't about to tell Jenkins that. "Yes. I believe my father mentioned it."

The smile was back. "Let's assume that you're going to continue to work for us after phase one. Depending on your specific position, we'll negotiate a new contract, but we're going to have to . . . adjust your salary. The $80,000 you're currently earning is much higher than we pay any of our employees doing similar work . . . especially those without much experience." He leaned forward again. "I realize that this might seem premature, David. But I wanted you to have all the information so you could . . . consider your options."

David knew he needed to get out of there. "Well, I certainly have a lot to think about." He stood up and offered his hand. Jenkins shook it, and said, "It really was a pleasure to meet you. I wish it had been under different circumstances."

"Just doing your job. I understand."

On the way down to get his car, David was having trouble deciding whether everything Jenkins talked about was simply "good business," or if he had a not-so hidden agenda—to use David, and then eventually force him out of the picture.

Regardless of Jenkins' motivation, David realized that he had to face the fact that his life was about to change dramatically – a new baby, a new apartment, maybe a new job, a cut in salary, and probably, no wedding.

It appeared that Alan Fenton's instincts had been right on target.

CHAPTER 25

A little over a week after David's meeting with Phil Jenkins, Jenna boarded a flight out of Long Beach and headed back to Boston. She hadn't told David that she was coming because she knew he would try to talk her out of it.

When she landed in Boston, Jenna called David's cell, but it went to voicemail. She didn't leave a message, but tried the apartment's landline instead.

"Hello."

"Hi . . . uh . . . Jeremy?"

"Yes . . . Jenna?"

"Yeah. Hi. How are you?"

"Fine. How are you doing?"

"I'm okay."

"David's not here. He went to visit his father."

"Oh. I tried his cell, but I don't think he had it on."

"Probably not. They prefer that you turn them off at the rehab facility."

"Do you have any idea when he'll be back?"

"I'd say, half an hour or so."

Jenna hesitated. "Would it be okay for me to come over and wait?"

"You're back in Boston?"

"Yeah, I just got in."

"David didn't mention that you were coming back today."

"He didn't know."

"This will be a nice surprise. He could use some good news."

"That's one of the reasons I came back early. I didn't like the way he's been sounding on the phone. Is he all right, Jeremy?"

Jeremy hesitated. "Well, it's been a tough few weeks. No question about that. But . . . uh . . . I think you better talk to David about that."

Jenna smiled to herself. "You're a good friend, Jeremy."

He deflected the compliment. "I hope you understand. I'm not sure it's my place to . . . ."

"It's okay. Don't worry about it." Jenna paused. "I'll be there in about twenty minutes, if that's all right."

"Yeah, sure. I'll wait for you out front. I can help with your luggage."

"I only have one suitcase. My mom is shipping the rest of my clothes to Tufts."

"Okay. I'll see you in a little while."

When he hung up, Jeremy called David's cell phone, but he still didn't pickup. Jeremy tried three more times over the next fifteen minutes with the same result. He then headed down to the lobby to wait for Jenna.

She arrived at about 4:30. And after a hug, a brief exchange about the flight, and some additional small talk in the elevator, Jeremy unlocked the apartment door and let Jenna go in ahead of him. After putting her suitcase down, he turned to get another look at her.

"I know I said it downstairs, but you look terrific."

"I suppose, if you're partial to people who resemble small buildings."

Jeremy smiled. "Oh, come on. You're not that big."

"I've still got four months to go." Jenna pointed to her stomach. "So this building is still going to be adding some square footage."

He smiled again. "Well regardless, I meant what I said. You look great. I think the pregnancy agrees with you."

"I wish you'd tell that to my bladder."

"All right, all right. No more compliments then." He paused. "Why don't you sit down? Would you like something to drink, or were you serious about the bladder remark?'

"Actually, some water would be great."

Jeremy returned a minute later with the water and sat down on the couch next to Jenna. She took a sip, and then said. "I tried David's phone again, but he still didn't answer."

"Yeah, I did too."

They were quiet for a few moments before Jenna spoke again. "Listen Jeremy, I don't want you to violate any confidences, but is David all right? He seems even more stressed out than he was before. What's going on?"

Jeremy shifted his position on the couch. "When I told you before that you needed to talk to David, it wasn't because he confided in me and told me not to say anything." Jeremy paused. "I've been sensing the same thing as you, but the only thing I know about for sure is what happened between him and his father. And you know all about that, right?" Jenna nodded as Jeremy continued. "Obviously, David was really upset over that whole situation, especially what his father said about you."

"What do you mean, what his father said about me?"

Jeremy looked embarrassed. "You know, when he asked . . . ." And then Jeremy stopped short as he realized from Jenna's expression that she didn't know anything about Mr. Whitcomb's question.

"Jeremy?"

"Oh Jenna, I thought David told you."

"Told me what?

"I'm sorry. I thought you knew." He paused. "I really don't want to get in the middle of this, Jenna. I shouldn't have said anything."

"It's not your fault, you didn't know. Can you at least . . . ."

The chime of her phone interrupted the question. She found her bag, fished out her phone, and glanced at the display. It was David.

Jenna flipped the phone open and answered. "Hi."

"Hi, yourself. I was visiting my father and turned my phone off. I thought I left it on vibrate, but evidently I didn't. Anyway, I saw that you had called. How're you doing?"

Jenna sensed from David's tone that he was forcing himself to sound upbeat, but she didn't let on. "I'm okay." She paused. "I'm back in Boston."

"What? Now? Today?"

"Yeah, today. Actually, I'm at your apartment with Jeremy."

"Really? You're serious?"

This time Jenna knew David wasn't forcing the happiness in his voice. "I'm just waiting for you to get back."

"I'm about ten minutes away. I just stopped to get gas. How come you came back early? I mean, obviously, I'm glad you did, but . . . ."

"I didn't like the way you sounded on the phone the last few times we spoke. I felt like I needed to be here."

There was silence for a moment before David responded. "I guess you know me better than I thought."

"You don't hide your emotions very well, David. I wish you wouldn't try to spare me from whatever's going on. I'm a big girl . . . ." Jenna decided to lighten the moment. "And getting bigger every day."

David laughed. "I really am glad you're back. I'll be there in a few minutes . . . and I promise we'll talk. Okay?"

"Okay."

"I love you."

"I love you too."

Jeremy had gone into his room once he realized that it was David on the phone. Although he had closed his door, Jeremy heard most of Jenna's side of the conversation. When he emerged from his room, Jenna noticed that he had changed his shirt.

"I'm going to go out for a few hours," said Jeremy.

Jenna protested. "You don't need to leave."

"You two should have some privacy."

"We can go into David's room."

"Jenna, it's fine. You guys need to talk. I'll see you tomorrow."

Jenna moved closer and gave him a kiss on the cheek. "Thank you."

"No problem."

David arrived a few minutes later. When Jenna heard the keys in the lock, she got up off the couch and headed for the door. David closed the short distance between them in three steps and took her in his arms, careful not to press against her stomach.

Jenna chuckled. "I'm not that fragile. You can give me a better hug than that."

He tightened his arms around her, but still kept a little distance. His lips found hers, and he gave her an extended kiss. After a few seconds he separated himself and said, "Let me look at you." He smiled. "Wow, you look great."

"Jeremy said the exact same thing. Hey, did the two of you rehearse that ahead of time?"

"How could we? We didn't even know you were coming," David said. "Where is Jeremy anyway?"

"He went out for a while." Jenna took David's hand. "Why are you so uptight? That was only a joke."

He expelled a mouthful of air. "I'm sorry. There's just a lot going on."

"That's what I thought. That's why I'm here."

He took her in his arms again. This time he held her closer and longer. As he was about to say something, Jenna beat him to it.

"David, will you please tell me what's going on? It's not fair to either one of us for you to keep it bottled up."

"You're right. I'm sorry. I should have told you everything before. I just didn't want . . . I don't know." He paused. "Let's sit down."

They sat on the couch half-facing each other with their knees touching and holding hands.

Despite what Jeremy had hinted at regarding something Mr. Whitcomb had said about her, Jenna knew that David had just come from seeing his father. She felt like she had to ask about him, even if it might lead to something awkward. "How's your father?"

"No change."

"I'm sorry. It must be hard seeing him like that every day."

"It is." He paused. "Actually, I don't go every day anymore. It was getting too difficult. I'd convince myself on the drive down that there was going to be some improvement, and it never happened. I go on the weekends and a couple of times during the week, but it's pretty discouraging."

Jenna squeezed his hand. "Are you still feeling guilty?"

"Yeah, somewhat. Although his doctor said the heart attack was probably inevitable. But I think he may have said that just for my benefit."

They remained quiet momentarily, and then Jenna decided to follow up on what she had heard earlier. "Jeremy and I were talking, and he mentioned something about a remark that your father made about me when the two of you were arguing. What's that all about?"

The color drained from David's face, and he didn't respond.

Jenna spoke again. "Don't blame Jeremy. He thought I knew. What did your father say, David?"

"It doesn't matter."

"It does to me."

David pursed his lips, and forced the words out. "When I told him you were pregnant, he asked me . . . if the baby was mine."

Jenna brought her hand up to her mouth and stifled a gasp. When she was finally able to speak, tears had formed in her eyes. "Why would he say something like that?"

David shook his head. "I don't know. I think it was just a knee-jerk reaction to everything I had just told him." He paused. "When he asked me that question—that's when I exploded and swore at him."

"So, the whole argument was about me, and what kind of person I am?"

"No! It was about him not being able to control everything I do."

"I don't understand. What was he trying to control?"

"I told you . . . everything. It's just so complicated."

"You need to tell me, David."

He stared at her. "You're right."

As David began to describe the events of the last several weeks, he felt as if floodgates were opening up. Even the speed at which he spoke accelerated as he moved from the topic of the trust fund, to the marriage clause, to Alan Fenton, and finally to Phil Jenkins.

Midway through David's explanation, Jenna closed her eyes and leaned back. It was as if all of this information possessed a physical weight pushing against her.

As he finished up, David looked exhausted. He expelled a mouthful of air as if he had just completed a marathon. "So that's where things stand."

"Oh David, this must have been awful for you. Why didn't you tell me?"

"I kept thinking I could figure something out. Find a way to fix it. I know I should have told you sooner. Maybe I have more of that control gene from my father then I'd like to admit."

Jenna reacted to the mention of Mr. Whitcomb. Despite everything David had told her, she still hadn't been able to get his insult out of her head. Plus, there was not going to be a simple solution to this, and David's father had put it all in motion.

David spoke again. "I'll do whatever you want. We can say 'the hell with the trust fund.' We can get married. I'll find another job."

"This is just so overwhelming."

"I know. But I told you, whatever you want to do, I'll do."

"This shouldn't just be up to me."

"I didn't mean it that way. I only meant that as long as we're together, I don't care about getting married . . . I mean . . . that didn't come out right. I don't know what I'm saying. I just want to do what's going to make you happy."

"I don't know what that is, certainly not yet."

Jenna started to fill up. "I can't believe this is happening." After a few moments she was able to reign in her emotions and think more practically. "And there's nothing Alan Fenton can do?"

"Not really."

"What about if you talk to Jenkins again and maybe get a better idea of what he's planning?"

"Even if I could find out more, it doesn't change anything about being able to get married. If I get married before I turn twenty-seven, I get nothing . . . *we* get nothing."

Jenna didn't mean for her words to sound so negative. But when she said them, David bristled. "Maybe your father really believed that the question he asked you was legitimate. Why else would he do this to you?"

"Come on, Jenna. There's no doubt that it was a horrible thing to say, but he was just trying to push my buttons."

"I'm not so sure."

David stood up. "This isn't getting us anywhere."

"No, it isn't."

"Maybe we should take a break from talking about this."

"That's probably not a bad idea."

They were quiet for a few minutes, and then Jenna grasped David's hand. "Please don't take this the wrong way, but I think I should go and stay with Trish at the dorm tonight."

"What? Why?"

"I need to let all this settle into my brain. Plus, I think it will help if I talk to Trish about it."

Jenna saw the effect her words were having on David, and she tried to reassure him. "David, I'm not mad at you. Don't look like I'm trying to punish you."

"How else am I supposed to take it?"

"I told you, I need to think about this by myself."

"But it's not by yourself. It's with Trish, or more specifically, it's *not with me*."

"I'm not trying to avoid talking about it with you. But we're not going to get anywhere tonight. Don't forget, you've had time to think about all this; I haven't."

"Is this because I didn't tell you everything sooner?"

"No, it's not. I'm just trying to digest everything that's happened; and I know Trish will help with that."

"Jenna, this shouldn't be like some pajama party. This is real life . . . *our life*."

"You think this is fun for me? You think I'd rather be with Trish than with you?"

With the slightest of pauses, David answered. "No, of course not."

Jenna realized that David's response wasn't as immediate as it should have been. "Why did you hesitate?"

"You're starting to read things into everything I say, or don't say . . . or don't say quickly enough."

"No, I'm . . . ." Jenna couldn't finish. She shook her head, reached for David's hand, and then spoke softly, but with resolve in her voice. "What are we doing, David? I hate this. Why are we fighting?"

"I don't know. It's just that I didn't expect to see you for a few more weeks, and then you're here, but you feel like you have to leave . . . ."

"I just know I'm going to be better able to deal with all of this if I go some place where I can clear my head."

David stared at her for a moment. "Okay. I can't say I completely understand, but if that's what you need to do, okay."

She leaned in and kissed him. "Thank you."

There was an awkward silence during most of the ride over to Tufts. David wanted to try to change Jenna's mind one last time, but thought better of it. He reluctantly accepted the idea that nothing he could possibly say would accomplish that. And in fact, it might make things worse.

When they arrived, he took her suitcase out of the trunk, brought it into Hutchinson House and on to the elevator. They gave each other a kiss goodbye that was more platonic than either of them intended.

David drove about fifty yards away from the dorm and suddenly stopped the car. He put it in park and sat there for a few minutes, trying to decide what to do.

His thoughts turned to his father and to Phil Jenkins. He slammed his fists into the steering wheel and half-shouted, "God damn it!"

He then shook his head and looked in the rearview mirror. He grabbed the gearshift lever, hesitated as he moved it passed the "R," then put it in drive and headed back to his apartment.

CHAPTER 26

Trish was waiting for Jenna when she got off the elevator on the second floor. She grabbed Jenna's suitcase, put it aside, and gave her a hug. "Hey, stranger. How're you doing? You look . . . ." Trish's voice trailed off as she saw the tension in Jenna's face. "What's wrong? Are you all right?"

"I will be. I just need a minute."

"Come on. Let's go in and sit down."

They sat on Trish's bed for a few moments in silence before Jenna spoke up. "David and I kind of had a fight. Well, not really a fight. It was . . . I don't know. There's just so much going on. That's why I called and asked to spend the night here. I felt like I needed to talk to someone . . . to you. And David got upset when I told him I wasn't staying at the apartment tonight." Jenna started to get teary-eyed.

Trish reached for Jenna's hand, trying to calm her down. "It's okay. It'll be all right."

Jenna tried to smile. "You know, when you say that, I almost believe it." Trish smiled back, and patted Jenna's hand.

It took a few more minutes for Jenna to compose herself, and then she told Trish the whole story. When she finished, Trish leaned back slightly and shook her head. "Wow, you guys have had a lot thrown at you."

"Yeah, it sure feels that way, and I have no idea what we should do."

Trish waited for a moment before speaking. "I'm not sure you're going to want to hear this, but for what it's worth, I think maybe you need to consider what *David's* been going through. Remember, he almost lost his father, and he still might. And from what you told me, he feels responsible."

"I know, and I've been trying to focus on that. But I'm also upset that he didn't tell me everything until today. It's my life, too. He shouldn't have shut me out."

"You're right. But you can't change that, and it sounds like he was trying to protect you, or at least find a way to fix it before he told you. I know it won't be easy, but I think you've just got to let it go. It's going to be hard enough to figure out what the two of you should do, never mind if you're going to dwell on the fact that he didn't tell you everything right away."

"It just so complicated."

"It is, but being angry at David is not going to make things easier."

"I can't help how I feel."

"Of course not. All I'm saying is that you've got to try to get past it."

Jenna thought for a moment. "You're right." She smiled. "You always seem to know what to say to me."

Trish smiled as well. "And my rates are so reasonable."

They both laughed, and then Trish continued. "Why don't we take a break and have something to eat? It'll give you a chance to calm down, and then we can talk some more if you'd like?"

"I'm not sure food is going to help solve any of this."

"Maybe not. But have you ever heard anyone say that they think better on an *empty* stomach?"

Jenna laughed. "That's true. Do you charge extra for the food?"

"No. It's included in my rates."

They used the break to talk about the baby, how Jenna was feeling, Trish's escalating romance with the news writer at the station, and then all sorts of entertainment trivia.

As they were finishing off some pretzels and flavored water, and running out of tabloid gossip to discuss, Trish said, "Now that we've solved all of the celebrities' problems, I think we're ready to tackle yours."

Jenna chuckled. "Mine seem harder."

"Maybe." Trish paused, and her expression became more serious. "I think the first thing you need to figure out is how important is to you to get married?"

"Very."

Trish nodded. "I understand. But considering how it impacts on everything else, do you still feel as strongly?"

"Emotionally, yes. I know it must seem old-fashioned, but I want to be married before the baby's born."

"How does David feel about that?"

"He said if that's what I really wanted, then we could get married, and forget about the trust fund."

"So, what's holding you back?"

"As much as I want to, I'm not sure it's the right thing to do."

Trish nodded. "Tell me again what happens if the two of you get married."

"If we get married before David turns twenty-seven then he forfeits the entire trust fund. He also could lose it if he quits his job."

"And you said David talked to a lawyer?"

"At least twice."

"Do you think David really doesn't care about the money?"

"Neither of us does. Except . . . ."

"Except what?"

"He's worried that if he quits, he won't be able to find a job right away, and with the baby coming . . . Plus, we have to find a new apartment, and we're going to need another car once the baby's born. I mean, I can postpone going back to school till the baby's older, but still, our expenses are going to be way up there."

Trish nodded. "From what you just said, it seems like you already know what you have to do."

They continued to talk for another hour. And while Jenna didn't firmly decide anything, she felt as if she was beginning to put things in proper perspective. Trish had been able to do just what Jenna had hoped – help her wrap her head around everything, and separate the emotional from the practical.

Deep down, however, Jenna knew that no matter what she agreed to, or what she said out loud to the contrary, the idea of not being able to get married would continue to bother her.

By the next morning when David came to the dorm to pick up Jenna, he felt much calmer than he had the previous night. Being by himself had allowed him to view things more rationally. He only hoped that Trish had been able to do the same thing for Jenna.

Both Jenna and Trish were waiting for him in the lobby. After Trish expressed her sympathy about David's father, Jenna gave Trish a hug, and thanked her for everything. David hugged Trish as well, and then he and Jenna headed for the car.

Once they were settled in, David said, "I'm sorry I was such a jerk yesterday."

"You weren't a jerk." She paused. "I should have been more sensitive about what you've been going through."

"Well, no matter what, I could have handled it better." He glanced over before continuing. "So, how did it go with Trish?"

"Really good. She helped me see things a lot more clearly."

"I'm glad. I had a lot of time to think about things also. Jeremy stayed over another friend's apartment last night, so I was by myself. It was actually pretty good."

They subconsciously avoided getting into a full-blown discussion during the twenty-minute ride back to Cambridge. And there were a few awkward moments once they were inside the apartment, neither of them knowing how to initiate the conversation.

Finally, David took Jenna in his arms and held her. After a minute, he broke the embrace and kissed her lightly on the lips. Jenna moved herself back into him and returned the kiss.

When they separated, she said, "I've missed you."

"I've missed you, too."

They found each other's mouths again, and began to kiss more passionately. After several minutes, Jenna said, "I think maybe we should postpone our discussion for a while." She took David's hand and moved toward the bedroom.

They both realized that the intensity of their lovemaking was borne more out of the need for physical release than anything else, but the reason didn't diminish the pleasure.

When they were both spent, Jenna rested her head in the crook of David's arm and shoulder, and eventually her breathing slowed. "I love you," she said.

David kissed her hair, and said, "I love you, too."

Jenna placed her arm across David's chest, and he held her closer. She exhaled a mouthful of air and said, "The more I think about it, David, I don't think you should quit your job . . . and, as much as I hate to say it, we probably shouldn't get married."

David started to change positions, but Jenna stopped him. "Can we please stay like this? I just want to be held right now."

"Okay." He was quiet for a moment, and then he said, "What changed your mind, at least about the marriage part?"

"I really didn't change my mind. It just seems to make more sense with the baby coming and everything. It gives us some security, especially if you stay working for your father's company. Plus I know how much you enjoy working there."

"Even so, we could still do one without the other. We could get married, and I could stay with the company."

Jenna hesitated before responding. "But there are so many things that could happen. I don't think we should take the chance."

"Are you sure?"

She hesitated again. "I think so."

David started to sit up. This time Jenna didn't stop him. As they faced each other, David put his hands on Jenna's shoulders. "You have to tell me how you're really feeling. I told you, if you want to get married, we will, end of discussion."

"It's not that simple."

"So, talk to me."

"I guess I want it both ways. I want to get married and I want the security of the trust fund."

"Come on, Jenna. That doesn't help. You've got to open up about this."

"I know." She paused. "Honestly, part of it is . . . what people think. I know it shouldn't matter, but it does."

"What do you mean?"

"I'm already getting looks from people when they see that I'm pregnant and don't have a ring on my finger. It's going to get worse when I go back to school, and even worse once the baby's born."

"It really bothers you that much?"

"Yes, it does."

"So, we'll buy you a ring."

"Don't make fun of it, David."

"I wasn't. All I meant was that if you were wearing a ring then maybe people wouldn't stare, and you'd feel more comfortable."

Jenna eyed David, trying to decide whether he was being patronizing. She decided that he wasn't. "But if we're watching our finances, we shouldn't be spending money on a ring."

David didn't respond immediately, obviously thinking about something. Finally, he said, "How about this? I'll stay working at my father's company, but I'll put out feelers to see what other opportunities might be out there.

If something opens up, we could consider getting married before the baby's born."

"So everything would remain the way it is now?"

"At least for the time being." He took her hands in his. "Except, we could get you an engagement ring . . . one that looks like a wedding ring."

"But that costs a lot of money?"

"They have rings that look just like diamonds that aren't very expensive. And then when we actually do get married, I'll get you the real thing."

He saw that Jenna was still processing all of this, so he gave her a moment before he spoke again. "This buys us some time, Jenna. A lot can change over the next few months." He paused. "Plus, we don't know what's going to happen with my father."

Jenna saw David's eyes start to moisten. She reached over and embraced him.

They held each other for a few moments and then David asked, "So what do you think?"

"Obviously, I wish things were more settled, but maybe this is the best we can do."

"You know me, Jenna. Normally, I don't like postponing things, but in this case, it probably makes sense."

She nodded. "You know, it's funny. This is kind of what Trish and I talked about last night. I don't mean the ring part, but about waiting."

"She'd make a good counselor."

Jenna laughed. "We talked about that, too." She leaned in and gave him a kiss before she spoke again, this time with a twinkle in her eye. "I'm not sure we should give her so much credit. I think it's just as likely that having sex before our discussion probably helped."

David smiled. "Could be. Maybe we should try it again and see if we can solve some more problems."

He kissed her on the lips and then moved to her neck. Her breathing became rapid, and that fueled David's arousal. He gently lowered her on to her back, and started to kiss her all over.

It had never been the case that when they were making love, Jenna's mind was any place but in the moment. However, in this instance her thoughts went elsewhere briefly. *I wish I could just accept not getting married better than I'm letting on. Nobody seems to understand how important it is to me. Maybe I just need some time. But shouldn't loving David and knowing that he loves me be enough?*

CHAPTER 27

David bought Jenna a half-carat cubic zirconia just two days after their conversation. He had debated whether to ask her to go with him but had decided it might mean more to her if he did it on his own.

She told him how genuinely touched she was by the gesture, and even more so by how quickly he had made the purchase. Still, David thought he saw something in Jenna's eyes that didn't quite mesh with her words.

He decided not to pursue it. They had agreed to postpone the wedding indefinitely. Revisiting that topic was not going to accomplish anything, especially after his phone conversation that morning with Alan Fenton.

David had dialed Alan's direct line, and on the third ring he answered.

"Alan Fenton."

"Hi, Alan. It's David Whitcomb."

There was a pause before Alan spoke. "Is everything all right? Your father?"

"No, everything's okay. I mean, he's about the same. Actually, I was calling about something else."

David could hear the relief in Alan's voice. "Sure. What can I do for you?"

"Jenna came back a couple of weeks early from California and we were able to talk things over. Neither one of us is thrilled with the decision, but for the time being, I'm going to stay with the company and we're not going to get married."

"I think you're doing the right thing. I know it probably goes against everything you're feeling emotionally, but . . . ."

"That's one of the reasons I called. I want to explore some other options."

David heard a wariness in Alan's voice when he spoke. "What do you mean?"

"As I said, for the time being I'm going to stay where I am, but I'd like to put out some feelers to see if there might be any positions opening up. Any suggestions?"

There was silence for a moment before Alan answered. "Are you sure you want to pursue that? Don't forget, if you quit and something happens to your father . . . ."

"I know, but it doesn't hurt to find out if anything's out there."

"I can't argue with that. Okay, let me make some calls."

"I appreciate it, Alan."

"I'll get back to you in the next day or so."

"Thanks."

"Oh, one more thing, David. I did some checking about borrowing against your trust fund. I'm afraid that doesn't look very promising. The people who do that kind of lending have been burned a few times recently and are a bit gun shy."

"That's okay. I think we're going to be all right, at least until phase one is completed. After that, who knows? That's another reason that I want to put those feelers out there."

"Okay. I'll talk to you in a few days."

As it turned out, Alan got back to David in less than twenty-four hours with the names of three local real estate developers. Although he knew it was a long shot, David sent out three letters of inquiry, expressing interest in positions that might be available either immediately or six months from now.

A week later Jenna moved back into the dorm with Trish to start their junior year. She was hoping to attend classes until the Christmas break—about two weeks before her due date. That would mean she'd only have a year and a half left to complete her degree, maybe less, counting the credits she had earned during the first summer session.

When Jenna registered for classes, she made sure to flash the ring David had bought for her. The ring itself was actually quite tasteful, not ostentatious at all. But Jenna knew that regardless of what it looked like, it really just served as a security blanket.

Still, whether it was her imagination or not, Jenna thought a number of older women after observing that she was pregnant, and then seeing the ring, had changed their body language to suggest a level of acceptance that hadn't been there a minute before.

When Trish first saw the ring on Jenna's finger, she simply asked, "Do you want to talk about it?"

Jenna responded. "Yeah, okay." She knew, however, that if she had said 'no,' Trish would have dropped it. Jenna continued. "I know it's probably silly, but it makes me feel better."

"Then it's not silly."

"But I feel like it shouldn't make a difference what other people think."

"You're not hurting anybody by wearing it."

"I took it off for a day, but I felt like people were judging me."

"Jenna, you need to stop being so defensive. If it makes you feel better, then you should keep it on."

"That's what I keep telling myself."

They ended the discussion, but Jenna's brain couldn't quite let it go. She looked down at the ring and thought – *This is a lie*. It reminded her of a soldier, wearing a medal he hadn't earned, or didn't deserve.

The last Friday in August, David went to see Phil Jenkins, ostensibly to update him on phase one of the project, but in reality he wanted to find out if Jenkins had made any decision about the second and third phases.

Jenkins opened up the meeting by making a reference to the recent monthly report David had filed. "So, I was reading that your roommate – Jeremy, right?" David nodded. "He won't be working for us anymore. Why is that?"

"He was only scheduled to work during the summer. He's starting his new teaching job soon."

"There's no need to replace him?"

"No. He did a great job, but I knew he was only going to be with us for two months, so I planned around that. If we need to, we can always give Darnell Smith some additional overtime."

"Don't get me wrong, I'm not complaining, but will the overtime you're talking about be enough?"

"It should be. If not I'll let you know."

"Okay." Jenkins paused. "As long as we're on the subject of your roommate, have you given any more thought concerning what you're going to do about the apartment?"

"I thought you said that we could stay there until December?"

"You're right, I did. I was just wondering if you'd definitely decided to do that. I mean, we have to clean it up and do some painting before we rent it out."

David had been surprised that the meeting thus far had been so civil. Jenkins last few comments, however, were much more reminiscent of what David had come to expect. Nevertheless, he kept his tone even. "Jeremy's started to look at some apartments on the South Shore, closer to where he'll be teaching, and I'll start looking soon. I figure we'll move out by the end of November. That should give you enough time to clean it up."

Although David spoke the last sentence with some intended sarcasm, Jenkins didn't react. He simply responded, " Excellent."

David was about to say something even more sarcastic, but changed his mind. Instead he decided to get to his real reason for being there. "Anything new on the likelihood of phases two and three going forward?"

Jenkins' smile and tone appeared even more patronizing, as if Jenkins were talking to a seven-year-old. "David, David, it's only been a few weeks since we talked about this. I'm still getting used to the Boston operation. Nothing's been decided."

David felt more foolish than upset. "Of course. I just thought . . . ."

"These things take time, David. You'll know when I know."

David doubted that. But he also knew that he wasn't about to get any more information out of Jenkins today. "Okay then, I guess I'll get back to the apartment complex." He paused. "I'd like to cut out a little early. I have to take my . . . ." David didn't know why, but he was about to say fiancée. "Uh . . . girlfriend to a doctor's appointment."

Jenkins' patronizing tone continued. "David, you don't need to ask permission to take personal time. Just make sure you call in and let my secretary know that you won't be on site. Anything else?"

"No."

As David was leaving he thought to himself. *I've been in this office hundreds of times with my father, and he was pretty condescending, but nothing like what just happened in there, not even close.*

After a few hours at the apartment complex, David picked up Jenna and headed for Braintree. It was Jenna's first visit with her new doctor.

"Are you nervous?" asked David.

"No, not really. My doctor in California knows Dr. Millwood pretty well. Plus I checked him out on the Internet."

"You can do that?"

"Sure. A lot of his patients wrote reviews. They were all very positive. Actually, Dr. Millwood's a bit of a throwback; he's an ob-gyn *and* a pediatrician. That's pretty rare today. But I like the idea."

"That's good." David paused. "So, we're still not going to find out the sex of the baby?"

"I told you. If you want to, you can. But, I'd rather be surprised."

"Yeah, like if I find out, I'm going to be able to keep it a secret."

Jenna smiled. "I can't help it if you're impatient."

David was going to wait until after the appointment before broaching the next subject, but since Jenna seemed to be in such a good mood, he changed his mind. "I was wondering, as long as we're in Braintree, I'd like to stop by and see my father. You don't have to come in, if you don't want to."

Jenna hesitated. "I'm not sure I'm ready to do that. I can't help it, but I'm still angry, David." She paused. "Let me see how I'm feeling after the doctor's visit."

Jenna liked Dr. Millwood very much. He was gentle, caring, and reassuring. It also didn't hurt that her pregnancy was textbook.

When they got back in the car after the visit, Jenna turned to David and said, "I think I'm going to try to come in with you to see your father."

"That means a lot to me, Jenna."

"I know."

David squeezed her hand and gave her a kiss on the cheek.

The rehab facility was about five miles away and took less than ten minutes to get there. When they exited the car, David took Jenna's hand, and he could feel it trembling. He glanced over, but didn't say anything.

They checked in at the front desk and then headed toward Mr. Whitcomb's room. Once inside, Jenna was convinced that they were in the wrong place. The man lying in the bed looked nothing like the imposing, larger-than-life figure she had seen only a couple of months before. This man with the tubes enveloping him and the gray pallor had to be someone else.

David moved toward the bed and spoke to his father in a whisper. Jenna remained where she was, unable to hear what David was saying.

After a few minutes, David asked if Jenna wanted to come closer. She shook her head.

Jenna noticed tears in David's eyes, and then she started to form some of her own. As David turned back toward his father, Jenna left the room. David came out a few minutes later. "Are you all right?" he asked.

"No, not really."

"What is it?"

"I don't know. I came in hoping that seeing him would make me less angry."

"And?"

"Maybe it helped a little, but not much."

"I understand. It's taken me quite a while. First, I had to get past the guilt I was feeling."

"I thought you told me that you *were* past that."

"I think I am for the most part. I needed that to happen before I could start to forgive him. Does that make any sense?"

"Of course, he's your father." She paused. "But, I hope you understand, David, I'm not there yet." She paused again. "When I saw how fragile he looked, I did feel sorry for him, but then I remembered how he treated you, how he treated us. Is it possible to feel sorry for someone and be angry with them at the same time?"

"Evidently, it is."

Jenna glanced at the fake wedding ring on her finger and felt a new wave of anger wash over her. *If he hadn't tried to control everything, then this ring would be real, and I wouldn't feel like such a hypocrite. I'm not sure I'm going to be able to forgive him any time soon. Maybe when the baby comes, or maybe when we get married . . . or maybe never.*

CHAPTER 28

Over the next several weeks, David visited the rehab facility less frequently. The initial sense of hope that he clung to—that his father would come out of the coma—had given way to the more realistic assessment that he very likely might remain in a vegetative state for the rest of his life.

Despite harboring those negative feelings, David never shared them with Jenna. Instead, every time he traveled to Braintree he asked her to come with him, hoping that being there might somehow change the way she felt about his father.

Jenna always approached the visits with the best of intentions. But each one tended to replicate the first time she had seen Mr. Whitcomb lying in the hospital bed – an equal combination of pity and resentment. But as the birth of the baby came closer and the wedding didn't, her resentment began to outweigh the pity. Without question, she knew that her reaction was more visceral than rational. But that made it even more difficult to deal with, not less.

In early October during one of these visits, the physician overseeing Mr. Whitcomb's case came into the room to speak with David and Jenna. "Nice to see you again."

"Hello, doctor. Is everything all right?"

The doctor answered tentatively. "Well, yes, but . . . ."

"What is it?"

"Nothing bad. It's just that one of the attendants brought something to my attention that made me wonder if something else might be going on with your father."

"What do you mean?"

"Have you ever heard of locked-in syndrome?"

"I think so, yeah. But I'm not sure exactly what it is."

"In essence, some patients in a coma can actually hear and understand everything that's being said to them. They just can't acknowledge it. They have no way of responding."

"You think that's the case with my father?"

"I don't know. Usually locked-in patients have had some sort of trauma to the brain, not simply a heart attack. Although in rare situations, if blood flow to the brain had been diminished, it could have the same effect."

"Are there tests you can do?"

"Not really. What we're hoping for is some sort of sign that he's understanding us."

"Like what?"

"Sometimes patients with locked-in syndrome are eventually able to blink or move their eyelids in response to some kind of outside stimulus." He paused. "Actually that's why we're even looking into this. One of our attendants who was giving therapy to your father was also talking to him at the same time. He thought your father might have been responding to things he was saying. The attendant paged me, and I came as quickly as I could."

"And?"

"I saw some eye movement, but it wasn't consistent. That doesn't rule it out, however. It simply may be that he was not able to respond each time. It's like the brain remembers what to do sometimes, and then it forgets . . . or this could be nothing at all—a spasm, a twitch."

"If he has locked-in syndrome, could that mean that he's starting to come out of the coma?"

"It could. But it's also just as likely that he'll remain in the locked-in state."

"Is there anything you can do, or I can do – visit more often, talk to him more, anything?"

"Those things certainly can't hurt. But as you know, we administer stimulation therapy a number of times each day. I've instructed that everyone who works with your father record notes on every real or imagined response."

The doctor could see by David's expression that his mind was racing. He put his hand on David's shoulder. "You have to understand that this condition is extremely rare. And even if your father does have locked-in syndrome, he still may not be able to communicate with us. Frankly, I debated even mentioning it to you. I didn't want you to get your hopes up."

"I understand. It's just that it's the first piece of good, well, possibly good news, since all this happened."

"Of course." He paused. "You have my number, if you have any additional questions. And certainly if anything changes, I'll contact you immediately."

After the doctor left, David spent the next fifteen minutes leaning on his father's bed, talking to him and looking for some reaction. Jenna quietly exited the room and waited in the lobby.

On the way back to Boston the only topic of conversation was Mr. Whitcomb. David's excitement and enthusiasm spurred his mind to consider all of the positive "what ifs."

With some reluctance, Jenna convinced herself that she needed to bring David back to reality. "Obviously, I hope that this turns out to be great news, but you heard the doctor. The chances are very small."

"I know. But I can't help thinking that if he comes out of the coma, or if he can communicate somehow, everything would be different. He could change the trust fund and then we could get married."

"And you know that nothing would make me happier." She paused. "But you have to be realistic, David."

Jenna knew that she was coming across as being completely negative, so she decided to drop it. In her mind, however, she continued to consider another possible scenario. *What if he does wake up, or can communicate, and then decides that he wants to leave everything the way it is. Wouldn't that be even worse? After all, he changed David's trust fund because of me. If he felt that way when he was supposedly thinking clearly, why would being in a coma change that?*

She pushed these ideas to the back of her mind, but knew that they would return front and center every time she thought about David's father.

David finally heard back from the last of the three real estate developers he had sent letters to. Although each of them expressed some interest in his services, none of them had any current or anticipated openings.

David called Alan Fenton and got five more company names. But before he sent out any new letters of inquiry, he called the rehab facility and asked if anything had changed with his father's condition. It hadn't.

He sent the new letters out the following morning.

Over the next several weeks, David and Jenna went apartment hunting. Initially they looked in Braintree and Weymouth in order to be close to Dr. Millwood's office, but nothing stood out.

On the way back into Boston on one of the trips, they took a detour through Quincy and quite by accident came across a complex that offered two-and three-bedroom townhouse-type apartments. They were almost exactly midway between Boston and Braintree.

They found the rental office on site, did a walk through, and decided on the spot to sign a rental agreement. The agent indicated that the two-bedroom unit would be available December first, but he could have it ready a week earlier since David wanted to move in over Thanksgiving weekend.

A few minutes later they were in David's car headed back to Boston. He opened up the conversation. "Well, that happened pretty quickly."

"I know, but I think we did the right thing. I like the apartment a lot."

"Yeah, me too. It's also great that we can move in over Thanksgiving. I think I told you; Jeremy's moving out that weekend. I'll get a couple of guys from work to help us, and we can move both of us at the same time."

"Where's Jeremy moving to again?"

"Rockland. It's about ten miles further south. It's closer to where he's teaching." David looked over at Jenna. "I know I'll be in the apartment by myself for a few weeks while you finish up at school, unless the baby has other ideas . . . ."

She smiled. "Dr. Millwood still thinks the end of December, but who knows?"

"Anyway, I was thinking that I could paint the baby's room while I'm in the apartment by myself." He hesitated. "Of course it would be helpful if we knew the baby's sex, so I'd know what color paint to use."

Jenna smiled. "Something neutral like yellow will be fine."

"How do you figure that yellow is neutral? I don't even own anything yellow."

"So that's the criteria – the color of your clothing?"

"No. But you have to admit, yellow is much more . . . little girlish."

"You just want to know if the baby's a boy or a girl. This has nothing to do with paint color."

"So?"

She smiled again. "Actually, I've been thinking that maybe I'd like to know ahead of time, too."

"What changed your mind?"

"I don't know. I'm not sure why I wanted to wait in the first place."

"So should I turn the car around and head back to Braintree?"

This time Jenna laughed. "I've got an appointment next week. We can find out then."

"Or, we could call?"

"You're unbelievable."

Jenna had always thought she was going to have a boy. So, even though she had given some consideration to girls' names, her focus had primarily been on boys' names – actually on one boy's name in particular – Robert, after her father. When she discussed it with David, he didn't seem to have any objections.

The following week when Dr. Millwood told them that they were, in fact, having a boy, Jenna thought for sure David would change his mind, and want his son to be named after him. And although David became very emotional, he dismissed the name selection as not something he felt strongly about. "I think he should have his own name. It'll make him independent more quickly." He wiped the tears from his eyes before he continued. "Wouldn't a psychologist have a field day with that last remark?"

After they left the doctor's office they went out to lunch, before heading over to the rehab facility. Dr. Millwood's pronouncement about the general health of the baby and the follow-up conversation at lunch had Jenna feeling very upbeat. Her mood helped provide the impetus for her to go inside with David.

As was usually the case, she knew she probably wouldn't be able to stay very long in the room, but it was important to David, so she made the effort.

After a few minutes the doctor who had spoken to them about locked-in syndrome showed up. They exchanged greetings, and then the doctor said, "I'm afraid we haven't seen anything that resembles what the attendant witnessed. Certainly nothing that would suggest your father understands anything that we're saying."

"But then why do you think he reacted like that the first time?"

"As I told you, we can't be sure that he was actually responding to what was being said." He paused. "We're not ready to give up on this yet. We'll continue to monitor him during the daily stimulation therapy, and hope we see some signs . . . ."

"Does the prognosis change if he doesn't have locked-in syndrome?"

"Not really. But the longer he's in a comatose state, the more unlikely it is that he'll recover." The doctor studied David briefly, and then continued. "Having said that, however, there are plenty of cases where people wake up after being in a coma for years. It's very difficult to know with any degree of certainty what's going on in any individual's brain."

David tried to smile. "We appreciate everything you're doing, doctor."

"You're welcome."

Jenna had remained on the periphery of the conversation, and although she took in everything that was being said, her mind was focused elsewhere. She had made an important decision over the last several hours, and she needed to tell David.

Certainly, now was not the time, but it needed to be soon.

CHAPTER 29

During the next several weeks, Jenna tried to find an appropriate time to talk with David about the decision she had made. Unfortunately, the opportunity never arose, or at least that's what she told herself.

On Thanksgiving morning David woke up just in time to say goodbye to Jeremy who was headed to his parents' house for a traditional turkey dinner. "Have a great time and say 'hi' to your folks for me."

"Will do. I'll be back on Friday night. Maybe we can load up a few things to save us some time on Saturday."

"That's a good idea. Okay. I'll see you then."

Later that day, David and Jenna had dinner out at a restaurant and then went back to the apartment. As they entered, they had to side step a number of boxes that were strewn about, as well as some of David's books and clothing that had yet to be packed. "You're not finished yet?" said Jenna.

"Almost. I'll take care of the rest of it tomorrow."

"If you'd like, we can do it now. I'll help you."

"I've got a better idea."

David took Jenna's hand and led her into the bedroom. His bed had been disassembled, but the mattress and box spring remained in the center of the room.

He began to remove her clothing, piece by piece, a ritual that never failed to excite her. When everything had been taken off, he eased her down onto the mattress. Jenna continued breathing heavily as David removed his clothes and lay down beside her. He gently kissed her neck and breasts, letting his lips linger.

Jenna had told him how unattractive she felt, but he knew that by taking things especially slowly, and having her excitement build, any notion that she was anything less than desirable, would disappear.

When they finished, they fell asleep holding each other.

They awoke around 3:00 in the afternoon within a few minutes of each other. Jenna spoke first. "That was a nice way to spend Thanksgiving."

"It sure beats watching football."

Jenna laughed. "I hope you were talking about making love and not sleeping."

David didn't respond immediately, appearing to think over his answer. Jenna jabbed him in the ribs, and said, "You're not funny."

David smiled and gave her a kiss. "I'm a little bit funny, don't you think?"

"Looks aren't everything."

"Ouch."

They were quiet for a moment before Jenna offered, "I hate to say it, but I think that this weekend might be the last time we'll be able to have sex until after the baby's born."

"Why do you say that?"

"I'll be at the dorm for the next few weeks finishing up the semester, and the baby's due ten days after that."

"I thought that was a myth that you aren't supposed to have sex in the ninth month."

"Maybe so, but I don't want to take any chances."

David shrugged his shoulders. "Not exactly what I wanted to hear, but obviously whatever you think is best."

David's last remark triggered something in Jenna, and the issue she had hesitated bringing up moved forward in her brain. Before she had a chance to stop herself, she blurted out, "Can we talk about the baby's name?"

David looked at her curiously. "I told you, I'm fine with Robert."

"I meant his full name."

"What are you talking about?"

"I'd like to name him Robert MacDonald, after my father."

The implication of what Jenna was suggesting began to register with David. "You mean that 'MacDonald' would be his last name? What about Whitcomb?"

Jenna lowered her eyes away from David. "I thought we could make 'Whitcomb' his middle name."

David appeared stunned. "His middle name?"

"I've been giving this a lot of thought, David."

"I guess so." He paused. "It might have been nice to have included me in the deliberations though, don't you think?"

"That's what I'm trying to do now."

"No you're not. You're telling me what you've already decided. It sounds like it isn't even up for discussion." He paused again. "Is this because you're still mad at my father? Well, it doesn't hurt him, Jenna. He doesn't know about any of this, and maybe never will. This only hurts me."

"I'm not trying to hurt you. Can I please explain?"

"Yeah, sure. I'd really like to hear what possible reason you could have."

Jenna continued. "I think my last name and the baby's should be the same, at least for the time being. When I take him to doctor's appointments, or meet people for the first time, it'll just make things easier if the baby has the same last name as I do."

"That's ridiculous. Do you think people at the doctor's office, or anybody else for that matter, cares about that? Is this the same hang-up you had about the ring?"

Jenna looked hurt. "It's not a hang-up. And don't forget, you're the one who brought up the whole idea of getting me a ring."

David raised his voice. "Only because I thought that's what you wanted. And I notice you haven't taken it off."

She glanced down at her left hand. "This is different."

"I don't see how." He looked at her intently. "Jenna, think about what you're saying. I mean, I could almost understand it, if you were talking about when he starts school. But he won't even be able to say his name for a year and a half." David shook his head. "So, what does this make me – a sperm donor?"

"Now who's being ridiculous? You're his father."

"And exactly how is anybody going to know that? These people you're so concerned with – at the doctor's office and . . . wherever; how are they going to know?"

Jenna remained silent, and David could sense that his last question was having an effect on her. He continued, but in a softer tone. "Jenna, I've listened to everything you've said. But there's got to be more to this that you're not telling me . . . or not telling yourself."

"I don't know, maybe." Her eyes softened before she spoke. "I guess I kept telling myself that it had nothing to do with your father, and not being able to get married, but maybe it does."

"I can understand that, but it's like you're punishing me because we can't get married.

"I told you, I'm not trying to punish anyone."

"Maybe you're not trying to, but the result's the same." He put his hands on her shoulders and looked directly into her eyes. "He's my son, too."

Jenna saw the pain in David's eyes. Any vestige of her convictions crumbled. "I guess in the back of my mind, I knew how you'd feel about this. That's probably why I didn't bring it up until now."

"Can you understand why I'm upset?"

"Yes . . . I don't know what I was thinking. I'm sorry."

"I know. Come here."

He took her in his arms, and they stayed like that for several minutes. When they separated, David brushed a tear off Jenna's cheek and kissed her lightly on the lips."

"I have an idea."

"What?"

"Why don't we make his *middle* name MacDonald? We can call him Robert MacDonald Whitcomb."

Jenna smiled through her tears, and nodded. "I'd like that."

Early Saturday morning, David, Jeremy and two paid recruits from Whitcomb Realty Trust loaded up the large rental truck with all of David and Jeremy's belongings.

Jeremy drove his car down to Rockland, and the truck followed. Jenna stayed behind to do some last minute light cleaning. By 10:30, Jeremy was all moved in, and the caravan headed for Quincy. By 1:00, all of David's things were in the new apartment as well.

David and Jeremy sat in the cab of the rental truck, each drinking a beer, waiting for Jenna to show up. Jeremy took a swig from his Budweiser and said, "That went pretty smoothly."

"Yeah, I figured we wouldn't be done until late this afternoon. Jenna was surprised too. I gave her a call when you went to get the beer. She should be here soon; she was just finishing up."

Jeremy took another sip of beer and looked over at David. "Are you all right? You were kind of quiet today. I know lifting a hundred and fifty pound bureau doesn't lend itself to a lot of conversation, but . . . ."

David took a drink before he answered. "I'm okay."

It seemed to Jeremy that David rushed to change the subject. "So, is everything still going well with the teaching job?"

"Yeah. I mean it's a lot of work. And it's not really the same as student teaching, or even being a leave replacement. Having your own five classes to prepare for is much tougher. But I love it."

David smiled. "That's great." He turned slightly in his seat. "Hey, remember when Trent used to get on your case about wanting to be a teacher?'

Jeremy smiled. "Yeah, he loved to bust my chops. How's he doing, by the way? Have you heard from him recently?"

"A few months ago." David raised his eyebrows. "He's gone all corporate."

"Trent?"

"Yup. It only took him about six months to become the fair-haired boy at the company."

"We're talking about your roommate before me, that Trent?"

"Yeah, he's got a condo in New York, and a Porsche."

"Really? Wow, I never would have thought that."

They were silent for several moments, and then David glanced at his watch. "I'm surprised Jenna's not here yet."

"Might have been some traffic." Jeremy paused, and then shifted topics. "Anything new with your dad?"

"No, not really."

"I'm sorry." He glanced over at David. "I was thinking about him the other day." He paused. "If only there were some way to let him know that he's going to be a grandfather . . . you wonder if that would change the way he felt about things."

"I've thought about that too, but unfortunately, I don't see that happening."

"You mean you don't think he's ever going to come out of the coma, or that it wouldn't make a difference, even if he did?"

"I don't know. We never really talked about it, but I think the idea of carrying on the family name was important to him." He paused. "Although that almost didn't happen either."

"What do you mean?"

"Jenna wanted to name the baby after her father."

"I know, you told me that."

"Not just his first name, his last name too."

"Really?"

"Yeah, but we finally got it all worked out. His name's going to be Robert MacDonald Whitcomb. Although for a while there, I wasn't sure the Whitcomb name was going to be anywhere to be found."

After Jenna finally arrived, David and Jeremy spent the next hour rearranging furniture, assembling the bed, and moving all the boxes into the appropriate rooms. When the apartment had some sense of order, Jenna emerged from the kitchen and said, "Thanks for helping out, Jeremy. You guys did a great job."

"You're welcome."

David spoke next. "I'm going to return the truck, and Jeremy's going to follow me in his car, and then bring me back."

"Okay. I'll just put a few things away while you're gone."

"No heavy lifting, all right?"

"You guys already did all of that. I'll take it easy, I promise."

On the way out the door, David gave her a kiss and said, "I'll see you in a little while."

Jeremy was right behind him. "You take care of yourself, Jenna." He touched her stomach and added, "And the little guy."

She smiled, gave him a kiss on the cheek, and thanked him again.

Jenna spent the next thirty minutes opening boxes and making sure she extracted all the items they needed to spend the night in some degree of comfort. She had just sat down to take a break when there was a knock on the door. She struggled briefly to get to her feet, using the arm of the couch to pull herself up.

Since she was alone in the apartment, she opened the door with some degree of caution. The woman who had knocked smiled warmly and said, "Hi, I'm Barbara O'Connor. I live in one of the apartments in the back of the building, number 108." She paused briefly. "I realize it's a bit old-fashioned, but I thought I'd just drop by and welcome you. I also brought an apple pie."

Jenna's initial expression reflected her surprise, but quickly softened. "That's very nice." She smiled. "I like old-fashioned, and I like apple pie. I'm Jenna, by the way, Jenna MacDonald. Why don't you come in?"

"I don't want to intrude. I know you're busy. I just wanted to say hello and welcome you to the building."

"You won't be intruding, please. I was just about to take a break. I'm waiting for my . . . uh . . . fiancée to get back."

"Are you sure?"

"Yes."

"Okay, for a few minutes." Barbara crossed over the threshold, and looked back over her shoulder. "So, when are you due?"

"In about a month."

"Your first?"

"Yes."

"Congratulations. Do you know what you're having?"

Jenna's face brightened. "A boy."

Barbara smiled. "Have you decided on a name?"

Jenna hesitated, the discussion she had had with David still fresh in her mind. "Robert, after my dad."

"He must be excited."

Jenna hesitated again. "He passed away when I was eight. After that, it was just my mom and I."

"I'm sorry."

Jenna nodded. "My mom lives in California; she's a teacher, but she's coming east during her Christmas break to help out with the baby."

"That's terrific."

There was a momentary lull in the conversation before Jenna asked, "Do you have children?"

"Yes, a son, Toby, but he's twenty-eight."

"Twenty-eight? You don't look old enough to have a twenty-eight-year-old."

"Thank you." Barbara smiled. "I think we're going to get along just great."

Jenna smiled back. "Well, it's true."

"Now you're embarrassing me."

"Does your son live locally?"

"Actually, he lives with me. He's a special needs adult. He has Down syndrome."

Jenna struggled to find the right words to respond. "Oh . . . I . . . really?"

Barbara jumped in to lessen the awkwardness. "Once you get settled in, I'll bring him by so you can meet him." She smiled. "I know I'm prejudiced, but he's a delight. Everybody loves Toby."

Jenna broadened her smile. "That would be nice. I'd like to meet him."

Barbara nodded, and started to stand up. "I think I'm going to take off. Anyway, welcome to the building. I hope you and your fiancée enjoy the pie."

"Thank you again. I'm sure we will."

Jenna closed the door behind Barbara, put the pie in the refrigerator, and returned to lie down on the couch. She closed her eyes, and in a few moments a number of ideas came into her head.

Barbara never even batted an eyelash when I called David my fiancée and not my husband. Maybe David's right. Maybe nobody cares about stuff like that anymore.

Her mind jumped to another topic. *Barbara was so matter-of-fact about her son having Down syndrome. That must be hard. I guess it's like a lot of things—you just learn to accept them. But still, it can't be easy.*

Before she could explore that idea any further, the baby kicked and took her thoughts elsewhere.

CHAPTER 30

David shuffled through the various envelopes and January white sale flyers he had just retrieved from the mailbox. His eyes came to rest on a letter from the city clerk's office.

He tossed the other pieces of mail onto the coffee table, and began to open the envelope he held in his hand. David was sure he knew what it was, but he still wanted to see everything in print, as if somehow that would make it all official.

The document inside said that Robert MacDonald Whitcomb had been born on December 27th. He weighed 7 pounds and 12 ounces, and was 20 inches long. His mother was Jenna MacDonald and his father was David Whitcomb.

As he read his name, David's thoughts drifted to his own father. It was becoming more and more apparent that his father was probably never going to wake up, never going to have the opportunity to make things right with Jenna, and never going to know that he had a grandson. It was like the document David was holding had not only acknowledged his son's birth, but had also confirmed his father's fate.

In the last several days something had shifted in David's outlook concerning his father's condition. Prior to that, he sincerely believed that his father would recover. Maybe it was the possibility of locked-in syndrome, or the anticipation of a new life coming into the world that continued to engender this hope. But now he could feel it all disappearing. Now, it would take a miracle. And David wasn't sure he believed in miracles.

He had just placed the birth certificate back in the envelope when he thought he heard a sound from the bedroom where Jenna and the baby were sleeping. David got up to check. The door was already slightly ajar as he peered in to make sure everything was all right.

Jenna was lying on her side with a quilt covering most of her. She had placed a pillow between her and the baby. David went back into the living room, picked up his cell phone and returned to take a picture.

He clicked the button and two seconds later he was looking at the photo. He noted that it was slightly off center. But all he did was smile and acknowledge to himself that he wouldn't change it for the world.

He returned to the living room, sat back down on the sofa, and picked up the remaining pieces of mail. As he thumbed through them, he began to reflect on the previous two weeks.

Jenna's mom had arrived the day after Christmas and had stayed for ten days. Sharon had been there to help Jenna through the delivery and through the first week of motherhood. When Jenna had trouble breast-feeding, Sharon had calmed everybody down, including the baby. Eventually, the doctor had suggested that they switch to formula, but Sharon's easy manner took the stress out of that transition as well.

David quickly became very fond of Jenna's mom. Besides the good advice and support she had given them, Sharon had never inserted herself into any discussion or conversation unless she was asked her opinion. That alone said so much about who she was.

David's thoughts shifted to another subject. This time it was about work. He had taken a week off, which had turned out to be less of a problem then it might have been, primarily because the weather had been so bad that a number of expected deliveries had been postponed. Still, David knew he would have to put in some extra hours each day in order to catch up.

His thoughts then moved to Phil Jenkins, who still hadn't told David what he was planning to do about phases two and three. It was probably time to try to get some answers.

As he picked up the phone to call Jenkins' office and make an appointment, he realized the picture he had taken was still on the screen. He stared at it for a full minute before he punched in Jenkins' number. As he waited for the call to go through, David thought about Jenna and the baby in the next room. It brought a smile to his face, and he acknowledged that at this moment, he was happier than he had ever been in his life.

He could only hope that whatever information he got out of Phil Jenkins wouldn't do anything to change that.

On Monday morning David arrived at Whitcomb Realty Trust a few minutes before 9:00. He waited about ten minutes before Phil Jenkins opened his office door and invited him in. "Hello, David. Let's have seat over here," said Jenkins, as he pointed to the less formal area of his office. "I'm behind that desk much too much."

He put his hand on David's back as he continued. "And congratulations again. I know I congratulated you on the phone, but I wanted to make sure I did it in person. Mother and son are still doing fine, I presume?"

"Yes. Thanks. I also appreciate you allowing me to take some time off."

"Don't give it another thought."

As they each settled into a chair, Jenkins continued. "So, what's on your mind, David?"

"It seems like we've been here before. But I was wondering if you've made a decision about phases two and three?"

"We have been here before, haven't we? Unfortunately, some things are still up in the air, and I haven't finalized my decision."

Although Jenkins' response did not have the same patronizing tone as it had during David's last visit, it still wasn't really an answer. David tried to keep himself calm, but it didn't work. "With all due respect, it's been six months. I think I have a right to know if I'm still going to be employed here a few months from now. If not, I've got to start looking for another job."

Jenkins didn't display any emotion, as he said, "Aren't you already doing that?"

David couldn't hide his shock, and before he could come up with a coherent response, Jenkins spoke again. "In many ways Boston's a small town, not like New York. You could have written a hundred letters in New York and I wouldn't have known anything about it, but in Boston, that's a different story." He paused. "I take it from your actions that you're not happy here."

David was still trying to find his voice. "Uh . . . No, no . . . I mean it's not that."

"What then?"

David started to form an answer that skirted the issue, but changed his mind. It was none of Jenkins' business, but maybe something closer to the truth would buy David a little good will.

"The only reason I sent out those letters was because there are restrictions on my trust fund, and especially now with the baby, I have to make sure my family is taken care of."

Jenkins appeared mildly surprised at David's candor. "Are you talking about the three million that was given to the company? Because, I'm afraid there's nothing I can do about that; those funds have already been invested."

David knew that wasn't exactly true, but he had given up trying to fight that battle. Instead, he said, "No, I'm not talking about that money. There's other money in my trust fund that I'm not able to access for a while." David decided that he had said enough so he shifted direction. "I need to know what my future is with the company, and I assume that's dependent on phases two and three going forward."

Jenkins didn't speak immediately, eyeing David carefully. "The truth is, I haven't ruled anything in or out." Before David could protest, Jenkins raised his hands as if fending off a verbal assault. "*However,* I am seriously considering extending phase one."

David hadn't expected that. "What do you mean?"

"As you know, phase one up to this point has gone very well." He hesitated. "Much of the credit for that goes to you."

David remained wary. His experience told him that Phil Jenkins had all the sincerity of a carnival barker. But he kept silent, deciding to see where this was headed.

Jenkins continued. "Anyway, I've been looking at a couple of our properties in the South End that were not originally scheduled to be part of phase one. You know the ones I mean?"

David nodded. "Yes."

"Well, the rents in that area have shot up. It's become a much more desirable place to live. If we upgrade those properties, we can easily raise rents by fifty percent."

"Where would you get the money to upgrade those properties?"

"Some of it would have to come from the money earmarked for phases two and three."

"So those phases *would* be eliminated?"

"No, not necessarily. Probably they'd have to be scaled back some."

David still wasn't buying it. "You'd have to take an awful lot of that earmarked money to do what you're talking about."

"Not if we make some changes to phase one."

"I don't understand."

"So far we've completed two and a half of the five apartment complexes, correct?"

"Yes, we should finish the third one in about six weeks, and then we've still got the two largest ones to go."

"Well, instead of upgrading those last two, I want to use the funds on the South End properties. We can refurbish every apartment there, and make them all upscale."

David was stunned. "But what about the other apartment complexes? We told those people we'd be upgrading all their appliances, putting in air conditioning . . . plus, don't we have contracts that we've signed?"

"I've already had some exploratory meetings with the contractors. They seem very willing to renegotiate. After all, phase one would be extended for six months. It puts more money in their pockets."

"But what do we tell the people in those other places?"

"This is business, David. And sometimes, you have to reevaluate what you're doing. Look at it this way, for the people in those apartments, their rent will stay the same."

"I've gotten to know some of those people, and now we're going to turn our backs on them?"

"If it makes you feel any better, tell them it's out of your hands. After all, it is."

David shook his head. "It sounds like this is a done deal."

"Pretty much. Actually, if you hadn't made the appointment today, I would have called you in at the end of the week to tell you all this." Jenkins sat forward in his chair. "Whether you can see it or not, David, this is good news." He paused. "I want you to oversee the extension of phase one, assuming that you aren't still trying to find another job."

David was having trouble processing all of this. His answer just tumbled out of his mouth. "No, no, I'm not."

Jenkins sat back. "Frankly, I thought you'd be more excited about this."

David got back some of his equilibrium. "I do appreciate the offer to oversee the extension. It's just that I feel like we're deserting some of the people we were trying to help. One of the reasons I agreed to use my trust fund was because of that."

"I understand, David, but things change. I told you, this is good business."

"I need to think about this some more."

"I'm not sure what you need to think about. You came in here worried about your job, and I just guaranteed that for at least another year. What do you need to think about?"

David realized that it wasn't in Phil Jenkins' makeup to understand why David wasn't jumping at this. On the other hand, accepting the offer would provide some of the security he had been looking for. "I still need some more time."

"I can give you two weeks. If you don't want the job, I've got to start looking for a replacement."

"I understand."

David got up out of the chair, and somewhat reluctantly offered his hand. After they shook, David said, "Thanks for seeing me."

"No problem. I hope you decide to continue with us."

David was surprised by the comment. "Can I ask you something?"

"Shoot."

"Why are you offering this to me? Wouldn't it be just as easy to let me go, and find somebody else?"

"I keep telling you, David. I base my decisions on what's best for the company. You've already done two successful upgrades. Why would I want to hire somebody else?"

David looked for anything in Phil Jenkins' expression that might suggest he was being less than truthful. He couldn't find it, or maybe he didn't want to.

Once David got back to the parking garage, he sat in his car for several minutes reviewing everything that had just happened. His immediate reaction was mixed. The idea of having a job he enjoyed for the next year was great news. But one of the reasons he enjoyed his job so much was because of the people he was helping. And now that part of the equation was going to disappear.

He continued to weigh all the different possible scenarios, and then finally reached into his pocket, took out his cell phone and punched in Alan Fenton's number. It was about to go to voice mail when Alan picked up. "Hi, David. How are you?"

"I'm fine."

"Any news on your father?"

"No, nothing good, anyway. I only visit once every two or three weeks now. Maybe I should go more often, but there doesn't seem to be much point."

"I know. It must be hard."

There was silence for a moment before Alan spoke again. "Is everything all right with Jenna and the baby?"

"Yeah, they're both fine. Actually, the reason I called is that I just left Phil Jenkins' office. I wanted to get some information about phases two and three, and as it turns out, he knew all about the letters I sent out."

"Really? Did he seem upset by that?"

"That's the funny thing. I don't think so. It was more like he wanted me to know that he was aware of what I had done, but it wasn't a big deal. In fact, in the next breath he asked me to stay on to oversee an extension of phase one."

"That sounds like just what you were looking for."

"Sort of."

"What do you mean?"

"He wants to scrap the upgrading of the last two apartment buildings we had scheduled, and instead, upgrade some properties in the South End. Obviously, the extension is good for me, but I feel like I'm letting down those people who thought they were going to have their apartments redone. Jenkins claims it's simply good business. But of course, that's how he rationalizes everything he does."

"It certainly does seem that way. I assume you want my take on this?"

"That's why I called."

"Off the top of my head, I'd say don't look a gift horse in the mouth. I know you feel like you're breaking a commitment to the people you mentioned, but that wasn't your decision. If you don't accept the extension, he'll just find someone else. You can't possibly have any influence over things down the road if you're not working for the company. And I hate to mention it, but if something should happen to your father, and you leave the company on your own accord . . . ."

"I know. But I can't help thinking about when we laid out the plans for the three phases. I was so excited about what we were doing, and now . . . now, it's much more like just a job."

"I understand that, but it's a job that you need."

"I think if the baby hadn't just been born, I'd tell Jenkins to forget it. I'm not sure I have that luxury now."

"I don't think you do either. Have you spoken to Jenna about any of this?"

"No. You're the first one I called. I think I might wait a few days before I bring it up. I want to have things clear in my own head first."

"Give me a call if you need to talk some more."

"Will do, Alan. Thanks."

David drove to one of the work sites where things had gotten a little behind because of the days he had taken off. Before he was aware of it, he was so engrossed in work that any thoughts of his conversations with Phil Jenkins and Alan Fenton had moved to the back of his mind.

Around noon, he gave Jenna a call to let her know that he would be home later than expected. She asked him how his day was going. David almost started to mention what had transpired earlier, but then decided to wait until he got home.

CHAPTER 31

David arrived home around 6:30. As he opened the apartment door, Jenna sat up on the sofa where she had been resting. David came over and gave her a kiss. "How long has the little guy been asleep?"

"About an hour."

"How's he been today?"

"A little fussy, especially when I tried to feed him."

"Really? You'd think that would be the time he'd be the least fussy."

"I know. Of course, things were kind of non-stop around here today. Maybe that had something to do with it."

"What do you mean?"

"Well, first Trish called. I was trying to feed the baby and talk to her at the same time. She offered to call back, but I haven't talked to her for a while, so . . . ."

"How's she doing?"

"Great. She's heading back to school next week, and then she said she's going to come out and visit." Jenna paused. "Right after I hung up with Trish, Barbara O'Connor dropped by with her son."

"Toby, right?"

"Yeah."

"Does he work at Shaw's Supermarket?"

"I think so. Why?"

"When I was in there the other day, there was a young man with Down's bagging groceries. I thought his name tag said Toby."

"It probably was him." Jenna smiled. "What a charmer. After we were introduced, he asked me what he should call me. He's about seven years older than me, but he said calling me Jenna wouldn't show the proper respect." She paused. "And you know what? For some reason, when he said that, it just hit me how silly I've been acting about this whole thing."

"So, what did you tell him to call you?"

"Promise not to laugh." She hesitated. "I started to say Mrs. Whitcomb, but then I changed it to Ms. MacDonald-Whitcomb. Finally I said, 'just make it Ms. MacDonald.' Poor Toby was totally confused."

A huge smile formed on David's face. Jenna jokingly slapped his arm. "I told you not to laugh."

"I didn't."

"Well, you were going to."

David held up his hands in surrender. "You can call yourself whatever you want. It's fine with me."

"You're enjoying this way too much."

David took her in his arms. "I'm just glad that you're not as uptight about this as you used to be."

"Yeah, I'm not sure why that is exactly. As I said, I guess I finally realized that nobody cares. Nobody's judging me. Anyway . . . ." She paused, "Did you eat anything? Do you want me to fix you something?"

"No. I picked up a burger on the way home." David changed the subject. "Was the baby awake the whole time Barbara was here?"

"No, he was only up for a few minutes. That was around one o'clock. After that he slept for almost four hours. And then just after he woke up, Jeremy dropped by."

"Jeremy? Everything all right?"

"Yeah. He just came by to say hello and see the baby. He thought you'd be home."

"Too bad I missed him. How is he?"

"He seems fine. He couldn't get over how cute the baby is. Oh yeah, and he told me to tell you that all your friends are relieved that the baby looks like me and not you."

David laughed. "No matter what I say to that, I'm going to get myself in trouble."

"Probably." Jenna pointed to the table in back of David. "He brought the baby a present."

David reached back and lifted the top off the box, and brushed aside the tissue paper to reveal a couple of outfits with sports decals and the name Bobby embroidered on them. "Wow, these are pretty cool." He paused. "Where would you even go to get something like this? I wouldn't have a clue."

"I think the mall has a place that does it. But still, it was really nice of him."

"Yeah, it was."

"I was a little surprised about how comfortable he was around the baby. He doesn't have any younger siblings, does he?

"No, he doesn't. It must be all that teacher training."

"I don't know. He just seems like a natural. Plus, I think there's a little bit of a difference between getting trained to teach high school students and knowing what to do with newborns." She paused. "Speaking of high school, he really seems to love his job. After I put the baby to sleep that's all he could talk about."

"Yeah, I've only spoken to him a few times on the phone, but he really does seem to like it. Of course, it doesn't surprise me. Ever since I've known him, that's all he's ever wanted to do."

David hadn't necessarily intended to raise the issue of his meeting with Phil Jenkins, but with all the talk about jobs, it popped into his head. As he started to say something, the baby monitor squawked.

"Uh oh, looks like he's awake."

"He didn't sleep very long."

Jenna glanced at the clock. "No, but I think all the interruptions today probably threw him off. He's scheduled to eat around now, anyway."

"I'll get him."

Jenna smiled. "Okay, I'll heat up the bottle."

David returned to the living room a few minutes later carrying the baby in his bassinet. He called into the kitchen. "I tried to pick him up, but he kept on squirming, and then he started to cry. He seems happier in the bassinet."

"He did the same thing with me earlier. I just think he hasn't settled into a routine yet."

Once the bottle was ready, David picked up his son, and after about ten seconds of flailing arms and legs, the baby found the nipple and calmed down. Jenna sat on the sofa next to David, and they both watched their little boy until he finished the entire bottle and closed his eyes.

After they put him back in the bassinet and carried him into their bedroom, they returned to the sofa. Jenna picked up the remote. "Do you want to watch the news, or just relax?"

"Actually, I wanted to talk to you about something." He paused as Jenna put the remote back on the coffee table. "I saw Phil Jenkins today."

"Oh, did he come out to the apartments?"

"No. He almost never does that. I went to see him at his office. I wanted to find out what's going to happen with phases two and three."

"Any luck?"

"Well, he hasn't decided for sure about them, but he told me he wants to extend phase one for an additional six months."

"How come? I thought you told me phase one would be finished by June."

"It's supposed to be, but he wants to substitute a couple of different properties for the ones we were scheduled to upgrade in the spring. These new properties will take another year to complete."

"So then when do the other ones get done?"

"That's just it. They don't." He paused. "The good news is he wants me to oversee everything, so my contract would be extended for at least half a year. On the other hand I've been working with some of these people for months, and now nothing's going to get done to their apartments."

"But that's not your fault."

"I know, but I still don't feel right about it."

"So what did you tell Jenkins?"

"I said I needed more time to make a decision. I have to let him know in a couple of weeks. But I don't see that I have much choice." David started to sit back when something else occurred to him. "Oh yeah, and here's the other thing—he knew all about the letters I sent out."

"How did he find out about that?"

"I have no idea. But he certainly wanted me to know that he was aware of it, although it didn't seem to bother him that much. Otherwise I don't think he would have offered to extend my contract."

"All this happened this morning?"

"Yeah. I called Alan Fenton right after the meeting, and then I tried to put it out of my head for the rest of the day."

"What did Mr. Fenton say?"

"He thinks I should accept Jenkins' offer."

Jenna hesitated. "For what it's worth, I think he's right. I can tell it bothers you, but it'll give us some additional security for a while longer."

"I know, and that's why I'm probably going to tell him 'yes.' I just wish I felt better about it."

A week later Phil Jenkins sent out an e-mail with a copy of the contract extension attached. David read it over carefully, and then forwarded it to Alan Fenton, asking for his advice. A couple of days later David received a phone call.

"Hi, David, it's Alan."

"Hi. Thanks for getting back to me. So, did you have a chance to look over the contract?"

"I did."

"And?"

"Everything seems in order."

"That's what I thought, but it kind of surprised me. Jenkins had warned me that down the road he was going to have to reduce my salary, but he didn't. I'm still trying to figure that one out."

"I may have some insight into that."

"Really? What?"

"After we spoke the last time, I contacted a few people at the company to try to find out what was going on. All three of them told me that Jenkins is quite impressed with the job you've been doing. He doesn't want to lose you. I told you before, David, Jenkins' reputation suggests that all he cares about is the bottom line. And it seems that keeping you on the payroll is good for the bottom line."

David's surprise was evident in his voice. "Really? Most of the time he's pretty condescending toward me."

"I think he's probably that way with a lot of people. Did he ever give you any reason to think that he was displeased with your work?"

"No, in fact, just the opposite. He's always been very complimentary. But I thought he was just blowing smoke."

"Evidently not."

David was quiet for a moment. "So after I sent out those letters, Jenkins thought I definitely wanted to leave?"

"I think he was concerned about it, yeah."

"When I met with him, I initially thought the same thing, but then . . . I don't know. He's hard to read."

"I know it may not have been what you intended, but it looks like sending out those letters was a good negotiating strategy."

"Yeah, that was my plan all along." Alan laughed as David continued. "So, you think that's why he's willing to keep my salary the same?"

"Probably, although I was also told that Jenkins plans to reorganize the upcoming summer work. He can save a lot of money by further reducing overtime. And with your experience, he probably doesn't need to rehire some of the summer help. I think that might include your friend, Jeremy."

"Yeah, I kind of figured that."

"With these newer apartment upgrades, Jenkins evidently feels that he can just give the tenants a week or so notification and then set up the appointments on-line. That means a lot less man hours."

"That's not very personal."

"I'm sure Jenkins doesn't think it's going to matter in this case. These people weren't expecting upgrades anyway. Switching dishwashers doesn't have to be warm and fuzzy."

"I suppose."

"David, I know you have some reservations about all this, but I think you have to try to be more detached. You may not like it, but this is the way Jenkins does business, and his track record is pretty impressive." He paused. "And frankly, I'm not sure your father would have done things much differently."

David started to protest, but stopped himself. After a moment of silence, Alan continued. "Anyway, I think you should sign the contract extension, and then sometime in the fall you can reevaluate where you are, and what you want to do."

David hesitated. "You're probably right."

"Okay. If you need anything else, let me know." Alan paused. "And David, I was serious before. The people I spoke with at the company all said that Jenkins has been singing your praises since shortly after he arrived in Boston."

"All right, if you say so. Listen Alan; I appreciate your advice. Thank you."

After he pushed the button to end the call, David couldn't help but reflect on Alan's last comment, and the irony it represented. Like most sons, David had always sought the approval of his father, and to some degree he had received it after he joined the company. But his father had never been particularly effusive about anything he'd done.

And now, a relative stranger who had known him for less than six months was giving David more positive feedback than he had gotten from his father in twenty years. David tried to convince himself that he didn't really care about that, but on a number of levels, he knew that he did.

Two days later he signed the contract extension.

CHAPTER 32

Over the next several months, with his new job security and his new son, David's life took on an equilibrium that he hadn't experienced in a long time. In order to maintain that balance however, he was forced to cut back on the number of visits he made to see his father. David convinced himself that seeing his father once a month was more than sufficient. Plus, he thought – *It's not as if he even knows I'm there.*

But somewhere in the back of David's mind he knew that his desire to please Phil Jenkins was at least partially at the root of the decision. If he was going to remain in Phil Jenkins' good graces, he felt that he needed to put in even more time at work, especially with the changes to phase one. And since he was not about to curtail his time with Jenna and Bobby, something had to give.

By the middle of May, David began to feel pangs of guilt regarding his infrequent stops at the rehab facility. He vowed that somehow he would find the time to visit more often. But that didn't happen.

Instead, something else that had been gnawing at him began to monopolize his thoughts and led him to spend every free moment at home. David was becoming more and more concerned about his son.

Holding your child in your arms, thought David, should be the most natural thing in the world. But with Bobby it almost always turned into a struggle. He would literally push David away, as if he didn't want any human contact.

But even as his concerns increased, David kept them to himself. He wasn't totally convinced that he was viewing the situation accurately, and he didn't want to worry Jenna. But unbeknownst to him, Jenna was feeling the same way.

Both of them continued to reject the possibility that anything might be wrong, as if denying it would somehow ensure that it wasn't true.

Eventually however, David's worries about his son became so pronounced that he had trouble concentrating at work; he had to force himself to smile, and he stopped being the one to feed Bobby, fearing that his touch would set him off. David knew that he couldn't go on like this for much longer.

One night in early June, shortly after Bobby was put down for the night, David asked Jenna to join him on the couch. He took her hands in his, and said, "Can we talk about something?"

He had expected to see some curiosity reflected in Jenna's expression, but there was none. It appeared to David as if she knew exactly what he was going to say. Her words confirmed it. "Is it about Bobby?"

"Yes."

Jenna nodded in understanding, and began to cry. David reached over and put his arms around her until her tears started to subside. Neither of them was able to form any words for a number of minutes.

When they finally separated, David spoke first. "How long have you thought something was wrong?"

"A long time I guess, but I just kept . . . ." Jenna began to cry again. After a moment she said, "What baby doesn't want to be held?"

"I know. I know."

Jenna took a deliberate breath as she tried to settle herself. "I talked to Barbara about it a couple of weeks ago, but Toby wasn't a typical baby, so she couldn't really tell me anything. She didn't know what to think." Jenna paused. "Bobby's not scheduled for another doctor's appointment for about three weeks. It's his six-month checkup. I wonder if I should try to move it up."

"Why don't you call the doctor and explain the situation, and see what he says."

"That's a good idea. I'll call first thing in the morning."

David took a few moments to gather his thoughts. "How about your mom? Have you talked to her about it?"

"Not really. I did mention it, but I kind of downplayed everything. I figured she was going to be here in a few weeks once her summer vacation starts, and I wanted to talk to her face-to-face anyway."

"What did you tell her?"

"Just that we were having trouble calming him down sometimes. That he seemed more content in the pack-and-play than being held."

"What did she say?"

"She mentioned about when I had to stop breast-feeding. She thought the two things could be related."

"How?"

"She wasn't sure. She also thought it could just be a phase he's going through."

"I don't really believe that. Do you?"

"No. I wish it were that simple."

They continued to talk for another fifteen minutes. There were no recriminations and no second-guessing that they hadn't brought it up to each other earlier. There was only concern about what their little boy might be facing.

The next day Jenna contacted Dr. Millwood's office about changing Bobby's appointment. She was told that the doctor was away at a conference and was not available except for emergencies. She decided to leave the date of the six-month checkup where it was.

After she hung up, Jenna logged on to the computer and began to Google various phrases – "babies not wanting to be held" and "babies who stopped breast-feeding." Invariably those searches led to other links about "tactile aversion" and "lactose intolerance." There were literally hundreds of thousands of postings connected to the topics she had entered.

After two hours Jenna felt more confused than anything else. Her suspicions spanned the spectrum from something Bobby would outgrow to food allergies to mental retardation. She shared all of this with David when he got home, and despite the frustration he knew Jenna had experienced, he began to Google a number of phrases as well.

The ritual of the Internet searches continued almost every night leading up to the doctor's visit. Both David and Jenna acknowledged that it was unproductive, but they couldn't help themselves. This was their child. Maybe the next online article would be the one that explained everything.

On the last Monday in June, David and Jenna sat in Dr. Millwood's waiting room with Bobby resting in his car seat. David couldn't help but notice that all of the other parents who had infants were holding them. He started to point this out to Jenna, but he could tell by her expression that she had observed the same thing.

David began to worry about what he should do if Bobby started to cry. He didn't feel as if he could just leave him in the car seat, but picking him up would probably make things worse. He decided that if Bobby started to fuss, he would take him outside.

David began to wonder if this was what his life was going to be like from now on—having to think two steps ahead to make sure he was prepared for whatever might occur with his son. His thoughts were interrupted by the nurse inviting them into the exam room.

Bobby seemed content with the change in scenery for the first few minutes, but then he began to whimper. After another minute the whimper turned into full scale crying. When David picked him up, Bobby immediately started to squirm, and his crying intensified.

Another few moments passed before Dr. Millwood entered the room. He smiled at Jenna and David, greeted them, and then turned his focus to the baby. He moved closer and said, "What seems to be bothering you, little man?"

David and Jenna exchanged glances. David was about to say something when the doctor continued. "My nurse told me about your phone call a few weeks ago. Is he still exhibiting some of the behaviors you were concerned about?"

David answered. "Yes. It seems that whenever we pick him up, it's like he's fighting us."

He turned toward Jenna "Is this something new? When I reviewed my notes from your previous visits, I didn't see anything to indicate that this was an issue."

Jenna responded. "No. I haven't mentioned it before. After I stopped breast-feeding, it seemed to disappear. So I didn't think that much of it. But it's gotten much worse recently."

Dr. Millwood reached over and grasped the baby's hand. He didn't react immediately, but then as if it were scripted, he tried to pull away, as he moved about in David's arms.

The doctor continued to watch Bobby as he slowly withdrew his hand. After a few moments he broke the silence. "I'm going to ask one of the nurses to come in and conduct a few tests. I'd like to observe how he responds."

David asked, "What kind of tests?"

"They're routine. What we normally do at the six-month visit. We check his weight and height. We also look at his ability to control his head, his ability to roll over, things like that."

David again: "Anything else?"

"A blood test for anemia and another round of immunization shots."

Some of the frustration David was feeling found its way into his voice. "It doesn't sound like any of that's going to help figure out what's going on."

Jenna was surprised at David's directness, but Dr. Millwood didn't appear fazed by it. "That's why I want to observe him. I want to see if there's anything in his responses that are inconsistent developmentally."

David realized that his previous comment had been too sharp. He tried to make amends. "I'm sorry. I didn't mean to imply anything."

Dr. Millwood clutched David's shoulder. "It's fine. Don't worry about it." He paused. "Let me get one of the nurses."

He was gone less than five minutes. During that time, David returned Bobby to the car seat, and went over and embraced Jenna. Neither of them said anything. They separated and composed themselves just before the nurse and Dr. Millwood re-entered the room.

After a brief introduction, the nurse got right to work. The exam lasted the better part of twenty minutes. And while the doctor took some notes, he said very little. After the nurse indicated that she was finished, the doctor invited David and Jenna to come back to his office.

Despite a pricked toe from the blood test and two immunization shots, the baby remained quiet in his car seat. Both David and Jenna looked over at their son as Dr. Millwood made his way behind the desk.

"Well, the good news is he seems very healthy. He's in the seventy-fifth percentile in both height and weight, and his physical development appears to be normal."

David said, "What's the bad news?"

"I don't know if there is any."

"But?"

"I do have some concerns about a couple of things." The doctor could see the anxiety spread over both David and Jenna's faces, so he eased into the substance of his remarks. "It may be premature to make anything out of it, but Bobby doesn't seem to make eye contact."

Jenna asked, "Do six-month-olds usually do that?"

"Yes, actually they do. Also, he doesn't seem to be very engaged in what's going on around him."

David spoke again. "What do those things mean?"

"Taken individually, maybe nothing. But when you combine them with his aversion to being held, it could indicate something else." Dr.

Millwood looked from David to Jenna and then back again. "It could mean that there's a developmental delay."

David continued to do most of the talking. "But I thought you said he was developing normally."

"He is, physically. But if there are issues, they're probably neurological. Unfortunately, there aren't any tests to definitively determine if there's a delay in a child this young. It's only been recently that the research has confirmed a link between eye contact and normal development." He paused. "I want to emphasize that it's still possible that this is just a reflection of Bobby's individual development. Not all babies walk at the same time, or talk at the same time . . . ."

"But obviously, you must believe it's something to be concerned about, otherwise you wouldn't have brought it up. What if it's not just an *individual* delay, then what could it be?"

The doctor appeared to gather himself to deliver the news. "If it's a more pervasive delay, then it could be something more serious."

Jenna interjected. "Are you talking about autism?"

The doctor looked directly at Jenna. "It's possible."

Jenna brought her hand up to her mouth. "Oh, my God."

David was too stunned to speak initially. Finally, he said, "There's no other explanation?"

"Look, I've known both of you since before Bobby was born. You know that I believe in being direct. That's why I answered your question the way I did, Jenna. But, we can't make a conclusive diagnosis until we know more."

David nodded and reached over for Jenna's hand before he spoke. "I know. I'm sorry if . . . ."

"You don't need to apologize. I know this isn't what you expected to hear today."

David nodded again. "So we just have to wait? There isn't anything that we can do?"

"Well, there are a few things that might help us get an early handle on what we're dealing with." The doctor paused briefly. "First, you should keep a journal. Write down any changes in Bobby's behavior. Record any instances of sustained eye contact. Anytime he seems to be participating in what's happening around him, make note of it. A paragraph or two each day is fine. There are a couple of excellent books on infant development. I'll give you the titles before you leave. Start comparing what it says in the books with what Bobby's doing. I want to see him every three weeks or so for the next several months. When you come in we'll go over the journal together."

David kept his voice calm, although he was feeling anything but. "How long do you think it will take before you know something more definitive?"

"Unfortunately, quite a while. It could be as long as a year. As I told you before, there aren't any tests for infants that can give us those answers." He paused. "They're doing some innovative things at the Developmental Diagnostic Center. But they won't consider doing an evaluation before the child is at least fifteen months."

Jenna was fighting back tears as she said, "I'm not familiar with that place. Is it in Massachusetts?"

"Yes, a few miles away in Canton. When the time comes, if it seems warranted, we'll make an appointment for Bobby."

David spoke up again. "So, you think they'd be able to tell us for sure whether he has a problem or not?"

"As I said, they're doing a lot of innovative things. They've got a national reputation, especially in regards to early diagnoses. So yes, I'd put a lot of stock in their findings."

"I know I'm getting ahead of myself. But if Bobby has . . . autism, what limitations will he have?"

"Maybe none. Part of that depends on where he falls on the autism spectrum."

David nodded. "There's no cure for autism, is there?"

"No." He paused. "But there a lot of excellent programs that help these children lead very productive lives. And some of the best ones are right here in Massachusetts."

"Do children with autism go to regular schools?"

Dr. Millwood was about to remind David that many of his questions were premature. But when he saw the pain in David's eyes, he decided to let him ask whatever he wanted.

Ten minutes later, Jenna and David left the office, each with a hand holding on to the car seat where Bobby lay sound asleep, and each using their other hand to wipe away their tears.

CHAPTER 33

After securing the seat belt around Bobby's car seat, David shut the back door, opened the driver's side door and slid in. He looked over at Jenna in the passenger seat, but she continued to face forward.

They remained silent for a few moments before David spoke up. "I don't know what I was expecting to hear, but it sure wasn't that."

Jenna continued to stare straight ahead. "No. Me either."

David looked over at Jenna again. "I think we should keep this to ourselves. I don't think we should tell anybody else, at least not yet."

This time Jenna turned to face him. "What do you mean? Why not?"

"I don't know. It's just not something I'm ready to talk about. I mean, we don't know anything for sure, so I think we should just wait."

"My mother's going to be here in a couple of weeks."

David interrupted. "I didn't mean your mom. Of course, we'll tell her. I just meant we shouldn't tell anyone else."

Jenna searched David's eyes. There seemed to be something he wasn't saying, but she couldn't figure out what it was. She proceeded cautiously. "I don't quite understand. I'm not sure what harm it will do to tell other people."

"I don't know about you, but it's going to take me a while to come to grips with this. I don't think I'm ready to try to explain it to someone else." He paused. "Plus, what would we say? 'Our son has autism. Would you like a cup of coffee?' "

Jenna sat more upright, surprised at David's tone. Instead of challenging him, however, she attempted to calm things down. "All right. If you think it's best."

"You don't?"

Again Jenna was surprised at how defensive David was being. "I'm not sure. But isn't it possible that Barbara, or Jeremy, or even Trish might know something about autism? Or maybe they might notice something that we miss."

David didn't respond immediately. Jenna could see that his emotions were still raw, and very close to the surface. When he spoke, however, he had them under control. "I doubt it. But even if they do . . . ." He hesitated. "Jenna, I'm just not ready to talk about it. Can we please agree to just wait?"

Jenna remained unconvinced, but decided not to push things. "Okay."

David started the car and they drove in silence the entire way home.

A few days later Jeremy dropped by unannounced, shortly after David had gotten home from work. Jenna buzzed him in and met him at the apartment door.

"Hi, Jenna." He leaned over and gave her a kiss on the cheek.

"Hi, Jeremy. So, to what do we owe this pleasure?"

He smiled. "It's the official start of summer vacation. I was over at the mall, and I thought maybe if you guys hadn't eaten yet, we could go out and grab something. My treat."

"That sounds like a nice idea. David's in changing. Why don't you run it by him when he comes out? I'm going to check on Bobby; his schedule is all off today."

A few minutes later David and Jenna came out to the living room together. David walked over to Jeremy and offered his hand. "Hey."

"Hi, David. How're you doing?"

"I'm doing okay. How . . . ." David stopped himself as he looked down and noticed a book in Jeremy's hand. It was one of the child development books that they had purchased on Dr. Millwood's recommendation.

Jeremy followed David's eyes to the book. He lifted it up and said, "I saw this on the table. It caught my eye because this was one of the textbooks in my Human Development class sophomore year."

David responded. "Really?"

"Yeah. It doesn't read like a textbook though. I enjoyed it."

David fumbled his words. "Uh . . . we just picked it up . . . a couple of days ago. You know . . . being new parents and all . . . ." David tried to change the subject. "Jenna says you'd like to go out and get some dinner."

"Yeah. My treat."

David took another quick glance at the book as he spoke. "What's the occasion?"

Jeremy brought the book up so that he was holding it with both hands, as if he were lecturing in front of a class. And in an exaggerated formal tone he said, "The successful completion of my first year of teaching."

David tried to smile. He was also trying to decide whether going out or staying home would lessen the chances of the conversation returning to the book. He hedged his bet. "I don't know if we can go out. We'll have to see how the baby's feeling when he wakes up."

"Sure. That's fine." Jeremy started to return the book to the coffee table when it opened to a dog-eared page. As it flipped open, he read the chapter heading to himself – *Autism.*

David looked at the upside down title and instinctively reached for the book. He stopped before it became obvious what he was doing. His only thought at that moment was to avoid the situation. "I'm going to check on Bobby again."

"Sure."

Jeremy watched David leave the room, and looked over at Jenna who was sitting on the couch. Despite the fact that she was across the room, Jenna knew what chapter the book had opened to, and David's quick departure confirmed it.

Her eyes met Jeremy's, and she could see a question forming. She debated with herself for a moment, as Jeremy glanced down at the book. When their eyes met again, she said, "We took Bobby for his six-month checkup a few days ago. The doctor thinks there's a possibility that . . . Bobby might be autistic."

Jeremy's mouth gaped open. He hesitated before responding. "Oh Jenna, I'm so sorry." He paused. "Are they sure?"

Jeremy turned as he heard David re-enter the living room. David gave a quick glance at Jenna and then responded. "No. They're not. It's just one possibility."

Jenna was about to counteract David's effort to downplay the doctor's statements, but instead offered an explanation. "Dr. Millwood's concerned about Bobby's lack of eye-contact and the fact that he's not engaged in what's going on around him." She paused, and tears began to form in her eyes. "And also that he doesn't like to be held."

Jeremy looked from Jenna to David. "I don't know what to say. Isn't Bobby awfully young to be diagnosed?"

David answered. "Exactly. That's why we're thinking it could just be a delay and not anything more serious."

Jenna again wanted to challenge what David was saying, but decided that it might embarrass him. Instead, she reached over to the end table next to her and picked up the journal that she was using to record Bobby's activities. "The doctor suggested that we write down our observations of Bobby's behavior. Then we're going to see the doctor every three weeks or so to go over the journal entries."

"How long will you do that for?"

Jenna continued to respond to Jeremy's questions. "About six months, and then we're going to have him tested in Canton at the Developmental Diagnostic Center."

"I've heard of that place. They have an excellent reputation. I'm pretty sure a couple of students at our school were treated there when they were younger."

David spoke up. "That's exactly why I don't want to jump to conclusions. We need to wait until he's tested. Right now, it could be a lot of different things."

Jeremy sensed David's denial, but decided to leave it alone. He could see how much pain his friend was in.

Jenna spoke next. "Jeremy, have you ever noticed anything about Bobby's behavior that didn't seem right to you?"

Jeremy answered carefully. "No, I don't think so."

In truth, Jeremy realized that he was holding back. He recalled that on a couple of occasions when he had held Bobby, the baby had pushed away from him quite forcefully. At the time, Jeremy had attributed it to the fact that the baby didn't really know him. But maybe there was another explanation. He was about to say something when he thought better of it. *They already know about that behavior. What good will it do to bring it up now?*

Jenna sensed that Jeremy was about to say something else, but it seemed to pass. She then asked, "Would you mind taking a look at the journal entries I wrote? It's only a couple of days worth, but I want to get an idea if I'm doing it right."

"I'm sure it's fine. I don't know what I should be looking for, but if you'd like me to read it, sure."

She handed the journal to Jeremy, and he began to read.

Bobby woke up at 7:30. While I changed him, he didn't make eye contact at all. I tried calling his name or making sounds, but he didn't seem interested.

When I spoon-fed him cereal, he did maintain some eye contact, but not when he took the bottle.

After he ate, I walked around with him for a few minutes. Most of the time he tried to wiggle out of my arms. Finally, I put him in the pack-and-play. He stayed in there for over an hour and seemed content. I tried to play with him, but he rarely responded to anything I was doing. He seemed to fixate on one of the patterns on the side of the pack-and-play.

He does seem to make eye contact if I hold a toy or a spoon up close to my face, and "force" him to look at me. It's rarely sustained though.

Jeremy looked up from the journal. "I'm not sure what the doctor wants, but whenever I have to write something about my special needs students, these are the type of anecdotal notes that they're looking for."

Jeremy was reluctant to read any more. Even though he had been invited to look at the journal, he felt as if he were invading David and Jenna's privacy. He handed the journal back to Jenna and asked. "How are you guys doing with all this?"

Jenna answered first after a quick glance at David. "I'm not sure it's completely sunk in yet."

David followed up. "I feel like we should do what the doctor advises, but until we know for sure what we're dealing with . . . ."

Jeremy could see from Jenna's expression that she didn't share David's wait-and-see attitude. There was an awkward silence for a few moments as Jeremy contemplated something. Finally, he spoke up. "If you'd like, I can speak with some of the special ed teachers I know from the elementary school and see what they think."

Jenna nodded and replied, "That'd be great. Thanks."

David responded as well, but without much enthusiasm. "Sure."

There was silence again before David said, "Listen Jeremy, I'm kind of tired and Bobby's not even up yet. Maybe we should do dinner another time."

"Yeah, absolutely. I understand."

They said their goodbyes and Jeremy left the apartment. After David was certain that Jeremy was gone, he spoke with some accusation in his voice. "I thought we agreed we weren't going to say anything."

"What was I supposed to do? The book opened to the chapter on autism. Jeremy's not stupid; he would have figured it out. I wasn't going to lie to him."

"That chapter could have just been where we stopped reading. It didn't have to mean anything. You should have waited to see if he asked about it."

"What difference does it make? And you heard him; he's going to talk to some of the special ed teachers."

"So, you think that they'll know more about this than Dr. Millwood? Besides, what's Jeremy going to tell them? We don't even know what Bobby has."

Jenna moved closer to David. "I know this is hard. It's just as hard for me. But pretending that there isn't something wrong doesn't do anybody any good." She paused. "I'm sorry if you think I jumped the gun on telling Jeremy."

David ignored the last statement. "I'm not pretending. You heard what the doctor said. Nothing's definite."

"If you mean we don't have an official diagnosis, you're right. But when we first talked about this, you said it yourself – this isn't just a phase Bobby's going through."

"Probably not. But that doesn't mean it's autism." David raised his voice further. "It almost sounds like you'd be relieved, if that's what it turned out to be."

"What? What are you talking about?"

Before David had a chance to respond, they heard Bobby on the baby monitor. Jenna headed into the bedroom. She looked back and said, "David, we need to talk about this some more."

David spoke more sharply than he intended. "Yeah, we do."

But they didn't. Not that night, and not for another week. Every time Jenna tried to bring up the subject, David dismissed it. "You've already made up your mind. I get that. But I haven't. What good is arguing about it going to do us?"

"I don't want to argue either. But don't you think we should *discuss* it some more?"

"What's there to discuss?"

Jenna touched David's arm and said softly, "Our little boy."

David stared at her for a moment, as tears began to fill his eyes. He started to speak, but couldn't. He turned away from Jenna and left the room.

When Jenna's mom came to stay for a week, David's outlook seemed to soften. He was much more attentive to Bobby, and even helped with some of the journal entries. After Sharon left however, there seemed to be a shift back to the way things were. It wasn't a dramatic change; it was much more gradual. But it was a retreat nonetheless.

A couple of days before Bobby's next scheduled appointment with Dr. Millwood, Jeremy stopped by after teaching a morning summer school class. He was carrying a bag of books. "I borrowed these from some of the special ed teachers I know. A couple of the books deal with early intervention strategies. I think Bobby may be too young for them, but I brought them anyway."

Jenna accepted the books, grasped his hand and said, "Thanks, Jeremy." She paused. "Come on in and sit down."

"Okay. Just for a minute though."

"Would you like something to drink?"

"Some water, maybe. That'd be great."

As Jenna headed into the kitchen, Jeremy went over to the pack-and-play where Bobby was lying on his back. He appeared to be looking at a colorful mobile featuring circus clowns. Jeremy reached down to touch Bobby's hand. "Hey, big guy." Bobby didn't pull away from Jeremy's touch. Instead he remained focused on the mobile.

Jenna re-entered the room with a bottle of water, and handed it to Jeremy. "Thanks." He took a drink and then asked, "How's he doing?"

"The last couple of days I think I saw a few positive things, but I don't know."

"He really seems focused on the mobile. When I touched his hand, he didn't react. That's probably a good thing, right?"

"I'm not sure. Some of the books mention being fixated on objects and shutting everything else out. So, I don't know. We're seeing the doctor on Friday. I've got a lot of questions I need to ask him."

They were quiet for a moment, before Jeremy spoke up. "How's David doing?"

Jenna looked away briefly. "He's having a real tough time with this, Jeremy."

"I could tell that from the last time I was here. Is there anything I can do?"

"I wish there were."

"I'd certainly be willing to talk to him. But in this case, I think maybe I'd have to wait for him to bring it up."

"Yeah, I agree." Jenna hesitated. "He doesn't even want to talk to *me* about it."

Jeremy looked surprised, but didn't respond. Finally, he said, "I hope it's not going to present any problems that I brought over the books. I don't want David to think I'm going behind his back."

"He'd never think that. He knows what a good friend you are."

"Well, I should be going."

They stood up, and Jeremy gave Jenna a kiss on the cheek. He then went over to Bobby, and rubbed his arm. "Take care, big guy."

Bobby broke his gaze on the mobile, and for the briefest of moments looked directly at Jeremy.

CHAPTER 34

Shortly after Jeremy left, Jenna began reading one of the books he had left with her. Most of the suggestions and strategies were definitely intended for children much older than Bobby. Still, she found a number of the ideas fascinating, and tried to imagine ways to modify them so that she could include them in the activities she did with her son.

Jenna wanted to tell David all about what she had been reading as soon as he got home, but wondered if that was a good idea. His mood had been so negative lately; maybe this would just make things worse.

She was trying to decide what to do when her thoughts shifted and she began to think about the last few weeks. Although she had raised the issue of David's denial with him, she hadn't really pushed it. She acknowledged that she was reverting back to the way she and her mother always dealt with uncomfortable issues – they tiptoed around them.

But this was too important; this was their child. Jenna decided that tonight she had to be more direct. If David got upset, so be it. She needed to shake him up and force him to confront what he was doing.

David got home around 6:00. He said hello and gave Jenna a perfunctory kiss. He went over to Bobby's bouncy seat and spoke to him for a few minutes before going into the bedroom to change.

When he came back out, he asked Jenna how her day had been, but it felt to her as if he were going through the motions, just like the kiss he had given her. She asked about his day and got the standard "same old, same old" response.

After a few more minutes of small talk, Jenna shifted her position on the couch and said, "David, we need to talk." She had uttered those very same words a number of times recently, so she followed them up with something stronger. "We can't keep going on like this."

That got his attention. "What do you mean?"

David's feigned ignorance about what she meant angered her. "You want a list?—You come home later and later; you haven't made a journal entry in weeks; you haven't even *read* the journal in weeks. You act like we're roommates sharing an apartment. And the only time you spend with the baby is right when you get home and when I put him to bed."

David stared at her for a moment before speaking. "I have to put in extra hours at work, Jenna. I wish I didn't, but I do. And when I get home, I'm tired."

Jenna interrupted. "Out of everything I just said that's your response?"

"It's the truth."

"No. I'm not letting you off the hook that easily. You can deny it all you want, but we both know this is about Bobby."

David started to protest, but then his shoulders sagged as he put his hands over his eyes and fell back against the sofa cushions. After a minute he sat up again. Tears were evident as he spoke. "You're right. I've been trying to sort everything out, but . . . ."

Jenna went to him, and they held each other for what seemed like a long time. When they separated, Jenna spoke first. "Please don't shut me out, David. We need to face this together."

David nodded and expelled a sigh. "I just don't know how I'm going to handle it, if it turns out that Bobby . . . ." He couldn't finish.

Jenna was about to interject, but she could see from his expression that he had more to say. "I feel like we keep getting kicked in the teeth. First, my father changes the trust fund, which means that we can't get married. Then he gets sick, and I've just started to accept the fact that he may never get better—and then this. It's like we don't have any control over our own lives." He looked away for a moment before resuming eye contact. "Somehow, I feel like I've been able to deal with all the other stuff, as tough as it's been. But this, with Bobby, I don't even know where to begin."

Jenna began to tear up as she grasped his hand. "I don't have any answers either, David. But shouldn't we at least be talking about it, and trying to figure it out together?"

He nodded. "It's just that—and I know that it doesn't seem like it—but right now, I'm doing the best I can." He paused. "I think about it all day at work. And then when I come home, I know it's stupid, but I expect to see some change, some miracle." He stopped again. "Most nights I just lie there pretending to be asleep, so I don't wake you."

A trace of a smile formed on Jenna's lips. "I do the same thing."

David gave a half-smile in return. "I don't know what to do. I've never felt so helpless in my whole life."

They were quiet for a few moments, and then something seemed to shift in David, like the tumblers on a lock falling into place. He looked intently at Jenna and said, "You do know that this doesn't have anything to do with us, I mean you and me?"

"I know that."

He stared at her and sighed. "Okay, I promise I'll try to do better."

At the doctor's appointment on Friday, there was nothing new. Dr. Millwood reviewed the journal entries and encouraged both Jenna and David to continue to do what they were doing. "We're probably not going to see much change in such a short amount of time, but over the course of several months, we may."

Jenna spoke up. "A friend of ours, who's a teacher, gave us some books about special needs children that outline some strategies that teachers use. Most of them are for children much older than Bobby. Do you think we should try them anyway?"

"I'd say yes. Early intervention has been shown to be crucial in helping children with developmental delays. But there are no conclusive studies involving children as young as Bobby. Still, that doesn't mean you shouldn't give them a try. They certainly can't hurt."

"Are there any specific activities you'd recommend?"

Dr. Millwood pondered the question briefly. "Did they mention 'floor time' in any of the books?"

"Yes, I think so." Jenna looked toward David. "You were reading some of them last night. Do you remember that?"

"Actually I do. But honestly, there didn't seem to be much to it. Isn't it just playing with the baby on the floor?"

Dr Millwood smiled. "In essence, yes. But it often forces the child to make eye contact and interact with the adult next to him. It tends to be more effective when the baby can sit up on his own. But regardless, I think this is something you could begin to use with Bobby."

True to his word of "trying to do better," as soon as they got home, David put a blanket down on the floor, gathered up Bobby and a bunch of toys and attempted to engage his son. David stayed on all fours for a full half hour, encouraging Bobby with both verbal cues and physical nudges. At the end of the thirty minutes, David made an extensive journal entry.

For the next few weeks, David made "floor time" a standard ritual at least three times a week. But soon after the next doctor's appointment, when there didn't appear to be much improvement, he started to pull back. Soon "floor time" was down to once a week.

Jenna confronted David again. However this time his reasons for backing off seemed to have some merit. "I'm not sure I see the point, Jenna. You see the way he is with me. He responds much better to you. I'll help out with other stuff, but it doesn't make sense for me to keep doing 'floor time' with him."

Jenna had to acknowledge that David's words had some validity, but she couldn't help wondering if his desire to pull back wasn't primarily emotional. It had to be difficult to continue to invest so much energy in what he was doing with Bobby, and then receive almost nothing in return.

A week later Jenna finally shared everything about Bobby's suspected condition with Barbara. As usual, she proved to be an exceptional listener. And despite the fact that Toby's limitations were not the same as Bobby's might turn out to be, the experience of raising a child with challenges had given Barbara a wealth of insight.

Midway through their conversation, Jenna said, "I feel like I'm doing this on my own. David is having a lot of difficulty accepting this. He's not as involved as he should be. Although part of me understands . . . how did you ever do it by yourself?"

Barbara smiled. "I don't know; you just do." Her smile faded. "My husband ran off with someone before Toby's first birthday, so he doesn't even remember his father. Then it was just the two of us, and he needed me, so . . . ." She paused, appearing slightly uncomfortable. "If I'm prying just tell me, but how do you mean that David's not really involved?"

"No, you're not prying. I brought it up."

Jenna went on to explain about her initial confrontation with David, and then all about the follow-ups, including the most recent discussion about "floor time."

Barbara then asked. "Do you think it's true that Bobby *does* respond better to you than to David?"

"Probably. No, I'd say definitely. But I can't help wondering if that's because I spend so much more time with him."

"That could be. Have you asked the doctor?"

"No I haven't; David's with me at every appointment. I don't want to embarrass him."

"I understand that, Jenna. But I think you need to find out about this. Why not give the doctor a call? He might even be able to talk to David about how important it is for him to be more involved."

"I think I'll give it a little more time, and then, if things don't improve, then that's what I'll do."

But July turned into August, and Jenna still hadn't made the call.

With only a few weeks before the end of summer, Trish came out to visit. Jenna fully intended to tell her best friend what the doctor suspected about Bobby, but she never got to it. Jenna could tell that Trish was excited about something as soon as she walked through the door. She wasn't inside the apartment for more than five minutes when she announced that she was engaged.

Jenna was genuinely thrilled for her former roommate, so it didn't seem right to rain on her parade with news about Bobby's issues. Jenna did acknowledge to herself however, that if she didn't have Barbara to serve as a sounding board, she would have told Trish everything.

It also helped that Bobby was on his best behavior during the visit. If he had thrown one of his temper tantrums, Jenna wasn't sure how she would have handled it.

Over the course of the summer, Jeremy stopped by on a weekly basis. On a couple of occasions before David had arrived home from work, Jenna opened up to Jeremy about David's detachment. Jeremy again offered to talk to David, but Jenna declined the offer, although she wasn't sure why.

She did ask Jeremy to read some more of the journal entries, which he gladly did. When he came across the words "floor time," he asked what that was all about. Instead of trying to explain it, Jenna showed him.

Jeremy took to it very easily. And by the end of August, Bobby seemed to be even more engaged with Jeremy than with either of his parents. It appeared that the amount of time someone spent with Bobby didn't necessarily correlate with his ability to be engaged. That realization was all the impetus Jenna needed to have another talk with David.

She was a little concerned that he might be upset, even jealous, about how well Bobby was responding to Jeremy. And at first, he did appear to be put out, but then his attitude changed. And during September and October he resumed spending additional time with Bobby. Although the progress they saw was slow in coming, both David and Jenna agreed that it was progress nonetheless.

At the doctor's visit a few weeks before Thanksgiving, Jenna and David heard some optimism in Dr. Millwood's voice for the first time. "It looks like we're seeing a spike in sustained eye contact. And although he's not talking, the sounds he's making are much more appropriate. Also from what I read in your journal entries, he seems to be much more responsive to outside stimuli – voices, the TV, things like that."

David asked, "So, what does all that mean?"

"It still appears that there are very significant delays, *but* because of what we're seeing, it may be that Bobby's going to be able to find some ways to compensate for some of his limitations."

David's range of emotions showed on his face. Finally, he asked, "So even though we're seeing all this progress, he's still going to have problems."

"Most likely. But the two of you are doing all the right things. I know that it doesn't necessarily sound like it, but what I'm telling you is good news, especially considering where Bobby was a few months ago." He paused. "After your last visit when we first started to see some of these positive signs, I called the Developmental Diagnostic Center. I asked if they would be willing to evaluate Bobby, even though, as I think I told you, they don't usually do that until the child is closer to eighteen months old. I heard back from them a few days ago. They've agreed to see Bobby the second week in February."

David's face brightened. "Really?"

The doctor nodded and smiled. "But it's important to focus on the purpose of the evaluation. The Center has an excellent reputation, and I suspect they're going to be able to give us a much clearer diagnosis." The doctor leaned forward. "Knowing with more specificity what Bobby's facing will help us going forward." He looked directly at David. "I believe we're going to be able to help your son, but we still have to be realistic.

There's a strong likelihood that these issues will be with him for the rest of his life."

Following the doctor's visit, and for the next two weeks, David was torn. Part of him wanted to just wait until February to find out what the Center had to say. But another part of him thought that continuing the regimen he had reestablished with Bobby would somehow change the evaluation results. He finally decided to go with the second choice, although if he had been pressed to explain why, he might have realized that it was more for Jenna's benefit than any other reason.

And then, a few days before Thanksgiving something happened which threatened to throw David and Jenna's life into further turmoil.

CHAPTER 35

David hadn't been to Phil Jenkins' office in nearly two months. They had talked on the phone and e-mailed back and forth a few times each week, but there had been no face-to-face conversations since the early fall.

"Thanks for coming in, David."

"Sure."

"I know you've been anxious about what's going to happen after your contract extension is up, and also about phases two and three. Well, I've finally been able to put together a plan that will get the company to where I want it to be." Jenkins smiled. "And I would like you to be part of that."

Although much of the wariness David felt toward Phil Jenkins had begun to fade, he wasn't able to shake it completely. He kept his response neutral. "Okay."

Jenkins appeared a little surprised by David's lack of enthusiasm, but he didn't allow it to deter him. "Let me outline what I have in mind, and then you can jump in with whatever questions you might have." He sat forward before continuing. "I've carefully analyzed both the Boston and New York properties that we own, and it's very clear that the potential profit margins are much higher in New York." Jenkins let that sink in for a moment. "So I've decided to utilize the money originally set aside for phases two and three in Boston and replicate the upgrades we did here to a number of our properties in New York."

David had suspected something like this might be coming. But hearing it directly, and so matter-of-factly, pulled him up short. He recovered enough to say, "I guess I'm not exactly surprised." He studied Jenkins briefly. "How soon are you talking about? What's the time frame?"

"A couple of months."

"You're going to start this during the winter?"

248

"Some of the preliminary work, yes. But the actual upgrades won't begin until the spring."

"How do I figure into all of this?"

Jenkins didn't hesitate. "I want you to supervise the entire operation."

"In New York?"

"Yes." He studied David, before continuing. "I anticipated there might be some reluctance on your part, so I'm prepared to make it worth your while."

"No matter what you're offering, I don't see how I can do that."

"Hear me out, okay?"

David was too shell-shocked to object. "Okay."

"I've given this a lot of thought, and there's no question in my mind that with your track record, you're the right person for this. So, I'm prepared to offer you a $10,000 a year raise and a two-year contract. If I'm not mistaken, from what you've told me, at the end of the contract you'll be very close to the time when your trust fund becomes available."

David was initially surprised by the terms of the offer, and then by the fact that Jenkins had remembered the details of his trust fund. As those thoughts flashed across his mind, he responded with a gut reaction. "I don't see how I can uproot my family no matter what the offer happens to be. I mean, I appreciate . . . ."

Jenkins raised his hands to slow David down. "I know how difficult any kind of change can be. I've just been through it myself. So, I'm willing to make the move even more attractive." He paused. "Obviously, we'll pay for all your moving expenses, but more importantly, we'll set you up in an apartment in New York where you can live rent-free."

"What?"

"One of the complexes we're planning to refurbish is just over the border in Nassau County on Long Island. It's in a very nice area. You can pick out the apartment you want, and we'll refurbish it any way you like. Before you move in, we'll show it to other prospective tenants as the model." Jenkins smiled as he emphasized what he had said earlier. "And you get to live there for free, including utilities."

David's initial reluctance to entertain any of what Phil Jenkins was offering started to waver. He had to admit the rent-free apartment was a very attractive bonus. And exactly what was holding him here? But then an image of his father's face entered his mind.

As if he could perceive David's thoughts, Jenkins looked at him and somberly added, "I'm sure it will be difficult being so far away from your father, but—and please don't take this the wrong way—I understand that his situation hasn't really changed much. Isn't that correct?"

"Yes, but . . . ." David started to say that he still visited his father once a week, but that hadn't been the case for months. He was trying to gather his thoughts when Jenkins spoke again.

"Frankly, David, I think if your father were able to, he'd encourage you to jump at this opportunity."

Although he hated to admit it, Jenkins' assessment made sense. Instead of acknowledging that, however, David changed direction. "What happens if I can't see my way clear to doing this, to move? What happens then?"

"I sincerely hope it doesn't come to that, but I guess I could keep you on for another six months. But that would still require you to go to New York. I'd need you to get the person we hire up to speed." Jenkins paused. "Look David, I really want you to oversee this operation. If there's something I haven't thought of that would make the transition easier, let me know and we'll work something out. But I have to tell you, I think a two-year contract with a substantial raise, plus a newly renovated apartment rent free is a very sweet deal."

David didn't speak right away. Jenkins could be very persuasive, but in this instance he didn't need to be—the offer spoke for itself. Finally, David asked, "When do you need an answer?"

"Soon. Let's say a couple of weeks."

"When would I have to be in New York?"

"Ideally, right after the first of the year."

"That's only six weeks from now."

"I know. That's why I said 'ideally.' I could probably stretch it a few weeks beyond that, if you needed the extra time."

"Obviously, I have to talk this over with Jenna."

"Of course. She's not from around here, is she?"

David looked puzzled. "No. Why?"

"I was just thinking that if she had family in the area, it would make things more difficult."

"I think it's going to be difficult no matter what."

Immediately after he left Phil Jenkins' office, David's inclination was to call Alan Fenton and then Jenna. But he resisted doing either. Instead, he left his car in the parking garage and walked to a coffee shop a few blocks away. He needed some time by himself to think about everything that had just happened.

The line at the coffee shop moved rapidly, and after a few minutes David was able to find a small table in the back that was intended for two people, but barely accommodated him and the large cup of coffee he had ordered.

The first thoughts that entered his mind as he sat down surprised him. *Maybe moving to New York isn't such a bad thing. Other than my father, there really isn't anything holding me here. And if Jenkins isn't going forward with phases two and three, I'd be out of a job anyway. Two years of employment in New York is a hell of a lot better than nothing here. Plus, Jenkins is right. Once I finish the two years, it'll only be a few months until I have access to the trust fund.*

His mind shifted. *But what about my father? I guess I could come back once a month or so. That's all I'm seeing him now, anyway.*

Another shift. *Jenna is going to hate this. She won't want any part of it. But what choice do we have? I'm sure the first thing she'll say is that we have to think about what's best for Bobby. But they've got to have excellent doctors in New York who specialize in this kind of thing.* He took a sip of coffee. *But then what about his evaluation? Maybe we could come back up here in February, just for that, if we need to.*

David shifted in his chair. *Why am I trying to find ways to make this work? Is this what I really want? I wonder if the fact that I'm even considering it has anything to do with not wanting to disappoint Jenkins. I don't know. But it's not as if everything in Boston has been so great for the last year. Maybe we could use a change."*

David spent an additional fifteen minutes nursing his coffee while focusing his attention on trying to anticipate Jenna's arguments and ways to refute them. Just before he left, he decided against calling Alan Fenton. Jenna had been somewhat upset the last time David had received big news regarding work, and he had told Alan first.

If David were going to convince Jenna that moving to New York was not such a bad thing, he didn't need any "who knew about this first" issue to get in the way.

As David opened the door to the apartment, Jenna was just entering the living room. She looked startled, as she raised her hand to her chest. "You scared me. Is everything all right? Why are you home so early?"

"I cut some things short because of Thanksgiving."

"That's not a problem?"

"No. Everything's fine. I planned on a short week, anyway."

"I wish I had known. I just put Bobby in for a nap. We could have gone out for lunch or something."

"It's fine." He paused. "Plus, it'll give us a chance to talk. Why don't we sit down?"

"Are you sure everything's all right?"

David ignored the question. "I met with Phil Jenkins today."

"Oh, was that today? I forgot about that."

"I didn't think it was a big deal either, but he's made some decisions that are going to affect us."

"Like what?"

"Well actually, most of it's good news. Once my current contract is up in a few months, he's offered me another two-year contract with a ten thousand dollar raise."

Jenna reached over and hugged David. "That's terrific."

After they broke their embrace, Jenna said, "You don't seem all that happy about it. What's the matter?"

"Well, there are some conditions."

"What conditions?"

David avoided the question. "Jenkins even offered us an apartment, rent free."

"You're kidding. A free apartment?"

"Yes."

Again, when David didn't show the enthusiasm she expected, she became wary. "So, what's the problem?"

"If I accept the offer, we have to move."

"To where?"

David avoided eye contact. "We'd have to move to New York."

"New York? Why?"

"Jenkins is going to use the money from phases two and three to refurbish property in New York. He wants me to oversee everything, just like I did here."

Jenna stood up. "We can't move to New York!"

"I know it's a shock. It was for me too, but then the more I thought about it, it didn't seem so bad."

"How can you say that? What about Bobby?"

"I know; that's the first thing that came into my mind. But I'm sure there are excellent doctors in New York."

Jenna stared at David, sensing that his response came so quickly that it had to have been rehearsed. "But he's making real progress here. And what about the Center in Canton? They don't have that in New York."

"I know, but if you want, we could come back up in February and still have the evaluation done here."

"Come back? When are we supposed to move?"

"Sometime in January."

"You can't be serious. That's a few weeks from now."

David forced himself to remain calm. "I know this came out of the blue . . . ."

"I can't believe you're even considering this."

This time when he spoke, a spark of anger was there. "And what choice do you think we have? If I don't agree to this, I'm out of a job. Then what are we supposed to do?"

Jenna stared at David a moment before she spoke. "There has to be another way."

"If you have any ideas, I'm listening."

Jenna shook her head. She didn't have a clue how to resolve this. But her instincts were telling her that she had to throw up every roadblock she could think of. "And what about your father?"

"I'll make time once a month or so to come up and see him."

Again, she felt certain that David's pat answer had been rehearsed. It angered Jenna, although she didn't mean for her words to sound as accusatory as they did. "You're barely seeing him that often now, and he's only a few miles away."

Jenna could see that her comment stung David. She reached for his hand and said, "I'm sorry, I didn't mean it the way it came out."

"It's all right."

They were quiet for a moment and then something else occurred to Jenna. She spoke calmly, trying to get her emotions under control. "What about health insurance?"

"What about it?"

"Well, Bobby's covered under your plan. But we don't even know if they have that plan in New York."

"I'm sure they must. But even if they don't, what difference does it make; we'll sign up for another one."

Jenna was having trouble keeping her frustration in check. "It's just not that easy, David; not all companies cover treatment for autism."

"Bobby hasn't even been diagnosed with anything yet."

"That's not the point!"

"I'm sure both states have the health plan. After all, Jenkins moved here from New York."

"He's living in your father's townhouse, but I'll bet his legal residence is still New York."

David raised his hands, and his tone became dismissive. "Okay, I'll check on the insurance, but I'm sure it's going to be fine."

"You don't know that! And what about me?"

"What do you mean?"

"Once my COBRA extension runs out, I won't have any insurance. Since we're not married, I can't be on your policy, remember?"

Now David felt as if Jenna were blaming him for the fact that they hadn't been able to get married. But he bit his tongue before he spoke. "Once your extension runs out, we'd have to buy insurance for you no matter where we live."

"But there are special programs in Massachusetts that they may not have in New York." Jenna expelled a mouthful of air. "I don't even know why I brought that up. That's the least of it. This has to be about what's best for Bobby, and moving to New York isn't it."

David started to protest, but realized anything he said at that moment to contradict Jenna would make things worse. Finally, he said, "I'm not sure what you want me to do, Jenna. This is exactly what I've been talking about for months. I don't have any control over my own life. It's like all the decisions I should be making are already made for me."

Prior to the meeting with Phil Jenkins, David had been looking forward to a quiet Thanksgiving weekend. Now, it was anything but. He and Jenna continued to hash out all of their options, which they both admitted were limited.

By Sunday night they had finally agreed on what had to be done. Jenna hated it, and David appeared not to like it much better. But as they both acknowledged – they really had little choice.

First thing Monday morning, David ran it by Phil Jenkins who didn't have any problem with what David was proposing. Jenkins did his best to seem empathetic, but David wasn't buying it. Jenkins seemed about as sincere as one of those automated voices that suggest, "Your call is very important to us," and then keep you on hold for twenty minutes. Nevertheless, David did appreciate Jenkins' willingness to tweak some of the terms of the contract to accommodate him.

In essence, the plan they had worked out had David moving to New York after the first of the year by himself. He would live in the apartment Jenkins had offered, and then he would travel back to Massachusetts each weekend.

After Bobby's evaluation in February, they would decide whether it made sense for Jenna and Bobby to stay in Massachusetts or move to New York.

Although she said she would keep an open mind, Jenna was certain that she wouldn't be moving to New York. The idea of David not being with her during the week was almost unbearable. But the thought of leaving everybody she had come to trust, especially Dr. Millwood, and thrusting her son into unknown situations with strangers was far worse.

CHAPTER 36

On the Saturday following Christmas, David and Jenna held a small party to celebrate Bobby's first birthday. Jeremy, Trish and her fiancée, Kevin, as well as Barbara and her son, Toby, were the only invited guests.

Considering that Bobby usually reacted negatively to having a lot of people around, and became even more distressed by the loud noise they generated, he tolerated the afternoon very well. Undoubtedly, part of the reason for that was the extended one-on-one time both Jeremy and Toby spent with him. Jenna wasn't surprised at how engaged Bobby was with Jeremy, but his positive interaction with Toby was something she hadn't expected.

About an hour into the party, Jenna and Trish were able to steal a few minutes in the kitchen to talk in private. Jenna opened up the conversation. "I really like Kevin."

"Me too," responded Trish. "I know it was silly of me, but I made that a prerequisite for anyone I was going to marry."

Jenna gave her a tap on the arm. "You haven't changed."

Trish smiled. "Actually, he is pretty terrific. He makes me laugh, and he's . . . just a nice guy. Plus, he's not too tough on the eyes."

Jenna smiled. "No, he's not. If nothing else, you two certainly have that in common."

"Well, thank you. But I think best friends and future maids of honor are supposed to say that."

Jenna hesitated briefly. "Speaking of that, have you set a date yet?"

"Tentatively, next September."

"Really?"

"Yeah, I wanted to wait until after graduation. Plus, weddings in the summer are so much more expensive; the fall seemed to work best. I hope that's not going to be a problem for you."

"It shouldn't be."

"You know, when we talked last week about David taking the job in New York, I wasn't just thinking about the wedding date."

Jenna put on a happy face. "Well, as long as you're planning on having the wedding on a weekend, then David should be available."

Trish smiled. "You know that's not what I meant." A pause. "Seriously, how are you going to handle everything with David being away so much?"

Jenna dropped the happy face. "I'm not quite sure. We went down to Long Island a couple of weeks ago to pick out some of the things for the apartment they're going to redo for David. It's in a real nice area."

Trish stared at her friend as she spoke. "Why did you make it sound like David's going to be there by himself? I thought you and Bobby were going to move down there too."

"When I talked to you, I was still trying to force myself to think that way. But I don't see how that's going to be possible."

"Why not?"

"Bobby's doctor is here, and the evaluation is in a few weeks. I can't imagine that things are going to change so dramatically that I'd be comfortable moving."

"Does David know?"

"Not really. I mean, I told him that we could decide after the evaluation, and we will. But I doubt my feelings are going to change."

"Wow."

"Yeah, wow."

"Listen Jenna, I'll try to come out as often as I can."

Jenna touched Trish's arm. "I appreciate that, but you're going to be on overload yourself – senior year and a wedding to plan." Jenna paused. "I think it's going to all right. Barbara's been great, and she's right here in the building. Plus, Jeremy said he'll stop by once a week or so."

"At least promise me that you'll call if there's anything I can do."

"I will."

They were quiet for a moment and then Trish said, "It was good to see Jeremy again. What's his story, anyway? Is he seeing anyone?"

"Nothing serious. I think he's dated a few teachers at his school, but that's it."

"That's too bad. He deserves to be with someone."

"Yeah, he does. And you should see how Bobby takes to him."

"I remember you told me that."

They were quiet again, and then Jenna broke the silence. "I guess we should probably get back to the party."

"Sure." Trish smiled. "But the guys were talking sports when we left. I'll bet they didn't even know we were gone."

A week later, David made the move to New York. He and Jenna spoke on the phone every night, and every night when they hung up, they were both close to tears. Having most of Saturday and Sunday together barely allowed them to survive the weekdays apart.

But after a few weeks, David at least, had begun to better adjust to the separation. The demands of his job allowed him to put the situation out of his mind for periods of time.

That wasn't the case for Jenna.

Her job was taking care of Bobby, which only served to magnify how much she wanted David to be there to help out.

If it hadn't been for Barbara and Jeremy, Jenna wasn't sure what she would have done. Barbara stopped by a few times each week, and Jeremy established a regular Thursday afternoon visit. Just the presence of another adult, and the conversation it brought with it, allowed her to hold on.

Bobby's evaluation was scheduled for the second Friday in February. David had planned to leave New York the day before at about 10:00 in the morning. A few minutes before that, Jenna received a phone call. She read the display and said, "Hi. Are you on the road yet?"

"No, it's a mess down here."

"What do you mean?"

"Snow. When I went to bed last night, they were calling for a dusting, but we must have at least eight inches on the ground. Anything up there?"

"No, nothing. And I don't think they're expecting anything. What are the roads like?"

"They're advising people to stay home, but I'm not going to miss the evaluation."

"David, if it's dangerous . . . ."

He didn't react to Jenna's concern. "I can't believe this."

"What's the forecast like?"

"They don't think it's going to let up until tonight."

"Then please don't think about coming up now. I'd be a nervous wreck the whole time."

"What I could do is get up real early tomorrow and head up then. The appointment's not until 11:00, right?"

"Yeah." Jenna hesitated. "I think I'd feel better if you did that."

"I guess. Okay." David paused. "Listen, I've got to make a couple of calls. I'll talk to you later."

Jenna's voice was filled with concern. "David, you're not planning . . . ."

"No, I promise. I really do have to make some calls. I'll talk to you tonight."

Jeremy showed up as usual that afternoon. Even before he started to play with Bobby, Jenna told him about her conversation with David.

"If he can't make it back for the evaluation, I'm off tomorrow. I can go with you," said Jeremy.

"How come you're off tomorrow?"

"School vacation week."

"Oh, I forgot about that." Jenna was obviously weighing something in her mind. After a moment she spoke up. "Well, I really would like to have someone with me. Are you sure you don't mind?"

"Not at all. Just give me a call in the morning, and let me know."

"That'd be great. Thanks."

"Not a problem."

When David called Jenna later that night, the news was not good. The New York area was expected to receive an additional eighteen inches on top of the foot they already had. It wasn't scheduled to let up until Friday afternoon.

"I don't know what I can do, Jenna. It doesn't look like I can drive. The airports are closed. The only possibility might be the train. But, there's nothing tonight, and I don't know if they'll be running tomorrow. I'm not sure I could get to the train station, even if they were." David paused. "Boston is still not getting anything?"

"No, it's all south of here."

"I guess that's for the best. I'd hate to see the evaluation cancelled; it took so long to get it." David's voice became filled with increased frustration. "God damn it. The one day I need to get back and this happens."

"Promise me you won't do anything foolish."

"It's just that . . . ."

"Please, David."

"All right, I promise." The frustration left his voice. "I'll call you early tomorrow morning and let you know what's happening."

"Okay." Jenna was silent for a moment. "I called the Center earlier."

"How come?"

"I wanted to find out if there might be an open date anytime soon, but there wasn't. The earliest we could reschedule is three months from now."

"We can't do that!"

"I know. I agree. I did find out one piece of good news. Even though they're doing the evaluation tomorrow, the results won't be ready for a few weeks. It's probably more important that you're available for that, rather than for the actual evaluation."

"It sounds like you're just trying to make me feel better?"

"No really, that's what they said."

"Well that's something, I guess. But I should be there for both of them."

"It's not your fault." Jenna wasn't sure why she hadn't mentioned it earlier, but she knew she had to bring it up before tomorrow. "Jeremy came by today."

"Oh right, it's Thursday."

"I told him about the storm, and he volunteered to come with me tomorrow if you can't make it."

David had a brief negative reaction to the news, but he kept it out of his voice. "Doesn't he have to work?"

"No, it's school vacation week."

David hesitated. "Well then, sure. That'd be great."

"I said I'd call him in the morning as soon as I heard from you."

David tried to keep his voice light. "I'll probably be calling pretty early; he won't mind?"

"He said it wasn't a problem."

"All right then. I guess I'll talk to you in the morning."

"Okay. I love you."

"I love you, too."

The prospect of Jeremy going to Bobby's evaluation instead of him ate away at David the whole night. While it made no logical sense that it should bother him that much, it did, and he barely slept.

A few times during the night he vowed to himself that he was going to drive to Massachusetts no matter what. But by the time daylight arrived, a quick glance out the window made him realize that trying to drive anywhere, never mind two hundred and fifty miles, bordered on a death wish.

He called Jenna at 4:45. She sounded relieved that he had decided not to attempt the trip. She assured him that she would write down everything that happened and would call as soon as she got back home. At the end of their conversation, she added, "The most important part of this whole thing are the doctor's findings, and you'll be here for that."

David tried to convince himself that Jenna was right, but wasn't very successful.

Jeremy picked up Bobby and Jenna at 10:30, and they arrived in Canton twenty minutes later. They were ushered into a doctor's office at exactly eleven o'clock. After introductions and some preliminary general health questions, the doctor explained what was going to happen.

"We'll take all of Bobby's vital signs, and then we'll observe his behavior for about fifteen minutes in a room with a two-way mirror. You'll be able to watch the whole time. The room will be filled with toys and various other objects with which he's familiar. The only thing we ask is that you don't say anything while we're observing him because the technicians have to take very detailed notes. We'll give Bobby a short break after that, and then you can ask whatever questions you might have."

Jenna asked, "What if he just sits there, or he just cries the whole time?"

"Well, that would tell us something, too. But that kind of behavior for that amount of time would be very unusual. Does he do that at home?"

Jenna was pleased that she could answer truthfully. "Maybe when he was younger, but not now."

The doctor outlined a number of additional activities that Bobby would be involved in, and then he talked about the last test that would be conducted.

"When human beings process information, even babies, they go through physical changes. The pulse rate increases and blood pressure is affected. So before we do the final activity with Bobby, which I'll explain in a moment, we'll put sensors on him to measure what's happening."

The doctor paused for a moment to make sure Jenna and Jeremy were following him. "For the last activity today, we'll place Bobby in front of a puppet theater. We'll roll a ball down an inclined track. At the end of the track will be some small bowling pins, which the ball will knock down. We'll repeat this two more times. On the fourth time we'll start the ball down the track, but then close the curtains to the puppet theater before Bobby can see what happens. One of the technicians will even stop the ball so there's no sound." The doctor paused briefly. "If Bobby is processing what's about to happen, then the sensors will record the physical changes."

Jeremy didn't want to overstep his bounds, so he looked at Jenna to see if it would be all right to ask a question. She anticipated what Jeremy was about to say and simply nodded.

Jeremy went ahead. "Wouldn't almost every child be able to mentally predict what was going to happen?"

"The vast majority, yes. But those that can't—they usually have serious cognitive limitations. We have to rule that out in order to make an appropriate diagnosis."

The doctor could see alarm on Jenna's face. He tried to reassure her. "I should emphasize that nothing I've read in Dr. Millwood's notes suggests that that's the situation here. We just need to rule it out."

Jenna asked a few more questions, and then it was time for the formal evaluation to begin. As she watched through the two-way mirror, she silently rooted for Bobby to do certain things. She mentally chided herself—*This is supposed to be an evaluation, not a contest.* But she knew that when it came to your own child, you couldn't help but compare him to what other children were doing. What parent didn't want their children walking before other children or talking before other children? Or in this case, just being able to anticipate that some small bowling pins would fall down?

CHAPTER 37

By the time the snow let up in New York it was Saturday night. David toyed with the idea of driving to Massachusetts early the following morning, but that would only have given him a few hours at home before he had to turn around and drive back. Making that effort would have assuaged some of the guilt he was feeling but would have accomplished little else. So he stayed in New York.

Over the next two weeks, Jenna had few waking moments when she wasn't thinking about what Bobby's evaluation might reveal. It was pretty much the exclusive topic of conversation with David, her mother, Barbara, and Trish. And with everyone but David, she was able to acknowledge that she was expecting Bobby to be diagnosed with some form of autism. Expressing that to David wasn't something she could bring herself to do.

Finally, the first Monday in March was upon them, and it was time to find out the results. Jenna was as nervous as she'd ever been in her life. It was as if she were in a courtroom waiting for the jury to return its verdict.

Outwardly, David appeared less nervous, but inside he was a wreck. He had arranged to extend his stay in Massachusetts for a few days, not only to attend the follow-up to the evaluation, but also to deal with whatever fallout there might be from the results.

David had made the suggestion that Jenna ask Barbara to baby-sit. He reasoned that Bobby's behavior during their meeting with the doctor could be a distraction. Jenna couldn't help but think that David had another motive for not wanting Bobby there – the more the doctors saw of Bobby, the more they might find his actions inappropriate. That notion hadn't come totally out of the blue. David had often expressed a similar idea prior to their appointments with Dr. Millwood.

David and Jenna arrived at the Center about ten minutes early and were immediately shown into a small office. A tall man dressed in a suit, who appeared to be in his fifties, greeted them. "Please come in and sit down. I'm Dr. Townsend."

They shook hands, and once David and Jenna were settled into their seats across from the doctor, he opened up a thick binder on his desk and said, "Before we begin there are a few things I wanted you to be aware of. The Center has been in existence for nearly twenty years, and I believe that it's one of the finest facilities of its kind in the country." He smiled. "Of course, you might expect me to say that. But most of the experts in the field all over the country seem to agree. Despite our reputation however, any institution that focuses on cognitive diagnoses, particularly in very young children, has to tread carefully.

"In many instances we have to make judgments based solely on observing symptoms because for many of the syndromes and conditions we're dealing with, their root causes still haven't been identified. That means that our diagnoses can't be as precise as we'd like. Having said that, however, our track record is still quite impressive. And what we've discovered over the last two decades is that even if we don't know what causes something, treating the symptoms of that condition can be nearly as effective."

Dr. Townsend paused to let everything sink in before continuing. "In your son's case there are some very positive signs. He's definitely processing information. For example, there were substantial physiological changes during the inclined plane activity with the bowling pins."

David looked puzzled until he remembered Jenna's description of the puppet theater. And although he felt a twinge of guilt as he was reminded of the fact that he had missed the evaluation, he gave a nod of understanding.

Dr. Townsend was about to offer an explanation until he saw David's expression change, and then he continued to describe some additional observations. "Your son's aversion to being picked up or even touched, as you recorded in some of your journal entries, seems to have dissipated substantially."

Jenna offered, "Yes, he's gotten much better about that."

Dr. Townsend smiled. "I'm sure that makes things a lot easier at home."

"Yes, definitely."

The doctor turned one of the pages in the binder and said, "We also observed that Bobby's interaction with some of the toys and other objects was more appropriate than we had expected, especially after reviewing Dr. Millwood's notes."

David sat forward, obviously pleased. "Like what?"

"Well, he actually played with the toy cars in a very appropriate manner. The same thing with the blocks and the cardboard books."

"And that's important?" asked David.

"Yes. Some children throw the cars or use the books to hit other objects, but he didn't. Undoubtedly, he was exhibiting learned behavior, but that in itself is significant."

Jenna questioned, "Why is that?"

"Because his actions are telling us that he can mimic what he sees other people doing. That's how babies learn, and we now know that Bobby has that capability."

David said, "All of this is good news, right? So are you saying that he may not have any of the delays Dr. Millwood talked about?"

"What I've described so far is definitely good news, especially in the long term." He paused. "However, some of our other observations revealed things that are more problematic."

David sat back, deflated.

Jenna glanced David's way and then spoke up. "What do you mean?"

Dr. Townsend spoke more deliberately. "On a number of occasions when Bobby was engaged in some activity, it was extremely difficult to get his attention."

David spoke again. "I thought you said it was a good thing for him to be more engaged."

"It is, but not to the exclusion of everything else around him. At times he seemed to withdraw into his own world, and it was nearly impossible to draw his attention away from what he was doing. That's not typical of children his age."

Jenna acknowledged to herself that she had seen Bobby exhibit the very same behavior at home. She was about to confirm that, but decided to let the doctor continue instead.

"We also discovered that when we were able to get his attention by calling his name, it appeared that he was really responding to the sound of someone's voice and not specifically to his name. In fact, when we called him by another name, or used a nonsensical word to try to get his attention, he responded in exactly the same way. Again, that's not typical. All toddlers tend to be egocentric, but Bobby doesn't appear to realize that he's a separate entity. He doesn't know that he's not part of the things around him."

David raised his voice slightly. "That doesn't make any sense. How could you possibly know that?"

"You're right, of course. We can't with a complete degree of certainty. But what all the research tells us is that children who respond as Bobby did usually have significant delays. They often have trouble understanding and internalizing causal relationships; they usually can't generalize very easily, and they have great difficulty interpreting non-verbal cues such as facial expressions or body language. The theory is that since they can't view themselves as separate beings, they're not able to conceive how their actions impact on anything around them."

As the doctor continued to explain other aspects of the theory, David sank into himself. The doctor's initial pronouncements had given David hope, but then the negative side of the ledger had quickly filled up.

Finally, as the doctor was concluding his remarks, David steeled himself to ask the question that he desperately wanted to know the answer to, but was truly afraid to broach. "What do you think is wrong?"

The doctor started to take exception to the word "wrong," but thought better of it. Instead he said, "We believe that Bobby is somewhere on the autism spectrum, but at this age it's very difficult to pinpoint exactly where."

Jenna had known in her heart of hearts that this was coming. But hearing the words out loud from an expert like Dr. Townsend, and in this setting, had more of an effect on her than she could have imagined.

Surprisingly, just at that moment her mind jumped, and she thought back to when she was a little girl. She had always loved rainbows. She had rainbow key chains, and rainbow sneakers, and notebooks with rainbows on the front. And then one day in school, she had learned that the scientific name for a rainbow was a spectrum. She remembered how disappointed she was – How could anything so magical have such an ordinary name?

She couldn't help but think that her disappointment as a little girl was a foreshadowing of this moment, and how the words the doctor had uttered—"somewhere on the autism *spectrum*" – would impact her life.

As the thought left her, she reached for David's hand. He took it in his, and said to the doctor, "I know there's no cure for autism, but is there any chance that Bobby will be able to lead a normal life?"

Again, the doctor had to force himself not to challenge the word "normal." But he knew what David meant, and correcting his vocabulary wasn't what David needed at that moment. "You're correct; there is no cure, per se. But there are some innovative and highly successful treatments available, many of them being offered right in this facility." The doctor hesitated briefly. "Bobby's not eligible to attend school here until he's around three, but there are a lot of things we can do to assist you until then."

David started to speak, but couldn't. When Jenna looked over at him, she began to tear up. After a few moments, David was composed enough to say, "I guess all I've been hoping to hear is that Bobby can be a reasonably happy, independent adult."

Dr. Townsend took a moment before responding. "I wish I could tell you that, David. But the truth is nobody can guarantee that for *any child*, regardless of whether they have limitations or not."

David and Jenna walked to the car in silence. David inserted the key in the ignition, but didn't turn it on. He looked over at Jenna. "Do you want to talk now or wait until we get home?"

"Let's wait. I'll ask Barbara to keep Bobby for a while longer."

If Jenna had known the effect the delay was going to have on David, she might not have postponed the conversation.

Coming to terms with his son's condition was not something David had been very successful at doing from the first moment he suspected something was wrong. Now with this further confirmation from Dr. Townsend, David felt backed into a corner.

Gradually over the half hour ride back to the apartment, David's distress and denial began to turn into anger. He knew he wasn't thinking rationally, but he couldn't help himself. He wasn't really angry at the doctor, or Jenna, or Bobby. He was angry at the situation, but he couldn't push back against a *situation*.

As much as he tried to calm down, he wasn't able to. His emotions got the best of him, and the first words out of his mouth back at the apartment were "I think we need to get a second opinion."

"What are you talking about?"

"You may be ready to just accept what they said, but I'm not. If Bobby had something physically wrong with him, we'd get another opinion in a heartbeat."

"So you think Dr. Millwood and Dr. Townsend—all the people at the Center—they're all wrong?"

"I don't know. But what harm will it do to find out?"

"You want to put Bobby through more tests? And us too? You want to go through this all over again? And not only that, where would we have another evaluation done? We've already been to the best place in the country."

"We could have another evaluation done in New York."

"New York?"

"Yeah, remember we said we'd talk about you and Bobby moving there after the evaluation."

"Yes, but you never mentioned anything about a second opinion."

"Well I am now."

Jenna started to react to David's tone, but caught herself. "Can we just back up a second? I know the news we got today was not what either one of us was hoping for, but it's not going to do any good to overreact."

"I'm not overreacting. I'm being very logical."

"No you're not!"

David ignored Jenna's comment. Instead he shifted the topic. "Be honest, Jenna, you never had any intention of moving to New York. And that's the main reason you don't want to have another evaluation, especially there."

Jenna couldn't respond immediately. David had struck a nerve. Finally, she said, "I admit I didn't think we were going to hear any news today that would make moving to New York the best thing for Bobby. And we didn't. You heard Dr. Townsend, they have proven treatments right here that can help him to . . . ." Jenna struggled to find the right words.

"What, to be normal? That's not going to happen."

"Don't say that! Why are you giving up on him?"

"I'm not. I just want to see what else is out there."

"I wish I believed that."

The remark stung David to his core. He stared at Jenna, and then once he recovered, said, "I'm going to head back to New York tonight."

"What? I thought you were staying until Wednesday? David, don't do this."

"I need to check out what's available for our son. Then maybe we can be together like a real family." With that he turned and went into the bedroom.

Jenna started shaking. "David, please . . . wait."

David didn't even look back over his shoulder. He kept moving toward the bedroom and said, "I need to pack."

David retrieved his suitcase from the corner of the bedroom and literally threw a few items into it, then stopped and went into the bathroom. He ran the cold water, splashed some on his face, and stared at himself in the mirror. He closed his eyes and thought – *What am I doing? Why am I acting like this?* He had no answer; he just knew that none of it felt right.

David returned to the bedroom and got a few more items out of his bureau. But instead of putting them in the suitcase, he tossed them back into the open drawer and sat down on the end of the bed.

He and Jenna rarely fought; they were usually able to talk things through and find common ground. He acknowledged to himself that this was mainly his fault, but he still believed the idea of a second opinion was a good one. Even so, he decided to go back out and apologize.

As he entered the living room, he started to say, "I'm sorry", but realized Jenna wasn't there.

He called her name, and when she didn't respond, his anger began to surface again. *She didn't even try to follow me into the bedroom, and then she just leaves. She probably went to get Bobby.* He glanced at the clock. *But that was ten minutes ago. She's probably down there telling Barbara everything that went on.*

But in fact, Jenna wasn't doing anything of the kind. When she arrived at Barbara's apartment, Bobby was sleeping. Her first inclination was to wake him up and get back to the apartment as soon as possible. But after she thought about it, she decided not to.

David needed time to cool off; he wasn't himself, and some of the things he had said had really hurt. But, she reminded herself, the two of them had always been able to work things out in the past, and she felt as if they'd be able to do that again, even though none of the other issues had been as serious as this one.

Jenna briefly described to Barbara what had occurred at the Center. She felt that Barbara sensed that something else was wrong, but she never pressed it, and Jenna didn't offer.

After another ten minutes, Jenna woke up Bobby, thanked Barbara, said goodbye to Toby, and headed back to talk to David. She started to compose what she was going to say, but as she passed one of the windows in the hallway that looked out over the parking lot, she saw David pulling his suitcase behind him heading for the car.

She brought her hand up to her mouth to try to stifle a gasp. Her legs started to buckle, and she had to lean against the wall to make sure she remained upright. The tears came immediately after that. And as she continued to cry, she gripped Bobby tighter and tighter.

He glanced up at his mother's face that was contorted with emotional pain, but didn't react at all.

CHAPTER 38

The drive back to New York provided an opportunity for David to reflect on what had happened at the Center, and then the fight with Jenna. Initially, he refused to think of it as a fight, but then he acknowledged to himself that that's exactly what it was.

Over the course of the four-hour trip, David had been able to purge himself of the anger he had originally felt, but a vestige of something else still lingered—Jenna's reaction to the fact that he wanted a second opinion.

Once he was inside the apartment on Long Island, David gave himself another twenty minutes to further settle down before calling Jenna. He had decided to apologize for everything that had gone on between them, except the notion of the second opinion. He was not going to give in on that. And why should he, he thought. Certainly, Jenna would eventually see that he was right.

Despite his resolve, David picked up the phone and put it back down three times before placing the call. He wasn't sure why he was nervous, but he clearly was.

Jenna answered after the second ring.

The first few minutes of the conversation were filled with apologies by both of them, followed by explanations as to why each of them had done what they had done – Jenna explained why she hadn't come back to the apartment right away, and David explained why he had left before Jenna had returned.

Eventually the topic of the second opinion moved to the forefront of the conversation, and whatever level of understanding they had come to started to evaporate. Although Jenna never specifically used the word, her tone suggested to David that she thought he was being unrealistic. And likewise, David never used the term, but it was obvious to Jenna that he thought she was being stubborn.

Jenna blinked first. She was too emotionally spent to resist any further. They finally agreed that David would check out facilities in the New York area, and if there were anything that looked promising, he would try to schedule an appointment for Bobby.

Once that was settled, they began another round of apologies, but they both sensed that something had changed. It was no longer possible to deny that Jenna's acceptance of Bobby's condition and David's reluctance to do that was affecting their relationship. Jenna felt the shift more deeply. It saddened her and scared her at the same time.

As soon as he hung up, David began to search the Internet for possible diagnostic facilities. He followed up the search with phone calls over the next two days, but without much success. In all honesty, he had to admit that none of the facilities even remotely measured up to the Center in Massachusetts.

When David spoke with Jenna on Wednesday afternoon, however, he didn't let on that he hadn't found anything worthwhile. Instead, he indicated that he was looking more closely at two or three different places that might provide what they needed. For some reason that he couldn't explain, David wasn't able to let go of the second opinion idea, despite the fact that it was making less and less sense at this point. Subconsciously, he acknowledged that this had become a battle of wills with Jenna more than anything else, but he still couldn't let it go.

After she hung up with David, Jenna sat quietly for a long time trying to sort through her emotions. She wanted to talk with someone about what was happening, but she wasn't sure she was ready to open up about it yet. Eventually, she came to the conclusion that the best person to talk to was Jeremy. He knew David better than anyone else; maybe Jeremy could help her figure out why David was acting the way he was.

Jenna gave Jeremy a call to confirm that he was coming by for his weekly visit the next day. He answered after a few rings. "Hello."

"Hi, Jeremy. It's Jenna."

"Hi." It was unusual for Jenna to call, so his first instinct was one of concern. "Is everything okay?"

She hesitated. "Uh . . . yeah. I just wanted to know if you were coming by tomorrow."

Jeremy sensed that something was wrong. "I was planning to. Are you sure you're all right?"

Jenna hesitated again, and before she could respond, Jeremy jumped in. "Jenna, what's wrong?"

She finally relented. "I need to talk to you about something."

"Do you want me to come over tonight?"

"No, no. It can wait until tomorrow."

"Are you sure?"

"Positive."

The next day Jeremy arrived around 3:30, a little earlier than usual. As soon as he came in, Jenna could tell that he wasn't himself. But before she had a chance to say anything, Bobby, who was playing on the floor looked up and said, "Me, me."

Jenna and Jeremy looked at each other, obviously puzzled. Bobby didn't often say anything, although every once in awhile, Jenna thought she could make out distinct words from the sounds he made.

As Bobby's gaze fixed on Jeremy, his face seemed to brighten and he repeated the words "Me, me." Jenna shook her head and glanced at Jeremy again, and then it dawned on her what might be happening. "I think he's trying to say your name."

Jeremy got down on the floor and made eye contact with Bobby. "Is that what you're trying to do?"

Bobby maintained eye contact and handed Jeremy a toy car. Jeremy accepted it. "Thanks. Can I play with the cars, too?"

Although Bobby gave no response, he continued to make eye contact and interact with Jeremy to an even greater extent than he usually did. For the next fifteen minutes Jenna forgot about the conversation she had wanted to have with Jeremy and just observed the two of them. Jeremy also appeared to have pushed whatever was bothering him out of his mind.

Eventually when Bobby's attention seemed to wane, Jeremy got up from the floor and sat on the couch. "Well, that was something, wasn't it?"

"Yeah, it really was."

They were quiet for a minute and then Jeremy said, "So what did you want to talk to me about?"

Jenna found that she had to ease into it slowly, but eventually she told Jeremy everything. After she finished, she said, "What I don't understand is why David's being so adamant about a second opinion. We've already been to the best doctors in the country. A second opinion's not going to change anything."

Jeremy waited a moment before responding. "He probably knows that. But David has always seen himself as someone who can fix things. Deep down I'm sure he knows he can't fix this. Maybe he's delaying coming to terms with it in the hopes that he can figure something out."

"I guess that's a possibility. But right from the beginning he had a tough time accepting any of this. I know he tried for a while, especially with the journal entries, but . . . ." Jenna fell silent briefly, and then declared, "It's like he and Bobby never connected."

Jeremy didn't know how to respond, so he didn't.

Jenna became emotional as she continued. "Bobby's his son. He needs to try harder."

"I don't think it's that easy, Jenna."

"Bobby responds better to you than he does to David!"

"I'm not sure that's true."

"Just look at this afternoon."

"Well, if that is the case, it's not because of anything I'm doing, or anything David's not doing."

"I wish I could accept that."

"But look at the way Bobby responds to Toby. Do you think Toby's doing something consciously to engage Bobby?"

"No, no I don't. But maybe Bobby can sense things." Jenna paused. "This whole situation is taking a toll on us, Jeremy. We never used to fight, but last Monday, and then on the phone . . . it's scaring me."

Jeremy looked directly at Jenna. "I'm certainly no expert, but I think you have to keep talking with each other about this."

"I thought that too, but lately everything turns into an argument."

"I still think that's what you need to do. I know you guys. Eventually you'll be able to work it out."

Jenna nodded her head in agreement. "I hope you're right."

After a few moments of tending to her son, Jenna's mind jumped back to when Jeremy had first entered the apartment. As she sat back down on the couch, she asked, "Is everything all right with you? Before you started playing with Bobby, you looked upset."

Jeremy protested. "It's nothing."

"I've known you as long as I've known David. I can tell when something's bothering you."

Jeremy tried to smile. "I'm that transparent, huh?"

"You want to talk about it?'

"No, really, it's going to be okay."

"That's not what I asked you."

Jeremy finally relented, and for the next fifteen minutes he related a situation he found himself enmeshed in at school.

"Last Friday I discovered that one of my students, a girl named Cindy, had plagiarized a paper. I was initially suspicious because of the sophisticated vocabulary. So I used some detection software, and found the same paper, nearly word for word, on a website that sells them.

"I asked her to see me after school. She denied plagiarizing anything at first, but then when I used my laptop to show her the paper on the website, she broke down crying, and admitted it.

"She said she was stressed out about her grades and sports. She's a good basketball player, and the playoffs are coming up. She begged me not to tell her parents. She said they'd freak out. I've met them, and she's probably right. It gets even trickier though, because her mother is on the school committee.

"Finally, I told her that her parents had to be informed; it's school policy. But I could give her a bit of a break. I told her that she was going to have to be the one to tell her parents. I gave her the weekend to tell them, and then I said one of them had to call me on Monday to verify that they knew.

"At first she didn't like the idea, but then I explained that she could pick the time and circumstances to tell them, which would probably be better than a phone call from me out of the blue. I also told her that after I talked with her parents, she had to redo the paper, and the best grade she could get was 50% of what she would have received if it were the original paper.

"Some teachers who catch students cheating just give them a zero, but making them do it over, and only giving them 50%, makes more sense to me. It gives them some incentive to do a decent job on the rewrite."

Jeremy had been wrapped up in the telling of the story, and hadn't shown much emotion, but as he continued, Jenna saw a change.

"Cindy's in my third period class. It meets around 10:00. So when I saw her on Monday, she told me that she had spoken to her parents and one of them would call me that afternoon. They never did.

"On Tuesday, I confronted her again, and she said her parents told her they forgot. I said that wasn't good enough. If I didn't hear from them by that afternoon, I was going to call them that night. She said she understood, but didn't think either one of them was going to be home. I think she could see that I was starting to get angry, so she offered to give me her mom's cell phone number, in case her mom didn't call and wasn't home later. I copied it down, and she left.

"Neither one of her parents called on Tuesday afternoon, so I waited until after supper and then called the number Cindy had given me. Initially, I didn't recognize the voice of the person who answered, but then I realized it was Cindy. I asked her why she had answered her mother's cell phone. She said she hadn't; it was her cell phone, and she must have given me her number by mistake. At this point I was furious, and told her that now one of her parents would have to come up to school in the morning, or I was turning it over to the principal. She didn't even respond; she just hung up."

Jenna could see that the retelling of this had shaken Jeremy, and she felt certain that the worst was yet to come.

"The next morning before homeroom, I was called to the main office. The secretary told me to go into Mr. Nolan's office. He's the principal. He invited me to sit down, and when I did, he told me that he just got off the phone with Cindy's mom, and she was very upset.

"He told me what Cindy had evidently told her mom. I couldn't believe it. Cindy lied to her about everything, but she told just enough of the truth that it sounded plausible.

"She told her mom that she had quoted a couple of sentences from the Internet in her paper, and I had overreacted and accused her of plagiarizing. Then supposedly, I had decided not to turn her in, and I had called her last night and . . . ."

Jeremy had to calm himself before he was able to continue. Jenna could see the start of some tears in the corner of his eyes.

"She told her mother that when I called, I said that since I had done something nice for her, how about meeting me and doing something nice for me."

At this point, Jeremy closed his eyes and buried his face in his hands. It took a full two minutes before he could speak again.

"Mr. Nolan asked me to explain what had happened from the beginning. I did, and then eventually I got to the part about calling Cindy's cell phone. I explained that Cindy told me it was her mother's.

"After I finished, Mr. Nolan said, 'This is a real mess, but I believe you're telling the truth. The problem is that Cindy showed her mother the screen that had your incoming call listed. And we can't prove what you actually said to her.'

"I told him that I still had Cindy's paper, and I could show Cindy's mother where it was copied from. But he said that didn't matter. Even if she had plagiarized the entire paper, the phone call was the problem."

Jeremy seemed to be able to steady himself as he was finishing the story.

"Anyway, Mr. Nolan said he was removing Cindy from my class, and that I shouldn't have anything to do with her for the rest of the year. He said he thought that might be enough to allow everything to eventually blow over."

Jenna put her hand on Jeremy's. "I'm so sorry. I can see what this is doing to you."

"You should have seen me yesterday. I'm actually a little bit better today, although saying everything out loud kind of brought it all back. But it really helped to talk to somebody. Thank you."

"Well, you helped me out too."

Jeremy was finally able to smile. "Okay, I guess we're even."

He stood up. "I think I'm going to go home, grade some papers, and go to bed early."

Jenna stood, and moved toward the door. "I hope everything works out. I know how much you love what you're doing." With that Jenna gave Jeremy a hug and a kiss on the cheek.

"Thanks." He paused for a moment, returned Jenna's kiss on the cheek and then said, "I wonder if David realizes how lucky he is."

CHAPTER 39

David didn't go back to Massachusetts the following weekend. It had nothing to do with what was going on between him and Jenna; it was about work. There was a major problem with one of the suppliers of building materials, and the only time that could be arranged for a special delivery was 8:00 Sunday morning. And David had to be there.

Although David was convinced that Jenna accepted the explanation as to why he couldn't come home, he also recognized that the timing couldn't have been worse. There was a palpable strain in every phone conversation between the two of them leading up to the weekend, regardless of the topic.

On the following Thursday Jeremy paid his weekly visit. And although Bobby didn't repeat the "me, me" sounds from the last time, he did seem more animated as soon as Jeremy walked in.

The two of them played on the floor for an extended period of time, with Jenna joining in for part of it. When Jeremy sensed that Bobby had tired of what they were doing, he got up off the floor and sat on the couch with Jenna.

They talked about Bobby for a few minutes and then Jenna said, "Any more fallout about that girl and the phone call?"

"No, not so far. I guess no news is good news. She's in one of my study halls, but I just check her attendance. I don't even call out her name. She usually goes to the library, so I don't have to have any contact with her."

"That's probably for the best."

"No question." Jeremy paused. "Thanks again for letting me vent last week."

"I'm glad I could help."

Jeremy remained quiet for a moment and then changed the subject. "How are things with you and David?"

"He couldn't come home this past weekend."

"Why not?"

"Work." Jeremy got a skeptical look on his face, so Jenna followed up with "It wasn't his fault."

"So you guys didn't have a chance to talk then?"

"Not really. I don't like trying to settle something like this over the phone. David's still trying to decide on a facility for a second opinion."

"You sound like you're a little more open to that then you were."

Jenna hesitated slightly. "I don't know. Maybe."

"Is he going to be able to come home this weekend?"

"He says he is." Jenna paused, realizing how judgmental her tone had sounded. "I mean, yes. I'm sure he will be."

"Well, that's good. Maybe you can get some things squared away."

"I hope so."

They talked for another ten minutes. Jenna invited him to stay for dinner, as she had done numerous times before. He declined again, as he always did.

Shortly after Jenna closed the door behind Jeremy, she thought back to the conversation they had just had. Why had she given Jeremy the impression that she was more open to the second opinion idea, or that things were better between her and David? Neither one of those things was true.

Jenna's mind shifted slightly, and she began to compare her recent conversations with David and those with Jeremy. They were like night and day.

With David everything felt like a struggle—trying to use just the right word, having to clarify what she meant. But with Jeremy, it wasn't like that. Every conversation was easy.

To be fair, she acknowledged to herself, talking to Jeremy was almost always face-to-face and didn't involve issues that affected both of them in the same way. Still, she thought back to the way things had been with David just a few months ago. That was the way it was with Jeremy now.

Jenna didn't allow herself to pursue that notion any further.

David arrived back in Quincy around 9:00 on Saturday morning, having gotten up very early, not only to avoid traffic, but also to try to make up for not having been home the previous weekend.

As soon as he walked into the apartment, he felt an awkwardness he hadn't expected. Jenna sensed it, and tried to ease things by offering a smile. But David still didn't seem to know what to do. Finally, he opened his arms, and Jenna did the same. "I missed you," he said.

"I missed you, too."

"I'm sorry again about last weekend. I really had no choice."

"I know. It's okay."

They didn't speak for a few moments, and then Bobby made a noise from his bouncy seat.

David and Jenna separated themselves. David went over to Bobby, plucked him out of the bouncy seat and placed him on the floor. David found a few toys close by, sat down, and began playing with his son.

It struck Jenna that David's actions seemed forced. She hated herself for thinking that, but she couldn't help it. It looked like David was playing with Bobby either to avoid talking, or to try to prove something to her, not because he genuinely wanted to be with Bobby.

As Jenna continued to observe the two of them, she couldn't help but compare David's interactions with Bobby with the way Jeremy interacted with him. With Jeremy things always seemed natural. Anyone watching would have no idea Bobby was autistic. With David, however, Bobby's whole body seemed to stiffen. Just the sound of David's voice appeared to make Bobby tense up, almost like every bone in his body was brittle, and could break at the slightest touch.

Over the course of the weekend both David and Jenna made every effort to try to smooth things over. They both initiated casual conversations, trying to ease into the subject matter that was really on their minds. But each time they tried to broach the topic of David's search for another facility, the conversation seemed to take on a physical weight, a heaviness that was more about the dynamic between the two of them than the topic itself. Not much got resolved.

Late Sunday afternoon David headed back to New York. Once again, the multi-hour drive gave him time to think. He tried to convince himself that although things were not quite back to normal, the gulf between Jenna and him had narrowed.

After all, he thought, we made love on Saturday night. That must mean something. *If things weren't getting better, Jenna wouldn't have gone along with that, would she?*

David's thoughts drifted to his inability to locate a place for Bobby's re-evaluation. Maybe he should just forget about it. It certainly would make the situation with Jenna much easier if he did. But was he ready to give up? He didn't know.

He turned on the radio and let his mind wander elsewhere for the rest of the trip. When he was a couple of blocks from the apartment, David stopped at a convenience store and picked up the last Sunday *Times* available. He was looking forward to lying in bed and reading until he fell asleep. It had been a long weekend and a long drive.

After arriving at the apartment, it took him about twenty minutes to change his clothes, check his phone messages, look at the mail, and grab himself a beer. And then he propped himself up on the bed and began to read.

He zipped through the first few sections of the paper, not finding much to hold his interest. The next section was labeled *Education*, not a section he usually read, but for some reason he decided to look through it. On the third page was an article about the Chambers Institute in New Jersey that treated children who were suspected of having "developmental delays." According to the article, *the founder of the Institute, Dr. Mark Chambers refuses to use the word 'autism,' claiming that it's an "over-diagnosed label that's meaningless."* After reading that quote, David sat up and pulled the paper closer.

The next several paragraphs focused on the Institute's mission and philosophy. It then segued into what a few of Dr. Chambers' detractors in the medical and education fields had to say about some of the treatment strategies being used at the Institute. The last paragraph in the article was a quote by Dr. Chambers responding to some of his critics. *"It's unfortunate that the powers that be in this field won't remove their blinders . . . Here at the Institute, we take great satisfaction in the fact that many parents who have been told by these very same experts that their children will have to live in the shadows of society . . . after attending our facility, find out that's simply not the case. We don't just provide hope, we provide results."*

It appeared to David that quite by accident he had found just what he was looking for.

For the next hour David searched the Internet, clicking on link after link related to the Chambers Institute. Although he didn't make a formal tally, David felt as if the positive and negative postings were about even.

However, the comments from the parents of children who had received treatment at the Institute, all contained glowing endorsements. After reading those, David didn't need any more convincing.

The *Times* article had generated so much interest that when David called the Institute on Monday he was on hold for thirty minutes before he was instructed to leave a message, and someone would get back to him as soon as possible.

"As soon as possible" turned out to be Wednesday. The voice on the other end answered a few of David's questions and then indicated that he would be sent out a packet of information. David was told to fill out all the forms enclosed with the packet and send them back. Within a few weeks he would be notified if the Institute were interested in setting up an interview with him. Following the interview, a decision would be made whether to schedule an evaluation for his son. The initial evaluation cost $1500 and was not covered by insurance.

David asked, "Isn't there any way to expedite this?"

The female voice almost laughed. "A few days ago that would have been possible, but not since the article appeared."

Despite the iffiness of the situation, David couldn't contain himself. He called Jenna immediately after he hung up. Her reaction was not particularly enthusiastic, which David had expected. But she promised to keep an open mind.

Jenna did ask a question that set him back on his heels momentarily. "So this wasn't one of the places you were already thinking about?"

"Uh . . . no. After I read the article, the other places just didn't seem to measure up."

Jenna forced herself to sound more upbeat. "Okay. I'll see if I can find the article on-line."

David threw out a caution. "Some of the blogs are pretty negative. But the ones from the parents are great. I'm really starting to get excited about this place." David paused. "Plus, we owe it to Bobby."

When they hung up, Jenna was more convinced than ever that David had lost sight of the supposed reason that he wanted the re-evaluation. Instead, it seemed as if his pride had gotten in the way. His focus had become proving the doctors and Jenna wrong, and himself right. Bobby's well-being had become an afterthought.

During the next few days, Jenna searched the Internet for everything she could find about the Chambers Institute. Thus far, she wasn't particularly impressed. But she knew that she wasn't approaching this with any degree of objectivity. However, since she had promised to keep an open mind, she decided to get some additional input from her mom, as well as Barbara and Jeremy. She even contacted Dr. Millwood, and left a message with Dr. Townsend at the Center in Canton.

After putting all the various pieces of advice together, she came to the conclusion that she should let David play things out. There was no harm in him going for the initial interview, if it came to that. And if she sensed that anything was not right, she could fight the battle then. But there was no reason to challenge things at this point.

Although she didn't believe for one minute that a new evaluation would discover anything different, maybe if she agreed to go along with it, and the diagnosis were the same, David would drop it, and things between the two of them could get back to normal.

She decided that she would tell David on Saturday that she would support whatever he wanted to do.

And then Dr. Townsend called her back.

CHAPTER 40

Jenna didn't recognize the phone number on the caller ID, so she answered more with a question than a greeting. "Hello?"

"Hello. Ms. MacDonald? Jenna?"

"Yes."

"This is Dr. Townsend from The Developmental Diagnostic Center in Canton. I'm returning your call."

"Oh, thanks for getting back to me, doctor. I'm sorry to bother you, but as I mentioned in the message I left, I was wondering if you were familiar with Mark Chambers."

"Yes. As a matter of fact, I am. What's this in reference to?"

Jenna went on for the next few minutes explaining what had transpired since Bobby's evaluation at the Center. She made it clear that she didn't share David's desire for a second opinion. But if it eventually came to that, she wanted to make sure that any facility they'd be taking their son to was a reputable place.

When she finished, there was silence on the other end of the line. Finally, Jenna asked, "Are you still there, Dr. Townsend?"

"Yes. I'm sorry. I was trying to decide how best to proceed."

"I'm afraid I don't understand."

"I have a bit of an ethical dilemma here, but I'd like to help you out. Can you give me a moment?"

"Certainly."

There was dead air for a full minute before Dr. Townsend spoke. "I think what I can do is to spell out a number of facts about Mark Chambers, and then you can draw your own conclusions. Would that be all right?"

Jenna wasn't sure where this was headed, but she agreed anyway. "That's fine."

"I'm sorry for all the cloak and dagger nonsense, but I wouldn't be comfortable offering my opinion on some things relating to Dr. Chambers. It might cross an ethical line that I'm not willing to cross."

Although Jenna was eager to hear what Dr. Townsend had to say, she offered him an out. "If you'd rather not discuss this, I understand."

"No, no. This will be okay. It's important that you hear some of these things, especially if you're considering having your son evaluated there."

"Are you sure?"

"Yes, definitely." He paused. "First of all, Dr. Chambers used to work here at the Center."

"He did? When?"

"About ten years ago." Dr. Townsend hesitated. "He was asked to leave."

"What? Why?"

"I guess you could say there were philosophical differences."

"What does that mean?"

"I have to be careful here, but I think it's fair to say that he doesn't share . . . well in essence . . . he doesn't believe that there is such a thing as autism."

Jenna's surprise was evident in her voice. "He doesn't? I read in an article that he thought it was over-diagnosed, but the article didn't seem to suggest anything beyond that."

"I know. I read the same article. But in other publications he's been much more explicit. In fact, his unwillingness to accept the existence of autism is the main reason that he was asked to leave."

"How can a doctor refuse to acknowledge something like that?"

"I don't have an answer for that. But I guess I should also point out that Mark Chambers is not a medical doctor."

"He's not?"

"No. He has a PhD in educational administration."

Jenna was surprised by the revelation, but she wasn't sure how she felt about it. She remained silent as Dr. Townsend continued.

"I didn't mean to imply that his lack of a medical degree was an issue, because it wasn't. He was hired by us to be a liaison with the local school districts, and he did a very fine job." He paused. "That is until he began to tell parents and school officials that some of the children being treated here could not possibly be on the autism spectrum because autism didn't exist."

"You're kidding."

"As you can imagine, it was a logistical nightmare. Various school districts refused to pay for special education services. Eventually, we straightened everything out, but it created a lot of problems."

"That must have been awful."

"It was. It's what finally led us to request that he leave."

Jenna was trying to process what all of this new information might mean for Bobby. "What else can you tell me?"

Again, Dr. Townsend hesitated. "How much do you know about the Chambers Institute?"

"Not much. Mainly what I've read on-line."

"Are you familiar with their fee schedule?"

"No. What fee schedule?"

"Well, the initial evaluation is fifteen hundred dollars, and unless something has changed very recently, it's not covered by insurance."

"Fifteen hundred dollars? David never mentioned that."

"Of course, that's just for the evaluation. Follow-up treatments cost between three hundred and five hundred dollars per session, and they usually recommend three or four a month."

"And none of that is covered?"

"I don't believe so."

"Not even once a child is certified as having special needs?"

"The state of New Jersey doesn't recognize the Chambers Institute as a valid educational center, so if school districts were to recommend that students in their district go there, the districts wouldn't get reimbursed."

"But I thought I saw some comments from parents of school-aged children."

"I suspect those parents are wealthy enough that they can afford to pay whatever the Institute charges. It's like sending your child to a private school. Some parents will often do that to avoid having their children labeled."

"But many of the comments I saw were very positive."

Dr. Townsend was quiet for a moment. "I'm afraid I've already delved further into the realm of opinion than I probably should have, but let me respond to that. The Institute treats children as young as ten months, which in the judgment of nearly everyone in the field, is much too early. There's no way to accurately diagnose developmental delays at that age."

"So why do they do it?"

"In one instance I'm familiar with, the parents were told that the initial evaluation was inconclusive, but that if their child received a year's worth of treatment, it would prevent anything from developing. I've seen the child's records. I'd stake my reputation on the fact that the child never had any issues to begin with. What parent wouldn't sing the praises of an institution that supposedly provided that kind of intervention?"

Jenna was about to interject, but she sensed that the doctor had more to say.

"In a number of other cases that I know of, the Institute simply claimed that it had to suspend treatment because the children came to them too late to be able to produce significant improvement." Dr. Townsend paused. "But usually by that time, the parents have paid thousands of dollars to the Institute."

"Are you suggesting that this is all about making money?"

"I won't comment on that."

Jenna decided to approach things from another angle. "Didn't I read that the Institute also treats older children?"

"Oh, yes. They have both middle school and high school programs. And if you only consider the data the Institute provides, it would appear that the students are achieving very well academically. But I would contend that that's an extremely subjective assessment. The curriculum is limited to a few subjects, and completely ignores socialization and independent living skills – the very areas where most of these young people need assistance." He paused, but Jenna could hear the agitation rising in his voice. "Did I mention that the tuition for middle school students is $30,000, and for high school students it's $35,000?"

"That's more than some colleges charge."

"Yes, it is." He paused again. "I've probably said too much already, but I'm reluctant to leave things the way they are. How about we do this? Why don't you e-mail me with any other questions you may have? That way I can take some time to formulate my responses, and make sure I don't answer inappropriately. Would that be okay?"

"Of course. I'm sorry if I've put you on the spot."

"Not at all."

Jenna's mind was swirling when she hung up the phone. She certainly would take some time to think things through, but her initial reaction was that she didn't want Bobby anywhere near the Chambers Institute.

She wondered how that would sit with David. On the other hand, why hadn't he told her about the fifteen hundred dollar evaluation charge, not to mention the treatment charges? Of course, she knew the answer to that. Those expenses were hardly selling points in David's quest to have her agree to the second evaluation.

Ultimately, Jenna decided to wait until David came home next weekend to talk with him about what she had just learned.

As it turned out, David called mid-week to let her know that he had been approved for an interview toward the end of April. Jenna almost broached the subject of her conversation with Dr. Townsend, but caught herself in time. "Okay, David, we can talk about the interview this weekend."

"What do you mean? What's there to talk about?"

"I just meant that . . . I don't know. It's just an expression."

David didn't respond immediately. "Okay, I'll see you on Saturday."

As he hung up, David wondered if he had overreacted to the phrase Jenna had used, but he didn't think so. His instincts told him that Jenna was going to continue to fight him on this.

Late Saturday night, after David offered some additional details about the upcoming interview at the Institute, Jenna finally mustered the courage to bring up her conversation with Dr. Townsend. "Actually, I've been doing some more research on Mark Chambers. I even called Dr. Townsend."

David looked surprised, but when he didn't say anything, Jenna continued. "There are a lot of people in the medical and educational communities who don't think very highly of what Mark Chambers is doing."

"I told you there was a lot of negative stuff out there. You know the Internet—anybody can post anything. Did you read the comments by the parents? They were all terrific."

Jenna ignored David's question. "Did you know that he used to work at the Center in Canton?"

David couldn't hide his surprise, but he recovered enough to offer, "So? What does that have to do with anything?"

"According to Dr. Townsend, he was asked to leave."

Jenna proceeded to tell David everything that Dr. Townsend had told her. A few times David interrupted and tried to refute some of the doctor's comments, but mostly he dismissed them as professional jealousy.

When Jenna asked why he hadn't told her about the fifteen hundred dollar fee for the evaluation, David responded by saying that it was a relatively small amount to pay, if it meant that they'd discover the truth about Bobby's condition.

"And what about the five hundred dollar treatments," asked Jenna?

"The treatments for children under two are less expensive than that."

"That's not the point."

"We can worry about that after the evaluation."

"I have a bad feeling about this, David."

"I know. You've made that pretty clear from the moment I mentioned it."

"That's not fair. I was willing to go along with the second opinion even though I didn't think it was necessary, but from what I'm learning about Mark Chambers . . . ."

"What? That he and Dr. Townsend don't see eye-to-eye on some things?"

"It's more than that."

"That's what it boils down to." David paused. "Are you trying to say that you don't even want me going for the interview?"

"I don't know. It sounds like once they get their hooks in you . . . ."

David was losing patience. "It's not a cult, Jenna."

"Don't patronize me."

"I'm not trying to, but you're being totally unreasonable."

"Because I'm looking out for Bobby?"

"And what am I doing?"

Jenna was about to say something she knew she'd regret. Instead she backed off. She wasn't sure why. Maybe she just didn't want to fight anymore. "All right. I guess it'll be okay."

"Well thanks for your permission."

"I didn't mean it that way. I just meant that there's probably no harm in the interview, but I don't think we should commit to anything beyond that, until we've talked some more."

For the next several weeks leading up to the interview, there was an uneasy truce between David and Jenna. Although there was an underlying tension, it never rose to the level of an argument because neither one of them would allow themselves to broach the topic.

The night before the interview, David phoned to say he would call Jenna as soon as he finished up the next day. During the rest of their conversation they both struck a conciliatory tone that they had independently vowed to carry over to the next day.

By 1:00 in the afternoon on Wednesday, Jenna still hadn't heard from David. She decided to give it another few minutes, and then she would place the call. But then at 1:10 the phone rang.

"Hello."

"Hi, it's me."

"I was beginning to get worried."

"Sorry. It took longer than I thought it would."

"So, how did it go?"

"Overall, fine. But there were a few things I didn't expect."

"Like what?"

"Well first of all, Mark Chambers sat in on the interview. In fact, he conducted most it."

"Really? Why?"

"I wasn't sure at first. But after a while, I figured out that it must have raised some red flags when they looked at Bobby's file and saw that he'd already been evaluated in Canton. I think initially Dr. Chambers was concerned that this might be a put-up job. You know, like I was an investigative reporter or something."

"You're kidding."

"I think it's possible. But once I assured him that all I was looking for was a second opinion, he seemed to accept that. In fact, he seemed eager to help us; he thinks that Bobby is an excellent candidate for the evaluation."

David could hear the sarcasm and suspicion in Jenna's voice. "I'm sure he does." A pause. "And why wouldn't he? It's a great opportunity to contradict the people at the Center."

"Jeez, Jenna, there's nothing sinister going on here. These people are in the business of helping kids." He knew he should have left it at that, especially because he was going to need her cooperation, but he couldn't help himself. "Why do you have to be so negative all the time?"

"I'm not. I just don't trust them."

"And what about me? Do you trust me?"

"That's not the issue."

"Yes, it is. I think the Institute would be a great place for Bobby to be evaluated."

"I wish I were convinced that that were true."

David hadn't intended to cut to the chase so quickly, but the words escaped from his mouth without him being aware they were going to. "I really need for you to go along with this, Jenna." He paused. "They'll only do the evaluation if we *both* agree to it. One parent's signature is not enough."

"Oh, David."

"There's that tone again. Why are you being like that?"

"Like what?"

"So stubborn."

"If that's what I'm being, then you know why."

"I know what you told me, but . . . I don't know what to believe anymore." David paused, trying to patch things up. "You should see this place. After Dr. Chambers was sure I wasn't some sort of plant, he showed me around. It's very impressive."

Despite her reservations, Jenna decided not to shut the door completely. "Can we wait and talk about it over the weekend."

"That's what we always seem to do, postpone conversations, but nothing changes."

"You really expect me to decide this right now, over the phone?"

"I think you've already decided. You're just pretending you haven't."

Jenna was hurt and angry at the same time, but she held her emotions mostly in check. "That's not exactly the best way to get me on your side."

"I didn't think there were sides when it came to Bobby."

This time her anger got the best of her. "This stopped being about Bobby a long time ago."

"What the hell is that supposed to mean?"

"I'm going to hang up now. I'll talk to you on Saturday."

Jenna spent a fitful night; her mind just wouldn't shut down. She regretted having spoken to David the way she had, but then just as quickly, she thought of some clever rebuttal she should have used. Before she finally was able to fall asleep, she decided it would help if she talked to Jeremy again. She was glad he was scheduled to come by the next day.

On Thursday afternoon shortly after he arrived, Jenna filled him in on everything David had told her. When she finished, she said. "I don't know what to do. I have some real concerns, especially about Dr. Chambers. Part of me thinks he's a scam artist and it's all about the money."

"Is that because of your conversation with Dr. Townsend?"

"Partly, and some because of what I've read on-line."

They were quiet for a moment before Jenna spoke, "It got pretty intense on the phone yesterday. We both said some things we shouldn't have. I'm really worried about where this is headed."

Jeremy tried to be reassuring. "You guys will get through this. You probably just need to remind each other to focus on what's best for Bobby."

"That's what I'm trying to do, but I'm not so sure about David." For the first time since Jeremy had arrived, Jenna was able to smile. "I guess David would say the same thing about me."

They talked for another fifteen minutes. Jeremy played with Bobby for a time after that, and then he left.

The next day around 4:00 in the afternoon, Jeremy buzzed the intercom. He identified himself, and Jenna said, "Hi, what are you doing here?"

"Can I come in? I'd like to talk to you."

"Sure."

As Jenna opened the apartment door she jokingly said, "So, you didn't get enough of the soap opera yesterday? You . . . ." She stopped in mid-sentence when she noticed Jeremy's expression. "What's the matter?"

Jeremy could barely get the words out before he broke down. "They let me go."

"What are you talking about?"

"The school. They're not renewing my contract."

"Oh, Jeremy. Is this because of that girl you caught cheating?"

"Yeah. I think I told you, her mother's on the school committee. And evidently, she wouldn't drop it. Supposedly, she told my principal that if I wasn't dismissed, she'd go after him."

Jeremy went on to explain that the principal suggested that he resign, instead of waiting to be dismissed. By doing that, when he applied for another position, Jeremy could honestly say he hadn't been let go. It was obviously the shock talking, but Jeremy added, "I don't know if I even want to teach anymore."

Jenna searched for something to say to ease Jeremy's pain, but every comment seemed insufficient and hollow. After another ten minutes of explanation, Jeremy went into the kitchen for a glass of water.

When he came back into the living room, he looked at Bobby playing on a blanket on the floor and smiled. He then got down on his hands and knees and engaged Bobby for the next fifteen minutes.

Jenna marveled at the change in Jeremy's demeanor. None of her words had made a difference, but a few minutes with Bobby certainly had.

When he got up off the floor, Jeremy said, "I think I'm going to take off."

"Why don't you stay for dinner?"

"Thanks, but I think I need to be alone for a while."

"Are you sure?"

"I'm not real sure about anything right now, but yeah."

Jenna opened up her arms, and Jeremy, fighting back tears, reached for her as well. After a moment, instead of kissing her on the cheek, he kissed her gently on the forehead. It was only a matter of a few inches, but the location of the kiss and its tenderness altered its intent from casual to sensual. They continued to hold each other much longer than either of them had expected to.

Finally, Jeremy stepped back. "I'm sorry. I better go."

On the way home, Jeremy tried to convince himself that what had just occurred was simply the result of the emotional upheaval his dismissal had caused. But somewhere deep inside, he knew better.

CHAPTER 41

As soon as she closed the door, Jenna's thoughts jumped to what had just happened. Initially, when she had opened her arms to Jeremy, it was simply to offer him comfort, but in the space of a few seconds as she continued in his embrace, it seemed to have become something else.

Had Jeremy felt it too? The last words he spoke—"I'm sorry. I better go."—could have meant any number of things. Was he apologizing for kissing her the way he did, for prolonging the hug, or simply because he had to leave? There was no way to know for sure.

She certainly couldn't deny that she had grown more and more fond of Jeremy, especially as she saw the way he interacted with Bobby. But she didn't believe that she had any romantic feelings toward him, at least not on any conscious level. But then why had she reacted the way she had?

Jenna knew she didn't have the emotional strength to explore that question right now. David would be back tomorrow, and she had no idea what to expect. Their last phone call had not gone well, and there was nothing to suggest the situation was going to improve.

She slept very little that night. Thoughts of David's pending arrival the next day and Jeremy's kiss kept insinuating themselves into her brain. Finally, at 5:00 she got up and made herself a cup of coffee. Bobby wouldn't be up for a few more hours. She decided that maybe if she glanced at a magazine or watched some mindless infomercial, it would stop the images and emotions that were pin balling throughout her, but it didn't.

And although it had always been Jenna's experience that things were much clearer in the light of day that was not the case this time. This time everything remained muddled.

David arrived back at the apartment around noon.
"Hi."

"Hi. How was your trip?"

"Not bad. A little traffic around Hartford. Bobby sleeping?"

"Yeah, his schedule is off a little, but I can get him up if you'd like."

"No, not yet." David hesitated. "We should talk."

"Okay," Jenna said, as she headed for the couch.

David sat down and leaned back, obviously tired from the long ride.

Jenna waited a moment and then said, "Would you like to hold off for a while? You must be exhausted."

David sat up. "No, I'm okay."

Jenna had spent part of the morning trying to figure out how she was going to say what she needed to say without being confrontational. To her surprise, when the moment arrived her words came out more spontaneously than she had anticipated they would. "I know how important the second opinion is to you, and I wish I didn't have such negative feelings about the Chambers Institute. But I just don't think it's the right place for Bobby."

David didn't want the conversation to deteriorate into a fight, so he spoke in an even tone. "I'm not sure you've given it a fair chance."

"I understand why you feel that way. But even from a practical standpoint, how would any of this work?" Jenna raised her voice slightly. "The Institute's in New Jersey. If they wanted follow-up treatments after the evaluation, we'd have to move. And then what about the Center in Canton?"

This time there was more agitation in David's voice. "Who said anything about moving? I just want another opinion. We don't ever have to go back there after that."

Jenna's tone matched David's. "So if the Institute says Bobby isn't autistic, but whatever issues he has could be eliminated by weekly sessions, you wouldn't push to have him go there?"

"Of course. And you wouldn't?"

"Only if I believed them. The more I read about Mark Chambers, the more I'm convinced he's a phony."

"You've never been willing to give this a chance."

Jenna forced herself to calm down, as she turned to face David more directly. "I know we don't agree on this, David. But there's got to be some way we can figure out a compromise."

David raised his voice even further. "And exactly what would that be? It's not a compromise if I'm giving up everything that I think is best, and you're not giving up anything."

Jenna had to admit to herself that David had a point. It forced her to be more conciliatory. "I don't want to fight anymore, David. I hated the things we said to each other on the phone." She paused. "Isn't there something we can do to make this right? Tell me what you want."

"You know very well what I want." David was quiet for a moment, and from the expression on his face, Jenna suspected he was preparing to continue the argument. But instead, his expression changed, and he looked toward the ceiling. He let out a sigh, and then a sadness came over him. He looked at Jenna as tears started to form in his eyes. "What I really want is for someone to tell me that my son doesn't have autism, that this is just a phase he's going through, that . . . ." He couldn't continue.

Jenna moved closer, and tried to console him. They remained silent until David started to get his emotions under control. "I know that's probably not what I'm going to hear, but doctors make mistakes, Jenna. This is our son we're talking about. He deserves a chance at a normal life. Shouldn't we be doing everything we can?" He broke down again.

This was the first time in months that David had opened up, and Jenna could see the obvious pain he was in. Although all of the logical arguments she had rehearsed were on the tip of her tongue, she couldn't bring herself to use them. She had vowed this morning—when she anticipated a moment like this—that she would stick to her guns. But she couldn't.

She wasn't sure where the idea and the words came from, but they seemed to flow naturally. "What about this, David? Let me do some more research to see if I can find some other facility that we can both agree on. And if I can't, then we'll have the evaluation done at the Chambers Institute."

David closed his eyes and tried to compose himself. At first he was only able to nod, but then through his tears he said, "Thank you."

They got up off the couch and opened their arms to each other. After a few moments, David separated himself slightly and kissed Jenna's forehead.

When things had calmed down, it occurred to Jenna that the hug and kiss on the forehead from David were the exact same things Jeremy had done the day before. It troubled her that although the physical gestures had been the same, her reaction to each of them should have been very different, but it wasn't.

The rest of the weekend went by uneventfully. For the first time in months, they seemed at ease with each other. As David was about to leave on Sunday, Jenna reiterated her pledge to look into some other facilities. And during the early part of the following week, much of Jenna's free time was spent doing that. A number of times each day she found herself thinking about Jeremy. In part she was wondering how he was coping with being let go, but inevitably her thoughts returned to the embrace they shared.

It was hard not to acknowledge that she was nervous about his upcoming Thursday visit. She wondered if Jeremy might find an excuse not to come. Or if he did show up, would things be awkward between them? On more than one occasion Jenna debated whether to call him just to break the ice before he came over, but she couldn't bring herself to do it.

After Bobby got up from his nap on Thursday afternoon, Jenna played with him for a while, and then did a little straightening up in anticipation of Jeremy's visit. But by 4:15, there was still no sign of him.

It may have been her imagination, but Jenna thought Bobby sensed that something was out of the ordinary. Or, she realized, he could simply have been reacting to her uneasiness.

At 4:30 there was a knock on the door. Jeremy usually had to use the intercom, so Jenna was a little surprised. As she was heading over to answer the door, Bobby repeated the words he had said a few weeks earlier – "Me, me."

There was no doubt in Jenna's mind that somehow Bobby knew that it was the day Jeremy always came to visit, and he was trying to say his name.

She looked over at her son, smiled broadly and said, "Yes, I think it is Jeremy."

But it wasn't. Instead, standing there in the corridor were Barbara and Toby. "Hi, Jenna. We were heading out to the store. I thought I'd see if you needed anything."

"Oh, no. We're fine, but thanks for checking."

Barbara poked her head inside. "Hi, Bobby."

It was unusual for Bobby to tune in to what was happening around him. But this time he had watched his mother walk over to the door, and after a moment he repeated what he had said earlier. "Me, me?" But this time Jenna was sure it was a question.

She was about to respond when Barbara interjected. "What did he say?"

Jenna wasn't about to try to explain any of this, so she simply replied, "I don't know. He's been trying out a lot of new words lately."

"Well, that's good."

"Yes, it is."

"You're sure you don't need anything?"

"Positive. Thank you."

Shortly after Jenna closed the door, the phone rang. "Hello."

"Hi, Jenna. It's Jeremy."

"Oh, hi." She hesitated. "I didn't recognize the phone number."

"My cell needs recharging. I'm using the phone in the Social Studies office at school."

Jenna was just about to ask if he was coming over, when Jeremy continued. "I won't be able to make it today."

"Is everything all right?"

"I have to meet with my union rep, you know, about my dismissal."

Jenna felt awful. How could she have been so insensitive? The first thing out of her mouth should have been to ask how he was doing. She started to say something, but Jeremy kept talking. "Say 'hi' to Bobby for me."

Jeremy's words made her forget what she was going to say, and triggered something else. She hadn't consciously intended to tell him what Bobby had said when Barbara had come to the door, but the words spilled out. "You should have seen what just happened. Barbara knocked on the door a few minutes ago and Bobby said 'me, me.' You know, like he did a few weeks ago. I really think that somehow he knew it was Thursday and he was expecting you."

As soon as the words left her mouth, Jenna realized how they might sound to Jeremy. Would he think that she was trying to use Bobby to make him feel guilty about not coming over? But Jeremy didn't seem to take it that way. In fact, she thought he sounded excited.

"Really? That's great. That's a big step, Jenna."

"That's what I thought."

Jeremy's next words came out more as an apology than anything else. "As I said, I can't make it today." He hesitated. "Would it be all right if I came by tomorrow?"

"Of course."

"I'll see you around 4:00."

"Okay. We'll see you then."

Jeremy started to say something, but stopped himself. "Uh . . . okay. I'll see you then." With that, he hung up.

Jenna sensed that Jeremy was about to bring up what had passed between them last week, but had second thoughts. She couldn't very well hold that against him; after all, she hadn't brought it up either.

Undoubtedly, there would be some awkward moments between the two of them on Friday. But with the way Bobby had reacted when he thought Jeremy was at the door, she was more than willing to put up with a little awkwardness for her son's sake.

As Friday morning turned into Friday afternoon, Jenna could feel herself becoming more and more nervous.

Jeremy arrived around 3:45. When Jenna let him in, he smiled at her, but avoided any physical contact.

"Hi. Sorry about yesterday."

"Don't be silly."

Jeremy looked past Jenna and focused on Bobby. "Hey, big guy. How're you doing?"

Bobby seemed to react to Jeremy's voice, and a full-fledged smile formed on his lips. Jenna and Jeremy looked at each other, clearly surprised. Jeremy said, "Wow, I've never seen him do that before! Have you?"

"No."

Jeremy got an exaggerated smug look on his face. "It must be part of the Baxter charm."

Jenna smiled. "Right." Any tension between the two of them seemed to disappear after that.

Jeremy stayed for another half-hour, spending most of the time playing with Bobby. And even when he did interact with Jenna, he never broached the subject of their embrace the previous week.

Jenna began to think that maybe she had misunderstood what had transpired between them. But then, when Jeremy was about to leave and he obviously avoided any physical contact again, she knew she hadn't.

She briefly put herself in Jeremy's shoes. He was probably David's best friend. Regardless of what he might be feeling, he wasn't about to act on it, or probably even acknowledge it.

For the time being, it appeared to Jenna that whether it was real or imagined, she had dodged one additional complication in her life.

CHAPTER 42

For the next several weeks, both David and Jenna pushed any thoughts of discussing the second opinion into the background. Neither of them wanted to revert back to the constant tension that had overtaken their lives. At some point they knew they'd have to confront the issue again, but for the time being, they were more than content to back off and take a breath.

Jeremy continued his weekly visits, and if anything, his relationship with Bobby grew stronger. And although he was just as friendly toward Jenna as he had always been, he continued to refrain from any physical contact.

On a number of occasions Jenna had started to bring up the subject, but thought better of it, trying to respect the fact that whatever Jeremy might have been feeling, he had decided not to pursue it.

Despite the initial awkwardness that each visit produced, Jenna found herself eagerly looking forward to having Jeremy stop by. She was able to convince herself that seeing Bobby's excitement whenever Jeremy showed up was the sole reason for the shift in her feelings.

But if that were true, she asked herself—Why hadn't she told David about Bobby's animated response every time he saw Jeremy? She could certainly have done that without mentioning any of the other tangential things that were going on. She didn't have an answer to that question, but something told her that she should still hold off mentioning anything to David. And so she did.

In early June shortly after Trish graduated, she came out to Quincy and spent the whole day with Jenna. Her wedding was a little more than three months away, and although everything was on schedule, the sole topic of conversation for the first half-hour was the wedding.

Bobby awoke from his nap shortly after that, and their attention turned to him.

"I can't believe how big he's gotten."

"I know. The doctor said he's in the eighty-fifth percentile for both height and weight."

Trish spoke tentatively. "How's everything else going . . . with him?

"Pretty well, actually. I've been e-mailing back and forth with Dr. Townsend from the Center in Canton where Bobby was diagnosed. He's been great about giving me suggestions about things to do, and we're definitely seeing a difference."

"He seems more tuned into things than he was the last time I saw him." Trish paused. "Do you take him to the Center on a regular basis?"

"No. Their programs are for three-year-olds and up."

"Really?"

"They used to have programs for younger kids, but the cost was prohibitive for most families. Insurance doesn't cover it, and local school districts don't start paying for those services until the child's been classified as having special needs. But as I said, Dr. Townsend has outlined a lot of different ideas that seem to help."

"Well, it looks like it's working. You deserve a lot of credit."

At that point Jenna almost mentioned Jeremy and his impact on Bobby, but caught herself. Bringing up that subject might have led to additional questions that Jenna hadn't been able to successfully explore with herself, never mind with anyone else. The rest of the afternoon wasn't anywhere near as serious, as they both easily slipped back into college roommate mode.

After Trish left, Jenna thought about how each of their lives had become so different. Less than two years ago they had been in exactly the same place.

Jenna found herself wondering if she would trade places with Trish if she could. It surprised her a little when she came to the realization that she wouldn't. Without question, she wished that certain things in her life were different, but most of those things she had no control over. All in all, she was happy with the choices she had made. She smiled to herself, and went into the bedroom to tend to her son.

Even though David hadn't brought it up recently, towards the end of June Jenna finally decided it was time to renew the search for an appropriate place for Bobby's re-evaluation. Her first call was to Dr. Townsend. She was able to schedule an appointment for later in the week.

"Thanks for seeing me, doctor."

"Of course. Please sit down, Jenna. What can I do for you?"

"First of all, I know I've mentioned it in my e-mails, but I wanted to thank you in person for everything you've done."

"You're quite welcome. So what else is on your mind?"

"Well, if you remember, I spoke with you a few months ago about David wanting a second opinion and . . . ."

"Right, right. I recall that. I take it that you haven't been able to convince him otherwise."

"No." Jenna appeared embarrassed. "As you can imagine, it's somewhat complicated. I finally agreed that if we can't find someplace we can both agree on, then we'd try the Chambers Institute."

Dr. Townsend didn't say anything immediately. Before the silence got too uncomfortable he said, "I think that would be unfortunate, but I understand. How can I help?"

The relief was very evident in Jenna's expression. "I really appreciate that."

Jenna removed some papers from her pocketbook. "I've made some notes about three places that are reasonably close by, and seem to have a good reputation." She handed the list to Dr. Townsend.

After looking it over briefly, he smiled and said, "You've done your homework. You're right; they do have good reputations."

They talked for another ten minutes, reviewing the relative strength of each facility. Eventually, Dr. Townsend indicated that his first choice would be the Concord Children's Center in New Hampshire.

"The only difficulty you may have is that they prefer that any child they evaluate is at least two years old. When will Bobby be two?"

"Not until the end of December."

"Well, they might make an exception because he's already had an evaluation. I'd be willing to give them a call on your behalf, if you decide that's where you'd like to go."

"Obviously, I need to talk with David. I'm not sure we're at that point quite yet. But thank you for offering."

"You're welcome. Just let me know."

Jenna hadn't planned to ask the question that started forming in her brain, but she went ahead anyway. "Can I ask you something else, doctor?"

"Of course."

"There seem to be two people that Bobby relates to better than anyone else, even more so than to me or David. Is that typical?"

"I wouldn't call it typical, but it's not uncommon. Unfortunately, we have no idea why it happens. If we knew why, we might be able to find a strategy to replicate the connection."

"It seems funny, because Bobby doesn't see these individuals all that often. One of them is a neighbor, a young man with Down syndrome, and the other one came with me to Bobby's evaluation – Jeremy Baxter. They see Bobby maybe once a week."

"Again, the frequency of time spent doesn't seem to make a difference. It's just another puzzling aspect of autism. But as we've talked about, the fact that Bobby is relating to *anyone* is a positive sign."

When David arrived back in Quincy the following weekend, Jenna brought up the issue of Bobby's re-evaluation. She approached the topic tentatively, avoiding any mention of her visit with Dr. Townsend.

David listened patiently, and then when Jenna indicated that the places she had looked at probably wouldn't be willing to see Bobby until he was at least two, David surprised her.

"There's a part of me that would like to get this settled, but the truth is I'm swamped at work; your mother's going to be here in a few weeks, and you're getting ready for Trish's wedding. It'd be okay with me if we wait a while."

Jenna's expression was filled with relief. "I think that really would be for the best, but are you sure?"

"Yeah. I mean, I still feel strongly about getting the second opinion, but I have to admit, it's been great over the last month or so not arguing all the time. Let's get through the summer, and then we'll figure out what we're going to do."

Jenna didn't say anything further. She went to him and threw her arms around his neck.

Toward the end of July, Jenna's mom came to stay with them for a week. If Sharon was disappointed that her grandson wasn't more animated toward her, she never let on. Instead, she pointed out all of the positive behaviors that Bobby exhibited that she hadn't seen before.

Jenna was tempted to tell her mom that she was in for an even bigger surprise when Jeremy came over later in the week. But she decided it was better to get her mother's reaction without any pre-conceived notion.

On Thursday morning Jenna tried to find some mindless chores to do prior to Jeremy's visit. Sharon noticed Jenna's inability to keep still. "Are you all right? You seem jumpy."

"I'm fine."

Jeremy showed up around 3:00. He stayed for more than an hour, about half of the time with Bobby. Jenna could see from the expression on her mother's face how surprised she was with the way Bobby became engaged in everything Jeremy did.

At one point she said, "He's amazing with you. He seems so at ease."

"I don't know what it is. It's kind of been like this for a while now."

"Well whatever you're doing, keep it up."

Jeremy got a smile on his face and offered a self-deprecating remark, "I'm really good with kids under three and senior citizens. It's the group in-between that I have trouble with."

Sharon laughed. "Somehow I doubt that."

After Jeremy left and Jenna put Bobby in for a nap, Sharon and her daughter had a chance to talk. "There's a real connection between Bobby and Jeremy, isn't there? Bobby's like a whole different child. David must be thrilled."

Jenna didn't respond right away. "Actually, David hasn't seen the two of them together recently." Jenna hesitated. "And I haven't told him about it yet."

"What? Why not?"

"I've been reluctant to say anything."

"I don't understand, Jenna."

For the first time Jenna found herself able to open up about what she had been feeling. She told her mom about the hug and kiss from Jeremy, the agreement about the second opinion, even about her own inability to sort out her feelings toward Jeremy.

"In the beginning I didn't tell David because I thought he'd blow it out of proportion. You know, like it proved that the initial diagnosis was all wrong. And then when Bobby was even more responsive to Jeremy, I thought David might see it as some kind of failure on his part. After all, *he's* Bobby's father and yet Bobby responds so much better to Jeremy."

"Do you really think David would care about that?"

"I don't know, but I didn't want to take the chance. I didn't want to hurt him. Plus, what if David got upset and didn't want Jeremy to see Bobby anymore?"

"You might not want to hear this, Jenna. But I think you're projecting things that are very unlikely."

"That may be true, but at the time . . . and now I've dug this hole for myself."

Sharon was quiet for a moment, and then asked, "Does any of this have to do with how you feel about Jeremy?"

"Honestly, I don't think so. I mean, when I see how happy Bobby is with Jeremy, naturally it makes me happy too. Doesn't it make sense that I would feel something for the person who does that for my son? Do I have feelings beyond that? I just don't know."

They were silent for a few moments before Sharon said, "I wish I could help you sort that out, but I'm not sure I can. But as far as telling David, I think you owe that to him, Jenna." Sharon paused. "Keeping secrets from one another—I don't think that's ever a good idea."

"I know. I've been wrestling with that every day for the last month."

Sharon smiled. "That alone should probably tell you everything you need to know."

When she went to bed that night, Jenna kept hearing her mother's words in her head, and was definitely leaning toward telling David as soon as he came home. But by the next morning the doubts had returned.

At around 11:00 the phone rang. It was Jeremy. "Hi. Is it okay if I come over for a few minutes?"

Jenna could feel her face flush as she responded. "Yeah, of course. What's up?"

"I'll tell you when I get there."

He arrived about forty-five minutes later. Bobby was sitting in his high chair having lunch when Jeremy came through the door. He said 'hi' to Bobby, who looked up and smiled, but then went back to his grilled cheese sandwich.

Jeremy glanced over at Jenna and her mother. "Not how he usually greets me, but I guess food trumps everything else. Remind me not to show up around lunch time again."

Even though she suspected he was joking, Jenna felt the need to jump in. "He's probably just surprised to see you. He knows you were here yesterday."

"I know. I was only kidding." He looked at Bobby again. "You get a pass this time, big guy. I'm in too good a mood."

Jenna asked, "Why's that?"

A huge smile came across his face. "I got a phone call a few hours ago. I've got a new teaching job."

"What? I didn't even know you had applied for . . . ."

"I know. I didn't say anything in case I didn't get it. And it's right here in Quincy at one of the middle schools. I would've preferred one of the high schools, but this'll be fine."

Without thinking about it, Jenna went over to Jeremy with her arms out-stretched. For the briefest of moments he hesitated, but then opened his arms as well.

Jenna quickly realized what she had done, withdrew awkwardly, but composed herself enough to offer, "That's terrific. I'm so happy for you."

Jeremy stayed for another fifteen minutes, sharing with both Jenna and her mom some additional details about his new position. As he was leaving, Bobby had finished his lunch and appeared ready to re-engage with him, but Jeremy had to go. He spoke to Bobby, but the words appeared to be for Jenna and Sharon's benefit. "I'm sorry, pal, I have to meet my new principal and sign some papers. I'll see you in a couple of days."

After he left, Jenna and her mother talked briefly about Jeremy's good fortune, and then decided to take Bobby out for a walk. They quickly drifted into small talk, which was fortunate for Jenna, because she would have had difficulty maintaining a meaningful conversation.

The renewed physical contact with Jeremy, no matter how innocent, had served to further entangle her feelings.

CHAPTER 43

The first few days of September felt more like the dog days of August — humid, hot and hazy. But by Saturday, the weather had done a one-eighty, and Trish had a picture-perfect day for her wedding.

David left work early on Friday afternoon and arrived back in Massachusetts that night. He got up early on Saturday to take care of Bobby and let Jenna sleep in. And while she appreciated the gesture, Jenna was much too excited to take advantage of it; she was up by 6:00.

Jeremy had received an invitation to the wedding as well, and was scheduled to arrive at the apartment sometime around 11:00 so they could all ride together. Although Jenna had to be at the church early to help Trish get ready, it made little sense to take two cars, let alone three.

When Jeremy called on the intercom at 10:30, Barbara and Toby were already there to baby-sit for Bobby, and Jenna was still getting dressed.

David greeted his friend at the door with a handshake. "Well hello, stranger."

"Hi. Yeah, it's been a while, hasn't it? How're you doing?"

"I'm good. How about you?"

"I'm fine."

David was about to say something else when Bobby, who had been playing with Toby on the floor, let out a squeal, "Jay me."

Both David and Jeremy turned at the same time.

Initially, David wasn't sure what Bobby had said, but when he saw his son get up off the floor and move toward Jeremy, he figured it out.

Jeremy met Bobby halfway, picked him up, and said, "Hey, pal, what're you doing? Playing with Toby?" Jeremy glanced over where Toby was sitting and said, "Hi."

Just then, Barbara came out of the kitchen and Jeremy acknowledged her as well. She smiled. "Hello, Jeremy."

David watched all of this unfold, too stunned to say anything.

It had only been in the last few weeks that Bobby had said anything even closely resembling 'daddy,' and even then David wasn't sure that's what his son had meant. And now, here he was clearly making an effort to say Jeremy's name. And not only that, Bobby had clearly wanted Jeremy to pick him up. David had never seen Bobby so animated. What is going on, he thought?

Jeremy's voice pulled David back into the moment. "Okay, Bobby. Why don't you go back to playing with Toby? Your mommy and daddy and I have to go somewhere."

It was obvious that Bobby didn't really understand what was being said to him. But nevertheless, when Jeremy lowered him to the floor, he eased out of his arms and went back over to Toby.

David was still struggling to process everything that had just occurred when Jenna emerged from the bedroom. To some extent he was relieved. It gave him a moment to pull himself together. Maybe this wasn't the best time to ask questions about what he had just witnessed, especially in front of all these people, but still . . . .

Jeremy spotted Jenna a moment later, and said, "Well, don't you clean up nice."

Jenna responded with a touch of sarcasm, "And aren't you the smooth talker. What a compliment." Jeremy smiled as Jenna continued, "Maid of honor dresses can be pretty hideous, but I really like this one."

Although David's mind was focused elsewhere, he was still able to tune into the conversation enough to say, "You do look nice."

Jenna assumed David was following Jeremy's lead. "Take it easy, guys; you're going to give me a big head."

Barbara followed up. "Ignore them. That color looks terrific on you. What is it, peach?"

"I think they call it 'orange blossom,' but it looks like peach to me."

Barbara again: "Well whatever it is, it's a great color for you."

"Thanks. Maybe you and I should go to the wedding and leave these two at home."

David forced a smile.

A few minutes later, they got into David's car and headed for the church in North Reading. Jenna insisted that Jeremy sit up front to give him more legroom. "Plus, I can stretch out in the back to make sure my dress doesn't get wrinkled." Although the seating arrangements in the car weren't conducive to any kind of serious discussion, David had all he could do not to bring up what was really on his mind.

The wedding ceremony lasted about forty minutes, and went off without a hitch. After some mingling in front of the church, everyone headed to the reception at the country club in Andover.

David and Jeremy were seated at a table with a group of twenty-somethings, all of whom Trish and Kevin knew from the TV station. As if on cue, they all went up to the open bar. And with Jenna outside with the bridal party having their pictures taken, David and Jeremy found themselves alone.

It certainly wasn't the question David really wanted to ask, but he offered it up anyway. "How's the new job?"

"The kids don't start until next week, but I think it's going to work out fine. I like the people I'm teaching with, and the principal seems like a good guy."

"That's great."

"How about you? Jenna mentioned that things are a little stressful."

David raised his eyebrows. "Yeah. That's putting it mildly. You know how it is; it's just like what we did a couple of summers ago. I've got to coordinate five different sub-contractors, so everything gets done in the right order. As you can imagine, it's even worse in New York than it is in Boston."

"Actually, I can't begin to imagine."

They both smiled. The silence lasted for a few moments, each of them trying to come up with something to talk about. Finally, Jeremy said, "I don't think I told you guys that I'm thinking of moving."

"Really? How come?"

"Right now it takes me about a half hour to get to school, which isn't too bad. But coming up Route 3, you never know what you're in for, especially during the winter."

"Yeah. That's true."

"I probably won't move right into Quincy itself, just close by."

"That makes sense."

It was getting increasingly difficult for David not to just blurt out the questions he had. And after a few more minutes, he couldn't hold back anymore. However, he was able to discipline himself enough to come at it from a slightly different angle. "By the way, thanks again for looking in on Bobby and Jenna each week."

It was obvious from his expression that the comment made Jeremy uncomfortable, maybe even embarrassed. "I'm . . . uh . . . glad to do it."

David ignored Jeremy's hesitation. "Well it's pretty clear that Bobby appreciates it."

Jeremy's expression brightened. "Yeah, he's a great little guy. And he's really coming along, don't you think?"

"No question."

"I'm sure Jenna told you. It probably started around the time he first tried to say my name. From then on, things just began to take off. He doesn't seem nearly as withdrawn as he used to. I think it has something to do with the new activities Dr. Townsend suggested."

David couldn't believe what he was hearing. He was about to try to get to the bottom of all of this when the twenty-somethings returned to the table, and any opportunity for that to happen disappeared.

Over the next several hours David thought of little else. He wasn't sure if he was more hurt or more angry. Somehow, he held it together throughout the rest of the reception and the ride home, never letting on that beneath the surface his emotions were churning.

Once they got back to the apartment he still had to wait for Barbara and Toby to leave, and then for Jenna to put Bobby to bed. David had intended to start the conversation calmly, but as soon as Jenna came into the living room, his anger got the best of him, and instead the words seemed to explode out of his mouth. "What the hell is going on? Why haven't you told me about what's been happening with Bobby?"

The color drained from Jenna's face. And although she knew exactly what David meant, she answered as if she didn't in order to give herself some additional time to think. "What do you mean?"

"Oh, come on, Jenna. I saw it with my own two eyes. Jeremy showed up while you were still getting dressed. Bobby actually said Jeremy's name and wanted to be picked up." David shook his head and expelled some air before he continued. "Jeremy said it's been going on for months. Obviously he assumed that you had told me all about it. And why wouldn't he?"

The last few sentences came out filled with anger, but as David continued, the hurt he was feeling pushed through. "Why didn't you tell me? How do you think it makes me feel that I don't know things about my own son?"

Jenna closed her eyes. "I don't know what to say."

David's anger resurfaced. "Well, try something."

"I don't want it to seem like I'm making excuses."

"Then don't. There aren't any, anyway."

Jenna realized that whatever she said would seem empty and defensive. But maybe David was right; there probably were no excuses. She would try to explain, and if it came across as making excuses, there wasn't much she could do about it.

She did make sure to look David in the eye, so he would know that she wasn't trying to hide anything. "At first, the changes seemed really small, and then when he started doing some other things, it was only with Jeremy. Honestly, I thought about saying something to you at that point, but that was right around the time you were pushing for the second opinion." Jenna looked away. "I was afraid you'd latch on to what Bobby was doing, and make it out to be something it wasn't."

"Of course I would have latched on to it. What I don't understand is why you didn't."

Jenna continued to try to defend her actions. "I told you why." She paused. "I did check with Dr. Townsend, and he said that it wasn't unusual for someone with Bobby's . . . condition to connect with one or two individuals. But it wasn't an indication that the underlying problem wasn't there."

David didn't respond directly to Jenna's statement. "Yeah, that's another thing. Jeremy mentioned Dr. Townsend too. How long have you been talking to him without telling me?"

"I told you about the e-mails."

"That was months ago. Are you saying that you haven't been in touch with him since then?"

"No. I have. He's been updating me on some new strategies to try with Bobby."

"This is unbelievable. Am I missing something here? I don't remember any new strategies."

"They only seem to work when Jeremy does them." She paused, and then the very words she vowed to herself she wouldn't say came out of her mouth. "I guess I thought that if I told you, you might get upset."

"What? Why, because it's Jeremy and not me? You think I would care about that? You really think that little of me?"

The words hung in the air, and they both recognized that this argument and what they had said to each other had changed things. They both felt it in the pit of their stomachs, as if a knife had been inserted and twisted.

The silence went on and on until Jenna lifted her head and made eye contact again with David. "I'm sorry, David. I thought I was doing the right thing, but obviously I wasn't. I really am sorry."

Although he knew Jenna was sincere, David was still reeling from everything that had just happened. Part of him wanted to accept her apology, but the overwhelming emotional pain he was feeling wouldn't allow it. Eventually, in a dispassionate voice he said, "I'm going to make the appointment for the evaluation at the Chambers Institute as soon as possible."

For the briefest of moments Jenna thought of objecting, but she had no fight left in her. "All right."

CHAPTER 44

The next day David got up early, wrote a note to Jenna, and headed out to visit his father. The entire time David was getting dressed, Jenna pretended to be asleep, not wanting to provide the opportunity for the argument from last night to be resurrected, at least not until she had time to gain some perspective.

David returned from the rehab center around noon. And while Jenna surmised he must have gone someplace else in addition to visiting his father, she decided not to question him about it.

"How's your dad?"

Given what had happened last night, David's voice and manner were softer than Jenna had expected. "Actually, he looks pretty good. His regular doctor wasn't there, so I didn't get a chance to talk to him. I'll probably give him a call during the week to get an update."

"You want some lunch?"

"No. I grabbed something when I was out."

David moved further into the kitchen where Jenna was feeding Bobby in his high chair. "Hi, pal."

Bobby reacted to his father's voice, but seemed to look past him to something on the far wall. Jenna tried to follow her son's eyes, but couldn't figure out what he was focusing on. A moment later he grabbed some cut up carrots off the tray in front of him and put them in his mouth. Evidently, whatever had drawn his attention ceased to be important.

Jenna stared at her little boy and wondered for the thousandth time – *What's he thinking about? What's going on in his head?*

She looked over and saw David watching her, as if he could read her mind. Or was he thinking about last night? She decided it was the latter. "After I finish feeding Bobby, would you like to talk some more?"

David's quick response suggested he was expecting the question. "I'm not sure there's much else to say. Is there? I'm not changing my mind about the appointment at the Institute."

"I know. I'm not asking you to." Jenna looked directly into David's eyes. "But lately it seems that no matter what I say, or how many times I apologize for something, it isn't enough."

David returned her gaze. "I'm not sure what you want me to say, Jenna. You were way off base on this. You didn't trust me, and that hurts more than anything else." He looked away briefly. "This is not something I can just shrug off; it's going to take me a while." He paused. "It's probably not a bad thing that I have to go back to New York tomorrow."

David hadn't intended for his remark to be so hurtful, but from Jenna's expression he knew that it had been. He tried to soften the impact. "What I meant was that it's going to take me more than a couple of days to get past this."

David saw tears forming in Jenna's eyes. He waited to see if she was going to say anything else. When she didn't, he offered, "I can't help it, Jenna. I'm still upset." With those words David went into the living room and opened the Sunday paper.

For the rest of the Labor Day weekend Jenna and David tiptoed around each other. On Monday morning as David was getting ready to leave, he kissed Jenna on the cheek and said, "I'll call you in a couple of days once I know about the appointment." And then he was out the door.

Jenna almost wished there had been some histrionics. Having David on such an even keel was more disturbing than any yelling he might have done. He had said he just needed time, but it didn't feel like time was going to be able to heal this. This seemed to have changed him.

As Jenna had done for the better part of the last two days, her thoughts revisited all of the things that she could have done differently.

Why didn't I tell David everything from the beginning? None of this had to happen, and now Bobby has to go to the Chambers Institute. I should have fought David on that . . . Who am I kidding? I wasn't in any shape to fight him on anything right then. Her mind went blank for a moment. When a thought began to fill the void, it involved Jeremy. *How does he fit into all of this? Is that the real reason I didn't tell David?*

Jenna realized she honestly didn't know the answer to that question.

What she did know was that she needed to talk to *someone*. She had things she wanted to say, things she wanted to explain.

As Jenna was about to pick up the phone to call Jeremy, she closed her eyes and took a deep breath. She had made a lot of mistakes over the last few months. Maybe having Jeremy come over would be another one?

She left the phone where it was.

David called Wednesday night to say that the earliest appointment he could get for Bobby was in January. Jenna felt a sense of relief wash over her. *A lot can happen in four months.*

David's voice interrupted Jenna's thoughts. "I know you still have reservations about the Institute, but this is something we need to do." If David had stopped there, Jenna would have assumed he was trying to ease the strain between them. But when he followed up with, "Plus, you owe me this," she had all she could do to not explode. Every instinct she possessed told her to resurrect her objections, but she knew where that would lead. Her desire to keep the peace won out. With a measured tone she said, "Don't I have to sign something for the evaluation?"

"I was about to mention that. They faxed me a form this morning. I'll bring it up with me this weekend."

Jenna was still smarting from David's remark. "Okay."

If David sensed that Jenna was upset, he didn't say anything. After a moment, he moved on to another topic. "I spoke to my father's doctor."

Jenna had trouble tuning in to this new subject, but was able to manage, "Oh, right. What did he say?"

"He didn't want to make too much out of it, but he's begun to notice some positive changes."

Jenna did her best to shake off her lingering resentment. "Really? Like what?"

"He seems to react to being touched, which hasn't happened in a long time. Plus, the doctor says he's responding to sounds, as well."

"And the doctor thinks that's significant?"

"He's not sure exactly what it means, but it certainly is a change. I'm going to talk with him some more over the weekend."

They spoke for a few more minutes, and then David said goodbye. Jenna tried to recall the last time David had ended a phone conversation without saying 'I love you.' She couldn't.

When Jeremy arrived on Thursday, he spent the initial half hour with Bobby, and then sat with Jenna on the couch, filling her in about the first few days at his new school.

Jenna had always thought Jeremy had very expressive eyes, but they took on a whole new dimension when he talked about teaching. After several more minutes he paused and said, "I'm sorry. I'm going on and on about all of this. It's just that I wasn't sure it was going to be anything like my other school, especially with the change in grade levels. But I think it might even be better. I know it's only been a few days, but . . . ."

Jenna smiled. "It's okay. It's great to see someone who loves his job so much."

"Quite a switch from a few months ago, huh? I was going to quit, remember?"

She nodded. "I once read somewhere that if you leave things alone for a while, sometimes they have a way of working themselves out." After she said it, Jenna wasn't entirely sure if her comment was aimed at Jeremy's situation or her own.

She was trying to find a way to ease into the topic of what was going on between her and David, but couldn't find an opening. And then Jeremy forced her hand. "Well, I think I'm going to head out."

As he started to get up off the couch, Jenna put her hand on his arm. "Could you wait a few minutes? I'd like to talk to you about something."

Jeremy got a look of concern on his face as he sat back down. "Of course. Is everything all right?"

For the next ten minutes Jenna outlined what had occurred after she and David had gotten home from the wedding. The only thing she omitted was any mention of how her possible feelings toward Jeremy might have impacted her decision not to tell David.

Jenna had become teary-eyed by the time she finished. Jeremy hesitated for a moment, but then took her hand and said, "I feel like part of this is my fault."

"What? No!"

"But I'm the one who told David about what Bobby was doing."

"And I'm the one who should have. Plus, he saw it for himself the day of the wedding."

"Still, I understand why David would think I was rubbing his nose in it."

"He doesn't blame you. This is my fault, Jeremy, not yours. I've made a real mess out of this."

"I think you're being too hard on yourself."

"I thought that too, at first, but not anymore."

They were quiet for a moment, and then Jeremy said, "Is David still okay with me coming over? I mean, if it bothers him . . . ."

"No. I told you. As far as he's concerned, this has nothing to do with you. I'm the one who kept it from him. Besides, we both see the way Bobby is with you. Do you think either one of us wants that to stop?"

"I just feel like if I had tuned into things better, then you guys wouldn't be fighting."

"Nothing about this is your fault."

"I wish I believed that."

"Well, it's true."

Jeremy waited a moment, and then said, "Are you going to be okay? Do you want me to stay a while?."

"I'll be all right. It helped just to talk about it." Jenna paused. "Plus, you must have lessons to prepare?"

Jeremy got a sheepish grin on his face. "All my lessons plans are done from now until Thanksgiving."

Jenna let out a little chuckle. "Why am I not surprised?"

Over the next several months there was an unspoken truce between David and Jenna. Although neither of them was completely satisfied with the way things had evolved, the thought of continuing to fight was out of the question. Better to avoid talking about it, than risk opening up the wounds again.

On a number of weekends David didn't make it back to Massachusetts. It was the weather, or it was work, or it was some combination. Initially, Jenna had become upset, but eventually she just accepted that this was the way it was going to be, at least until David decided to forgive her.

The problem was that in his own way, David *had* forgiven her. But forgiving someone and getting past what they had done, were not the same thing.

For Jenna's part, although she acknowledged that their relationship was in this place mainly because of her mistakes, she was nevertheless resentful. Most of all she resented David's insistence on the Chambers Institute. She felt that she had been bullied into agreeing, at a time when she was overwhelmed with a sense of guilt and unable to stand up for herself or for Bobby.

Periodically, Jenna thought back to a few months ago when she and David had enjoyed just being in the same room, when they knew what the other person was going to say before they said it, when there was a shared intimacy. But that had all disappeared. Even making love was more perfunctory than passionate. She wondered if she were to blame for that too.

Jenna realized that the only time she laughed anymore was with Jeremy or during the occasional phone conversation with her mother or with Trish. She also realized that quite possibly, she missed the laughter as much as anything else.

In mid-December, about two weeks before Bobby's second birthday, David got a call asking him to come by the rehab center when he returned to Massachusetts. He was assured that nothing was wrong. In fact, there had been some additional positive developments regarding his father's condition.

David drove up early Saturday morning and went directly to the rehab facility. He met with one of the doctors for a half-hour, sat with his father for another twenty minutes, and then headed to Quincy.

As he came through the apartment door, Jenna said, "This is a surprise. I didn't expect to see you until this afternoon."

"I left New York early so I could stop off to see my father." As he finished crossing the living room, David bent down and gave Bobby a kiss on top of the head and Jenna a peck on the cheek.

Jenna spoke next. "How's he doing?"

"I think he looks better than he has since he went in there." As David took off his coat, he continued. "The doctor even said that although there's a limited amount of medical documentation on it, my father's exhibiting some behaviors consistent with a patient who is ready to come out of his coma."

"Seriously?"

"I know there are no guarantees, but it's been so long since I thought there was even a chance . . . ."

Jenna went to him with her arms outstretched, and David didn't hesitate as he embraced her. After a brief time they separated and David continued. "The doctor said they'd like to consider moving him to a

319

facility in Westchester, just outside of New York City. They're doing some experimental treatment there that might speed up his recovery even more. There are still a lot of details to work out, and I have to call Alan Fenton and make sure he agrees. But from everything the doctor told me, my father's an ideal candidate."

Jenna thought David was getting ahead of himself. But this was the most animated and excited she had seen him in months. She wasn't about to say anything to put a damper on it. "That sounds terrific, David."

"Wouldn't it be great if things started to turn around for us?" He paused. "But at least, once he's transferred, I won't have to go back and forth to Massachusetts."

Jenna looked puzzled. "What do you mean?"

"Well, after my father is moved to Westchester, there's no reason to stay here. You and Bobby can come to live with me in New York."

Jenna wouldn't have been able to speak, even if she had wanted to. Her stomach knotted up, and then it extended to her whole body.

She felt paralyzed.

For the next several minutes, although Jenna could hear David's voice, she had no idea what he was saying. He might as well have been speaking in some ancient language. Eventually, she recovered enough to retrieve one of the thoughts she had had a few moments before.

"I know you're excited, David, but we probably need to hold off making any decisions until we know more."

David nodded. "Yeah, you're probably right about that."

Jenna breathed an inaudible sigh of relief.

CHAPTER 45

David called Alan Fenton the first thing the next morning, telling him about his father's improvement and possible move to the facility in Westchester. Alan responded with some excitement in his voice. "I went to see him a few weeks ago, and I thought I saw some positive signs too, but not to the extent you're talking about. Obviously, if there's any chance that your father could come out of the coma, we have to do whatever it takes."

"I got the impression that it wouldn't be until well after the first of the year, but that's still pretty soon. I think I'd like to take a look at the place before we okay the move."

"I agree."

"All right, Alan. I'll keep you posted."

David scheduled his visit to the Westchester facility on the Martin Luther King holiday, several days before Bobby's evaluation at the Chambers Institute. By doing that, he could bring Jenna and Bobby back to New York with him on Sunday, and they could all spend time together before the evaluation.

Although David's plan allowed them to be together as a family, Jenna was still hesitant to agree. It might give David the idea that she was willing to entertain moving to New York permanently.

She wondered to herself: When had she started to view things with such suspicion? Why had the fact that David wanted her to spend time with him in New York seemed like some sort of calculated ploy? She hated that she felt that way, but she couldn't help it.

David was very excited when he returned from the visit to the Westchester clinic. Everything was state-of-the-art, and the doctors were upbeat and optimistic about the results they were getting with quite a few of their patients.

David had become so wrapped up in his father's situation that, in the evenings when he came home from work, there was very little discussion of Bobby's upcoming evaluation.

That was all right with Jenna.

There was little traffic on the ride down the Garden State Parkway to the Chambers Institute, so they arrived about thirty-five minutes early. They spent a few minutes walking around the grounds, which Jenna had to admit were beautiful.

David's voice interrupted her thoughts. "We probably should head inside."

The receptionist directed them to the office where they were meeting with the doctor prior to the evaluation. Jenna wasn't sure if it was a good omen or a bad omen that the receptionist never mentioned Mark Chambers. But evidently, he wasn't scheduled to participate in the meeting.

They waited in the office for about ten minutes before the doctor showed up. He introduced himself, had David and Jenna sign some additional forms, and then proceeded to outline what was going to happen.

Right from the beginning, Jenna had a sense of déjà vu. Nearly every activity the doctor described was in essence the same activity Bobby had done almost a year ago in Massachusetts.

As they finished up with the doctor, Jenna started to make that point to David, but remembered that he hadn't been at the first evaluation. She decided to back off and not say anything. If David thought she had already made up her mind, they would be arguing again before Bobby even started the evaluation.

While it became more and more difficult for Jenna to hold her tongue as she observed the various activities, David's reaction was at the other end of the spectrum. "He's doing really well, don't you think?"

"He is." Jenna hoped her response sounded sincere, but the truth was Bobby had been performing similar activities to the ones they were observing for months now. Of course he should be doing well; this wasn't an evaluation as much as it was an extended floor time exercise for him.

By the time Bobby got to the last activity of the day, Jenna knew for certain that nothing productive was going to come out of the evaluation.

The final activity was exactly the same as the final activity at the first evaluation, except instead of live-action, they used a video to depict the ball rolling down the tracks and crashing into the miniature bowling pins.

When Jenna looked over at David, he seemed to have an expression on his face that suggested even he remembered having this activity described to him. But he didn't comment.

Bobby didn't seem all that interested in what was going on, until the final time the ball rolled down the tracks and the screen went blank. Even though he couldn't see what happened, he shouted, "Boom!"

The technician in with Bobby laughed out loud, as did David on the other side of the two-way mirror. "Wow, that was amazing, wasn't it?"

Jenna smiled. "Yeah, it was." She started to say something else, but held off, realizing that David had never seen it before.

Again, Jenna felt like Scrooge at Christmas. It would have been very easy to get caught up in David's enthusiasm, but Jenna had witnessed Bobby do something similar to that a hundred times – Jeremy had taught it to him.

Whenever he and Bobby played with blocks, they would construct a tower, and then Jeremy would roll a toy truck toward it. The first two times he would stop the truck before it reached its destination, but on the third time, he would let it crash into the tower. Jeremy had taught Bobby to yell "boom" just as it hit.

To the people at the Institute as well as David, all of Bobby's responses must have seemed very appropriate, thought Jenna. But she knew better. Bobby was giving those responses because he had done that activity so many times that his response was automatic. It probably wouldn't do any good to say anything to the people at the Institute, but what about David?

Do I bring it up on the ride home? Wait for the results in a few weeks? And what about the fact that Jeremy was the one to teach Bobby to say, "boom?" David said that didn't matter to him, but was he telling me the truth?

Jenna recognized that her *m.o.* lately had been to postpone talking about anything that was the least bit uncomfortable. She had convinced herself that she was just buying time, but deep down she knew she was avoiding things.

She resembled an air traffic controller who wouldn't allow any planes to land because of inclement weather. At some point, however, she understood that she had to permit them to touch down; they couldn't circle forever.

David waited until they had gotten into the car before opening up the conversation. "I thought Bobby was incredible today."

Jenna hesitated, but then decided to let one of the smaller planes approach the runway. "He really was."

"That video with the bowling pins, and him shouting, 'boom,' that was great."

Jenna steeled herself before giving the go-ahead to lower the landing gear. "It was." She paused. "But I think we need to remember that he's a year older, and he's talking now."

"I know, but still . . . besides the doctors will take that into consideration."

The plane had descended and was starting to level off. "I'm a little concerned that it's going to be difficult to get an accurate diagnosis."

"Why?"

"Well, Bobby's done a lot of those activities before, even during the first evaluation."

"So? What does that matter? What are you trying to say?"

"I'm not sure. It's just that if you practice the same thing over and over again, you're bound to get better at it."

"Isn't that the point?"

"Not for an evaluation."

"Why are you downplaying this?"

"I'm not trying to. I'm just worried that the report isn't going to be as helpful as we'd like." Jenna pulled up the nose of the plane at the last possible instant. "But I guess we should just wait for the results and not jump to any conclusions."

"I thought that's what we were going to do."

"Okay."

It appeared that the plane would have to wait a while before making another attempt.

The preliminary results from the evaluation arrived three weeks later at the apartment in Quincy. The accompanying letter strongly recommended a follow-up visit to review the report in detail.

Jenna waited until Bobby went in for a nap before she started to read it. The initial paragraphs described each activity contained in the evaluation, and what it was supposed to measure. Jenna was fairly impressed with that part of the report. However, when it came to the results, it was much less comprehensive. Jenna assumed that was to ensure parents would schedule a follow-up appointment.

The most specific information came toward the end.

It appears that the subject has some developmental delays, but they don't present as significant. He is slightly delayed in verbal pronouncements, but appears to be processing information consistent with children close to his chronological age.

Jenna wished with all her heart that she could just accept those statements at face value, but her head wouldn't allow it. The Institute had given him the same "test" that he had been given a year ago. *Of course* the results were going to be better.

And what about the things that the people at the Chambers Institute had never seen—the temper tantrums borne out of Bobby's frustration at not being able to communicate, the perseverative behaviors, the inability to make sustained eye contact, the lack of affect, the inability to show affection, the intense focus one minute, and the inability to concentrate on anything the next?

She knew her child better than anyone else. Tears welled up in her eyes as she admitted to herself that the report she held in her hand was a lie.

She had really tried ever since the first evaluation to look at things differently, to see all the positive things Bobby was doing, and dismiss the abnormal things as insignificant, but she couldn't. What good would that do?

She didn't want to become the kind of parent who pretended everything was fine, when she knew that it wasn't. Nor did she want to go to the other extreme and become one of those parents whom she heard her mother talk about, the ones who exaggerated their child's disability because then it made the parent into a victim and worthy of other people's sympathy.

She simply wanted to be realistic, to understand her son better, accept him for who he was, and help him overcome whatever obstacles had been thrown in his way.

Is that what David wanted too? It should be obvious that he did, but Jenna wasn't sure. She hoped that the next few weeks might help answer that question.

As it turned out, the very day David and Jenna were given for an appointment at the Chambers Institute for the follow-up visit, was the same day David's father was scheduled to be transferred to Westchester. Despite numerous phone calls to both facilities, David was told that it would be impossible to switch dates. The Westchester facility didn't have any idea when they would have another empty bed, and the Chambers Institute was booked solid for months.

David called the Chambers Institute for the fourth time, again explaining his predicament. An hour later he got a call back from one of the doctors, who said he had gotten clearance from Mark Chambers to arrange a conference call with Jenna and David instead of the face-to-face review. "It's not going to be anywhere near as comprehensive, but it's the best we can do."

The call was placed on the third Friday in February just before noon. David was already back in Massachusetts to oversee his father's transfer later that day. David picked up the landline in the kitchen, and as soon as he confirmed it was the Institute, Jenna went into the bedroom and listened in on the extension.

The doctor spoke to them for nearly half an hour. For the most part, it was a recitation of the findings contained in the written report they had already received—no mention of autism, just mild delays; Bobby's verbal skills were near average; he seemed to be processing information in an age-appropriate way, etc.

David and Jenna both asked a number of questions which the doctor answered in very general terms. And then came what Jenna had fully anticipated – the sales pitch.

In order to catch Bobby up to where he should be, the Institute strongly recommended hourly sessions at least every other week, more often if possible. The cost per session was approximately $300.

The doctor went on to explain that in order to achieve the desired outcome for Bobby, a minimum of six months worth of treatment would be necessary.

Jenna was sure that the sales pitch she was hearing would have been much more effective face-to-face. Over the phone, the doctor sounded like any other telemarketer hawking some "truly exceptional offer."

At the conclusion of the call, David thanked the doctor, as did Jenna, who then hung up the phone, went into the living room, and sat on the couch.

David joined her. "So, what did you think?"

Jenna would have preferred to have David give his opinion first, so she would have had a better sense of what she was up against. She tried to maneuver the conversation in that direction anyway. "You already know how I feel."

"I'd still like to hear it."

She looked away briefly. "I'd give anything if there was some way to make Bobby's . . . condition disappear. But I've come to accept the fact that that's not going to happen."

David looked surprised. "But the people at the Institute believe they can do that. You heard the doctor."

"Don't you think I want that to be true?" Jenna paused. "But it's not."

"I don't understand how you can keep saying that. You saw what he did at the evaluation, how much he's improved."

"You're right, he has improved, but a lot of that is simply because he's older. I don't know how we're supposed to trust some place that doesn't even acknowledge that there is such a thing as autism."

"I thought you didn't like labels."

"It's not a label; it's a diagnosis."

David was getting more and more upset, and his anger wasn't far from the surface, but he was still able to keep it from boiling over. "I don't get it, Jenna. They tell us our son has only mild delays which they can correct with six months worth of treatment, and you don't want any part of it."

"Because they're wrong."

"And what if *you're* wrong?"

David's question was the same one she had asked herself over and over again. And despite how strongly Jenna believed that she was right, she hesitated for a moment before responding. "I've read everything I can get my hands on, and I've spoken to Dr. Townsend probably fifty times. I've watched other two-year-olds at the playground and at the mall—Bobby's not like them." She looked directly at David. "I'm not wrong about this."

Jenna's remarks blunted some of the anger David was feeling, but he wasn't ready to concede anything yet. "So you're completely dismissing everything in the report."

"Bobby has more than mild delays. And $300 treatments at the Chambers Institute aren't the answer."

"So now it's about the money."

"Stop it. You know that's ridiculous."

David tried a new tack. "You agree with what I'm trying to do for my father, right? How is that any different from what the Institute wants to try with Bobby?"

"You're really asking that question? Your father's in a coma; nobody disputes that. The only chance of him coming out of it may be this new treatment, so of course you should try it. Bobby was already diagnosed with a form of autism, and then we get a second evaluation that basically repeats the first one, and lo and behold, he does better. And then this place wants to charge us $300 a session to do the same things I can do at home with him for free. I'd say there's a huge difference."

David ignored Jenna's answer. "We talked about this before. What harm will it do to try the treatments, and see how it goes, just for a few months? It would work out perfectly – my father being transferred to Westchester, and you and Bobby moving to New York."

And there it is again, thought Jenna. This time she raised her voice even more, "The two people in the world that our son relates to best are Jeremy and Toby, and you want to take him away from them?"

"If the treatments at the Institute can help him, then yes."

"Jeremy and Toby are a big part of the reason Bobby's made so much progress."

David's anger started to show through. "You know, I'm a little tired of hearing that."

"What? You're the one who got so upset because I didn't tell you about how Bobby was doing with Jeremy."

Again, David ignored her comment. "We need to do this."

"No we don't." Jenna looked David in the eye. "We're not moving to New York."

David was stunned by Jenna's tone. He started to respond in kind, but thought better of it. "I've got to go check on the arrangements for my father. Why don't we let things cool down?" He paused, but couldn't resist trying to regain control. "But, we're not done talking about this."

"We are if it involves moving to New York."

David didn't say another word. He grabbed his coat and left.

An hour later, Jenna studied her reflection in the mirror. Surprisingly, she wasn't able to detect any sign of the tears that had been there earlier. She tilted her face even closer, scrutinizing every feature. Although the tears weren't visible, the overwhelming weariness was. And despite the fact that she felt it throughout her entire body, it was almost like it traveled through some invisible transit system and collected in her eyes.

She thought for a moment that maybe it was just sadness. But no, it was much more encompassing, much more deeply felt. Certainly sadness was a part of it, but . . . Before she could complete the thought, a recurring question pushed its way to the forefront. *I'm only twenty-three-years-old; how did all this happen?* Of course there was a simple answer, one that she had come up with a hundred times before. But like most simple answers to emotional questions, it wasn't totally accurate, and it wasn't particularly helpful.

After several more minutes of reflection, her mood shifted again and the sorrow returned. She knew that she was powerless to stop another crying onslaught, but she steeled herself and tried anyway.

Just at that moment she heard a stirring in another part of the apartment. She held her breath and remained perfectly still, listening intently to make sure she hadn't imagined it. No, there it was again. She rubbed her eyes with the heels of her hands and moved toward Bobby's bedroom, as she acknowledged to herself that tending to her son was the only thing in the world that could have halted her tears.

CHAPTER 46

Sunday and Monday went by, and Jenna still hadn't heard from David. To some extent it was a relief—She wasn't sure what to expect the next time they spoke, or how she was going to react when they did.

On Tuesday night when the phone rang, Jenna felt a knot in her stomach as she glanced at the caller ID. She was able to keep her voice steady however. "Hello."

"Hi, it's me."

"Hi."

"I'm sorry I didn't call until today. Work's been hectic, and then I've had to go over to see my father each day. This is the earliest I've been back to the apartment since Saturday."

Jenna decided not to comment on the excuses David offered. Instead, she asked, "How's your father doing?"

"No problem getting him settled in, but I had to sign a lot of papers, and then I had to meet with a couple of the doctors so they could explain about his treatment."

They were both quiet for a moment before David spoke again. "About the other day . . . I . . . uh . . . I'm sorry. I shouldn't have yelled like that. I think with my father and everything, I just overreacted."

Jenna was thankful for David's apology, but she was still wary as to where the conversation was headed. She limited her response. "I'm sorry for yelling, too."

David was hoping that Jenna would continue. When she didn't, he said, "I feel like I need to say a few things. All right?"

"Okay."

"I still think we should give the Chambers Institute a try." Jenna started to protest, but David charged ahead. "*But* . . . I also understand that it's not very practical right now. With my father's situation and work,

330

trying to move you and Bobby any time soon just doesn't make any sense. I spoke with somebody at the Institute yesterday, and he said that there would still be an opening for Bobby in a few months. So I'm willing to hold off, but I need you to promise me that you'll at least consider it down the road."

"I'm not sure what you expect me to say, David. I appreciate that you're not pushing for this right now, but I don't see how I'm going to feel any differently in a couple of months."

It wasn't the answer David wanted or expected, but he tried to extend the olive branch anyway. "I know I kind of sprang the idea of moving on you, and I really didn't give you much time to think about it. I guess I'm asking you to do that now, that's all."

Jenna knew David was trying to smooth things over, but all she could think of was—*We've done this dance before*—*pretending that if we postpone things, one of us will change their mind. And I'm probably as guilty as he is, but I'm not going to give him some false hope about this.* Her mind shifted to something else David had said. *It's interesting that he found time to call the Chambers Institute, but not me.*

Before she could say anything, David continued. "I thought I'd take a ride down to the Institute and find out specifically what they can do to help Bobby. Then we can talk about what they're offering – no yelling, just talking."

Jenna thought it was like they were having parallel conversations. David hadn't heard anything she had said, not just today, but for weeks. She couldn't hide her exasperation. "They're going to tell you whatever you want to hear; nothing's going to change, David."

"You don't know that. Why won't you give this a chance? I've been going back and forth for a year, and now we have an opportunity to be together as a family. It's like that doesn't matter to you."

"That's not true, David, and you know it."

"So then let's give it a try. What do we have to lose?"

"*We* don't have anything to lose, but Bobby does."

"So you're not even willing to hear what else they have to say?"

"If you want to go talk to them in person, go ahead. But unless they've recently discovered a cure for autism, I don't want Bobby anywhere near that place."

David matched Jenna's response with his own sarcasm. "It's nice to see you're keeping an open mind about this."

"When it comes to what's best for Bobby, you're right, my mind's already made up."

"Well, I'm still going to talk to the people at the Institute."

"Do what you have to do."

Jenna didn't want to end the phone call like that, but before she could come up with anything more conciliatory to say, David jumped in. "I probably won't be able to make it up there this weekend. Give Bobby a kiss for me."

And then he hung up.

For the next hour, Jenna replayed the phone call in her head. *What was happening to the two of them? Every time they spoke, it turned into World War III.*

She tapped into the philosophical corner of her brain, and extracted the idea she had come up with a few years ago – how emotions weren't on a linear spectrum, how they only had to travel back to a crossroads before taking another path. That would explain why her feelings toward David had seemed to shift so much in such a relatively short amount of time—Every discussion lately meant another step back to where her emotions started to branch off in another direction.

On Thursday when Jeremy came over, Jenna shared everything that had been going on between her and David. At the very end she said, "I'm afraid I put you right in the middle of this again."

"What do you mean?"

"I told David that one of the main reasons I wouldn't even consider moving to New York was because I didn't want to take Bobby away from you and Toby." Jeremy remained silent as Jenna continued. "It's the truth, but I'm sorry I brought you into it."

"Don't worry about it. And for what it's worth, I think you're doing the right thing. I just don't understand where David is coming from. Is he in that much denial?"

"I think that's a big part of it. You know, if you refuse to accept something, then somehow it isn't true."

"That's not really like David."

"Under most circumstances, I'd agree with you, but not when it comes to this."

"So how were things left?"

"Up in the air. But as I said, he's going to see the people at the Institute. After that, I don't know what's going to happen."

Jeremy was quiet for a moment before offering, "Can I make a suggestion?"

"Of course."

"I think you should get some advice from the doctors at the Center in Canton. And if you'd like, I can probably arrange for you to talk with some of the special ed staff in Quincy. Bobby's not eligible for any services from the school system until he's three, but you might be able to have the testing done earlier."

"Wouldn't David have to sign off on that?"

"No. Only one parent needs to sign."

"I don't know. I'd be going behind his back again. Why do you think any new testing would make a difference?"

"If you have another independent test that comes to the same conclusions as the Center did, it might convince David to think twice about the Institute."

Although David called several times each week, he didn't make it back to Massachusetts for three weekends in a row. The phone conversations between Jenna and David were civil, primarily because neither one of them raised the issue of the Chambers Institute or the move to New York.

It seemed that after each phone call, Jenna continued to ask herself the same question – Was this the way other couples acted when they had a disagreement – barely talking to each other?

She thought back to her own parents. She never remembered them even being cool to one another, never mind fighting. But she was only eight when her father died. Maybe she was too young to notice, or maybe things seemed more idyllic than they really were. She suspected that when you lost a parent at such a young age, it was almost impossible to view them as having any human frailties.

Unfortunately, none of Jenna's thoughts helped her resolve anything.

Toward the end of March, David called to say he would finally be able to make it up to Massachusetts over the weekend. He also brought up the topic of the Chambers Institute, indicating that he hadn't been able to find the time to go down there yet.

Jenna accepted the information matter-of-factly, not mentioning that she was going to contact Dr. Townsend, or that she planned to talk with the local special ed personnel.

David asked about Bobby, and Jenna asked about David's father.

As they were about to end the conversation, Jenna went on to a new subject. "I think there's something wrong with the dryer."

"Why? What's the matter?"

"The drum isn't turning right."

"Can it wait until I come up on Saturday?"

"Maybe. But are you sure you're coming home?"

Jenna realized immediately how her last comment must have come across. "I'm sorry, David. I didn't mean it the way it sounded."

David didn't acknowledge either statement by Jenna. "Why don't I have somebody from the maintenance crew in Boston come out and take a look tomorrow? Okay?"

"That'd be great. Thanks."

After she hung up, Jenna realized that despite the issue of the Institute being brought up, their conversation had been the most non-confrontational one they'd had in weeks.

Tuesday came and went with no sign of the maintenance man. On Wednesday the dryer died completely. That night Jenna called David, but it went to voice mail. She left a message, and he finally called back Thursday morning.

David explained that he had tried to contact the maintenance crew on Tuesday morning, but he was put on hold; then he got disconnected and forgot to call back. He promised to get right on it. "I'll have someone there by the end of the day."

No one showed up.

That night Jenna had trouble getting to sleep. She kept projecting the scene on Saturday when David came home. He'd make some additional excuses as to why the maintenance guy hadn't shown up. He'd accuse her of overreacting, and maybe even try to turn it around so that somehow it was her fault. Jenna became angrier and angrier.

Sleep finally came to her around 3:00 in the morning. When she awoke about four hours later, the anger had subsided with the thought that certainly someone would show up today, and everything would be fine.

She glanced at the clock every few minutes throughout the morning and the early afternoon, each passing hour increasing her frustration.

At around 2:00 she called Barbara, but she wasn't home. Jenna left a message – *Hi Barbara, it's Jenna. I was wondering if you could come over and watch Bobby for a little while. My dryer's broken and I need to use the one in the laundry room downstairs.*

For the next hour she tried to put things in perspective – she was seething over the fact that she couldn't dry some clothes – how ridiculous. But deep down, she knew that her anger was about more than the dryer.

Shortly after 2:30 in the afternoon, Bobby was showing signs of needing a nap. Jenna decided that a nap might do her some good as well. She put him in his big boy bed with the safety sides on it, and then went into her own bedroom. But after tossing and turning for fifteen minutes, she got up and went into the living room.

There wasn't another thought in her head but that David had promised something, and hadn't delivered on that promise. There were no clean clothes for Bobby, or for her, for that matter, and David would be home in less than twenty-four hours.

There was a load of wash still sitting in the machine that she had finished in anticipation of Barbara being able to baby sit. On impulse, Jenna unloaded it into the laundry basket.

She then checked to make sure Bobby was asleep, grabbed her purse, and quietly opened the apartment door. She double checked the lock, and then hurried down to the laundry room.

She started to turn around twice, thinking that leaving Bobby alone, even for a couple of minutes was a huge mistake. But her anger at the situation overwhelmed her common sense.

When she got to the laundry room, she checked the two dryers and found the larger one empty. She tossed in all of the wet clothes, deposited the requisite number of quarters, set the dials, and waited a few minutes to be sure everything was working properly.

She left the laundry room and glanced at her watch as she waited for the elevator. When it hadn't come to the basement floor after a minute or two, she decided to use the stairs.

As she was climbing the single flight, she realized that although her anger was totally out of proportion, the simple act of drying some clothes had calmed her. She definitely felt better.

That feeling was short-lived however. As soon as she turned the corner in the first floor hallway, she looked toward her apartment door.

It was wide open.

CHAPTER 47

The sight of the open door caused Jenna's knees to buckle. She dropped the empty laundry basket and brought her hand up to her mouth, trying to prevent a scream from escaping.

She partially fell against the wall about thirty feet from the apartment. But her instincts overwhelmed the panic she felt, and she was able to right herself and run toward the open door.

As she crossed the threshold, a pleading cry emerged, "Bobby, Bobby!"

There was no immediate response in the split second that followed, and then she heard a woman's voice. "We're in here."

Nothing registered at first, and then Jenna realized it was Barbara. She ran into the bedroom, and there on the floor was Bobby playing with Toby. Jenna stood just inside the doorway, her whole body shaking. "Oh my God. Oh my God."

Bobby looked up at the sound of his mother's voice, but then quickly went back to what he was doing. Jenna went over and scooped up her son. She looked over at Barbara. "What happened?"

"I'm not exactly sure. Toby and I got back from a doctor's appointment a few minutes ago. He went on ahead to get the mail, and when I caught up to him, he was standing next to your apartment door holding Bobby's hand. I called to you, but . . . ."

"I went down to dry some clothes. I was only gone a couple of minutes. Bobby was asleep when I left; I didn't think he could climb over the sidings on his bed, never mind open the door."

Jenna turned Bobby in her arms. "How did you do that?"

Bobby started squirming, trying to push away from his mother. "Down, down."

Jenna's heart was still racing, and she didn't want to let go of her son under any circumstances. But it was obvious that he didn't really understand what all the fuss was about. She gave him his wish and placed him back on the floor with Toby.

Jenna looked over at Barbara. "I don't know what I was thinking. The dryer's broken. Someone was supposed to come fix it, but they never showed up. I got so upset . . . ."

Barbara moved closer and put her hand on Jenna's arm. "It's okay, Jenna. Nothing bad happened. Everything's okay."

"I can't believe I left him alone."

Barbara half smiled. "I don't know of any parent that hasn't done something similar."

"I feel so stupid."

"Join the club."

That got a brief smile out of Jenna.

Barbara continued, "Why don't I make us some tea? That'll give you a chance to calm down."

"Thank you."

Once the tea was ready, they all moved into the living room. Barbara and Toby stayed for another fifteen minutes until Jenna found her bearings.

Shortly after they left, the thoughts of what horrible things could have happened overtook Jenna's mind. She started shaking again, and couldn't stop. Another wave of regret started to overwhelm her.

She picked up the phone and dialed Jeremy's number. He answered on the second ring. "Hello."

"Hi. Are you still at school?"

"No. I'm home, but I have to go back to school later. I'm chaperoning a dance. What's going on?"

"It's okay, never mind."

Jeremy could hear the concern in her voice. "Jenna, what is it? What's wrong?"

"I was hoping you could come over. Something happened, and I . . . ."

"Are you all right? Is Bobby all right?"

"Yes, but . . . ." At that point her voice cracked.

"Give me a few minutes to change, and I'll be right there."

After she hung up, Jenna put Bobby in to take the nap that he hadn't finished. She needed to talk to Jeremy without any interruptions. She felt sure that he would know what to say to get her back on an even keel; she couldn't afford to be an emotional wreck tomorrow when David got back.

As soon as Jeremy arrived, Jenna told him everything that had been going on for the last few weeks, even repeating some things he already knew. When she finished, there were tears in her eyes and the shaking had returned.

Jeremy went to her and held her for a full minute. His embrace seemed like the most natural thing in the world, and she wanted to stay in his arms for the rest of the day.

Eventually, Jeremy began to separate himself. "Are you feeling any better?"

"Yes, but I can't stop thinking about what could have happened."

"But it didn't."

"I know, but still."

"You need to stop beating yourself up about this."

Jenna didn't respond immediately; and then she said, "After I knew Bobby was all right, all I kept thinking was—What's David going to do when he finds out?"

"What do you mean?"

"I told you how it's been between us lately. What if he decides to try to take Bobby away from me? We're not married. I don't even know what my rights are."

Jeremy looked surprised. "David wouldn't do anything like that."

"Probably not, but I still can't stop thinking about what if he did."

Jeremy appeared to be considering something before he spoke. "Then maybe you shouldn't tell him."

It was Jenna's turn to look surprised. "You really think so? But then what if he finds out anyway? Won't that make it worse?"

"How's he going to find out? Not from Bobby or Toby. And Barbara's not going to say anything."

Even though Jenna was dreading having to explain things to David, she didn't automatically take up Jeremy's suggestion. She had been burned before by keeping things to herself. "I don't know."

"I understand. I'm just not sure anything good is going to come out of telling him."

They were quiet for a few minutes before Jeremy spoke again. "Have you contacted Dr. Townsend yet?"

"No."

"You know what you said before about David? Well, if you think there's even a remote possibility that he'd try to force you to move . . . or worse, Dr. Townsend's definitely someone you should have in your corner."

Jenna nodded. "I know. I think I've held off because I didn't want to believe that David would keep pushing things." With that, she took a deep breath and her body shuddered.

"Are you going to be okay? I could try to find someone else to fill in for me tonight."

"No. You promised the kids. I'll be all right."

Jeremy got up and started toward the door. About halfway, he turned around and faced Jenna. He placed his hands on her upper arms. "I need to tell you something."

Jenna remained silent, as Jeremy continued. "You know how upset I got when you told me that David wanted you and Bobby to move to New York? Well, that wasn't just about Bobby." He looked directly into her eyes. "The thought of you not being in my life . . . I don't know what I'd do." He paused. "I'm sorry. I know this makes things more complicated for you, but . . . ."

Instead of saying anything else, he drew Jenna toward him, kissed her lightly on the lips. "I have to go."

That night Jenna's brain wrestled with all the implications of what Jeremy had said. It easily overwhelmed the issue of whether to tell David about the incident with Bobby.

In the twilight of consciousness before she fell asleep, Jenna's mind drifted back to a number of months prior when she had first suspected that Jeremy had feelings for her. At that time she had thought of it as a complication, the very same word Jeremy had used. But now . . . .

Jenna awoke shortly after 7:00. She remained in bed for a few minutes, vaguely remembering a dream she had had. She wasn't able to recall the details, but Jeremy was a part of it. An involuntary smile formed on her face.

Her reverie was interrupted by Bobby calling to her—something he had just started doing over the last several weeks. "Mommy." The smile on her face broadened.

But in the few seconds it took to walk into her son's room, the smile disappeared. She felt a twinge in her stomach as she recalled what had happened the day before, and the fact that she still hadn't decided whether to tell David or not.

Jenna continued to play a mental game of ping-pong for the next several hours, going back and forth as to what made the most sense. And then around 10:00 the intercom buzzer rang.

"Hello."

"Hi. I was sent from Whitcomb Realty Trust to fix your dryer."

Jenna hesitated before the words registered. "Oh, right. I'll buzz you in."

It took about forty-five minutes for a pulley and belt to be replaced, and then another five to vacuum out the dust and lint. Jenna gave the worker a ten-dollar tip, thanked him, and he was on his way.

For some reason, the fact that the dryer was now fixed helped Jenna make up her mind about what to do. There just didn't seem to be much of an upside in telling David, whereas there could be a huge downside.

David arrived back at the apartment around 4:00 in the afternoon. He offered two apologies – one, for not having arranged to have the dryer fixed until that morning, and two, for not being home earlier. He only elaborated about the second apology.

"It's so frustrating, Jenna. I go to the facility in Westchester three or four times a week. Nothing's changed. In fact, it's like my father's in a nursing home instead of some cutting edge treatment center. That's why I was late. I was trying to get some answers, but the regular staff and most of the doctors are all off on the weekends. At this point, I wish I hadn't moved him at all."

David's pre-occupation with his father's situation left little time over the weekend to discuss much of anything else. The incident involving leaving Bobby alone began to fade quickly into the back of Jenna's mind. To her relief, it was replaced with the idea that maybe David would give up on the notion of having them move to New York, considering how dissatisfied he was with the Westchester facility.

Also occupying her thoughts was Jeremy. Although he hadn't explicitly expressed what he was feeling, there was little doubt what he meant. And again she was faced with a dilemma – *Should I pretend nothing happened unless he brings it up? And what if he does bring it up? Then what do I do?*

Ultimately, Jenna decided it wasn't a conversation she should initiate, nor one she should prepare for ahead of time. If Jeremy brought it up, she'd respond in whatever way her heart told her to.

Despite that decision, Jenna continued to replay Jeremy's words in her head, not only those about his feelings, but also those about contacting Dr. Townsend. The first thing Monday morning she called his office, and was able to schedule an appointment for Wednesday.

Dr. Townsend greeted her with a broad smile. "It's nice to see you, Jenna. Please sit down."

"Thank you." She paused. "I'm a little embarrassed. I feel like I'm constantly bothering you with my problems."

"Well you're not. I'm glad to help in any way I can."

Jenna decided not to hold anything back. She offered additional details about the Chambers Institute; she told him about David's desire to have them move to New York, and her concerns about Bobby's progress if he wasn't around Jeremy and Toby.

Dr. Townsend listened intently, never interrupting even once. When it was obvious that Jenna had finished, he leaned forward and said, "You and David certainly have been dealing with a lot." He paused. "I'm probably not telling you anything you don't already know, but the challenges of having a child with autism can impact the parents' lives in ways most people can't begin to anticipate."

They explored that topic for several more minutes before Jenna switched gears. "I guess what I'm looking for is some assurance that I'm doing the right thing."

Dr. Townsend leaned back and folded his hands in front of him. "There's no doubt in my mind that you are, Jenna. As I mentioned to you when you first asked about the Chambers Institute, I admit I'm not objective." He paused. "But that doesn't mean I'm wrong. All my professional judgment suggests that Bobby will continue to make progress if you continue to do what you're doing and if he has additional interaction with the people here at the Center."

Jenna let out a sigh. "I think that's exactly what I needed to hear. But how do I convince David of that?"

"Well, that could be difficult. Parents in denial are often quite irrational when it comes to their children. On the other hand, if we can provide some strong evidence that Bobby's making progress, maybe David will come around." He paused. "I do have an idea that might help in that regard. The April school vacation is coming up soon. Why don't you bring Bobby here to the Center during that week?"

"Really?"

"Yes. We operate on the same schedule as the public schools, so we tend to have fewer students during school vacations. He'll be younger than most of the other children, but we'll find an appropriate group for him."

"That would be terrific." Jenna's expression changed to one of concern. "But won't that be expensive? And our insurance won't cover that, will it?"

Dr. Townsend shook his head. "Probably not. Most insurance companies won't cover treatment for autism until the child is at least three years old. But the truth is we have a number of very generous benefactors, so we're able to keep treatment costs quite reasonable."

Jenna's expression continued to convey her concern. Dr. Townsend picked up on it and added, "On occasion we have parents who are willing to volunteer at the Center while their children are receiving services. We then apply those volunteer hours to the cost of the treatment. It usually balances out. Do you think that's something you'd be interested in?"

Jenna's face brightened. "Yes. Absolutely."

"Excellent. Problem solved."

"I can't tell you how much I appreciate everything you're doing. Thank you."

Dr. Townsend smiled. "Don't thank me yet; we work our volunteers pretty hard."

Jenna returned his smile. "You're not going to scare me off."

"I didn't think for a minute that I would."

They continued to talk about some more of the details for a few minutes, and then Dr. Townsend said, "During the week that Bobby's here, I think I'd like to schedule another assessment, partially for David's benefit. If it shows the kind of progress I suspect it will, it might make a difference in how he views things."

Jenna spent much of Wednesday night and Thursday morning thinking about her meeting with Dr. Townsend. She couldn't remember being as excited about anything relating to Bobby in a long time. But as Jeremy's Thursday afternoon visit approached, her excitement gave way to apprehension, as she once again found herself unsure of what to expect once Jeremy arrived.

The last time something appeared to be happening between the two of them, Jeremy had backed off. But this time, while he hadn't said anything directly, the implication was clear. Still, Jenna decided to go with her original instinct – let Jeremy take the lead on whether to bring it up or not.

At around 3:30 when she buzzed Jeremy in, she realized that the chain on the door was still in place, which meant that she couldn't just call to him to come in. She would have to open the door, and the two of them would be only a few feet apart, standing face-to-face.

The knock came a moment after she slid the chain out of its holder. Jenna waited briefly, took a deep breath, and turned the knob. If Jeremy was surprised that she had responded to his knock so quickly, he didn't show it.

"Hi," he said with a smile.

"Hi," Jenna said, as Jeremy stepped inside, and she closed the door behind her.

"How's Bobby doing today?"

"He's fine. He just went into his room."

"And how are you doing?"

"I'm fine, too."

Jeremy continued to smile. "I'm glad." With that he reached for Jenna's hands, clasped them in his, and appeared to be ready to kiss her. But after a moment of gazing into her eyes, he pulled back, let go of her hands, and said, "I'm going in to see Bobby."

A number of thoughts and emotions flooded Jenna's mind. As she sorted through them over the next few moments, several things became apparent – Unlike the last time when they had been in a similar situation, Jeremy hadn't avoided physical contact this time. On the other hand, his actions suggested that he wasn't about to rush things either. And maybe most importantly—at this point, it appeared that he wasn't asking anything of her.

A minute later Jeremy and Bobby came into the living room. As they began to play, Jenna told Jeremy about her visit with Dr. Townsend. The more she spoke, the more excited Jeremy seemed to get.

When it was time for him to leave, he stood up, gave Bobby a kiss on the head, and went over to Jenna. "That really is great news about the Center. I think it's going to be terrific for Bobby."

"I do too."

As before, Jeremy took her hands in his and said, "I guess we'll have to wait and see what happens."

It was obvious to Jenna that he wasn't just talking about Bobby.

CHAPTER 48

Despite her excitement about Dr. Townsend's invitation to bring Bobby to the Center, Jenna still had some trepidation. Any change in routine for Bobby often resulted in a major meltdown. And three hours each day at the Center would certainly qualify as a change in routine.

She recalled a number of unscheduled trips to the mall and the supermarket where Bobby's outbursts had led to stares of recrimination – the expression on the faces of strangers seeming to ask, "Why can't you control your child? What kind of mother are you?"

Jenna mentally chided herself—*Obviously, the Center isn't the mall. Bobby will be surrounded by trained professionals who understand children like him; and who won't be judging me. But still . . . .*

During the two weeks leading up to the visit, Jenna's anxiety gradually eased. Although she had trouble acknowledging it to herself, without doubt part of the reason for that was because there would be no confrontations with David over the next few weekends.

In what was becoming more and more frequent, David called to explain that he wouldn't be returning to Massachusetts for a couple of weeks. He had to work on the next two Saturdays and Sundays to make up for the time he was spending at the Westchester facility. He was still involved in the protracted dispute with the administrative staff as to whether he had the right to move his father, given that he had signed a six-month contract.

Just before they concluded their conversation, David asked about Bobby. And even though a discussion about their son might have proven contentious, the notion that Bobby appeared to have become an afterthought to David saddened Jenna. It also forged her decision that she wouldn't mention anything to David about the upcoming visit to the

Center until after the fact. But it wasn't a decision she came to lightly—the list of things she was keeping from David was continuing to grow.

A few days before the trip to the Center, Jenna received an e-mail from Dr. Townsend outlining the upcoming week's activities, and asking her if she had any questions or concerns.

Jenna debated briefly whether to mention how changes in routine affected Bobby, but concluded that the people at the Center had probably seen it all. She did include in her response how much she was looking forward to the week, especially for what it might mean for Bobby.

At the bottom of the e-mail, Jenna asked if it would be all right for Jeremy to come with her on one of the days, explaining that he was a teacher and had the week off. In his return e-mail, Dr. Townsend replied that Jeremy was more than welcome and then added jokingly that he shouldn't be surprised if they ended up putting him to work.

When Jenna arrived on Monday morning, Dr. Townsend indicated that she would be staying with Bobby for the entire three hours as a means of easing him into the situation. But for the rest of the week, she would be assisting with another group of children elsewhere in the facility.

He went on to explain his rationale. "In addition to working with Bobby on specific skills, we'll also be assessing his progress in various areas. Having a parent in the room while we're trying to do that can often skew the results."

"I understand."

"But what we have arranged beginning tomorrow is for you to conclude your day at 11:30, and then to come observe Bobby until he finishes up at noon."

Each morning for the next few days, Jenna fully expected that she'd have a difficult time focusing on the group of children she was working with, anticipating that her thoughts would constantly be with Bobby, but that turned out not to be the case. Instead, she found herself so engaged with her own group that Bobby only entered her thoughts periodically.

When Jeremy came by the apartment on Thursday afternoon, Jenna filled him in on everything that had transpired since Monday. Although most of it centered on Bobby, she also spent a substantial amount of time talking about what she had been doing.

By the end of her explanation, Jeremy had a huge smile on his face.

"What are you smiling at?" Jenna asked.

"You."

"What does that mean?"

"Well it's pretty obvious how much you're enjoying yourself."

Jenna's smile got bigger. "I really am." She paused. "There's this one little boy, Ethan, and a couple of times this week, you could just see it in his eyes that something clicked. It was amazing."

"You're preaching to the choir, you know."

"Right. I forgot."

Jeremy's smile turned into a smirk. "I'm really looking forward to seeing you in action tomorrow."

Jenna gave him a playful slap on the arm.

They were quiet for a moment, and then Jeremy said, "You know, once Bobby's in a full-time program, you should look into becoming a teacher assistant."

Jenna looked at him skeptically. "Can I do that without a degree? I mean, I was hoping to go back to school and finish up, but we can't afford that until David's trust fund becomes available, and that's not for another year or so."

At the mention of David, the trust fund, and the future, Jenna saw Jeremy's expression change dramatically. She was trying to come up with something to say, but then Jeremy seemed to steady himself. "I'm pretty sure you only need a couple of courses to get certified."

After playing with Bobby for another half hour, Jeremy's mood seemed to bounce back. When he said goodbye to Jenna, he did it in the same way he had for the last several weeks – with some physical contact, but nothing more overt. Although with increasing frequency, Jenna was certain she saw something more in his eyes.

On Friday morning Jeremy picked them up around 8:30 and drove to Canton. Once they arrived and dropped Bobby off with his group, they headed for the other side of the building.

Jeremy stayed with Jenna and her group for most of the morning, even joining in on some of the activities. Jenna marveled at how effortlessly he eased into the group, and how quickly the children gravitated toward him. Even the staff members commented on it.

At 11:30 Jenna and Jeremy went to observe Bobby behind the two-way mirror. After a few minutes Dr. Townsend joined them.

Jenna saw him first. "Hi doctor. You remember Jeremy."

He offered his hand. "Of course. Why don't we go back to my office? I've arranged for one of our staff to stay with Bobby in case we need some additional time to talk."

After they were seated, Dr. Townsend began the conversation. "Before we get started, I wanted to ask how you enjoyed your week."

"It was amazing. I was telling Jeremy how much I looked forward to coming each day. It was very rewarding, and your staff is terrific."

"Thank you. That's nice to hear."

As Dr. Townsend continued, he opened a folder in front of him. "I think I have some very good news for you."

He looked up and smiled. "Bobby has shown much more language growth than we would have expected. But the most significant development appears to be his use of inflection and intonation in his speech. He doesn't do it with any degree of consistency, so we can't be sure that it's intentional."

"I understand about the language growth, but I'm not sure I understand about the rest of it."

"It's possible that what we're seeing is Bobby making connections between what he's feeling and his speech. If that's true, it's a major step forward. As you know, many children on the autism spectrum have difficulty not only relating to what others are feeling, but also with expressing what *they're* feeling." He paused, obviously searching for the best way to explain what he meant. "For most people, besides the descriptive vocabulary they employ, they learn to use inflection and intonation to convey the highs and lows of their feelings. Usually, individuals with autism aren't able to do that until they become adults, if at all."

"And you think Bobby's doing that already?"

"It's possible. We've mainly seen it at times when he gets excited." Dr. Townsend smiled. "Not unlike what you just did when you asked the question."

Jenna returned the smile as Dr. Townsend continued, "I think the next few weeks could be a critical time for him. We need to be sure that what we're seeing isn't just an anomaly. If it's real, then we need to do everything we can to foster those connections. I don't want to overstate the case, but this could be life-changing."

Jenna brought her hand up to her mouth, and tears started to form as Dr. Townsend outlined what he had in mind. "Ideally, we'd like Bobby to continue coming to the Center on a daily basis for the foreseeable future."

Jenna was still processing the words "life-changing," when the implication of Dr. Townsend's last sentence hit her. "What about—?"

Dr. Townsend had anticipated what Jenna's concerns might be. "I've already spoken to some of our financial people, and assuming that you're in agreement, we'll find a way to make this happen."

The relief on Jenna's face showed through her tears.

Dr. Townsend continued. "I've been considering a number of options. One possibility is to do a formal assessment, which I'm sure would conclude that Bobby is somewhere on the autism spectrum. If that were the finding, then an intervention program would be the natural recommendation. The problem is, as I've mentioned to you before, getting the insurance company to agree."

"What if they don't?"

"Then I think the next best thing would be periodic visits here to the Center coupled with specific activities done at home. We can walk you through those to make sure you're comfortable with what you're going to be doing."

Jeremy looked over at Jenna, and then entered the conversation. "I usually see Bobby at least once a week, but I'd be willing to see him more often if you think it would help."

Dr. Townsend turned toward Jeremy. "I think that would be a real plus. Jenna's told me how well Bobby relates to you. There's no question that he'd benefit from any additional time you can spend with him."

The doctor turned back to Jenna. "Let's do this. Why don't you bring Bobby back next week? We'll start with Monday, Wednesday, and Friday. You can do the same thing you did this week – volunteer for a couple of hours, and then we can show you some of the strategies you can use at home. In the meantime, I'll contact your insurance company and try to get a sense of whether they'd be open to any of this."

Jenna had trouble speaking. "This is a lot to take in. I can't believe everything you're doing: it's just overwhelming. Thank you doesn't seem like enough."

Dr. Townsend smiled. "It'll do."

On the car ride back to the apartment, Jenna and Jeremy continued to discuss everything that Dr. Townsend had shared with them. A few times Jenna had to fight back tears as she thought of the possibilities as to where all of this might lead.

Again, Jeremy seemed just as excited as she was. He offered to come by on Tuesdays as well as Thursdays, whether the insurance company decided to cover Bobby's continuing treatment at the Center or not.

After Jeremy dropped them off, and Jenna got Bobby settled in, her thoughts turned to how comfortable the conversation in the car with Jeremy had been. Months ago she and David might have had a similar conversation about their son, and what was best for him, but not anymore. Now, nearly every interaction between the two of them had an edge to it, a sense of one-upsmanship, a desire to "win" rather than compromise. Jenna was fearful that when she saw David tomorrow, despite the incredible news she had gotten today, her thoughts would prove prophetic.

As David came into the apartment on Saturday afternoon and called to Jenna, she could hear the weariness in his voice.

She called back. "Hi, I'm in here."

The weariness she had detected in David's voice was even more evident in the way he carried himself as he entered the bedroom. Jenna didn't comment on it, but asked in a compassionate tone. "How're you doing?"

"I've been better. I've been fighting with the administrators in Westchester for two straight weeks, and they won't budge. It's all about money for them."

Jenna's mind flashed back to the conversation they'd had months ago regarding the Chambers Institute and money, but she kept it to herself. She then asked, "They're still holding you to the six-month contract?"

"Yeah. And in the meantime they're not doing anything for my father. When he first got there, they said they thought he was on the verge of coming out of the coma. And now, here we are months later, and he seems worse off than he was."

"Is there anything else you can do?"

"Maybe. I'm going to stay up here in Massachusetts for a few days. I already cleared it with Phil Jenkins. I'm going to talk with Alan Fenton on Monday to see what he can do from a legal standpoint."

David's words started Jenna's mind racing. As excited as she was about the past week at the Center, she still wasn't sure how David was going to react. She wanted to wait for just the right moment to tell him, even if it meant holding off for a week or more. But now that David was going to still be around on Monday—the next scheduled visit to the Center – it appeared that she had to move up the timetable.

In the next split second something else pushed its way into Jenna's thoughts—Although she understood that David was dealing with his father's situation, it still bothered her that he hadn't even asked about Bobby. Of course it was possible that when he first came in, David had checked the other bedroom and saw Bobby sleeping. She decided to give him the benefit of the doubt.

Jenna was about to say something, but then David spoke again. "I've looked into a couple of other facilities hoping that Alan can figure out a way to get out of the contract."

Jenna tried to keep the concern out of her voice. "Oh? Whereabouts?"

"There are a few possibilities on Long Island and one in New Jersey."

At the mention of New Jersey, Jenna blanched. David didn't seem to notice as he continued, "I'm not going to look into them any further until I'm pretty sure I'll be able to move him."

David expelled a mouthful of air. "Anyway, I've made an appointment to see Alan at 10:00 on Monday, and then when I get back, I thought we could all go out for lunch. It'd be nice to spend some extra time together over the next few days. I know I've missed a bunch of weekends recently, and . . . ."

This time David picked up on the concern in Jenna's expression. "What's the matter?"

"Can we go into the living room? I need to talk to you."

David looked puzzled. "Okay."

As they passed Bobby's room, David asked, "Is he due to get up soon?"

"Not for a while." David had asked the question so naturally that Jenna was sure he must have checked on Bobby earlier when he came in. Although that made her feel better, it wasn't going to make the upcoming conversation any easier.

As they sat down, David spoke first. "So, what's this about?"

Jenna tried to put on an air of confidence that she didn't possess. "A few weeks ago I called Dr. Townsend."

"Why'd you do that?" David asked in an accusatory tone.

351

Jenna hadn't expected that particular question. Her mind scrambled to come up with an explanation that didn't include the real reason – that she needed an ally in case David tried to force them to move to New York . . . or worse. Just before the silence had gone on too long, a plausible answer occurred to her. "I hadn't spoken to him recently, and I wanted to get some more ideas about some activities to do with Bobby."

To Jenna's relief, David seemed to accept that. "Okay, so?"

"Well, I ended up going to see him, and . . . ."

For the next ten minutes, Jenna explained about the volunteering, the informal assessment, and the plans for next week and beyond. And then she inadvertently mentioned that Jeremy had been with her yesterday. David raised his eyebrows, and she could see him getting more and more upset. Jenna wasn't even sure David heard her when she used the phrase "life-changing."

In an attempt to diffuse the anger that was evident in David's expression, Jenna offered an apology of sorts. "I know I should have said something sooner, but you were already dealing with so much with your father."

David's voice seemed to explode. "Don't bring my father's situation into this. It has nothing to do with him. It's the same thing all over again, Jenna. You do what you want, and then tell me about it afterwards." He stared at her. "I'm curious. Would you have bothered to mention any of this to me, if I weren't still going to be here on Monday?"

With some defensiveness evident in her voice, Jenna opted for less than the truth. "I was planning on telling you as soon as you got home, but there wasn't much of an opportunity."

David's sarcasm surfaced. "Yeah, I know. My father's situation always seems to get in the way."

Jenna's anger was starting to match David's, but she pulled back. "I understand why you're upset, but can you please try to focus on what Dr. Townsend had to say?"

"You mean that Bobby's progressing like a typical two-year-old? Isn't that what the Chambers Institute told us months ago?"

"What?"

"I know you don't think that they know what they're doing, but it's kind of interesting that they came to the same conclusion as your Dr. Townsend."

"No they didn't. It's not the same thing at all. How can you even think that?"

"Oh, I don't know, maybe because you never tell me anything about my own son. Jeremy knows more about Bobby than I do."

The words flew out of Jenna's mouth before she could stop them. "If you were here more often, maybe that wouldn't be a problem."

David appeared stunned. "You really think if I had a choice, I wouldn't be here?"

Jenna remained quiet, primarily because she had blurted out something unintended a moment before, and didn't want to do it again. But David took the hesitation to mean that she wasn't sure of the answer.

He got up off the couch, picked up his jacket, and headed for the door. "I'm going out."

"David, wait."

"I need to get some air, and clear my head. I'll call you later."

Jenna watched the door close as David's words started to register. He hadn't said, "I'll see you later." He had said, "I'll call you later." Did that mean that he wasn't coming back home tonight?

At first Jenna was shaken, but then the stark realization set in that she truly wasn't sure how she felt about that.

CHAPTER 49

David called a few hours later as he said he would. After stilted "hellos" back and forth, both he and Jenna were at a loss as to what to say. Eventually, David broke the silence. "I'm sorry we got into it like that."

"I am too."

"I think it's best if I stay in Boston tonight."

"You don't need to do that, David."

"I appreciate you saying that. But I think I need some more time by myself to sort things out." He hesitated, and Jenna could hear the words catch in his throat. "The last few months . . . I almost feel like I've become this other person with you, and I'm not sure I like him very much." He paused. "It'll just be for tonight; and then I'll come by tomorrow so we can talk. Okay?"

This was a side of David that Jenna hadn't seen in a long time; she responded in kind. "Of course. But are you sure you wouldn't rather come back tonight?"

"I don't think so. I'm hoping that if I sleep on it, things will make more sense in the morning." David forced a laugh. "Although I don't expect I'm going to get much sleep."

"I don't think I will either."

There was silence again before David said, "Okay, I'll see you tomorrow." There was another brief hesitation and then David added. "I know it probably doesn't seem like it, especially the way I've been acting lately, but I really do love the both of you."

Before Jenna could respond, David ended the call, as if he was fearful of what she might say in return.

Throughout the night, thoughts of David, Bobby, and Jeremy swirled together in Jenna's head, but David's last words before he hung up caused her the most difficulty. Not because she didn't believe them, but because ever since things had started to become strained between them, she had forced herself not to think about David's feelings.

It seemed that their life together had become like a giant labyrinth. And whenever a decision had to be made as to which way to turn, she had rationalized that since David's focus was on his father and his job, he didn't care about anything else. It was easier to relegate him to an onlooker, to someone who was on the periphery and didn't feel things to the depth that she did, especially when it came to their son. Of course, deep down she knew that wasn't true, but black and white was always easier to deal with than gray.

Sometime close to dawn, Jenna thought about the argument that she and David had had hours earlier. She truly wondered how they were going to get past the things they had said to each other. But then she thought about the follow-up phone call. It certainly sounded as if David was willing to try to make amends.

At that point Jenna vowed that for her part, when David came home later in the day, their conversation would be different. She would try to really listen to David, to consider what *he* was going through, and not to judge him at every turn.

And although she convinced herself that she would stick to those ground rules, something in the back of her mind quickly began to create a fissure in her resolve – She knew that regardless of her good intentions, her protective instincts toward Bobby would ultimately determine what she said and did.

When David arrived around 11:00, he gave Jenna a kiss and then inquired about Bobby. Jenna explained that she had asked Barbara to watch him while they talked. David nodded and then sat down; Jenna joined him.

David turned slightly to face her. "I'm sorry, Jenna." Although he didn't specify for what, Jenna accepted the apology as sincere, and waited for him to continue.

"I really hate how it's been lately. It seems like we're always at each other, and I just don't even know how we got to this point." He paused. But I did some soul searching last night, and I came to the conclusion that a lot of it's my fault."

Jenna was caught off guard by David's admission. In her heart of hearts she probably believed that the words he had just spoken were true, but that wasn't what came into her head at that instant. "We're both responsible."

After a moment David said, "I want to fix this, Jenna. We *need* to fix this."

Jenna's mouth tightened as she fought to stay in control of her emotions. She could only manage a nod in agreement.

"I think we should get away, just the two of us. Maybe down the Cape for a few days, and not think about anything else."

Jenna kept her voice gentle. "I want to fix this too, David. But how can we go away? What about Bobby?"

"I thought maybe we could ask Barbara."

Jenna's first thought was that even if Barbara were available, going away would mean that Bobby couldn't go to the Center. But instead of expressing that concern, she opted to put the ball back in David's court. "What about your father and the meeting with Alan?"

"I thought we could leave right after that, either Monday night or Tuesday morning, assuming Barbara can watch Bobby. If she can't, then we'll have to figure something else out."

David looked like he was barely hanging on, and Jenna didn't want to say anything to force him over the edge. But the very instinct she had thought of last night – protecting her son—kicked in. "The only thing I'm worried about is that this is such a critical time for Bobby. I hate to have him miss any time at the Center."

David spoke calmly. "I understand that. I heard what you said yesterday." He paused. "I told you I did a lot of soul-searching last night. I decided I'm not going to fight with you anymore about the Chambers Institute or the Center in Canton. If you think it's best for him to go there, I'm okay with it."

Jenna arched her eyebrows in surprise, and a sense of relief showed on her face, as David continued. "I know you said that it's a critical time for Bobby. But don't you think that it's a critical time for us too?" David's voice had started to become louder, but then he softened it. "He'll only miss a couple of days."

Jenna could see tears forming in David's eyes, as he tried to go on. "I'm really afraid that if we don't do something . . . ."

Jenna could hear the pleading and desperation in David's voice, and she filled up as well. "You're right. Let me talk to Barbara when I go get Bobby."

David reached out for her, and she moved into his arms.

Jenna went to Barbara's apartment a few minutes later. When she returned, she told David that Barbara had said she'd be able to watch Bobby on Tuesday and Wednesday. David went to Jenna again and held her. "We're going to work this out."

For the next hour, David made a concerted effort to engage Bobby, but with only limited success. As Jenna watched the two of them, she was pleased that David was doing what he was doing, but she couldn't help but make a comparison with the way Bobby interacted with Jeremy. But she also acknowledged to herself that that wasn't David's fault.

Later on when Jenna headed off to bed, David indicated that he was going to stay up for a while to watch some TV. A couple of times during the night Jenna came out into the living room and found David fast asleep.

She wondered if not sleeping in their bed was intentional on his part.

As Jenna awoke the next morning, she was vaguely aware of water running. It took her a moment until she realized it was the shower in the other bathroom.

She lay there in bed staring at the ceiling, trying to imagine why David had decided not to shower in their bathroom. Maybe it doesn't mean anything, she thought. Just like not sleeping in our bed didn't mean anything. Or was David trying to avoid any situation that could lead to making love? That was possible. He knew that whenever they had had a serious argument in the past, it took her a few days before she wanted to become intimate again.

But obviously, she thought, they both understood what going away together implied. And wasn't that part of the point to begin with? Maybe David wanted to wait until he was pretty sure what her response would be. Maybe that was it. If he had pursued anything last night and she had resisted, no matter how gently, he might have assumed that it meant something that he wasn't prepared to face.

Then another thought found its way into her consciousness. She had been so consumed with analyzing David's actions that she hadn't even considered how she would have reacted if he had come to her.

Initially, she told herself that she really didn't know what she would have done. But then a clearer picture started to emerge. She saw herself telling David that she wanted to wait until they were away together.

It frightened her a little that she was able to conjure up an excuse for something that had never occurred, and that those feelings were so close to the surface.

Jenna got out of bed a moment later and went into Bobby's room. He was awake, playing with a foam cutout of a train. She smiled at her son and said, "Hi there, sleepyhead." Bobby looked up, but didn't respond, and then he turned his attention back to the train.

Shortly after that, David poked his head into the room and said, "Good morning."

"Hi."

"I'm sorry I fell asleep on the couch last night."

"It's okay."

"I'm going to go in and get dressed. I used the other shower; I didn't want to wake you."

It seemed to Jenna that David was trying too hard to explain things that under most circumstances shouldn't need explaining. "I was just about to get breakfast for Bobby before we head out to the Center. Do you want anything?"

"No. I'll grab something on the way into Boston."

Twenty minutes later David emerged from the bedroom and came into the kitchen. He walked over to Bobby and tried to find a spot on his face that wasn't covered with cereal. He finally opted for his forehead, where he planted a kiss. "I'll see you soon, pal. Be a good boy for mommy."

David went over to Jenna, and gave her a kiss on the forehead as well. "I should be back before noon. How about you?"

"Around then. Maybe a little later."

"Good luck with everything today."

"You too. Say 'hi' to Alan for me."

As the door closed behind David, all Jenna could think of was how uncertain her life had become.

CHAPTER 50

Jenna pulled up to the Center at around 8:45. She dropped Bobby off with his group, which she noticed was now a little larger following school vacation week. She also saw two additional staff members who evidently had been assigned to help out with the increased numbers.

She watched through the two-way mirror for a few minutes before going to meet her group. She knew it was unlikely, but Jenna was hoping that she'd see something that would further validate what Dr. Townsend had talked about. She smiled at herself for even entertaining such foolishness. Even so, she took one last look over her shoulder as she left.

Jenna's group had also added some children, as well as one additional staff member. The new person was already involved in some of the activities that Jenna had helped out with the previous week. So for a short while, she had a few minutes to herself.

The unencumbered time allowed Jenna's mind to turn to thoughts of David and the trip to the Cape. It had all come about so quickly that she hadn't had time to figure out how she truly felt about it. On some level she realized that she had agreed to go away with David out of a sense of obligation.

She remembered when David had used the phrase "You owe me this," about taking Bobby to the Chambers Institute. She had resented those words at the time. But now, in this context—trying to repair their relationship—she did owe him something, and probably herself as well.

Jenna's thoughts were interrupted by one of the staff members asking for some assistance. She eagerly joined the small group of seven-year-olds and continued to help out for the next hour and a half.

At around 11:20 she left the group and went to observe Bobby. When she arrived, he was sitting with a young woman whom Jenna recognized from the previous week. The woman was showing Bobby some pictures, and initially it appeared that he was interested, but then after a few minutes his attention seemed to wander.

Shortly after that, the woman put the pictures away, selected a book from the table and began to read it to Bobby. Jenna watched for a little while, and then when she saw some of the children and staff members beginning to cleanup, she walked into the room, and went over to Bobby.

The woman working with him had just finished reading the book as Jenna approached. "Hi. I'm Jenna, Bobby's mom."

"Hi. I'm Pam. Nice to meet you."

"Could I speak with you for a moment?"

"Certainly."

"Bobby won't be back until Friday. I was hoping that you could show me what you've been working on, so I could make sure I continue doing it at home."

"Oh, sure." Pam looked over at Bobby and saw that he was still holding the book she had been reading to him. She pointed to it. "As I'm sure you know, he loves trains. Usually after he's been working at an activity for a while, as a reward, we offer to read him the train book. Do you have that one at home?"

"No. We have a lot of other things having to do with trains, as you can imagine, but not that particular book."

"You might want to pick it up. Bobby really likes it. And it seems as if he's beginning to understand that if he at least attempts an activity, then he gets to have the book read to him."

"Really? I was watching when you were showing him the pictures. Toward the end, it didn't look like he was being all that cooperative."

"I think he was just getting tired. Actually, I was quite pleased. I wasn't sure he was ready for that particular activity."

"Why? What is it?"

"I'll show you." Pam went over to retrieve the folder off the table. She opened it, and selected one of the pictures. "As you can see, this is a photo of a man laughing. We show these to the students, hoping that they'll make the connection between the man's facial expression and the concept of laughter. Eventually, we hope they take it one step further and realize that laughing represents being happy. But for most of the children we work with, that last step is way beyond them at this point. All abstractions tend to be."

Pam fanned out some more of the photos for Jenna to see. "Here's a little boy who's angry, and a little girl who's crying."

Jenna said, "Dr. Townsend mentioned to me about trying to help Bobby make connections, but I thought it was mainly about his speech."

"Not entirely. As I said, the first step for children with autism is getting them to be able to decipher what facial expressions mean. Once they figure that out, then we try to get them to connect it to empathetic speech. It's almost like they have to learn how to feel."

Jenna felt a quick sadness come over her, but she didn't show it. "Can I borrow these?"

"Sure."

"I'll bring them back Friday."

"No rush. We have plenty."

On the way home, Jenna stopped at a local bookstore, went into the children's section, and was able to find a copy of the train book. As soon as Jenna took it off the shelf, Bobby grabbed for it. But instead of asking for the book, he repeatedly made a guttural sound, similar to one he used to make before he had any language. Jenna shook her head. "Use your words."

But Bobby would have none of it. And despite some judgmental glares from people outside the children's section, Jenna held her ground. "Use your words," she said again, as she held the book out of Bobby's grasp.

He repeated the guttural sound and got on his tiptoes as he reached for the book again. Jenna tried twice more, and was about to give in, when Bobby finally said, "Book. Tray book." Jenna bent down, gave him a hug, and handed him the book. She let him continue to hold it even after she paid for it and they headed out to the car.

As she buckled Bobby into his car seat, Jenna realized that some of her anxiety about leaving him for a few days was beginning to fade. She'd explain about the pictures and the train book to Barbara, and then when she got back home, Jenna would do some more follow-up.

David had been back at the apartment for almost an hour, when Jenna opened the door and she and Bobby came inside. The TV was off, and David was sitting on the couch. He waited a moment before he stood up. "Hi."

Immediately, Jenna sensed that something was wrong. "Is everything all right?"

"Yes and no."

"What's the matter?"

David expelled a mouthful of air. "I went to see Alan this morning."

"Right."

"Well . . . ."

At that moment, Bobby interrupted. "Bobby eat."

Jenna replied, "Just a second, honey."

David looked at his son. "No. No, it's okay. Get him settled first."

Bobby repeated himself. "Bobby eat."

Jenna ushered him into the kitchen. "Come on, mommy will make you a sandwich." With that pronouncement, Bobby headed for his high chair.

Jenna looked over at David. "We can talk while I get his lunch. So, what happened?"

"I filled Alan in on everything I've been going through trying to move my father. He thought it was ridiculous too. Anyway, he made a few phone calls, and eventually they agreed that I could transfer him."

Jenna was puzzled by David's lack of enthusiasm. "What am I missing? Isn't that what you wanted?"

"Yes, but I have to make the arrangements immediately. They only agreed to this because they have someone on the waiting list. I've got to find some place that will take him as soon as possible."

A split second elapsed and then Jenna understood. David said it out loud. "We have to postpone our trip until I get back." He hesitated. "I hate doing that, but I don't have a choice."

A small part of Jenna was relieved. Postponing the trip, considering the tension that had recently existed between the two of them, wasn't all bad. But that emotion quickly disappeared, and was replaced by something harsher—This was just another instance where David put his father before everything else. She kept those feelings to herself, and responded by saying, "I understand," although, in reality, she didn't.

"If I leave shortly, I can probably make it to one of the facilities on Long Island by late this afternoon. If I can work something out with them, I should be back by Tuesday night—Wednesday at the latest. I've already cancelled the reservation for the Cape. Can you talk to Barbara and see if she's available next week? I'm just going to tell Jenkins that I have to take some more time off, and we can go then."

Jenna's emotions were swirling around like they were in a melting pot—a mixture of disappointment, sadness, and anger. But she didn't allow any of them to find their way to the expression on her face.

David went to Jenna and embraced her. "I promise we're going to be all right, Jenna. Once I take care of this, nothing's going to get in the way from now on."

He gently pulled away from her. "I really have to go, if I'm going to make the ferry in New London." With that, he kissed her on the lips and said, "I'll call as soon as I know something. I love you." He went over to Bobby and kissed him on the top of the head. "I'll be back soon, pal."

Jenna stood in the kitchen for the next several minutes trying to process everything that had just happened. She felt a numbness come over her that seemed to prevent any single emotion from coming to the surface.

She sat down next to Bobby's high chair. A moment later there were tears running down her cheeks. Bobby looked at her and said, "Mommy cry."

Jenna looked at her son, and thought back to her conversation with Pam. It didn't seem that there had been any inflection in Bobby's voice when he had spoken those words. So it was doubtful that he had made any connection between her crying and what she was feeling.

But then again, neither had she.

When Jenna awoke on Tuesday morning, she tried to refrain from analyzing what had gone on the day before, but to no avail. Eventually she was able to convince herself that the best course of action was to wait until David got back and then try to come to grips with everything.

Later that morning she took Bobby to the playground for an hour, and when she returned there was a light blinking on the answering machine. She pushed the necessary buttons and heard David's voice. "Hi. I tried your cell, but couldn't get through for some reason. I just wanted to let you know that I've got another meeting with the administrator of one of the facilities on Long Island this afternoon. Things are looking pretty good. I expect to be back on Wednesday. I love you. Give my love to Bobby, too.

Hearing David's voice triggered something in Jenna, and again she found herself trying to make sense of what she was feeling. But there were too many emotions colliding together for that to happen. She busied herself with as many mindless tasks as possible, and eventually the need to confront her feelings subsided.

Around 3:30 in the afternoon, the intercom buzzer rang. It took a moment for it to register that it was probably Jeremy. With all the turmoil of the last several days, she had forgotten that he had said he'd be coming by on Tuesday.

When he came in, Jeremy gave her a kiss, took off his jacket, and went to see Bobby. "How're you doing, big guy?"

Bobby looked up briefly, but then turned his attention back to the foam trains he had been playing with. Jeremy smiled. "It's tough to compete with those trains. I think you might have a budding conductor on your hands."

"I know. I just hope Amtrak is still around in another twenty years."

Several minutes went by and then out of the blue, Bobby said, "Mommy cry."

Jeremy glanced at Jenna. "That's new. Where did that come from?"

Jenna was equally surprised by Bobby's comment. She struggled to come up with a believable answer. "It must be from the activity he was doing at the Center." She reached for the folder off the end table, and began to explain it to Jeremy. When she finished, he said, "What a great idea. It looks like he picked it up pretty quickly."

"Evidently."

As Jenna responded, Jeremy thought he detected something amiss in her body language. He stared at her, and then asked, "Was Bobby right? Were you crying?"

Jenna appeared even more uncomfortable than she had been. And she found that she couldn't lie to Jeremy. She opted for the partial truth. "Uh . . . No, not just now."

"I'm sorry. That was none of my business."

She was quiet for a moment, not sure if she wanted to get into it or not. And then without being aware she was going to, she said, "The last couple of days have been kind of difficult."

Jeremy put up his hands in a benign gesture. "It really is none of my business."

"It's okay. Maybe it'll help if I talk about it."

For the next twenty minutes, that's what they did. Jenna opened up about everything that had gone on since the previous Saturday. She saw

Jeremy cringe a number of times when she told him that his name had been brought into the argument.

When Jenna finished, Jeremy looked troubled. He shook his head slightly. "I just don't want to be the cause of any problems between you and David." He paused. "You know how I feel about Bobby, and . . . ." He looked away briefly. "And, I'm pretty sure you know how I feel about you. But I don't want to feel responsible or *be* responsible for whatever might happen. I can't do that to David." He seemed to steady himself. "That's why I backed off a few months ago. I can't be in the middle of this, Jenna." He paused again. "I offered before to take a break from seeing Bobby. Maybe that would be best until you and David figure things out."

Jenna's voice filled the apartment. "No! I told you before, neither one of us wants that."

"I'm not sure that's true, Jenna. And I don't blame David. Put yourself in his shoes. He has to be away all the time, and then when he comes home, he tries to catch up on all the things Bobby's been doing that he's missed, things that you and I know all about, and he doesn't. How do you think that must make him feel? Besides, now that Bobby is going to the Center . . . ."

Before Jeremy could finish the sentence, Bobby appeared next to him with a book in his hand. "Daddy, read book."

Jeremy looked at Bobby, knelt down in front of him, and smiled. "Is that right? Your daddy read this book to you?" Bobby didn't respond. Instead, he thrust the book toward Jeremy.

Jenna was still trying to come to terms with what Jeremy had said, but Bobby was being so insistent that she briefly turned her attention to him. "No, honey, Daddy didn't read that book to you."

She offered an explanation to Jeremy. "I bought that book for him yesterday, just before we came home. And then David left shortly after that. I'm not sure why Bobby said that."

As if he understood his mother's question, Bobby again held the book at arm's length toward Jeremy and said, "*You* daddy. *You* read tray book."

Both Jenna and Jeremy were so stunned that they were unable to speak. Although it had taken a moment for Bobby's words to sink in, there was no mistaking what he meant.

Jenna looked over at Jeremy and saw that his eyes were closed. After a moment he opened them, and smiled again at Bobby. "Okay big guy, *Jeremy* will read the train book to you."

365

Jenna waited until Jeremy finished reading, and then said, "I know this is difficult, but Bobby needs you. You heard him. You know what he meant."

Jeremy had trouble looking at Jenna. "I know. But maybe that's exactly why I should take a break for a while. Obviously, he's getting confused about things. That's not fair, not to David and not to Bobby."

CHAPTER 51

Jeremy stayed for another twenty minutes, but nothing Jenna said could move him to change his mind. The best she could do was to get him to agree to reconsider once she and David returned from the Cape. Of course, that assumed the issues between them had gotten resolved. Jenna was devastated by the prospect of Jeremy being out of Bobby's life, and she knew that somehow she had to figure out a way to prevent that from happening.

Jenna's mind shifted to the positive things that had come out of Tuesday afternoon – Bobby's identification of her crying and his use of inflection. In view of what else had occurred, however, Jenna's enthusiasm was quickly dampened. Nevertheless, she was eager to share what Bobby had done with Dr. Townsend.

Jenna found him in his office on Wednesday morning after she brought Bobby to his group. The door was open, so she knocked softly on the doorjamb. "Excuse me, Dr. Townsend. May I speak with you for a moment?"

"Of course. Come in."

"If this is a bad time, I can come back."

"No, it's fine. Actually, I was about to come looking for you anyway. I wanted to give you an update on the insurance situation." He put his hands on the desk in front of him. "Initially, I didn't think it looked very promising, but then the person I was speaking with intimated that if the results of the formal assessment turned out to be as compelling as I think they will be, then the company would come around. Given that, I'd like to do the assessment as soon as possible, probably next week. Is that all right with you?'

Jenna hesitated, thinking about the postponed getaway with David. "Uh . . . that would be fine."

The doctor didn't appear to pick up on any reluctance on Jenna's part. "I'll try to schedule it for Monday. If for some reason we can't, then either Wednesday or Friday, but definitely next week." He made a note on the pad in front of him. "I'm not sure how long it will take before we hear back from the insurance company, but we'd like Bobby to continue at the Center, at least until we do."

"Thank you, doctor. That's incredibly generous."

He smiled in acknowledgement. "You're welcome." A pause. "What was it that you wanted to see me about?"

Jenna had decided that when she related the two incidents to the doctor, she would alter them slightly; they were just too personal. "A couple of days ago, Bobby saw me . . . laughing, and he was able to identify what I was doing. A few minutes later, he followed that up by emphasizing a word, as if he wanted to make sure I knew what he meant. At least, that's what it seemed like."

"Tell me more about the second situation."

Jenna hadn't anticipated having to provide additional details. She scrambled to come up with something. "Well . . . uh . . . Jeremy and I were with Bobby. And evidently, he wanted Jeremy to read him a book, so he gestured toward Jeremy, and said, '*You* read the train book.' " It sounded to me just like the inflection you were talking about."

"It certainly does. What we have to hope for now is that he continues doing it on a more regular basis."

"What about the other situation where he identified the laughing?"

"That's a positive step as well, but nowhere near as significant as his use of inflection."

Jenna wanted to know more, so she pushed a little further. "Do you think it was significant that Bobby was talking to Jeremy?"

"It's certainly not surprising, considering what you've told me about their relationship."

Jenna thought back to what had actually happened, and shifted positions in her seat to cover up her discomfort. Dr. Townsend continued. "If I recall correctly, the staff here has only heard Bobby use inflection in reference to things, not people. So it's possible that in the incident you described, that Bobby's feelings toward Jeremy may have been a factor." The doctor looked pensive for a moment. "But in actuality, it doesn't matter. It's doubtful that we would recommend changing any of the activities Bobby would be doing either here or at home, even if we knew for sure."

Jenna received Dr. Townsend's assessment with mixed emotions. On one hand, Bobby was showing signs of real growth. On the other hand, Jeremy might have been the reason for that, and Bobby was about to lose him. She silently vowed again that she wouldn't let that happen. It certainly appeared that her upcoming discussion with David was going to resemble a high wire act. And there was no safety net in sight.

On the way home, Jenna decided she had to impose on Barbara once again to watch Bobby. She simply couldn't afford to have her attention diverted; there was too much at stake. Not to mention, that at this point, she had no idea what might come out of Bobby's mouth.

David showed up about fifteen minutes after Jenna had taken Bobby to Barbara's. When he came through the door of the apartment, she had trouble reading his expression. "How'd you make out?" she asked.

"As far as moving my father, that's going to work out okay, although I have to go back to Westchester tonight and finish making the arrangements. They're going to transfer him at the end of the week. That's the good news." David expelled some air. "After I got that squared away, I called Phil Jenkins to tell him that I needed a few more days off, plus next week. That didn't go over too well."

"What do you mean? Why?"

"He said that if I wanted the next few days off, I should forget about having next week off too." David paused to gauge Jenna's reaction. She didn't seem as upset as he had expected, but then again, she hadn't heard the rest of it.

David continued the story. "There's some issue with the subcontractors that has to be taken care of. Anyway, without telling him our business, I said I had to have at least part of next week off. He said that wasn't an option; this week had already cost the company a bundle. I knew if I kept talking to him, I was going to lose it. So I said I'd get back to him, and hung up. At that point, I was only about thirty miles outside of Boston on my way here. I decided to take a detour and go see him in person."

"What happened?"

"By the time I got there, I had calmed down some, but that didn't last long. We started yelling at each other." David looked at her more intently. "I threatened to quit. He called my bluff and said, 'Do what you have to do.' We continued going at each other pretty good, and then finally he asked me what was going on. I just said it was personal. He pressed some more, and I told him that I was tired of being away from home so much. We kept talking, and then finally he made a proposal – If I finish overseeing the upgrade of the project we're working on, then he'll transfer me back to Massachusetts permanently."

Jenna's expression changed. "Really?" A pause. "How long will it take to finish the project?"

David dropped the other shoe. "If I push it, I think three months, maybe less."

"Three months!"

"I know it seems like a long time, but . . . ."

While David was trying to explain, Jenna began to weigh things in her mind. Long term, this was great news. Short term, it was anything but – no chance for the getaway any time soon, and therefore no chance to iron things out with David so that Jeremy would be willing to come back.

And then an idea struck her. "Why don't we just go away this weekend?"

"I thought of that, but I can't. If we don't move my father before Monday, he has to stay in Westchester for the next two months. I have to get him out of that place. It's horrible. They're doing nothing for him."

Jenna nodded as if she understood, but once again, she didn't. Was the Long Island facility so much better than the one in Westchester?

Her thoughts turned back to the proposal. "When you said you could get the job done in three months if you 'push it,' what did you mean by that? Weekends?"

David looked uncomfortable. "Probably, some."

Jenna's patience was thinning. "I'm not sure I can keep doing this by myself, David."

"I know. That's why I agreed to the proposal. It's only three months, and then I'll be home for good."

"Right now, three months seems like forever."

"You could come to New York."

"We've talked about this. You know I can't. Bobby needs to continue going to the Center. Plus, Dr. Townsend wants to do a formal assessment for the insurance company next week."

David looked at Jenna with some suspicion. "So we couldn't have gone away next week anyway. When were you planning on telling me that?"

"I wasn't trying to hide anything, I just found out a few hours ago."

He stared at her for a moment and then seemed to accept her explanation. "So then come down to New York after the assessment."

Jenna's exasperation got the best of her. "Bobby is making real progress. I'm not going to jeopardize that."

It was David's turn. "I don't know what you expected me to do, Jenna. Should I have quit my job?"

"No. Of course not."

"Then what?"

"I don't know. It's just that over the last several days, things have gotten more complicated."

"What are you talking about?"

It was now or never. "Jeremy thinks he should take a break from seeing Bobby."

"When did this happen?"

"Yesterday."

"Why?"

To spare David's feelings, Jenna avoided telling him the whole truth. "Bobby wanted Jeremy to read him a story . . . and . . . he ended up calling him 'daddy.'"

There was a shift in David's posture, as his shoulders sagged perceptibly. "Obviously, I'm not thrilled about that, but I'm not sure what it has to do with anything?"

"Jeremy thinks that because he spends so much time here, Bobby's getting confused." Jenna paused. "And he knows that we've been having some problems."

David raised his eyebrows and started to say something, but didn't.

Jenna explained further. "Jeremy said that he doesn't think it's a good idea to keep coming here, if it's going to affect your relationship with Bobby."

"How is accidentally calling him 'daddy' going to damage the relationship I have with my son?"

Jenna's breath caught as she heard the word "accidentally." She took a moment to respond, hoping to come up with something coherent to say. "Jeremy just doesn't want to be in the middle of anything."

"What's he in the middle of?"

She felt trapped. "I'm just telling you what he said."

David looked at Jenna as if he were going to pursue it further, but then stopped short of that. "I don't know what he thinks he's in the middle of, Jenna." He paused, then offered sarcastically, "But by all means, tell him he can still come over . . . every day, if he wants."

Jenna knew she should leave it at that, but she felt like she had to defend Jeremy. "He's trying to help, David. But he doesn't want to hurt you. Why are you being like this?"

"Being like what? I said it was fine."

"It doesn't sound like it's fine."

"I can't help how it sounds. It'll have to do."

"Jeremy's not going to accept that. And then the only one who suffers is Bobby."

David's voice increased a few decibels. "How many times do you want me to say it? Should I put it in writing?" And then the real focus of David's anger came out. "I don't know what else I'm supposed to do, Jenna. I gave in about the Chambers Institute; I offered to quit my job; you refuse to come down to New York . . . ."

Jenna tried to buffer David's anger by remaining calm. "I know, and I appreciate all that, but none of those things is going to get our life back to the way it was."

"That's exactly why I made the deal with Jenkins. Three months and it *is* back to the way it was."

For the first time since the conversation began, the predominant emotion in Jenna's heart was sadness. "Even if that's true, what happens in the meantime?"

David lowered his voice. "It's three months, Jenna." David looked directly into her eyes, and hesitated before he asked, "Do you still love me?"

"Yes," she responded immediately.

"Then we'll get through this."

Jenna's emotions exploded to the surface, and she was unable to speak. David put his arms around her, and she didn't balk. He continued to hold her for the next few minutes, and then he went into the bedroom and got his suitcase. He placed it by the door, and came to her again. "I'll give Jenkins a call, and see if he'll agree to shorten the time I have to be in New York. But no matter what, it's going to be okay. I promise."

Jenna was too emotionally drained to do anything but nod. David kissed her, picked up his suitcase and left. As she watched him head out the door, Jenna's only thought was *I want so much to believe him.*

She took a few more minutes to pull herself together, and then went to Barbara's apartment to get Bobby. She stumbled through the next several hours, never fully able to get a handle on what she was feeling. She kept staring at the clock, willing the digits to change more quickly. She wanted it to be 7:00, 4:00 West Coast time, when she knew her mother would be home.

Jenna usually talked to her mother at least once a week; most recently, it had been more often than that. But in none of the conversations had she shared the depth of the problems that she and David were dealing with.

As soon as Jenna spoke her first words, Sharon knew something was seriously wrong. And before the first minute was up, Jenna's tears had returned. It took her almost ten minutes to explain everything to her mother. "I don't know how I can possibly keep doing this by myself. Not for three more months, and without Jeremy, and for the most part without David."

"I know it's not exactly the same, but I could come help out for a few weeks in July."

"That'd be great, mom. I'd appreciate that." Jenna let out an audible sigh. "You know, there's a part of me that believes it's not just the three months or trying to do everything by myself. I told David that I wanted things to be like they used to be, but I'm not sure that's entirely true. What I really want is for him to put Bobby and me first. Since the day I met David, his father has had this control over him. And it's *still* going on. It doesn't seem to matter that he's in a coma."

"Have you told David how you feel?"

"Not in so many words."

"I think you need to tell him, Jenna." Then Sharon offered a caution. "But I wouldn't do it until you're sure that you know what you want from him. It's not fair to lay out the ground rules and then change them."

"I know."

Sharon paused, and then decided to move in a different direction. "How does Jeremy fit into all this?"

"You've seen how Bobby is with him. Especially now with what Dr. Townsend told me, it's more important than ever that Jeremy be in his life."

"And what about you?"

Jenna didn't answer right away. "We've already had this discussion."

"I know. I was just wondering if anything's changed."

"No. I still tell myself that any feelings I have for Jeremy are because of the way he is with Bobby. But, whether that's true or not, I don't know."

"Do you think David senses any of that?"

"We've never really discussed it."

"Was that your choice or his?"

"It's just never come up. We only talk about Jeremy in terms of his relationship to Bobby."

"I know it's going to be difficult, Jenna, but I think you need to figure out how you feel about Jeremy before he comes back into Bobby's life."

"It doesn't matter what my feelings are. Bobby needs him."

"I don't doubt that, but it sounds like Jeremy being there already complicates things. Pretending that it doesn't is not going to change that."

"I know what you're trying to say. But if need be, I'll push my feelings into the background."

"Even if you find yourself falling in love?"

Jenna was silent for quite a while, and then, "I remember something you said to me just before Bobby was born. You said, 'You can't imagine that you could possibly love anything as much as you love your child. You'll make any sacrifice you have to for him.' Of course, you were right. So if I have to . . . ."

Jenna wasn't able to finish the sentence.

CHAPTER 52

(Eight months later, two days after Christmas)

Despite the fact that she wasn't fully awake, Jenna was still aware of something wonderful enveloping her. It was as if each of her senses had come together to create the same emotion, like five small streams combining to form a powerful river.

She was reluctant to open her eyes, not wanting to end the dream, if in fact that's what it was. As the remnants of sleep finally left her, she realized it hadn't been a dream at all. The powerful river of emotion she was feeling was simply contentment. Without consciously connecting the two things, she glanced at her left hand and saw the diamond engagement ring she had received on Christmas Eve.

She smiled as she thought about how much her attitude toward rings and what they represented had gone back and forth over the last several years—how important it had been to her when she first found out she was pregnant to have a symbol on her finger; and then ironically, after Bobby was born, how it didn't seem to matter; and now, maybe because she wanted more order in her life, how it had become important again.

As Jenna completed that thought, the bedroom door was pushed open, and Bobby rushed in. He ran over to his mother and said, "My birfday."

"Yes it is."

And then a voice came from behind the bathroom door. "Whose birthday is it today?"

Bobby scooted around the bed and positioned himself beside the bathroom. "*My* birfday."

375

"You're absolutely right. It is your birthday. Daddy'll be out in a minute, and then we can get some breakfast, okay?"

Bobby nodded, but didn't say anything out loud.

"After that, how about I take you to the mall and you can pick out a present?"

"A train."

"Now there's a surprise."

At that point, Bobby flew out of the bedroom and headed for the kitchen.

Jenna called out. "You can finish up in there. I'll get his breakfast."

"No. It's okay. Go back to sleep."

"Are you really thinking about taking him to the mall this morning? It's going to be a madhouse with people returning Christmas gifts."

"Not at the toy store."

Jenna smiled. "You might be right about that. Do you want me to come with you?"

"No. You've got to get ready for the party. Plus, isn't Trish coming over early? I figured I'd give you two some time to talk."

Her smile faded. "It's just that . . . I know Bobby's behavior out in public has been much better lately, but you never know."

The bathroom door opened, and Jeremy came out dressed in a robe, drying his hair. He went over to Jenna and kissed her. "If it happens, I'll deal with it. But I'm sure it's going to be fine."

Jenna smiled again because she knew it would be. She then feigned a serious expression and said, "Actually, at some point, I do need to go to the mall, though. I have to return this gaudy ring I got for Christmas."

"Can't do it."

"And why not?"

"They don't have a Cracker Jack store at the mall."

After Jeremy and Bobby left, Jenna treated herself to a hot bath, got dressed, had a cup of coffee, and waited for Trish to arrive. Jenna had spoken to Trish a couple of times since the breakup with David, but she hadn't shared all of the details. Now that Jenna had some additional perspective on what had happened, she thought she'd be much more comfortable telling Trish the full story.

Trish showed up around 11:00 carrying two large bags containing Christmas and birthday gifts. She put them down, gave Jenna an extra long hug, and then started to take off her coat.

Jenna said, "Here, let me help you with that."

Trish had just finished removing an arm from one of the sleeves, when she spotted the ring. "Oh my God, Jenna, let me see. When did this all happen?"

Jenna smiled and extended her hand. "Christmas Eve."

Trish hugged her again. "I'm so happy for you. Congratulations!"

After a few more minutes of engagement and wedding talk, they went to the couch and sat down. Trish asked, "Have you told David?"

"Not yet. I'm expecting him to call today to wish Bobby a happy birthday, but I'm not going to say anything. I think he'll be all right with it, but it's Bobby's day. I don't want anything getting in the way of that."

"That's probably a good idea."

"How's David doing, anyway?"

"I haven't talked to him in a few weeks. He's in Florida; did I tell you that?"

"No. What's in Florida?"

"Evidently, the company's looking to possibly expand down there, so David went to check out some of the properties they're considering. He's going to be there until May. But he's scheduled to get his trust fund around then, so I don't know if he's going to stay with the company after that."

Trish changed topics. "How's his father?"

"Pretty much the same. David moved him to Florida so he'd be close by for the time being."

"I guess some things never change."

Jenna looked pensive. "You know, it's funny. In the last few months I've been able to look back, and I see some of David's actions differently."

"How do you mean?"

"Well, after he agreed to finish up the project in New York, and then got his father settled in at the facility on Long Island, it was like he was a new person when it came to Bobby and me—He went to talk to Jeremy and asked him to continue to see Bobby; he made it home every weekend for two months in a row; he even went to see Dr. Townsend at the Center in Canton. Things couldn't have been better between us. But then he came home one day, and said he wanted to look at a new place in New Hampshire for his father.

"At first I was upset, but then I realized that once David transferred back to Massachusetts, he'd want his father to be near by. It only made sense. But one weekend in New Hampshire turned into three, and then when he finally came home after that, he dropped the bombshell.

"He told me that the New Hampshire facility wasn't what he was hoping it would be, so he felt as if he had to keep looking. He said his father had been so close to coming out of the coma when he went to Westchester that he couldn't give up now. So, after he finished with the assignment in New York, instead of coming back to Massachusetts, he was going to take a leave of absence and go all over the country, if need be, until he found some place that could help his father."

Jenna shook her head. "He apologized over and over again, but said it was something he just had to do; it had been eating at him ever since he transferred his father out of Westchester." She hesitated. "Of course, that was exactly what I had been afraid of – that David would revert to putting his father ahead of everything else, including Bobby and me. I think because things had been going so well just prior to that, it caught me totally by surprise. I was stunned . . . and hurt. I tried to get him to change his mind. I told him that we had already gotten through two months, and I'd be able to hold everything together until he got back. But his mind was made up. I didn't realize it at the time, but now I'm convinced that he had been planning the whole thing for quite a while."

Trish spoke for the first time in several minutes. "What made you think that?"

"I found out later that he had asked his boss for a large advance against his trust fund. Then he prepaid the rent on the apartment for a year. He started depositing extra money in the checking account each month. He even paid off the money we owed the Center in Canton for Bobby's treatment. You don't wake up one morning and all of a sudden decide to put those things in motion."

Jenna continued. "The last time I saw him, I asked him about it, but he avoided the question. He simply said that once he made up his mind what he had to do, he wanted to make sure that I didn't have to worry about anything. He said that at some point down the road, after he found the right place for his father, he'd come back. And then, if I wanted to, we could try to start over. But I could see it in his eyes that he knew that wasn't going to happen."

Jenna started to fill up at the memory. Trish put her hand on Jenna's. "I can't imagine how painful that must have been . . . for the both of you."

"It was. At times, it still is. I mean, I have Jeremy, and Bobby has Jeremy. But David doesn't have anybody, not even his father, really."

"But that's also the choice he made."

"It certainly seemed like that at the time, but now I think there was more to it."

"Why do you say that?"

"I found out from Jeremy that David had gone to see him before he even talked to me. He told him some of what he was planning, but asked him not to say anything until he had the chance to tell me himself."

Jenna struggled to keep her composure. "There's no way I'll ever know for sure; I doubt that David even knows for sure. But I have a hard time believing that he would have chosen to leave, if it were just about his father. I think after David spoke to Dr. Townsend, he realized that if Bobby was going to make the kind of strides he needed to make, then Jeremy had to be an even bigger part of his life. And the only way that was going to happen was if David left. I think he understood that if he came back to Massachusetts, Jeremy would feel like he had to stop coming around so much." Jenna paused. "I don't think either his father's situation or Bobby's situation by itself would have been enough to make David leave . . . and give up his family. But when he was faced with the reality of the both of them . . . ."

Trish had always been able to be direct with Jenna, so she started to respond, but then held back. Jenna looked at Trish, and answered the question that she was sure her friend had been about to ask. "I know. It's also possible that I'm rationalizing this whole thing, because I can't accept the fact that David would choose his father over us."

They were quiet for a few moments, and then Jenna said, "But regardless of why he did it . . . I was thinking this morning that I've never been this happy in my entire life. Jeremy and I are going to get married. I see Bobby doing things every day that I didn't think I'd ever see. We had his special education meeting, and he's going to start the pre-school program at the Center in January. And I'm going to be a part-time teacher assistant at the same school where Jeremy teaches—and then I thought about David. It seems so ironic that if he did leave for Bobby's sake, then in the end, the two of us were just trying to do the right thing for our son, and yet we couldn't do anything for each other."

Jenna's tears became more pronounced.

A moment later the apartment door opened and Bobby bounded in, followed by Jeremy. Before anyone could offer any greetings, Bobby was showing his new train to his mother. He stared at her briefly, and then turned to Jeremy. "Mommy crying."

Jeremy moved closer, and was about to ask Jenna if she was all right, when Bobby asked, "Why mommy sad?"

Somehow, Jenna knew what Bobby was going to say before he said it. And as soon as she actually heard the words and understood their significance, she thought again of David – not with sadness this time, but with love and gratitude for the sacrifice he had made for their little boy.